A HEAVY TOLL

The narrow bridge over the gorge looked kind of flimsy. "Think it'll take your horse's weight?" I asked Gilbert.

The young squire scanned it with a practiced eye. "Aye, if I dismount."

"Good enough." I started across.

"Nay, Wizard Saul!" he yelped. "First we must test for—"

"Ho! Ho!" something rumbled.

I glanced at the sky. "Thunder?"

Hands as wide as bread boxes slapped onto the railing. Something huge and smelly swung up in an arc and landed with a shock that made the bridge sway. I held tight to the railing and stared, totally dumfounded.

It was bigger than a bear, eight feet tall and shaped like a turnip, with legs as thick as kegs coming out of the narrow end. Eyes the size of dinner plates stared hungrily down at me; beneath them a huge slice of mouth opened in a grin set with shark's teeth.

" 'Tis a troll!" Gilbert cried. "Flee!"

THE WITCH DOCTOR

Book III of
A Wizard in Rhyme

Christopher Stasheff

A Del Rey® Book
BALLANTINE BOOKS • NEW YORK

A Del Rey® Book
Published by The Ballantine Publishing Group
Copyright © 1994 by Christopher Stasheff
Excerpt from *The Secular Wizard* copyright © 1994 by Christopher Stasheff

http://www.randomhouse.com

Library of Congress Catalog Card Number: 93-22129

ISBN 0-345-38851-8

Printed in Canada

First Hardcover Edition: February 1994
First Mass Market Edition: January 1995

With thanks to Phil Strang,
who read *Her Majesty's Wizard* and asked,
"What would happen to a man in that universe who
was exactly half good and half bad?"

and

To Lester del Rey, who answered,
"He'd last about thirty seconds!"

CHAPTER 1

What can you say about a friend who leaves town without telling you?

I mean, I left Matt sitting there in the coffee shop trying to translate that gobbledygook parchment of his, and when I came back after class, he was gone. I asked if anybody'd seen him go, but nobody had—just that, when they'd looked up, he'd been gone.

That was no big deal, of course—I didn't own Matt, and he was a big boy. If he wanted to go take a hike, that was his business. But he'd left that damn parchment behind, and ever since he'd found it, he'd handled it as if it were the crown jewels—so he sure as hell wouldn't have just left it on the table in a busy coffee shop. Somebody could have thrown it in the wastebasket without looking. He was just lucky it was still there when I got back. So I picked it up and put it in my notebook. "Tell him I've got his parchment," I told Alice.

She nodded without looking up from the coffee she was pouring. "Sure thing, Saul. If you see him first, tell him he forgot to pay his bill this morning."

"Saul" is me. Matt claimed I'd been enlightened, so he called me "Paul." I went along—it was okay as an in-joke, and it was funny the first time. After that, I suffered through it—from Matt. Not from anyone else. "Saul" is me. I just keep a wary eye for teenagers with slingshots who also play harp.

"Will do," I said, and went out the door—but it nagged at me—especially since I had never known Matt to forget to pay Alice before. Forget to put on his socks, maybe, but not to pay his tab.

When I got back to my apartment, I took out his mystical manuscript and looked at it. Matt thought it was parchment, but I didn't think he was any judge of sheepskins. He certainly hadn't gotten his. Well, okay, he had two of them, but they hadn't given him the third degree yet—and wouldn't, the way he was hung up on that untranslatable bit of doggerel. Oh, sure, maybe he was right, maybe it *was* a long-lost document that would establish his reputation as a scholar and shoot him up to full professor overnight—but maybe the moon is made of calcified green cheese, too.

Me, I was working on my second M.A.—anything to justify staying around campus. Matt had gone on for his doctorate, but I couldn't stay interested in any one subject that long. They all began to seem kind of silly, the way the professors were so fanatical about the smallest details.

By that standard, Matt was a born professor, all right. He just spun his wheels, trying to translate a parchment that he thought was six hundred years old but was written in a language nobody had ever heard of. I looked it over, shook my head, and put it back in the notebook. He'd show up looking for it sooner or later.

But he didn't. He didn't show up at all.

After a couple of days, I developed a gnawing uncertainty about his having left town—maybe he had just disappeared. I know, I know, I was letting my imagination run away with me, but I couldn't squelch the thought.

So what do you do when a friend disappears?

You have to find out whether or not to worry.

The first day, I was only a little concerned, especially after I went back to the coffee shop, and they said he hadn't been in looking for his damn parchment. The second day, I started getting worried—it was midnight and he hadn't shown up at the coffeehouse. Then I began to think maybe he'd forgotten to eat again and blacked out—so I went around to his apartment to tell him off.

He lived in one of those old one-family houses that had been converted into five apartments, if you want to call them that—a nine-by-twelve living room with a kitchenette wall, and a cubbyhole for a bedroom. I knocked, but he didn't answer. I knocked again. Then I waited a good long time before I knocked a third time. Still no answer. At three A.M., when the neighbor came out and yelled at me to stop knocking so hard, I really got worried—and the next day, when nobody answered, I figured, Okay, third time's the charm—so I went outside, glanced around to make sure nobody was looking, and quietly crawled in the back window. Matt really ought to lock up at night; I've always told him so.

I had to crawl across the table—Matt liked to eat and write by natural light—and stepped into a mess.

Look, I've got a pretty strong stomach, and Matt was never big on housekeeping. A high stack of dishes with mold on them, I could have understood—but wall-to-wall spiderwebs? No way. How could he live like that? I mean, it wasn't just spiderwebs in the corners—it was spiderwebs choking the furniture! I couldn't have sat down without getting caught in dusty silk! And the proprietors were still there, too—little brown ones, medium-sized gray ones, and a huge male-eater with a body the size of a quarter and red markings like a big wide grin on the underside of its abdomen, sitting in the middle of a web six feet wide that was stretched across the archway to the bed nook.

Then the sun came out from behind a cloud, its light struck through the window for about half a minute—and I stood spellbound. Lit from the back and side like that, the huge web seemed to glow, every tendril bright. It was beautiful.

Then the sun went in, the light went away, and it was just a dusty piece of vermin-laden debris.

Speaking of vermin, what had attracted all these eight-legged wonders? It must have been a bumper year for flies. Or maybe, just maybe, they'd decided to declare war on the army of cockroaches that infested the place. If so, more power to them. I decided not to go spider hunting, after all. Besides, I didn't have time—I had to find Matt.

The strange thing was, I'd been in that apartment just three days before, and there hadn't been a single strand of spider silk in sight. Okay, so they're hard to see—but three days just isn't time enough for that much decoration.

I stepped up to the archway, nerving myself to sweep that web aside and swat its builder—but the sun came out again, and the golden cartwheel was so damned beautiful I just couldn't bring myself to do it. Besides, I didn't really need to—I could look through it, and the bedroom sure didn't have any place that was out of sight. Room enough for a bed, a dresser, a tin wardrobe, and scarcely an inch more. The bed was rumpled, but Matt wasn't in it.

I turned around, frowning, and scanned the place again. I

wouldn't say there was no sign of Matt—as I told you, he wasn't big on housekeeping, and there were stacks of books everywhere, nicely webbed at the moment—but the pile of dirty dishes was no higher than it had been, and he himself sure wasn't there.

I stepped out into the hall and closed the door behind me, chewing it over. No matter how I sliced it, it came out the same—Matt had left town.

Why so suddenly?

Death in the family. Or close to it. What else could it be?

So I went back to my apartment and started research. One of the handy things about having some training in scholarship, is that you know how to find information. I knew what town Matt came from—Separ City, New Jersey—and I knew how to call long-distance information.

"Mantrell," I told the operator.

"There are three, sir. Which one did you want?"

I racked my brains. Had Matt ever said anything about his parents' names? Then I remembered, once, that there had been a "junior" attached to him. "Matthew."

"We have a Mateo."

"Yeah, that's it." It was a good guess, anyway.

"One moment, please."

The vocodered voice gave me the number. I wrote it down, hung up, picked up, and punched in. Six rings, and I found myself hoping nobody would answer.

" 'Allo?"

I hadn't known his parents were immigrants. His mother sounded nice.

"I'm calling for Matthew Mantrell," I said. "Junior."

"Mateo? Ees not 'ere."

"Just went out for a minute?" I was surprised at the surge of relief I felt.

"No, no! Ees away—college!"

My spirits took the express elevator down. "Okay. I'll try him there. Thanks, Mrs. Mantrell."

"Ees okay. You tell him call home, sí?"

"Sí," I agreed. "Good-bye." I hung up, hoping I would see him indeed.

So. He hadn't gone home.

Then where?

I know I should have forgotten about it, shoved it to the

back of my mind, and just contented myself with being really mad at him. What was the big deal, anyway?

The big deal was that Matt was the only real friend I had, at the moment—maybe the only one I'd ever had, really. I mean, I hadn't known Matt all that long; but four years seems like a long time, to me. Four years, going on five—but who's counting?

It's not as if I'd ever had all that many friends. Let me see, there was Jory in first grade, and Luke, and Ray—and all the rest of the boys in the class, I suppose. Then it was down to Luke and Ray in second grade, 'cause Jory moved away—but the rest of the kids began to cool off. My wild stories, I guess. Then Ray moved, too, so it was just Luke and me in third grade—and Luke eased up, 'cause he wanted to play with the other kids. Me, I didn't want to play, I was clumsy—I just wanted to tell stories, but the other kids didn't want to hear about brave knights rescuing fair damsels. So from fourth grade on, I was on decent terms with the rest of the kids, but nothing more. Then, along about junior high, nobody wanted to be caught talking to me, because the "in" crowd decided I was weird.

What can I say? I was. I mean, a thirteen-year-old boy who doesn't like baseball and loves reading poetry—what can *you* say? By local standards, anyway. And in junior high, local standards are everything. Made me miserable, but what could I do?

Find out what they thought made a good man, of course. I watched and found out real quick that the popular guys weren't afraid to fight, and they won more fights than they lost. That seemed to go with being good at sports. So I figured that if I could learn how to fight, I could be good at sports, too. A karate school had just opened up in town, so I heckled Mom until she finally took me, just to shut me up. I had to get a paper route to pay for it, though.

It only took six months before I stopped losing fights. When school started again in the fall, and the boys started working out their ranking system by the usual round of bouts, I started winning a few—and all of a sudden, the other guys got chummy. I warmed to it for a little while, but it revolted me, too. I knew them for what they were now, and I stopped caring about them.

It felt good. Besides, I'd connected with karate—and from it, I got interested in the Far East.

One of the teachers told me I should try not to sound so hostile and sarcastic all the time.

Sarcastic? Who, me?

So I learned to paste on the smile and sound cheerful.

Didn't work. The other kids could tell. All I succeeded in doing was acting phony.

Why bother?

Of course, things picked up a little in high school, because there was a literary magazine, and a drama club, so I got back onto civil terms with some of the other kids. Not the "in" crowd, of course, but they bored me, so I didn't care. Much.

So all in all, I wasn't really prepared for college. Academically, sure—but socially? I mean, I hadn't had a real friend in ten years—and all of a sudden, I had a dozen. Not close friends, of course, but people who smiled and sat down in my booth at the coffee shop.

Who can blame me if I didn't do any homework?

My profs, that's who. And the registrar, who sent me the little pink slip with the word "probation" worked in there. And my academic counselor, who pointed out that I was earning a quick exit visa from the Land of Friendship. So I declared an English major, where at least half of the homework was reading the books I'd already read for recreation—Twain, and Dickens, and Melville. I discovered Fielding, and Chaucer, and Joyce, and had more fun. Of course, I had to take a grammar course and write term papers, so I learned how to sneak in a few hours at the library. I didn't take any honors, but I stayed in.

Then I discovered philosophy, and found out that I actually *wanted* to go to the library. I started studying without realizing it—it was so much fun, such a colossal, idiotic, senseless puzzle. Nobody had any good answers to the big questions, but at least they were asking.

My answers? I was looking for them. That was enough.

So I studied for fun, and almost learned how to party. Never got very good at it, but I tried—and by my senior year, I even had a couple of friends who trusted me enough to tell me their troubles.

Not that I ever told them mine, of course. I tried once or twice, but stopped when I saw the eyes glaze. I figured out that most people want to talk, but they don't want to listen. It followed from that, logically, that what they liked about me was that I listened, but didn't talk. So I didn't. I got a reputation for being the strong and silent type, just by keeping my mouth shut. I also found out, by overhearing at a party, that they thought I was the Angry Young Man.

I thought that one over and decided they were right. I was angry about people. Even the ones I liked, mostly. They wanted to take, but they didn't want to give. They cared about fighting, but they didn't care about brains. They spent their time trying to get from one another, and they didn't care about why they were here.

Oh, don't get me wrong—they were good people. But they didn't care about me, really. I was a convenience.

Except for Matt.

Matt was already working on his M.A. when I met him, and by the time I graduated, he was making good progress on his Ph.D.

So what was I going to do when I got my degree? Leave town, and the one good friend I had? Not to mention the only three girls who'd ever thought I was human.

No way.

So I started work on my master's. Physics, of course.

How come? From literature and philosophy?

Because I took "Intro to Asia" for a freshman distribution requirement, and found out about Zen—and learned about Shrödinger's Cat in "History of Science." Put the two together, and it made a lot of sense.

Don't ask. You had to be there.

Then Matt ran into a snag on his doctoral dissertation. Do you know what it's like to see a real friend deteriorating in front of your eyes? He found that scrap of parchment, then got hung up trying to translate it. Wasn't in any known language, so it had to be a prank. I mean, that's obvious, right? Not even logic—just common sense.

Matt didn't have any.

Now, don't get me wrong. Matt's my friend, and I think the world of the guy, but I'm realistic about him, too. He was something of a compulsive, and something of an idealist, as well—to the point of . . . Well, you know the difference between fantasy and reality? Matt didn't. Not always, anyway.

No, he was convinced that parchment was a real, authentic, historical document, and he wasted half his last year trying to decipher it. I was getting real worried about him—losing weight, bags under his eyes, drawn and pale . . . Matt, not me. I didn't have any spare weight to lose. Him, he was the credulous type—one of the kind that's born every minute. I'm one of the other kind, two born for every one of him. I mean, I wouldn't believe it was April if I didn't see the calendar. Forget about that robin pecking at the window, and the buds on the trees. If I don't see it in black and white, it's Nature pulling a fast one. Maybe a thaw.

So he had disappeared.

I thought about calling the police, but I remembered they couldn't do anything—Matt was a grown man, and there hadn't been any bloodstains in his apartment. Besides, I hadn't been on terribly good terms with the local constables ever since that year I was experimenting with recreational chemicals.

Still, I gave it a try. I actually went into the police station—me, with my long hair and beard. Nobody gave me more than a casual glance, but my back still prickled— probably from an early memory, a very early memory, of my father saying something about "the pigs" loving to beat on anybody who didn't have a crew cut. Of course, that was long ago, in 1968, and I was so little that all I remember of him was a big, tall pair of blue jeans with a tie-dyed T-shirt and a lot of hair at the top. I hated that memory for ten years, because it was all I knew of him until Mom decided to get in touch with him again, and I found out he wasn't really the ogre I figured he must have been, to have left Mom and me that way. Found out it wasn't all his idea, either. And I had a basis for understanding him—by that time, I had begun to know what it was like to have all the other kids put you down.

"I'm sorry, kid," he told me once. "I didn't know alienation was hereditary."

Of course, it wasn't—just the personality traits that led to it. I wouldn't say I ever loved him, but at least I warmed to him some. He had shaved and gotten a haircut, even a three-piece suit, by then, but it didn't fool anybody for very long. Especially me. Maybe that's why I wear chambray and blue jeans. And long hair, and a beard—like my early memories of him.

And early memories stay with you longest and deepest, so I really felt as if I were walking into the lion's den.

The cop at the desk looked up as I approached. "Can I help you?"

About then, he could have helped me out of there, and I might have needed it—but I said, "I hope so. A friend of mine. He's disappeared."

Right away, he looked grave. "Did he leave any message?"

I thought of the parchment, but what good is writing you can't read? Besides, he wasn't the one who wrote it. "Not a word."

He frowned. "But he was over twenty-one?"

"Yeah," I admitted.

"Any reason to think there might have been foul play?"

Now, that question sent the icicle skittering down my spine. Not that the idea hadn't been there, lurking at the back of my dread, mind you—but I had worked real hard not to put words to it. Now that the sergeant had, I couldn't ignore it anymore. "Not really," I admitted. "It's just not like him to pick up and pack out like that."

"It happens," the sergeant sighed. "People just get fed up with life and take off. We'll post his name and watch for him, and let you know if we find out anything—but that's all we can do."

I'd been pretty sure of that. "Thanks," I said. "He's Matt Mantrell. Matthew. And I'm—"

"Saul Bremener." He kept his eyes on the form he was filling in. "Three-ten North Thirteenth Street. We'll let you know if we hear anything."

My stomach went hollow, and my skin crawled. It doesn't always help your morale, finding out that the cops know you by name. "Uh . . . thanks," I croaked.

"Don't mention it." He looked up. "Have a good day, Mr. Bremener—and don't take any wooden cigarettes, okay?"

"Wooden," I agreed, and turned numbly about and drifted out of that den of doom. So they remembered my little experiments. It makes one wonder.

The sunlight and morning air braced me, in spite of the lack of sleep. I decided they were nice guys, after all—they'd left me alone until they could see if it was a passing fad, or something permanent. Passing, in my case. So it was smart—they'd saved taxpayers' money and my reputation. I wondered if there was anything written about me anywhere.

Probably. Somewhere. I mean, they had to have something to do during the slow season. I began to sympathize with Matt—maybe blowing town suddenly wouldn't be such a bad idea.

Get real, I told myself sternly. Where else would I find such sympathetic cops?

Back to the search. Maybe *they* couldn't do anything officially, but *I* wasn't official.

So I searched high and low, called the last girl Matt had been seen with—back when I was a junior—and started getting baggy eyes myself. Finally, I took a few slugs of Pepto-Bismol as a preventative, screwed my disgust to the nausea point, and went back into his apartment.

I scolded myself for not having moved that table; just lucky Matt hadn't left anything on it. I laid my notebook down on the desk next to the phone and gave a quick look at the table, the kitchenette counter, and the miniature sofa. Nothing there but dust and spider silk.

Then I went through that apartment inch by inch, clearing webs and squashing spiders. Or trying to, anyway—I must have been dealing with a new and mutant breed. Those little bug-eaters were fast! Especially the big fat one—I took my eyes off it for a second to glance at the arachnid next door, and when I glanced back, it wasn't there anymore.

It wasn't the only thing that wasn't there—neither was any sign of where Matt might be. I mean, *nothing*—until I turned and looked at the kitchenette table and saw the parchment.

I stared. Then I closed my eyes, shook my head, and stared again. It was still there. I could have sworn I'd put it back in my notebook—so I picked up the notebook and checked. Yep, the piece of sheepskin was still in it, all right.

That gave me pause. Practically a freeze, really, while I thought unprintable thoughts. Finally, slowly, I looked up and checked again.

It was on the table.

I looked down at the notebook, real fast, but not fast enough—it was back between the lined sheets. I held my head still and flicked a glance over to the table, but it must have read my mind, 'cause it was there by the time I looked. Then I laid down the notebook, real carefully, and stepped back, so I could see both the notebook and the table at the same time.

They each had a parchment.

Well, that settled that. I gave up and brought the notebook over to the table. I set it down beside the parchment. Yep, they were both still there—Matt's parchment in my notebook, and a brand-new one where none had ever been before. At least, a few minutes before—I had checked the table as I crawled across it. I frowned, taking a closer look at the new parchment.

It was written in runes, and the "paper" was genuine sheep-skin, all right.

How come runes?

Because runes are magical.

I tried to ignore the prickling at the base of my skull and told myself sternly that runes were just ordinary, everyday letters in somebody else's language. Okay, so it was an old language, and a lot of the items written in it had been ceremonial, which was why they had been preserved—but that didn't mean they were magical. I mean, the people who wrote them may have *thought* they could work magic—but that was just superstition.

But it was also something that made the scholar in me sit up brightly and smack his lips. I mean, literature had been one of my undergraduate majors—justified an extra year on campus, right there—and although it wasn't my main field anymore, I was still interested. I'd learned at least a little bit about those old symbols—and I knew Matt had a book around here that explained the rest. I hunted around until I found it, blew the dust and webbing off, and sat down to study. I looked up each rune and wrote its Roman-letter equivalent just above it. I tried pencil first, but it just skittered off that slick surface, so I had to use a felt pen. After all, this couldn't really be anything old, could it?

After three letters, I leaned back to see if it made a word. H-e-y.

I recoiled and glared down at it. How dare it sound like English!

Just a coincidence. I went to work on the next word.

P-a-u-l.

I sat very still, my glance riveted to those runes. "Hey, Paul"? Who in the ninth century knew my name?

Then a thought skipped through, and I took a closer look at the parchment. I mean, the material itself. It was new, brand-new, fresh off the sheep, compared to Matt's parchment, which was brittle and yellow—several years old, at least. Something inside me whispered *centuries*, but I resolutely ignored it and went on to the next word.

I wrote the Roman letters above the runes, refusing to be sidetracked, resisting the temptation to pronounce the words they formed, until I had all the symbols converted—though something inside me was adding them up as I went along, and whispering a very nasty suspicion to me. But as long as I had another rune to look up, I could ignore it—even after I'd already learned all the runes again and was looking each one up very deliberately, telling myself it was just to make sure I hadn't made a mistake.

Finally, though, I had written down all the letter equivalents and I couldn't put it off any longer. I stayed hunched over the parchment, my hands spread flat on the table, trying to grip into the plywood as I read the translated words.

H-e-y P-a-u-l g-e-t i-n t-o-u-c-h I-v-e l-o-s-t y-o-u-r a-d-d-r-e-s-s.

Or, to give it the proper emphatic delivery: *"Hey, Paul! Get in touch! I've lost your address!"*

I could almost hear Matt's voice saying those words, and I swear my nails bit into the plywood. What kind of a lousy joke was this? Friend? You call that a friend? First he leaves town without a word, and then he sends me *this*?

I was just realizing that he couldn't have sent it, when I felt the pain in the back of my hand.

"Damn!" I snatched it back, saw the little red dot in the center, then the big fat spider standing there with that big wide grin painted on its abdomen, and so help me, it was laughing at me. Anger churned up, but the room was already getting fuzzy. Still, I tried to hang on to that anger, tried to lift a hand to swat—the blasted thing had no *right* to . . .

But before I could even finish the thought, the haze thickened, wrapped itself around me like a cool blanket, rolled itself up, and bore me away to someplace dim and distant, and I almost managed to stay conscious.

CHAPTER 2

When I came to, the mist was gone, and I felt amazingly well. I mean, I had never felt that whole, that healthy, since I was a kid—and I hadn't been aware of it then, of course. It was like waking up on an April day, with the air fresh and warming from the night's chill, and the sun painting the day in primaries as you watch, and knowing it's your birthday.

But it wasn't April, it was November, and I was inside Matt's apartment. Only I wasn't, I was out in the open—and it wasn't November anymore, it really *was* April. Either that, or it was Florida.

Florida, with mountains stabbing up from the horizon? And not gently rounded mountains, like the Appalachians, but jagged granite obelisks, with snow on top?

Of course, they were off in the distance. Close by, all I could see was a field of wheat, with two or three little hedges cutting it into odd shapes. Whoever lived here, they could use some lessons in geometry.

I was just beginning to wonder how I'd come here, when I saw the knight.

Well, I knew about the Society for Creative Anachronism, of course, but I also knew they didn't go in for tilting, and this guy was carrying one of the most authentic lances I could have imagined. Plus, he was riding a Percheron—and I don't know any SCA types who could afford the upkeep on a pony, let alone a beer-wagon bronc. And, of course, there were the half-dozen men on foot behind him, all wearing more or less the same combination of brown and gray, with steel bands glinting

13

on their hats and long spears in their hands. They raised a whoop and pointed at me. The knight turned to look.

He saw me and perked up right away—dropped the point of the lance to horizontal, aimed the war-horse at me, and kicked it into a gallop.

Must have been the long hair and the beard. Mine, I mean. Either that, or he had something against blue jeans and chambray.

His men raised another whoop and came pelting after him like children hearing the bells on an ice cream truck. I just stood there, staring at all that scrap iron and horse meat thundering down at me, trying very, very hard not to believe any of it.

Then I realized the tip of the lance had come close enough so that I could see it was sharp and made of steel, and I had to believe that much. I jumped aside. The rider tried to swerve, bellowing some nasty things, but his Percheron didn't have that tight a turning radius, and he went crashing into the underbrush.

Underbrush?

I whirled around and, sure enough, there it was, just stunted trees and bushes, a little thicket in the middle of all those fields, presumably where the ground was too poor to grow anything. Or maybe around a creek—I braced myself, hoping to hear a splash.

Instead, I heard a crack that filled my whole head, along with a piercing pain. The scene went dark for an instant, then came back full of bright little shiny lights. I would have fallen down, but a big rough hand was holding me up by the arm while a voice guffawed, "He is nothing, only a scrap of skin and bone! Here, Heinrich, you try him!"

And I was spinning and staggering across the grass, dazed and amazed to realize I could understand the words, though I knew damned well they weren't English.

Then I slammed into something else meaty and with foul breath. He slammed a fist into my gut. I doubled over, my stomach trying to climb up my throat, and a huge bellow of laughter filled my ears. Then something hard slammed into my bottom, and I heard another nasty laugh. I moved my legs fast, just barely managing to catch up with my top half in time to keep from falling—but behind me, I heard an outraged shout. "It was not your turn, Rudolf! Remember your place!"

Then I slammed into another wall of leather and sweat that

made an evil laugh and pushed me back far enough so that I could see the fist swinging at me. Reflex finally took over, and I squirmed aside so that the fist hit my shoulder, not my head. It spun me around enough so that I could see Heinrich belting Rudolf one. Rudy went down to his knees and stayed there, rubbing his chin—and behind them, the knight was sitting his horse with his visor up, nodding and laughing.

Then another tough snarled, "My turn!" and grabbed me.

But another clunk grabbed my other arm and yanked back. I yowled, but I could still hear him bellowing, "Take a lower place, Gustang! I will not be forborne!" And he swung a quick left hook into Gustang's gut.

I couldn't believe it. Not only were they beating up a total stranger, just for fun—they were fighting over me, too, about the pecking order.

But the wrangling had taken just long enough for me to collect a little bit of my wits, and it was the part that held the memory of my karate training. What would I have told my teacher, if he'd been here? "Sorry, Sensei, I was watching the scenery?" Sure.

Time to remember I was a trained killer. I'd never killed anything larger than a mouse, of course, and that was only with a trap—but that didn't change the training.

I spun around, slamming into the guy who had my arm and snaking my leg around his in the process, shoving and kicking back. Down he went, and I spun to the next one, who was so surprised he was slow getting his guard up—only it wasn't a guard, he was just swinging at me, not even trying to block. I ducked and kicked, and he went down.

The other four finally woke up to what I was doing and fell on me with an outraged roar. I sidestepped, ducked, punched, whirled, and kicked, recovered and chopped. The adrenaline was singing, and if I was bruised and groggy, I didn't realize it. Two of them were down, and the other two hesitated, uncertain—at a guess, I decided they weren't used to having their toys play back.

Then the knight shouted and slammed down his visor— obviously time to restore a little order here. His men relaxed, stepping back and leaving it to Papa.

All the outrage I felt boiled up as I saw the Percheron plodding forward and beginning to pick up speed. This was no way to treat a stranger, at least one who hadn't even offered an insult! As the huge beast lumbered into a trot, I shouted, "What are you doing, jumping a stranger just going his way? Are you out of your brains, have you nothing but hay? Do you have any sanity? Any common humanity? You should feel what it's like to be crashed up this way!"

The huge horse tripped. It tumbled. It hit the ground hard and rolled. The knight bellowed in alarm, and just managed to kick free at the last instant.

I stared.

So did his men.

Then somebody hissed, "Zabreur!" and the knight began to kick his arms and legs—he was on his back, trying to turn over.

But he was out of action long enough for me to make some headway against his men. I turned to them, advancing—if I tried to run, it would restore their self-confidence.

But that was very thoroughly shot. They moaned and backed off fast, then turned, stumbling, and started to run.

I stared, thunderstruck. They couldn't be that scared, just because the horse had hit a gopher hole and tripped! Okay, so it was a lucky coincidence that I had just finished yelling something—but that shouldn't have scared them that much.

The knight didn't think so, either. "Hans! Klaus! You worthless, good-for-nothing blobs of dog meat! Come back here and aid me, or I'll . . ." Then he caught sight of me limping toward him, frowning, curious, and I guess I must have looked pretty bad, being mussed up with my shirt torn and all, because he moaned and made some sort of sign. "You cannot prevail! My master is an Earl of Evil!"

Some force staggered me, making my head ring. He must have thrown something I hadn't seen. Anger surged, and my instinct sent me to kick his head in—but prudence took over at the last second, pointing out that I should get as far away from him as possible, and not add homicide to any other charges the local authorities might dream up against me. This was especially true because he obviously *was* one of the local authorities. I had laid off smoking grass for similar reasons, and it had apparently paid off, since I hadn't been arrested. I slowed and nodded. "Right. I love you, too, sweetheart. Remind me to return the hospitality someday." Then I turned and went away, walking fast—or as fast as I could; I seemed to have developed a limp.

I glanced back a couple of times, but no one was showing any great interest in following me. That made me curious after a while, so I shinnied up a tree until I had a line of sight back to the little forest we'd been near. I was on the other side of that woods now, but I could see the knight and his boys trudging off toward the castle way up high across the valley. That was both good and bad—good, because it meant I had some time to find a hiding place, or get farther away; bad, because it meant they'd apparently decided I was too much to handle and were going back for reinforcements.

Of course, they could just be cutting their losses. Maybe they were planning not to mention me to anybody again—but somehow, I doubted that. Might have had something to do with that word somebody'd hissed when the knight went down— "Zabreur." My German was a little rusty, and that probably wasn't real German, anyway—but didn't the word mean "male witch"?

Possible.

I shinnied back down, turning thoughtful. Chambray and blue jeans probably looked like luxury fabrics, to them—now that I thought about it, their cloth had looked pretty much homemade. And my styles were certainly odd, by their standards. The belt and boots alone would be enough to mark me as above peasant rank, and weird—tooled leather with a huge metal buckle, and high heels. No, from their point of view, I was familiar enough to be real, odd enough to be special.

I set off uphill again, deciding I'd better stay alert. The "magician" pose was a good idea—it could help protect me, and I sure didn't have anything else to do the job. Well, no, I had a large clasp knife in my pocket—I like 'em big enough so that "jackknife" seems like an understatement. I decided I'd better use it to help me make something better in the way of a weapon. I stopped off at the next woodlot, hunted around, and found a fallen branch that was still pretty solid. I whittled away twigs as I walked and, pretty soon, I had a serviceable staff. I'd hung around with some SCA guys and learned a little about quarterstaves from them—but I'd learned a bit more from my sensei. I wasn't an expert, mind you, but I was capable, and it was better than nothing.

I looked around me then, finally letting the scenery sink in, instead of just taking a quick glance to know which way to go. There were rugged mountains in the distance, big hills nearby, with sheep grazing on the slopes and every more-or-less horizontal spot taken up by grain. I couldn't have told you one cereal from another unless it came in a box, but this stuff looked too hairy to be wheat.

Finally, it hit—I wasn't in the Midwest anymore. In fact, I doubted I was even in America—and judging from what I'd seen of the locals, I wasn't even in the twentieth century.

Time travel? Space zapping? Impossible! I had to be dreaming.

But those punches had sure hurt. A dream, this wasn't.

Hallucination?

Possible—but if it were, it would've had to have been the most detailed trip I'd ever heard of, and the most enduring. Besides, I had sworn off all chemical experiences years before.

Flashback?

Again, possible—though I didn't think I'd taken anywhere near enough drugs, ever, to have caused a spontaneous trip to happen, and certainly not one that lasted this long. Still, it was a possibility. I closed my eyes and willed myself back to my apartment.

But there were no psychedelic patterns inside my eyelids, only darkness—well, redness; I was standing in sunlight. I groped for my identity symbol, but my hands were empty, except for the staff. In desperation, I put my left hand on my belt buckle and started tracing the patterns of the Native American symbols I could feel there.

Nothing happened.

I sighed and gave up, opening my eyes. I was stuck here, wherever "here" was—and I was going to have to live by the local rules, whatever they were. Denial wouldn't help, and it might be a quick road to disaster. Whether that disaster was psychological or physical was kind of a moot point—it would be very unpleasant, either way.

Unless there was some evidence to the contrary—and I couldn't see any—I had to assume that the knight and his bullyboys were genuine, not modern people putting on some incomprehensible show. Those guys couldn't have been SCA members—they weren't polite, they weren't friendly, and their weapons weren't padded. So, somehow, I'd landed in the middle of some sort of medieval culture, from what I could see of it—and if they thought I was a magician, that could explain a few things.

I wondered where I was. I couldn't offhand think of any place on Earth that was still living in the Northern European Middle Ages. Okay, there were some isolated islands where the living was still pretty limited—no TV, even—but so far as I knew, they didn't run to knights.

A medieval fair, being held to attract the tourists? No; you don't beat up on tourists.

I sighed, deciding that I just didn't have enough information to figure out where I was, how I'd been brought there, or why. I shelved it until I could learn more. There were more immediate problems that needed tending to, such as survival.

I set off up-slope. A few hundred yards later, I passed a berry bush—and I was amazed to realize I was hungry. I stopped and stepped closer, inspecting the berries carefully, and decided that I couldn't be all that badly off, if I could still want food. I'd tied in with a local back-to-the-basics group for a year or two, going out on field trips into the countryside to learn how to survive in the wild, or at least without grocery stores; I hadn't quit until they started talking about setting up a commune. So I knew which plants were edible and which weren't, and the all-important rule: If you're not sure it's good to eat, don't touch it. But these looked to be perfectly ordinary raspberries, so I took a chance, and a handful. They tasted good, so I took another handful.

As I was munching, I noticed a very big spiderweb, glowing with the sunlight behind it—in fact, several of them; the neighborhood must have been saturated with flies. The biggest web, though, had an eight-legger the size of a quarter, an exact double for the one that had stung me. Anger rose, and my hand tightened on my staff—but I told myself that it couldn't be the same bug, and I turned away.

Bad year for spiders, folks.

The land was still sloping upward. I decided I must be in the foothills of the mountains I'd seen in the distance. After a little while, I came to a woodlot that went on and on. I stayed on the fringe, just this side of the underbrush, and kept a wary eye on it—for all I knew, a dragon might have come charging out any second. On the other hand, I wanted to be able to duck into it quickly, if Sir Overbearing and his boys decided to come hunting, after all.

Then, suddenly, the shock hit. I stopped dead still, leaned on my staff, and waited for the feeling of desolation to pass.

It didn't.

I lifted my head, looking out over that strange, strange view, and Kullervo's lines from *The Kalevala* sprang into my mind.

I chanted them aloud, hoping the sound would make me feel better:

> "And the friendless one reflected,
> 'Wherefore have I been created?
> Who has made me and has doomed me,
> Thus without a sun to wander
> Through the starry wastes forever?' "

It worked. Just the sound of a human voice helped, even if it was my own—and the feeling of kinship, the knowledge that somebody else had felt this way before, somewhere, somewhen, and that a lot of other people had to have felt the same way, too, to keep that verse alive down the centuries. I wasn't a total oddball, and I wasn't completely alone. Culture can be a great consolation.

Consolation enough to put some spirit back into me. I straightened up, squaring my shoulders, and set off again.

Light blossomed—an actinic, piercing light that seemed to lance though my eyes.

I fell back, raising a forearm to protect them. Panic surged through me—the only thing I'd ever heard of that made sudden light like that was a bomb.

But there was no explosion. Instead, I seemed to hear, very faintly, the sound of a chiming gong—but it could have been imagination.

In fact, it had to be—and so did the strange, vague, anthropomorphic shape at the center of that light burst, where the glare was strongest. As I watched, it coalesced, becoming clearer and more humanlike.

Then I caught my breath. It had turned into the shape of a young man, swallowing up all the light so that it still shone faintly, even though I could see through him. Just barely.

He wore a glowing robe, and there was a shimmering behind him, a suggestion of huge folded wings—and his face was very severe.

No. It couldn't be. An angel?

"I am even so," the being responded, "and the one who hath known thee even since the day of thy birth, Saul."

Well. That brought me back to my senses, a little. "If you've known me that long," I said, "how come I've never seen you before?"

"In that dull world to which thou wert born, naught of the

spirit can be seen, save to those few souls that do glow with goodness. Here, though, the world of the spirit is open to men, if they do but seek."

"World?" I frowned. "You mean I'm in a totally different world from the one I've lived in all my life?" Somehow, that didn't seem like news.

"Even so," the angel agreed, but he was still frowning.

Then the other part of his message registered. "But," I said, "I'm not particularly interested in the world of the spirit."

"How little thou dost know thyself, Saul! And how greatly dost thou seek to hide thine own nature from thyself. Thou hast ever been preoccupied with the things of the spirit, and 'tis even thy aching search for truth that hath led thee away from the churches of men."

I just stood there for a second while that sank in. Then I said, "I thought you boys were supposed to think the churches had a monopoly on truth."

"The religions they serve have truth within them, and therefore do the churches, also—yet the folk who constitute each church are but human, and as fallible as any among thee. How intolerant art thou, to excuse thine own failings and condemn them for theirs!"

I lifted my head in indignation. "I haven't condemned anybody!"

"Hast thou not turned from them because thou hast judged them to be hypocrites? Yet surely thou must needs see that their faith is a striving after perfection."

I nodded, not following.

"Therefore, if they do strive for perfection, they cannot already have attained it."

"Now, wait a minute!" I held up a hand, seeing where he was going.

"Thou hast learned it," he said, nodding. "If they are not perfect, thou canst not blame them for their imperfections."

"But I haven't judged anybody!"

"Hast thou not but now judged even thy Creator? Hast thou not blamed Him for creating thee doomed to loneliness?"

"Oh," I said. "*That's* what brought you here."

"Even so," the angel confirmed. "In this world—nay, this universe—prayers are answered more obviously than in thine own, and verses are prayers, or petitions to the Adversary."

Suddenly, I was very glad I hadn't sung "Sympathy for the Devil."

Then the rest of what he'd said sank in. I frowned. "What do you mean, 'this universe'?"

"Hast thou not perceived it with thy vaunted reason?" he taunted. "Thou art no longer in the universe of thy birth. Thou hast been transported to another, in which magic rules, and physics is superstition."

I stared.

"Yet the God of All is the One God here, as well as in thy home," the angel said inexorably, "and of all the universes that be; for 'tis He who made them, and doth maintain them by the force of His will. It is this mighty and majestic God whom thou dost blame for thine own failings!"

"But I wasn't talking about the Judaeo-Christian Creator," I objected. "I was reciting a quotation from the Finnish national epic! If you want to look for the 'creator' I was talking about, go look among the gods of the Finns! Besides, I didn't even make a statement! I just asked a question!"

The angel waved the objection away with an impatient gesture. "'Tis immaterial. Thou art in a universe in which the only true Creator is Jehovah, and thou must needs align thyself either with God, or with the Devil."

"Are you trying to say God didn't make me to be lonely?"

"Nay, nor to wander. If thou dost lack friends and home, that is the consequence of thine own deeds and choices. If thou dost not wish it so, thou canst choose otherwise."

I frowned. "Choose to go back to my own world?"

"Even that, though thou shalt have to seek the means, and labor long and hard to earn or learn the way. Yet I spoke more of thy grieving for friends and place."

"I've been looking for friends all my life!"

"They have been there," the angel said inexorably. "Thou hadst but to live as they did, to learn their ways and follow them."

"Wait a minute! You're saying that if I wanted to be part of a group, I had to do as everybody in that group did?"

"Thou hadst need to abide by their rules," the angel said. "There are many such that I have rejoiced to see thee turn away from—yet there were others who were good folk, whose customs thou didst disdain."

I remembered the kids in grade school, who thought fighting and sports were everything. "Damn right!"

The angel's face flared in wrath. I shrank back. "Uh, sorry, there. *Darn* right."

He diminished to a slow burn.

I collected the pieces of my wits and said, "They were so phony! And their standards were, too! Thinking that how well you could hit a ball really mattered!"

"It did," the angel said, "to them."

"Not to me! Reading books counted! Knowledge counted!"

"Thus thy books meant more to thee than friendship. Thou hadst made thy choice; thou hadst small room to rail 'gainst God."

"Oh, yes I did! I should've been able to have friends *and* books—other kids who liked to read, liked to learn! Then I would have been part of a group! We might even have learned how to play baseball together!"

"Dost thou not wish to be rare?"

"No!" I exploded, and was shocked to hear myself say it—but I'd worked up too much momentum to be able to stop. "I'd love to be normal! To have friends! To be a social animal! And I tried! I did learn their ways, at least a little bit—but it was too late! I couldn't acquire the instinct! And they knew I was faking!"

"Yet nonetheless would have given thee toleration, if thou hadst continued to strive."

"To try to be something I wasn't? To be a phony? I thought you guys were supposed to value truth!"

"As indeed we do," the angel returned, "and I rejoice that thou hast chosen the more truthful way. Yet 'twas thy choice, not God's doing."

"Sure, but look what He gave me to choose from!" I drew a deep breath and reined myself in. Harmony, balance; center yourself ... "I thought having more brains was supposed to give you a big boost toward Heaven."

"Nay," the angel returned. "Heaven is open to all, to the lame as well as the nimble—and to the moron as well as the genius. 'Tis the soul that is of concern to God, not the mind."

I stared, shocked.

Then I said, "But I thought people with better minds had a better chance of coming closer to the truth! And that's God, isn't it?"

"That is an aspect of God," the angel said, "or a description of it. 'Tis no more the whole of Him than is His omnipotence. Oh, a man of greater intellect can come to a fuller and more complete knowledge of God, if he doth strive lifelong—yet his way is more torturous, for his mind can see more obstacles to faith in God than can the man of less nimble wits."

"But the smarter man can do more holy works!"

"Not 'more,' " the angel corrected me, "only ones that others cannot see. Yet his temptations to error are greater, for if he does not apprehend the truth in an instant, he is like to say it doth not exist, and turn away."

"So," I said slowly, "that's why the student went to the rabbi and said, 'Teach me the whole of the law while I stand on one foot.' "

"That is an allegory," the angel agreed. "Yet if thy mind is the means of coming closer to God in the end, it hath also its own forms of obligation."

I turned wary. When someone says obligation, they're trying to get you to do something you don't want to do. "Such as?"

"To use thy mind to labor for the good of thy brethren," the angel said. "To never rest till thou hast come to see the Truth of God—and, till thou hast attained that clarity of vision, to hold fast in the faith that 'tis there."

I turned very cold. "You're asking me to believe in something I don't know is there."

"If thou didst know it," the angel returned, "there would be no need for faith."

"Nice twist to the logic." I dismissed the argument with a wave. "But if I can't prove it, I won't accept it."

"Yet thou must!" The angel stepped closer, face creased with anxiety. "For this world to which thou hast come is a domain in which spirit rules, and if thou art not dedicated to God and His goodness, thou wilt slip toward Satan and evil."

"Ridiculous!" I scoffed. "I've heard that before, too—'You've got to commit yourself. There's no middle ground.' "

"There is not, here. With each deed thou dost to any other human being, thou dost commit thyself to good, or to evil! Thou canst not remain poised between! Thy smallest action will doom thee, if thou dost not choose God as thy goal. Thou canst not stand alone!"

"Well, I blasted well intend to!" I snapped. "I'm not about to commit myself to anything! Or anybody! All my life, people have been telling me, 'You've got to sign up! You have to join! You can't just stand by yourself!' But I didn't believe them—I learned early that being part of a group always results in having to do things you don't believe are right. I refused to do those things before, and I'll refuse again!"

"And therefore wilt choose to be alone," the angel warned.

"Yeah, I've been ostracized! Sometimes directly and openly, sometimes subtly and covertly—but always cut off, snubbed. If that's the price I have to pay for being my own honest self, I'll pay it—and I have! I've been doing just that for twenty-four years now, thank you, and doing just fine!"

"Thou hast not," the angel contradicted. "Thou dost endure in loneliness and instability."

"Well, if that's the price of freedom, I'll pay it! And if you think you're going to do anything to punish me for it, you'd better just stop talking and get to the thunder and lightning!" I braced myself, ready for annihilation, and found myself hoping that I'd been right about God, and that He was on my side after all.

The angel looked unutterably sad as he studied me, then seemed to rally a little. "Nay. My power may not be spent 'gainst the living, and most especially not 'gainst the mortal who was placed in my care. I shall repel devils who seek to torment thee with all of my power, as I have in the past—but thy choices are thine own to make, by God's decree. And thou hast made them."

I stood still, waiting for the adrenaline rush to wear off.

The angel turned stern again. "Yet henceforth do not rail 'gainst Heaven for thy loneliness—for 'tis thou who hast chosen it."

Suddenly the light exploded outward, enveloping him. It dwindled, rising and soaring upward, but faded out before it had gone very far.

I just stood staring after it, feeling the stiffness ebb from my limbs, feeling the weakness begin, and letting myself realize that I had just seen my guardian angel.

But I intended to go on griping all I wanted. I might have to accept loneliness as the price of freedom and integrity, but I didn't have to be happy about it.

On the other hand, I *wasn't* accepting it, either. "You *can* have friends and still be yourself," I muttered to myself. "It's just that friends who like you the way you are, are few and far between."

Which reminded me of Matt.

I turned and started trudging uphill again. If I'd been transported into a different universe, maybe he had, too.

Same different universe?

I hauled up my sinking stomach. There was a good chance

of it, wasn't there? After all, I'd been looking for him when
that damned spider had bitten me and sent me into this world.

How could a spider bite transport you between worlds?
Death?

Or hallucination. Which reminded me of the angel. Had to
be a hallucination. Couldn't possibly have been anything else.
The berries, I realized—they may have looked like ordinary
raspberries, but they had probably contained a hallucinogen of
some sort. They'd just opened up a channel for my subconscious to speak to me, in the form of my guardian angel.

Which meant my subconscious was religious.

I definitely didn't like that notion.

I could almost hear it speaking. *Sub to conscious. Come in,
conscious.*

No. I refuse. I'll stay outside.

And I would, too.

CHAPTER 3

As I walked, I tried to reason it out—after all, forty credits' worth of philosophy ought to be good for something, and if it wasn't any good in this situation, it never would be, anywhere. I resisted the personal, supernatural view of the local phonemena—angels weren't real, and neither was magic. Well, okay, something that sure looked a lot like magic was going on here—but magic wasn't a person, with emotions and a personality; magic could much more believably be just a force, a kind of energy, impersonal and . . .

My train of thought derailed as a flicker at the corner of my eye caught my attention. I glanced that way, but it had disappeared, of course. No, there it was again, like a glitch in my field of view. A wild stab of panic hit; this would be a very, very bad time to lose my vision! But it passed, with a little shove from my common sense—and just in time, too, because the glitch widened, and I felt the impulse to reach out and adjust tracking. Silly, of course—because it not only widened, but swelled, turning into a zigzag tearing that reached downward to the ground and churned up a cloud of dust.

Then the membranes in my nose stood on end, and wrung themselves dry as the stench hit them with a rotten egg. "Guardian angel," I muttered, "if you're anything more than a hallucination, now would be a great time to show yourself!"

It didn't, of course—hallucinations don't usually come on demand. But I did feel a surprising surge of confidence, almost reassurance. Shouldn't have surprised me, I suppose—the mind plays funny tricks on itself, and this was just my subconscious'

27

way of getting itself to believe it could cope with whatever was coming. I suppose.

But I happened to notice a tickling in my thumbs.

The dust cloud died down, and there sat an ancient crone in a gown of charcoal gray.

That, I could live with, given the milieu—I had seen her before, in my extreme youth, in dozens of illustrations in books of fairy tales. What threw me, though, was that she was sitting at a desk, with papers strewn all over it, and a quill pen in an inkwell.

"You have cast two unauthorized spells in the space of half an hour."

Two?

Spells?

The crone wheezed on. " 'Sobaka,' said I to meself, 'there's nothing for it but to come hither and gaze—and aye, there he be! Yonder he stands, flaming with zeal to oust the palsied old witch-woman from her bailiwick and take her peasants for his own! If there's aught I cannot abide, 'tis a bursting new magus!"

"Hey now, wait a minute!" I was beginning to get angry again. "I don't want anybody's 'bailiwick'—and you can't own people!"

"Blasphemy!" she cried. "Not only a magus, but also a liar! As if 'tweren't a plentitude of folk in the art one must struggle with as 'tis! Aye, a body's no sooner believing she's secure in her place, to lord it over her own trembling churls in easy breath, when, *whoosh!* Another young'un crops up, with cheek and with challenge, to be put in his place. It's no wonder the land's going to the pigs, with half the peasants turning to bandits, and a good number of them trying to out-evil their own township witch! And all from letting delinquents get out of hand! Ahe, for the auld days! When younglings knew their places, or we had leave to fry them!"

"Leave?" I glanced at the desk again. "Who gives you leave to blast people or not?"

"Why, my master, fool, Queen Suettay!"

"Sweaty?" I stared; it struck me as an odd name for royalty.

"Nay, fool—Suettay! And be sure you do not take her name in vain, or she will surely appear to blast you!"

That gave me back some composure. I smiled, not too nicely; I'd heard that before, though usually about a personality a bit higher than an earthly monarch—that you have to talk nicely about Him, or He'll strike you with a lightning bolt. But I've seen and heard an awful lot of people saying nasty things about God, and I've never noticed any of them running afoul of large doses of electricity—except for the one who was working on a live wire at the time, and he didn't start cursing until after he got zapped. "Okay, so she's Queen Suet-ty." I had a mental image of a very, very fat lady looking like an awning pavilion with a crown on top.

"Suettay!" the old witch snapped. "Speak her name properly, crack-pate, or she will wish you ill indeed!"

Now I had it—the French word for wishes, intentions, as in, "I wish you a good day." The pronunciation had thrown me off, that was all. "Whatever. And this Queen Suettay will zap you, if you zap me?"

"Without showing you the error of your ways, aye. I am the bailiff of this bailiwick, given authority to see to its taxes and enforce the queen's laws o'er it! 'Tis for me to see you are noted in its book, and deal you work to do that will give the queen crops—or, if I have no need of you, to another."

I bridled instantly. I mean, had I left my own civilized universe, with running water and modern medicine, just to come to a godforsaken medieval backwater that still made me cope with a bureaucracy? "Okay," I snapped, "so you've got the authority to issue me a travel pass, or whatever, because you're the witch in charge of the local parish . . ."

"Bailiwick!" she screamed. "Speak not in the words of the Flock!"

I frowned. Flock? Then I remembered the parable of the Good Shepherd, and that "ecclesia" literally means "flock," and I understood. So anything having to do with Christianity was anathema to her, huh? Maybe I could use that—but I kept it in reserve. After all, calling on the saints, or making the sign of the cross, or anything like that, kind of rankled; I hadn't been about to cop out to religion back home, and I didn't intend to here. Besides which, it might require conviction, which I definitely did not have.

She must have seen that in my eyes, because she gave me a gap-toothed grin. "Ah, then! You shy from those words yourself, eh? Well, then, come! Prick your finger, write your name in my book, and swear to serve the queen and her master, or I'll call upon his power, and you'll writhe in flames!"

Outrage kindled. "No way!" I snapped. "I've heard about that book—and I'd end up writhing in flames either way, until this hallucination wears off! I won't be a slave, and I won't accept any master!"

She answered with an evil grin. "Excellent," she crooned, "most excellent! For if you'll serve no master, then you cannot be protected by any—and the Other Side will not ward you!"

I felt the hair rise on the back of my neck.

"I felt your first use of a spell and said to myself, 'Sobaka, what bother is this?' and began to tidy up my work to spare time for a visit—but ere I departed, I felt the nerve-grating shimmer that could only have come from an agent of the Other Side, and withheld my visit till that grinding had ceased . . ."

Translation: she'd sensed the visit from my guardian angel and had been so scared that she'd burrowed under the bedclothes. I felt a little more confident.

"Yet cease it did," she crowed, "and totally—there was no shred of it left! Therefore did I come here, and sure enough, I see no particle of the aura of the Other Side about you! You have not aligned yourself with them, and have not their protection!"

The temperature of my precious bodily fluids began to fall again.

" ' 'Tis an idiot, surely,' I said to myself, 'an idiot who doth think to gather magic as if he were a windmill, gathering power from the gale and wielding it to grind what he will! Ay, such a fool I can twist right easily!' So come, addlepate, and sign in my master's book, or die in agony!"

Somehow, for a second, I didn't doubt that she could do as she'd said, and my heart sank down to join the caterpillars that were trying to turn into butterflies in my belly—but mostly, I felt the hot anger of indignation. How *dare* this old witch try to push me around! "No way will I get on your hook!" I snapped. "Keep the fire for your blasted book!"

She let out an outraged squawk, just about three-quarters of a second before her book burst into flames. She screamed, jumping back.

All I could do was stand there and stare.

That was too bad; it gave her a chance to recover from her surprise. "Vile recreant!" she screamed. "The records of all who owe my master are destroyed!" Then she hooked her fingers into claws, chanting,

> "By the most vile of obscene names,
> Follow that book into the flames!"

And she threw a whammy at me.

Only this whammy took form very fast, some unseen energy gathering itself together until it materialized about halfway between us as a roaring globe of fire. I shouted and leapt out of the way, but it swerved to follow me. I jumped again, in a forward somersault, but came up to see it still following.

I ran.

Behind me, the hag's cackling almost drowned out the roar of the fireball—and it was gaining. In a rush of adrenaline, I suddenly realized I should be trying verbal acrobatics, not physical—she had brought this phenomenon into being by versifying; I sure hadn't seen her pulling the pin on a grenade. I ducked behind a boulder; it followed me, and it was roaring, but so was I, tapping myself on the chest and chanting,

> "Put out the light, and then put out the light.
> If I quench thee, thou flaming minister,
> I can again thy former light restore,
> Should I repent me; but once put out thy light,
> Should I, consid'ring, find it sinister
> I can leave it dark and quenched forevermore."

I had to do a little rewriting there, since rhyme seemed to be important here—but under the circumstances, I didn't think Shakespeare would mind.

The fireball dimmed, darkened, and took a nosedive for the ground. By the time it hit, it was only a smoking cinder.

Sobaka stared at it.

Then she snapped her glare up to me, and I have never seen so much malice in a pair of human eyes. "Villain! Aroint thee! If you wilt not bend to my will, you shall break!" She began to move her hands in some sort of jagged pattern, chanting in a language I didn't know, though it sounded like Latin.

I gave her a grim smile. She must have thought that if I didn't know the words, I wouldn't realize she was versifying—but I could recognize rhymes when I heard them, and the meter was strong enough to slice up for seasoning. Well, if she wanted to have a contest slinging verses, that was okay with me.

Or maybe it wasn't. There was a huge rumble, and the ground heaved beneath my feet. I fell, instinctively turning to land on my side and roll as Sensei had taught me—and saw a jagged crack opening the earth where I'd been standing. The

hair on the back of my neck prickled. How had she known an
earth tremor was coming?

But it was my turn, and the minor chasm made me remember
an old hard-times song. I made a few modifications:

> "Well, if I had it, why, you could have it,
> But I ain't got it—I'm down and out.
> And now I've had it—with you, I've had it,
> So now I'll send it, and end this bout.
>
> She gave me trouble
> On a scale that's Richter,
> So from the rubble
> Now I have picked her.
>
> And I will drop her
> Into a deep hole
> That will stop her
> From hurting people.
>
> And this old clown
> Will be unfound
> As she sinks down, down, down."

The earth rumbled again, and a hole opened right under the
old woman's feet. She dropped like a stone.

I stared.

Sobaka screamed.

I was so flabbergasted, I couldn't think of anything to do
until she had disappeared. Then I came to and leapt over to the
hole to tell her not to panic, I'd dig her out—never mind that
she'd been threatening to kill me—but she was wailing, "Air!
Nay, give me air!"

I looked down the hole and saw two very wide and frightened eyes peering up out of the darkness about ten feet below
me. "The earth, the earth presses in all about me! Spare me,
Wizard! I shall trouble you no more! Only release me! Do not
let the earth fall in on me, I pray!"

"Holy cow!" I gulped. I had just put a claustrophobic in a
hole. "Enough, right now!"

I heard a moo.

I froze. I didn't want to look up.

But the wailing down below roused my guilt; I had to do

something. I looked up slowly, straight into the big brown eyes of a lean-looking bovine female. It had a hump on its back—a Brahma cow.

Coincidence. Pure coincidence. Obviously, I was closer to India than I had thought.

I turned back to the hole, assured that the cow wouldn't bother me. "Just keep calm! We'll get you out of there!"

"Be quick," she wailed, "before my master seizes the chance to take my soul!"

I froze again.

Then I said, "No taking of souls allowed. Not while the person's still living."

"Aye, but death might happen thus! The master needs but a slight chance, a crumbling of the earthen wall, to bring about a natural death! Then he can take me, and I am doomed forevermore!"

"He?" I frowned. "You're talking about the Devil?"

"Do not say his name!" she wailed. "Or you will hear the rustle of leathery wings!"

I was about to object, saying that was only a superstition. Then I remembered the cow, and decided I didn't want any more coincidences. "Look, as long as you've lived a good life by your own beliefs, you've got nothing to be afraid of."

"But I have not!" she wailed. "I have been as evil as I might! I have sold my soul for power over my fellows!"

"Sold your soul?" I stared. "Why the hell—uh, heck?—would you do a dumb thing like that?"

"I was ugly, and small, and shrewish, and all shunned me. 'Sobaka,' they said, 'you are so ugly, even the swine will spurn you! You are stupid, Sobaka—step aside.' ' 'Tis done badly, Sobaka—you can never do anything right!' 'Not even I could love you, Sobaka, and I am your mother!' 'Do not sing, Sobaka, you have the voice of a crow!' Until, at last, hate waked like a burning coal in my breast, and I swore I would someday have power to make them all suffer, to rue the day they had mocked me! But I could see no way to it, till the master appeared to me in a dream!"

I couldn't believe it. Not only a paranoid with a five-star inferiority complex—it had blossomed into raving delusions. She had actually convinced herself that she had sold her soul! All of a sudden, I could understand how come she had dug herself under when she'd heard my verse—it had fitted into her delusional system and had convinced her subconscious that she'd been overwhelmed by a spell. And since I wouldn't sign up with the Devil, presumably I had the force of good behind me, which is always stronger than evil in the end—at least, in the sort of medieval culture this seemed to be—so she'd been convinced my spell had taken over anything she could dream up.

Selling her soul was a metaphor for having dedicated herself to evil, of course. She had probably managed to become a minor bureaucrat just by toadying to the people in power—but she had convinced herself she was damned.

I couldn't let her die in that kind of agony, no matter what she'd been trying to do to me. "Look," I said, "even if you sold your soul, you can still get it back. All you have to do is repent, tell God you're sorry and won't do it again!"

"But what if I should live?" she cried, in an agony of indecision. "If I should repent and live, I would be the lowest of the low! All whom I have wronged would rise to smite me down! The master would send agents to deprive me of what life I'd have left—though 'twould be precious little; I am more than an hundred years old already!"

Delusion again—she couldn't have been a day over sixty, judging by looks. This being a medieval culture, she was probably only forty—life aged them fast, back then.

"Look," I said, "just because you were small and plain didn't mean everybody hated you."

"Yet they did! All need to know there is one lower than they! How could they fail to despise me?"

"By your being good, way down deep," I reasoned. "Sure, they're cruel—but if they saw you were really good inside, trying hard to make up for everything mean you did, they'd start liking you."

There was silence down at the bottom of that hole. Then, almost shyly, "Do you truly think so?"

Well, no, I didn't, actually—just from the clues, I had a notion she had been maximally mean to everybody she'd ever known, and people aren't that quick to forgive. So I changed the subject. "It doesn't get done in a day, of course—you have to earn trust, earn forgiveness by proving you've reformed—and proving it again and again for years and years. They'll punish you at first, sure, but you deserve it by now, don't you?"

"I did not when I was a maiden!" she said hotly. "Where was their goodwill then?"

"That was then," I reminded. "How much punishment do you deserve now?"

It was quiet, down there in the dark. Then she began to cry.

I hate the sound of a woman crying. "Please," I said. "Please don't cry. I'll get you out of there somehow."

"I have been so evil!" she wailed. "I deserve death, slow and agonizing death! Nay, what if they were to do to me as I've done to them?"

"Maybe it would be quick," I suggested. Inside me, my blood ran cold. Just how wicked had this woman been, anyway? "Maybe they'd be so angry, they'd just kill you out of hand."

"Then I would be damned!" she howled.

"Not if you'd repented." Then I remembered my Dante. "Sure, you'd spend a long time in Purgatory—but at least it wouldn't be Hell. Besides, the more they hurt you before they killed you, the less time you'd spend in Purgatory." I hated that kind of logic—I had a notion it had resulted in a lot of people torturing themselves, and certainly refusing painkillers when their last hours could have been a lot less agonizing—but it would help in this case.

"I cannot face it," she wept. "I cannot face the tortures I have meted out."

There was a rustling noise, just in front of me.

I froze. Then, very slowly and much against my better judgment, I looked up.

He was very toothy in the grin, very red in the skin, very black in the wings, and very sharp in the horns.

Sobaka saw him and wailed so hard she almost jarred the earth loose.

I found my voice. "Is this your master?"

"Nay!" she howled. " 'Tis his minion!"

Or some peasant, I realized, come to get revenge by scaring the life out of her.

"Get back, slave," he sneered. "This soul is forfeit!" And he jabbed at my face with his pitchfork.

I recoiled, but reflex took over; I grabbed the pitchfork and yanked, hard. I took him by surprise; he stumbled into the hole and fell flat on his face.

Dirt cascaded down inside.

Sobaka screamed in terror.

I realized I had to work on her delusional system—nothing

else was going to work fast enough. "Get out of here," I snapped. "You can't take her soul till she's dead!"

"I shall see to that, too." The devil bared his teeth in a snarl, rolling up to his knees, crouching to spring. "I shall cave in the hole. Fear not—she's already buried." And he sprang at me.

I leapt to the side, rolling. Oh, well, what the hell—I had a delusional system, too. "Guardian angel! This is where violence is authorized!"

"It is indeed!" a steely voice sang. "Avaunt thee, hell spawn! Or I shall rend your ectoplasm asunder!"

There he was, my guardian angel, twisting the pitchfork into a pretzel and throwing it at the devil. The horny one howled in terror and disappeared.

I wondered just what had been in those berries.

"Only juice," the angel assured me. "I am real, Saul. Remember."

I was thinking at a frantic pace. "Uh, before you go, could you step over to that hole, for a second?"

"Wherefore?" The angel frowned down at the hole—and then, bless him, he stepped up to the brim and called down. "Sobaka! Call on God, and He shall yet send your angel to ward you! I have banished your demon, but he will not stay gone when I go!"

I couldn't take a chance on any more hesitating. I began to chant,

> "Aid me now, insightful Freud,
> To help this woman to avoid
> Paranoia stemming from
> Insecurities that come
> From toxic parents, spiteful peers,
> And all anxieties and fears
> They bred, that are a key
> That locked inferiority
> Into her soul, therein to fire
> Hot into a complex dire.
> Vengeful fantasies, begone!
> Grandeur-delusions, all be done!"

I swear to this day, I don't know where that verse came from. I mean, if I'm really up for it, I can improvise—but not like that.

Then I remembered the tried and true.

"Day by day, in every way,
    I'm getting better and better."

"I repent me!" Sobaka wailed, deep down in the hole.
"Alas, my soul! All these years, I have sought revenge for
naught! For insults that need not have hurt me! Ah, what a
monster I have been!"

Well. Results already. What had been major wounds suddenly seemed like minor irritations. It didn't matter what people said to her, because she knew she was good.

Now.

But why was my guardian angel looking at me that way—I
mean, surprised?

I shoved the question aside. The memories of her cruelties
would swamp her newfound self-esteem, if I didn't give her an
out.

"What's done cannot be undone,
    But what's broken can be mended.
    Remorseful sinners can atone
    For all the hurt intended."

"Yet there is hope!" the voice cried from the hole. "I can
make amends—some, at least! Those whom I've slain, I
can give aid to their survivors! And if 'twill restore some faith
in goodness to them, to see me suffer as justice dictates, why
then, let them hurt me!"

I wasn't sure I liked the sound of *that*—but it would probably give her the strength she needed, to endure the transition
back to goodness. Seeing herself as a martyr was better than
the fire of her own self-damnation—I meant, *con*demnation—
and if I ever came back this way, I could see to it that she
moved on from suffering to service.

"I repent me!" she cried again. "Dear Lord, save my soul!
Inflict what trials Thou wilt, what sufferings Thou dost deem
just! Only let me come into Thy presence!"

There was a howl of rage and frustration somewhere, distant, but ringing. I looked up, surprised, but I didn't see anybody except my angel.

He was smiling a very smug smile, though. "That, Saul, was
her personal tempter. You cured her mind, and she saved her
own soul."

I stared.

Then I gave my head a shake. Whatever sort of dream this was, working within its rules was working very well. "Okay," I said, "but we'd better hurry up and save her life, shouldn't we?"

"Should we? For the longer she lives, the greater the chance that she'll slip back into sin."

I looked up at him, scandalized—but he wasn't even looking at me, he was talking to empty air on the other side of the hole. I felt the gooseflesh rise.

"Indeed, you are right," he said with regret. "If the Lord doth wish her home, naught we can do will save her."

"So if we can save her," I said, "that means it's not her time."

He looked down at me in surprise. "Indeed, Saul. You see it most clearly."

Well. I wasn't impressed. I'd figured that one out, long ago. Hadn't he been watching? "So how do we get her out?"

"Try a verse," he suggested.

"Ridiculous!" I snapped. "You can't make things happen just by talking!"

"Speak of that to Madison Avenue," he retorted. " 'Twas you put her down there, did you not?"

I just glared at him. I always hated it when the other guy was right.

But he *was* right—so I sighed and called down into the hole,

> "The day doth daw, the cock doth craw,
>   The channering worm doth chide!
> 'Gin you must be out of this place,
>   Though in sore pain you may bide!"

And she was standing beside the hole, looking about her in surprise that very quickly became major fear. "How—how did you achieve *that*?"

"By poetry," I said impatiently, "or at least a very, very old folk song. What's the matter—don't you even know the rules of your own universe?"

She shook her head, faster and faster, stepping away from me, hands coming up to fend me off. "I know only the rules of good and evil!"

That stonkered me. "Then how did you work magic?"

"Why, by reciting the spells my mas . . . doomer gave me."

Rote memorization. Parrotlike repetition. Coincidence and

association. She hadn't understood anything about what she was doing. No wonder she was a minor functionary. "There are other rules," I said. Then I remembered. "But you don't need to know them anymore."

" 'Tis true." Her hands came down. "All I need now is the justice of God, and the need for faith in Him."

Suddenly, she was on her knees, clutching at my jeans. "And 'tis you who have rekindled that faith! 'Tis you who have cured my soul of the curdled anger called hatred, that did drag it down! 'Tis you who have freed me to suffer for the right and seek to aid my fellow creatures! Oh, a thousand thanks, young Wizard, and a thousand blessings!" Then she remembered herself and dropped her hands. "If the blessings of a corrupted soul may be of benefit to you."

I was hugely relieved. I just don't like having things clutching at me—unless they're young, female, and shapely; and even then I'm wary. This one may have been female, but she was anything but beautiful, and I could have sworn she was growing older by the second.

"Your soul shines like newly minted silver," my angel said.

I looked up at him, startled. Compliments were one thing, but this . . .

Then I realized he was prompting me. "Say it yourself," I snapped. "No way am I going to deliver a line like that!"

"To whom do you talk?" Sobaka quavered.

I looked down at her, then looked up quickly at the angel. No, he was still there. "Him," I said, pointing. "Can't you see?"

She looked where I was pointing, and fear creased her wrinkled face, not that it made much difference. "Nay," she said. "There is none there."

"Well, there is," I sighed, "even if he's invisible to you."

"A familiar!" Her tones quaked.

"No, an angel," I said quickly, and started improvising; anything to give her the guts to keep going. "You've got one, too, and he—"

"She," my angel prompted.

"She," I corrected. Maybe the Quakers had been right. "She is watching you every second."

Sobaka glanced around her, fear turning into wonder on her face. "Can you see her?"

"No," I said, "but she's there."

"She is very happy just now," my angel informed me.

"She's very happy just now," I told Sobaka. "Don't make her sad again, okay?"

"Oh, I shall not!" She turned away, heading off downslope. "Oh, bless you, unseen angel, for never having despaired of me! Oh, stand by me and lend me strength, for I now must undergo the strongest trials of my life!" She turned back to call to me. "Ever shall I praise you in my prayers, healer of my soul!"

I shuddered, but managed to fake a smile. "Pay it back to other people," I called. "You don't have much time left. Better get busy."

"I shall! Oh, I shall!" And she headed off down the hill, caroling her joy.

I winced; a singer, she wasn't. "At the rate she's aging," I muttered, "I don't think she'll even make it to the bottom of the hill."

"Even if she dies, she will be on the road to Heaven," my angel assured me. "Her angel thanks you, too."

"Tell her she's welcome." I turned to him, frowning. "So angels come in sexes, too?"

"Well, no," he admitted, "but it makes you humans think of us more easily if we seem to. You term it 'identification' and 'self-image.' Call it 'gender.' "

"Identification!" I looked up, understanding something I'd been wondering about. "So that's why you've dropped the 'thee' and 'thou' form."

"That you might better understand me, aye."

"Understand, my foot! You want me to identify with you, to emulate you! Hey, I'm not even supposed to be able to *see* you!"

"You did call upon me," he reminded.

"And Sobaka didn't, so she couldn't see her angel? Is that who you were talking to, about whether or not to get her out of the hole or let her die?"

"Her guardian angel, yes." He nodded. "You have made three most happy today."

"Three?" I looked around, frowning. "I only count two— Sobaka, and her guardian angel. If you say so."

"Three," he said proudly. "Count me, also. You have struck a blow for the angels today, Saul. You are on our side, after all."

Why did that send such a thrill of panic through my veins? Why did I snap out, "No way! If I did something that worked for your side, it's just because it was the right thing to do under the circumstances! Don't bet I'll do it again! If something else comes up that I think is right, I'll do it, even if it's for the other side—by your rules!"

A look of apprehension crossed his face. "Nay, nay! Do not sin for no reason other than my having said you are on the side of the angels!"

"Very funny," I said bitterly, "considering who's talking. If it seems right, I'll do it, even if it's against your side—but don't worry, I won't murder, loot, or rape, just to keep from signing up with your team, either. I won't go out of my way to commit what you think is wrong." I turned on my heel and stalked away.

"You have lied," he called after me, "with that speech."

"See?" I said over my shoulder. "I've started already."

CHAPTER 4

The nice thing about being past Sobaka's checkpoint was that I was able to keep on trudging up-slope. I didn't know where I was going, except that it felt right—especially since it was out of her domain. Maybe, if I was lucky, I could get out of this massive hallucination. Or else find Matt . . .

Another nice thing about getting up in the world, was that I kept stretching out the sunset. Finally, I came to a pass at the top of the mountain. Down below me, the valley was in shadow—twilight, to them. I could even see a few lights appearing—fires of some sort. Maybe smoke-holes in huts? Had these people invented the chimney yet?

Then I looked up and saw one of the most glorious sunsets of my life. The only ones to beat it had been out in the Great Plains, where the landscape is mostly sky. Here, I was high enough up to have a lot of sky again, though not quite as much. Everything looked golden and rose, every mountaintop—and there were a lot of mountaintops. I wondered where I was—the Pyrenees? The Alps? Was I even in Europe?

Or even on Terra?

I shelved that thought, but it shook me enough so that I stopped contemplating the sunset. I turned back to the pass, saw its huge granite walls towering to either side, and decided I wanted to be through it before the light completely failed. I hurried, with a wary eye above me, glancing from side to side—I'd heard that mountaineers, historically, tended to be rather territorial. I'd also heard that they had reasons. But if they were watching, I guess they figured I was no threat, or was too small a fly to swat, because nothing happened. In fact, the only living creature I saw was a kind of mountain goat, who watched me for a while, then jumped into a shadow and disappeared. He was beautiful, but the experiences of the day made it seem rather spooky.

So, as I came to the other end of the pass, I was wondering what I was going to do about being alone in a strange country, in what was promising to be an extremely dark night.

I was very glad to see the campfires below me.

Not very far below, and I could tell they were campfires because of the tents. But the hallucination was still on—the men between the tents and the fires were wearing armor covered by long white tabards, and leading Percherons.

I sighed, squared my weary shoulders, and started the downhill hike.

One of the younger ones looked up, saw me, and called out, "Stranger!" He lugged out a sword the size of the Eiffel Tower and brandished it as he came toward me, demanding, "Friend or foe?"

"Either one," I snapped—that sword got my back up. "Take your choice."

He frowned at me—it wasn't one of the expected answers. But his buddies dropped what they were doing and came clustering around; I hadn't seen that much steel in one place since I'd crossed the Golden Gate Bridge. "Declare yourself," one of the older ones demanded.

That was exactly what I had been trying not to do. "Saul Delacroix Bremener," I told them, and nothing more.

"Saul Delacroix?" He frowned at his companions. "Named for the king or the apostle, and one of the cross."

"But Paul was not of the cross," one of the others objected. "He never knew the Savior, in life."

"Still, 'tis a goodly name," another said, then moved aside quickly as a tall, broad-bodied man with grizzled hair stepped through. He had a face like tanned leather and a jaw like a vise. The commander, at a guess.

He looked me up and down and pronounced, "His attire is odd, but he has no horse or arms. He cannot be a gentleman; he must be a peasant." Then he turned away, dismissing me with a gesture. "Let him stay; but he must draw water and fetch wood for the fire." He glanced back at me. "See to it, fellow."

The command did it. "Peasant" got to me, and the bit about

menial labor made it worse—but the command made my anger turn cold and active. "Fetch it yourself," I snapped. "I may be a commoner, but I'm no serf—and I am a gentleman." Which was true, on a technicality—I was a scholar, after all. By their standards.

"Oho!" A glint came into the commander's eye. "If you are a gentleman, then you are a gentleman-at-arms—for there is no other sort!"

Great. To be a gentle man, you had to be capable of violence. Oddly, the idea appealed to me; it fit into my configurational pattern of contradictory concepts. Hypocrite? Who, me? I just calls 'em as I sees 'em.

"Yet he is clearly not a knight, or he would wear a sword. Ho, Gilbert! You aspire to knighthood—prove yourself! Test this stranger for me!"

A kid with only a smallsword grinned and stepped up to me, dropping into a wrestler's crouch and beckoning.

I was appalled. He was at least six years younger than me, certainly still a teenager, and the top of his head was bald. "You've got a tonsure!" I said.

"All monks do," he agreed.

"But you're a knight!"

"Only a squire." His lip curled at my ignorance. "I am not yet worthy of my final vows. Will you fight, or talk?"

Well. Monks were obviously different here than they were at home. I dropped into karate stance, circling my hands and coming up ready to catch or chop. "Ready."

He stared at my actions, then frowned and lunged.

He telegraphed the move—I saw the half step forward on the left—but I resisted the urge to dodge, staying in to test the waters, so to speak.

He hit, and he hit hard. It was like slamming into an opening door. He grabbed me in a bear hug and hoisted—it had to be the crudest move I'd run into since grade school.

But effective—he was very strong. I found myself rising high, then slamming down at the ground, while all around me, those monks-cum-knights were cheering.

I twisted, landing on my side, and rolling back up to my feet to see the kid grinning as he came back in for more. But this time, I sidestepped at the last second. "That was your freebie," I told him. "Now I get my turn."

He didn't like that; he turned with a bellow and charged. I grabbed his arm and turned, put a hip against his, and flipped him. He swung up and down like a Ferris wheel. I figured he wouldn't know how to fall, so I held on to his arm and pulled up, to make sure he landed on his side, without too much force. The knights rumbled at that—they didn't like the look of it. I let go, and the kid scrambled to his feet again, face red, boiling mad.

Good. Angry, he'd make mistakes.

But he didn't charge again; he was smart enough not to make the same error twice. He shuffled in, hands circling, hunched over, watching for an opening.

I decided to give him one. I dropped my guard and put my hands on my hips, looking exasperated.

Sure enough, he bit. He went for my knees. I shoved against his shoulders, pushing myself back. That made him madder; he charged forward, trying to catch my knee like a donkey going after the carrot that's hanging from the pole. But he only took a couple of steps before he went for my crotch and arm, trying to hoist me. That meant he was coming up; I stepped back just long enough for his momentum to take him up far enough so that I could grab his tunic, lifting him a little bit as I hooked a leg behind his, and pushed as I kicked back. He fell—harder this time, since I wasn't trying to break his fall for him. He scrambled up, eyes blazing, and sent a fist shooting toward my face.

Oh, so he wanted to box. I blocked, and the blow went wide as I counterpunched. He hit my shoulder, and pain jolted the joint, but nothing big. On my other hand, his head rocked back, and I brought the left down, fingers stiffened, and jabbed him in the solar plexus.

That took the fight out of him, along with the breath and the legs. He folded around a center of agony, fighting for breath. I relaxed with a sigh of distaste—I really didn't like doing this to anybody, but especially not to a guy who really hadn't had a chance to fight back. Then I stepped around behind him, massaging his back and sides right opposite where I'd hit. The ring of men let out a shout of outrage, but the biggest guy held up a hand. "Nay. He but seeks to give aid to a fallen foe." He turned to me. "Yet give over, good man—let us tend to him."

"No," I said, "I don't think you know the technique. I broke it, I'll fix it." I heard a hiss of breath below me and looked down at Gilbert. "You okay now?"

"I will mend," he gasped. "You are a doughty fighter."

"Just had a little training," I assured him. "You're very strong, did you know that?"

"Strength is not enough," he groaned.

"True." I grasped his arm and pulled. He followed and came to his feet. From the heft of that biceps, I knew I'd done right to try to stay away from him. It was a good thing he had used that bear hug to throw me; if he'd just kept squeezing, I'd have been out like a light.

"You have fought bravely," the commander assured him, and beckoned a couple of other squires. "See to him."

They took him away, one on either side, and the ring of men began to break up as they turned back to their tasks, eagerly discussing the bout—what there had been of it. I noticed several guarded glances in my direction, but none of them seemed contemptuous.

I sighed. It was the same old story all over again. Just win a few fights, and they'll accept you. Wasn't there anything more to a man than his fists?

"You are welcome among us now," the commander assured me.

Of course.

But he was still watching me warily.

"Thanks for your hospitality," I said wryly. "I assure you, I won't start attacking without an invitation."

He shrugged the comment away. "We have swords enough. As to this wrestling, 'tis a peasant's sport—yet you do it well."

"Maybe too well?" I hazarded, from the look on his face.

"Mayhap." He turned, glowering. " 'Tis a most strange manner of wrestling. Where did you learn it?"

"In the East," I said. Okay, so America was west of here, assuming I was in Europe; but Japan was west of America, wasn't it? And it was the East. So I had learned it in America, but it was Japanese, and America was east of Japan, so I had learned it in the East.

"Ah." His face cleared; he nodded grimly. "The land of the paynim. Any rarities might come thence."

He meant the Near East, I was pretty sure—but Muslim culture was just different enough from his that, for all he knew, anything, but anything, might be there. It struck me with sudden inspiration—an excellent means of explaining any way in which I didn't fit in. "I lived in the distant land for many years," I said. "I'm a scholar, and not terribly interested in the things of this world—but their wise men taught me that training of the body has to come before any really advanced training of the mind."

"There is truth in that," he allowed. "With what weapons were you trained?"

"Only the staff," I said. "They drew their scholarship from holy men, who taught that it was wrong to use edged weapons."

"As do ours." The commander nodded. "Save for we few who are sworn to defend the True Faith by force of arms."

"I was wondering about that," I said. "You have tonsures. Are you monks, or knights?"

He frowned more closely at me. "How long have you been away from Christian lands?"

"Since I was very young," I admitted. After all, the American public schools fit that description, these days.

His face cleared. "Small wonder, then. Know that we are knights of the Order of Saint Moncaire—yet monks, also."

Well, now, that rocked me. I mean, I'd learned about the Knights Templars in school and read about them in *Ivanhoe*, and been thoroughly scandalized by the mere notion that a man who is purportedly dedicated to God could also be dedicating himself to smashing up his fellow human beings with a Clydesdale and a mace. But I tried to be tactful. "Uh . . . isn't that kind of a contradiction in terms?"

Instantly, the frown was back. "Why, how mean you?"

"Why," I said, "a monk is dedicated to love of his fellow human beings, and to upholding the Commandments—including 'Thou shalt not kill,' and 'Love one another.' But a knight is dedicated to hurting those same people."

"Assuredly, you cannot mean it!" He paled, and I could have sworn he was genuinely shocked. "Do you truly know so little of your own faith?"

"Of my own civilization, you mean." I frowned up at him. "You forget I've spent most of my life in a foreign land."

"Aye, I had forgot." He gathered composure around him, but still seemed rather shaken. "Know, then, young man, that we, as knights, are dedicated to the protecting of God's people from those who worship evil. And they who are dedicated to evil, scruple not to kill and maim in their lust to capture all that they can. It is therefore necessary to take arms against the minions of Satan; only major force can stay them."

I braced myself and tried to smile. I was hearing the rationalization that had allowed medieval Christians to mount a crusade against their own countrymen, for no better reason than that they had come up with a different version of Christianity.

The commander turned away and began to stroll through the camp, glancing around him to see all was in order—but he was still talking, so I tagged along. "Know, too," he said, "that in these lands of Christendom, many folk have fallen under the sway of Satan and his minions. Allustria, where we are now, is sunk in the bog of corruption; it is ruled by a sorcerer-queen. Ibile is only lately freed from a similar fate, and Merovence is free only because a most powerful wizard came to the aid of the heir, Queen Alisande, and fought off the evil spells of the usurper's sorcerer, so that her armies might cleanse the land of the false king Astaulf and his twisted knights."

Well, usurpation I could understand, even if it was saturated with superstition. "I take it you come from this, uh, Merovence?"

"In truth, we have."

"Ibile"—that had a familiar ring. The Iberian peninsula? If so, the "reign of evil" would probably have been nothing more than the Moorish Empire—to medieval Spaniards, the Muslim Moors seemed like pagans, therefore worshipping false gods. So I took the rest of it with a grain of salt. "Allustria" sounded like "Austria" with a couple of *l*s thrown in—maybe "Allemagne," which was Germany, combined with Austria? I knew of a pretty demonic figure in recent history who had tried to do just that—but he wasn't medieval. So I decided to reserve judgment on the evilness of Allustria's queen. But Merovence—would that be France, or Italy? Or maybe Poland or Russia? At a guess it was the land of the Merovingians, which would have been France.

Why not ask? "I'm kind of turned around," I said. "Which way is Merovence?"

"Why, ahead of you," said the commander, surprised. "You are near its border. Did you not know you had come out of Allustria?"

Suddenly, the business about Allustria being under the reign of an evil queen gained credence—at least, judging by the reception I'd had there, and the things Sobaka had said. "I hadn't known," I said. "Wherever it was, though, I was trying to get out of it."

"In that, you succeeded. Know that you have come into the mountains, and even though the queen of Allustria claims them, her writ does not truly run—though she has folk stationed in pretense of governance. If these hills are held by anyone, they are held by the mountaineers who call themselves Switzers."

Suddenly the geography clicked into place, and I frowned. "But aren't you kind of going the long way around? To go through Switzerland to get into Allustria?"

The commander nodded. " 'Tis even so. Yet there is no other way to come upon the minions of Queen Suettay unawares. Even coming down from the mountains, we may be espied."

"I think not," I said slowly. "If you go down through the pass I came from, you may find that the functionary who's supposed to watch that crossing point may not have been replaced yet."

He glanced at me keenly. "Have you slain him, then?"

"Her," I corrected, "and no, I didn't do any killing. Persuaded her to see the error of her ways, you might say." I didn't like the way he looked at me then, and I added quickly, "Don't get any ideas. I'm not a missionary."

"You must have a silvered tongue, then, to have so swayed one of Queen Suettay's liege men!"

I noticed my correction about gender hadn't taken, and I wasn't surprised. People tend to see what they want to see, and the Middle Ages kind of locked people into certain expectations, blinding them to anything they hadn't been taught. I recognized this whole business about needing to take arms against evil as just another excuse for doing what Christianity forbade, which amounted to hypocrisy.

I wasn't about to say that out loud, though. Standing for truth is one thing, but saying it when you haven't been asked is another. I had no desire to get pummeled, or to become the subject of an impromptu beheading.

But I was still kind of dazed by the notion of an order of military monks. I wondered what their monastery looked like. Did it have a gate, or a portcullis?

"Strange that you know so little of your own land," the commander sighed, "from sojourning so long among the paynim. Yet you are a scholar, and therefore also a gentleman—though you know not the weapons of honor."

Again, I nodded. I knew something of late medieval society. A gentleman was below the aristocracy, but above the peasantry—upper middle class, in my own day's terms.

Knights qualified, but by the eighteenth century, so did squires, even if they never became knights. They owned enough land to have several tenant farmers, and generally had more education than most. At this point in history—assuming it to be about 1350; I didn't dare ask, for fear of betraying ignorance that might make me suspect—that meant being able to read and write, and knowing table manners and strict rules of protocol.

Not that these boys seemed all that big on class distinctions, though—I saw knights in their gambesons, fetching buckets of water and lighting campfires, right along with their squires. "Uh," I said. And, "I notice that your men are fetching and carrying, right along with their squires."

"Aye," he said. " 'Tis a lesson in humility."

"But," I said, "when I came up, you said all I was good for was fetching and carrying."

"Aye, and I regret the haste of my words—yet by your appearance, who was to know your quality? Still, friend, though peasants may be fit only for hewing wood and drawing water, a knight is fit for any task, short of those fit only for royal blood, or appropriate to a monk."

"But knights can draw water and gather wood, too, eh?" I nodded; it made sense, within their worldview. You can always do less than you're able—and to them, it was a gesture of humility—but you can't do more. The idea raised my hackles, especially since I knew damn well that any man could learn to ride or swing a broadsword—though I would have been the first to admit that some can learn it better than others. It was just that my enlightened age believes that every task is as honorable as any other—or tries to, anyway. "But you're monks, too."

"Aye, and like other monks, we labor at menial tasks as well as great, to make us mindful that we, too, are only mortal, and must strive lifelong if we would become saints in Heaven."

Something about that struck a faint resonance of rightness within me. I tried to ignore it. "Meaning that all people are equal in God's eyes?"

He stared at me as if I had spoken treason. "Nay, nay! Only that all may become saints, after death!"

But some saints were greater than others, no doubt. I had a vision of Heaven with everyone walking around with different sizes of halos, and smaller houses for the peasant-saints but bigger houses for the gentry-saints, and of course palaces for the aristocrat-saints. My mouth quirked, and I had to bite my lip to keep from laughing, then speak quickly to cover up. "In that case, do you mind if I help?"

The commander smiled slowly. "Why, how is this? Will you now freely offer to do what you refused, when commanded?"

I looked up at him, amused. "Kind of answered your own question, haven't you?"

The commander laughed and clapped me on the shoulder. "Aye, you are indeed a gentleman! We will be glad of your aid."

"And I'm glad of your hospitality," I rejoined, "for which, my thanks. Even with the opening wrestling match, you're a lot more friendly than the last bunch I ran into."

The tension was back, suddenly; he was alert all over again. "Who were they, and where?"

"A knight and his men-at-arms," I answered slowly. "Don't know their names, but his shield had a torch turned upside down and mashed flat."

"Sir Hohle of the Tarn," he said, his face grim. "I know him by repute, and all of it is evil. Where did you meet him?"

"On the other side of the pass, and a long way down, before the climbing became really steep."

" 'Tis well; his horses could not follow. What manner of welcome did they give you?"

"None at all; they used me for a punching bag, until I got mad and started hitting back."

"Mad? You are a berserker, then?"

"No, no!" I closed my eyes, then looked up at him with a forced smile. "I meant 'angry.' I knocked down a couple of them, and the knight decided to flatten me—but his horse crumpled underneath him, and the fall knocked him out."

"Sheer happenstance?" The commander frowned. "I trust it not. What spirit wards you?"

That brought a chill trickle of familiarity through my vitals, but I shrugged and said, "Just the usual guardian angel, as far as I know."

"Then it must have been something you said," the commander mused. "Are you a wizard?"

Again, that cold trickle—I couldn't think why. "Not as far as I know." I didn't bother mentioning what had happened to Sobaka; surely that must have been my guardian angel at work. Or my hallucination . . .

Hallucinations that happen to somebody else?

"It may be that you have an inborn talent for magic," the commander said, brooding. "If so, walk very carefully! The merest misstep might cast you into the power of the Evil One—for folk who have such gifts draw either on the power of Satan, or the power of God, though they know it not. Beware, lest you evoke a power you wish not to worship."

That got my back up. I wasn't about to worship any source of power, no matter where it came from. After all, who'd worship Niagara Falls, just because it produced electricity? "Thanks for the advice," I said, though. I've always tried to be polite, but at the moment, I had extra reasons.

" 'Tis scarcely a matter for astonishment, that you had so ill a greeting," he said, "since you were coming out of Allustria. In truth, I am amazed you could walk through that benighted land with no more unpleasantness than such as they gave." He stopped by a stack of leather buckets and handed me a couple. I braced for another scene, but he picked up two himself and started walking toward the stream that was gurgling nearby.

Mollified, I followed. "I wasn't in Allustria very long." That much, at least, was true.

He nodded. "You came through the Balkans, then?"

I didn't want to tell a real lie, so I said, "I wasn't about to ask for hospitality there." I looked up sharply at a sudden thought. "Wait a minute! That's why you insisted on that wrestling match, wasn't it? To see if I'd pull any tricks!"

"We did test you," he admitted. "Think not harshly of us, I prithee. You were coming from Allustria—we marked you as soon as you came forth from the pass—and you wear outlandish garments. Who knew but you might be a sorcerer come amongst us?"

I stopped, frowning. "How do you know I'm not?"

"Why, a sorcerer would have used foul magics to best his opponent, before ever the man had struck him—or, at least, would have used foul blows and no slightest mercy. You accorded your opponent first strike and did what you could to lessen the impact of his fall."

So he had noticed why I'd held on to the kid's arm. I nodded slowly; for the first time in my life, starting with a fight made sense. Almost.

Suddenly, I felt bad about deceiving him, especially if I was going to accept his hospitality. What had happened to my obsession with truth? "Actually," I said, "I didn't go into Allustria by my own choice. I was in my homeland, thousands of miles away, and a very large spider bit me. I blacked out, and when I came to, I was on the other side of that mountain." I gestured behind us.

The commander stopped in his tracks, staring at me. "Were you truly? Then you have been transported hither by some great magical power!"

"One that works through spider bites?"

He glanced to either side and lowered his voice. "I have heard of such—of a Spider King, whom no one knows to be either good or evil."

Instinctively, I liked this arachnid autocrat. "Where can I find him? Maybe he can send me home!" Could I dispel the hallucination by working through its own terms?

"None knows, nor do I think he would send you hence, for he must have brought you here for a purpose of his own." He frowned down at me for a few seconds, then forced a smile. "Still, be of good cheer! It may be you were transported here by a saint!"

I shuddered, deciding that, saint or Spider King, I was dealing with superstition.

That was what this whole scene was, of course. Was that what was really underneath my rationalist mind—a superstitious subconscious?

The commander turned away and started walking again. "Still, if you waked in Allustria, whatsoever it was that brought you must have work for you there. Mayhap you should not be fleeing that benighted land."

"Or maybe I should," I gritted. "After all, I didn't apply for the job. I wasn't even consulted."

"We do not always choose our paths." He knelt by the river and filled each leather bucket with a single swing of his arm, then stood again.

"Have you?" I asked. "Chosen your path, I mean."

He nodded slowly. "We have chosen to go into Allustria, no matter the risk. There do be yet a few good folk there, who strive to maintain their virtue in a sink of absolute corruption. The sponsor of our order, Saint Moncaire, came to our abbot in a dream a fortnight agone, to reveal the plight of one such poor family, who hold by God and goodness, though they dare not do so openly . . ."

I felt the anger of outrage ring through me. Superstition or not, people have a right to worship as they please, without having to hide it. "But they've been careful, so they haven't been bothered?"

"Oh, nay! They were gentry, but over the span of generations, they suffered again and again, because their rulers sought to rob them of their faith by driving them into despair—first by taxes, then by spells."

"But how'd these rulers know about them?"

"Because the good souls of this household never left off doing good for their neighbors and aiding those who were poor or beset. Thereby did the witches and warlocks who were given jurisdiction over their parish know them for what they were and seek ways to bedevil them."

"Sounds like some petty bureaucrats I know." I nodded, with a bad taste in my mouth.

"Now," the knight said, "they live without land and are tenants on the acres their ancestors owned—for they were squires, and their holdings held a whole parish within their boundaries. All its people, following the example of this family's goodness, forsook their dog-eat-dog ways and persevered in the face of all the harassments and abuse their masters did heap on them. Those harassments have grown more and more frantic as the decades have passed, for such fortitude and perseverance in virtue is bound to attract the attention of the queen, who will no doubt punish her henchmen for failing to drive these virtuous folk into sin. Therefore they will harry this family out, root and branch—for they persevere in their faith and charity, even though they are poor and must ask aid of others, which none dare grant. One child is dead of poor food and chill; another is ailing. They are at wits' end and near to despair. Therefore hath our abbot sent us forth, to win glory by bringing these poor folk out of the land of spiritual misery, and into the light of Merovence."

"That could be dangerous," I suggested, "if there really are so many evil sorcerers around—and even more, so many evil knights."

"Most dangerous indeed, and 'tis quite possible we shall lose our lives in the attempt." His jaw firmed and his eyes flashed. "Yet 'tis for us to seek to ward the godly, unheeding of the peril—and if we die, we die. Spending our lives in so worthy a cause, we shall surely not linger long in Purgatory, and it may be that we shall even be accorded the crown of martyrdom."

I winced; I wondered how many people had been lured into unnecessary suffering and early death by that promise.

" 'Tis not death we should fear," the commander said, "but that we might fail in the attempt—for we must bring that family out right quickly, ere they despair and are subverted and dishonored, or slain."

"*Should* fear," I said softly. "But what you really do fear is the evil that you have heard is in that land. Right?"

"We should be fools if we did not." His whole body tightened so much that I knew it was closer to terror than fear. Privately, I gave him credit for being either a hero, a saint, or a fool. I didn't think he could really qualify as a saint, since he was using a sword—so, all things considered, I strongly favored the last option: a fool. Not that I was about to say so, of course.

So I accepted their hospitality for the night, helped with the camp chores, and joined in the sing-along on the less-religious songs—I always did like "Amazing Grace," but I wasn't too good on the Gregorian stuff. I was a devoutly agnostic Protestant, and the God I didn't believe in was Calvin's, so I didn't do too well on the Latin—only one year in high school, and it didn't sound much like theirs. Different dialect, no doubt.

Then I bedded down at their fire, helped with the morning chores, hauled a bucket of water to help douse the fire—and held up an open hand in salute. "Well, it's been fun. Thanks a lot for your hospitality, Sir Monk—but I gotta be going now."

"Assuredly you will not ride alone!" He seemed to be genuinely dismayed. "You are not yet past the reach of Queen Suettay. Wizard or not, a lone man is a marked man; you will be easy prey for whatever evil forces she may send against you!"

"I've managed okay so far," I objected.

He sighed. "You have indeed—yet you slept among armed monks last night. How many other nights have you spent in Allustria?"

I swallowed thickly, remembering what superstition claimed about nighttime. "None," I admitted. "Only one day."

"Even so." He scowled. "And in that day, you did work magic?"

"Well, I wouldn't have said so, but . . ."

He chopped off my comment with a sideways sweep of his hand. "What you would say matters little; what you did, is all.

Be assured that Suettay knows of your presence—or that her underlings do."

That, I could believe, whether or not magic really did work here. Sobaka's boss was bound to notice she was missing, sooner or later—and if she were at all efficient, it would be sooner. First thing I knew, I might have bloodhounds on my track, and I had a notion that in this world, the emphasis was on the blood. "I'll be okay," I protested.

"You mean, 'well enough,' " he interpreted, "and in Allustria, there is no such state. You are either holy enough to withstand the assaults of the satanic, or you will succumb to their temptations and become yourself an ally of evil."

"No way!" I glared up at him. "I don't buy it, Captain! You don't *have* to be either a saint or a devil—you can just be yourself, human and humane. A man can stand alone, and I intend to! I refuse to commit myself!"

"Mayhap that is true in the land from which you came, but it is not, in Allustria." He clapped and beckoned. The knights and squires looked up in surprise, and he pointed at Gilbert, the guy I'd wrestled yesterday, then beckoned. The kid dropped his horse's reins and came over.

"This foolish wizard seeks to ride alone, still within Queen Suettay's reach," the commander explained.

The kid went wide-eyed, staring at me as if I had just volunteered to be the main course at a state dinner.

"It's not really that bad," I protested.

"Nay, it is!" he said. "You will be corrupted or slain ere you see another dawn!"

My stomach sank, but I stood up a little straighter and said, "Look, I'm not the superstitious kind, but I'm no fool, either. If I see trouble coming, I'll hide, and if it won't pass by, I'll fight."

" 'Tis praiseworthy to die fighting," Gilbert admitted, "yet foolish to spend your life needlessly."

The commander nodded. "Buy some advance in grace, at least, if you must give up your life. Nay, I cannot let you ride fully unguarded. Gilbert, do you ride with him, as his shield and buckler."

The kid stared at him as if he'd been wounded. "But, my general! To lose my chance for glory in our quest—"

"Is what I require of you." The commander's tone was iron.

Gilbert flushed, then slowly bowed his head, but his back was ramrod-stiff.

" 'Tis not so vile as it may seem." The commander's tone softened. "I have had a dream that has shown me that this man is a hinge—upon him will turn great events, and if he can be held to the path of goodness, I doubt not he will aid greatly in the overthrow of the evil queen, and the establishment of the reign of goodness in Allustria."

Gilbert looked startled, then glanced at me.

"Don't look over here," I said. "It's news to me, too."

"A stalwart man with a rugged face did speak to me as I lay sleeping," the commander said. "He wore kingly robes, and a cap with leaden images of saints all about its rim. He told me that this man Saul will be the lever that topples the throne of Allustria, even as the disciple Paul was transformed from the sword that slew the early Christians, to the share that plowed the field of Gentiles." He turned to me. "You are fortunately named."

I wasn't about to disagree with him, but I did think his metaphors were a little odd. "Who was this saint you saw in your dream?"

But the commander shook his head. "Some holy man of Allustria's age of virtue, belike, who lived in humble obscurity and died unknown; not all the saints were famed, or even known. He was none of whom I have ever heard. Yet his face did not shine, so he may be a blessed one, not a saint."

I frowned. "How do you know he isn't a devil masquerading in disguise?"

Everybody in hearing range looked up with a gasp, and the commander stared, offended. "Why, for that I am in a state of grace!"

"Uh, sorry." I swallowed and forced a smile. "But even in a state of grace, you could be tempted."

"Mayhap," he said slowly, "but a devil would not wear saints' medals on his hat."

I gave it up. He was so certain about it that he couldn't even consider being wrong. "But look—I really don't need an escort. This young man has important work to do."

"My work is what my captain commands," the kid assured me, "and if he says that accompanying you is of greater import than our quest, he must be right."

That grated. Faith is all well and good, but so is skepticism.

But the commander was nodding. "Import there is, and the danger will be no less—mayhap greater. Nay, there will be

great chance of gaining glory in this mission—and, win or
lose, you will gain your spurs."

The kid's eyes fired.

"Dead or alive," I muttered.

"How do you say?" the young man asked me courteously.

"That this really isn't necessary," I snapped. I had to admit
that I liked the idea of an armed escort, but I have this thing
about close and continued contact with people I don't know
well. "Look, I really appreciate the offer, but I travel alone." I
grabbed his hand and pumped it. "Nice wrestling with you.
Have a good trip." I dropped his hand, gave the commander a
curt bow. "Thanks for your hospitality, sir. I wish you well on
your quest—and good-bye." Then I turned on my heel and
strode away.

Behind me, I heard him call, "God be with you, too, Wizard," and to somebody else, presumably the squire, "Why do
you wait, Gilbert? Take sword, buckler, and horse, and go with
him!"

I walked faster. If the kid had to pack, I had a few minutes
to get lost, at least. There was a line of evergreens ahead; if I
could make it to the trees, I could hide well enough so that he
might miss me.

I was about ten yards away from the first fir when I heard
the hoofbeats behind me.

CHAPTER 5

Look, I hate jocks—or, well, not jocks as people, just jocks as a class; and you couldn't have any better example of the jock-ocracy than medieval knighthood.

"Ho, Wizard!"

I sprinted.

The evergreen boughs closed around me. I heard a blundering behind me, and a cry, "Wilt thou not wait?"

No. I wouldn't. At least, not if I had any choice. I dodged to the left, since he'd probably be expecting the right, and plastered myself behind the largest trunk I could find.

"Wizard? Wizard!"

I tracked his voice and, as he moved forward, I sidled around backward, trying to keep the tree trunk between us. I must have succeeded, because he blundered around for an awfully long while, coming up with all sorts of swearwords that had to be so clean they were almost antiseptic—things like, "By blue!" and "Bones!" and "Blood and iron!" I resolved to remember them if I ever had to cure an infection. When he was far enough away, I sprinted to a little thicket I had seen and crawled in. He kept crashing around, coming up with an amazing variety of expletives that had absolutely no need to be deleted, while I tried to stifle my laughter.

Finally he gave up, blundering back out the way he had come, lamenting his failure loudly and at great length. I felt sorry for him, a little, then reminded myself sternly that he was probably better off with his buddies—and in any case, this was my chance for a getaway. I crawled out and started walking fast, heading downhill. Twice I struck a trail wide enough for

a horse, but I sheered away from them—that was exactly the
kind of road he'd be likely to take, if he hadn't given up looking for me yet. They angled across my path, instead of going
straight down, which I figured was a plus.

Finally, I came out onto a clear road, wide enough for two
horses side by side. It was still trending downhill, but at an angle opposite to the trails I'd seen, and I decided to chance it.
The kid had either given up by now, or passed me by. But I
kept a wary ear tuned as I went down the dirt track, walking
fast, alert for the slightest sign of him. So the first time, Gilbert
saved my bacon without even being there—because I was listening for him, I heard the sudden rustle in the leaves just behind me, and had already leapt forward before I heard the thud
on the ground. I whirled, chopping at the point where a guy's
neck would be if he were crouching. I was a little high; I
caught him on the side of the head, and he yelled as he went
sprawling.

I whirled back to the front, having a hunch he wouldn't
have dared jump an able-bodied man if he were alone. Sure
enough, another specimen was just coming out of his crouch
from having dropped from the branch ahead of me, as four of
his buddies stepped in from the sides, two with battle-axes,
two with arrows drawn.

Let me tell you, these were not the nice, clean boys from
Sherwood Forest—or, rather, if there really was a Robin Hood,
this is probably what most of his merry men really *did* look
like. Their clothes were patched and filthy—I could actually
see the dirt—and the only one of them who shaved had been
neglecting that art for several days. The others looked as if
their beards got trimmed once a year, and that had been January first. Their grins showed rotten teeth, and they smelled to
high Heaven.

The one in front uncoiled from his crouch and sprang at me
with a shout. I didn't try to get out of the way, just gave
ground fast, so that he didn't slam into me terribly hard. I
nearly kicked him away from sheer disgust; the stench of him
was more likely to knock me out than his fighting. But the
archers wouldn't try a shot, if he was real close, so I ignored
the stench and grappled him. Unfortunately, he grappled back,
throwing his arms around me and squeezing. I whirled him
around with the pain in my ribs getting worse and worse—all
he knew was a bear hug, but he was *strong*! I'd caught him

with one of my arms up, though, so I waltzed him over toward
his buddies at the side of the path, hoping my wind would last
until I was next to one of the hatchet men.

Max the Axe saw me coming and backed off, keeping just
far enough away for a swing, worse luck, and I was starting to
see spots, so I stamped on my hugger's instep. He howled and
loosened up; I broke his hug and hit him with three quick
punches to the face. He let go with an oath that would have
blistered paint, if they'd had any, and I staggered away, just accidentally stumbling into the axeman.

He saw me coming and shouted, swinging his blade up, but
I slammed into him in a body block, and we both went down.
I grabbed the axe handle and twisted as I rolled. He yelped,
and I came up holding an axe in both hands.

A stick cracked down on my right-hand fingers. I yelled as
the fingers went numb, and somebody twisted the axe. My hurt
hand fell loose, but I yanked hard on the other one and kicked.
I got him in the gut—he was the first one I'd chopped, getting
back into the fight. He gave a loud grunt and fell away, and I
started whirling the axe, as if it were a propeller blade. The
four who were still on their feet backed away—they didn't like
the look of that, and the archers didn't look too sure about trying a shot.

I was just realizing that one was missing when the blow
caught me on the back of the head, and for a minute, I couldn't
see. Somebody grabbed the axe out of my hand; somebody
else kicked me in the gut, and I went down with that awful
dread that the final blow is coming, that I was just about to
gain empiric evidence as to whether there is an afterlife.

But there was a lot of yelling going on still, and some very
odd ringing noises. I heard heavy, dull, staccato sounds with
some howling thrown in, and managed to pull myself up, my
eyes clearing, to see three of the bandits trying to scramble
back into the brush, three of them lying crumpled on the
ground in front of the horse's hooves, and my old buddy Gilbert, with a little round shield on his left arm and a large sword
in his right, hefting and glaring after them as if trying to decide
whether to go chasing.

"Don't try it," I croaked. "Once you're off the road, they've
got the advantage. They can just sit up in the trees and throw
rocks at you, even."

"Friend Saul!" he cried, whirling toward me. "You are
hurt!"

"Just a mild concussion." I hoped I was as well as I was try- ing to sound. "Y' know, I think I'm glad you decided to tag along, after all."

Then things got kind of dim, and my knees folded.

He was there before I hit the ground, leaning down from his horse, holding me up.

"I'll ... be all right," I managed. "Just ... need to get my bearings."

"You should rest."

"Just a little while." I looked up into his broad, open face, saw the frown of concern, and decided maybe there was some- thing to be said for jocks, after all—if they were on my side.

Well, what could I do? Tell him to go home to Papa, after he'd saved my life? Right.

So we went along together. Gilbert insisted that I ride the horse, and I insisted that I didn't—if it doesn't have brakes and a gear shift, I'm not interested.

"You shall have to learn to ride, if you stay long in our land!" he remonstrated.

"I'm not planning to," I assured him. "What's a nice kid like you doing in the military, anyway?"

"Why, for that good folk need protecting!" He was mildly scandalized that I even asked.

Well, that made sense. "But why as a monk?"

"I felt the call," he said simply. "I have a vocation."

I'd always wondered about that. "What's it feel like—the call? Did you have a dream? A sudden moment of enlighten- ment?"

"I have heard of such," he said slowly, "yet in my case, 'twas simply that there was a famine when I was so small that all I can remember is the great gnawing in my belly, and the kindly face of the monk who came at last to give my family a loaf of bread. In the rush of gratitude that came then, I wished to be like him—and that wish never left me."

"Just a good example." I frowned. "Didn't it bother you, when you were old enough to know what was going on, to find out that some monks were greedy and lustful?"

His face hardened. "I did hear of such, aye, though we only knew of one, ourselves—but we did learn of a whole abbey full of them, miles away, and heard that other abbeys did visit grinding rents upon their tenants, the whiles their monks did live in luxury. Yet the monks who dwelt nearby us lived in a cloister they had built with their own hands and which they themselves had enlarged and repaired. They farmed, even as we did, and would not accept gifts of any more land than they themselves could till."

"Sounds like the Franciscans," I said.

He frowned. "I know none of that name. Their example has shone down the years of my life, though. I cannot condemn all clergy for the mistakes of a few, aye, or even of many, when those I have met myself are good and godly men."

I nodded. "Then why didn't you join their order?"

"Alas! As I grew older, I found that I was fond of fighting. The good monks did rebuke me, and I strove hard to contain my anger at others' taunts; but when they struck at me, I felt outrage at their injustice and smote them down. Then did I come near to despair, thinking myself fit only for the plow and never for the cloister—but the monk who came to say Mass for us, every Sunday, did learn of this and told me of the Order of Saint Moncaire. 'If you must needs strike a blow,' quoth he, 'let it be the minions of Satan that you smite, so that you may protect the poor and weak.' Thereupon my heart did thrill, and I gave my poor parents no rest till they agreed to let me try my vocation, and I went to the monastery as a squire."

I nodded. "So you like fighting, but you wanted to be a monk, and the Moncaireans let you combine the two. Very neat. And you wanted to be a knight?"

"What lad does not? Yet I knew I could not, for I was base-born; I wished only to be a squire, and never thought I could be more."

"Oh." I frowned. "So that's how it goes here, is it? You have to be born a knight in order to become one?"

" 'Tis possible that a lowborn squire may be knighted for great courage and prowess," he pointed out, "yet 'tis rare."

"A battlefield commission, huh? And of course, he'll never really be accepted by the other officers."

"Your terms are strange—yet 'tis so. His children, though, will be ranked with any, for they will have grown with other knights. Natheless, 'tis otherwise, in my order—any lad may become a knight of Saint Moncaire, if he proves his vocation. Yet it will take great deeds to win my spurs." He flashed me a grin. "Therefore, lead me into danger, Wizard Saul! For I would prove my worth!"

"I'll try not to arrange it," I assured him, but I had this secret, nagging dread that he was going to get his wish.

Maybe right now. We came to the top of a rise and saw a huge crack in the ground right in front of us. It was a gorge, and it stretched away out of sight to the right and left.

But there was a bridge over it. Very narrow, but it was a bridge. "Well, at least there's a way over." As we came up to it, though, I developed doubts—it looked kind of flimsy.

"Looks like single file," I told Gilbert. "Think it'll take your horse's weight?"

He scanned it with a practiced eye—I guessed he'd been trained in military engineering. "Aye, if I dismount."

"Good enough." I started out across.

"Nay, Wizard Saul!" he yelped. "First we must test for—"

"Ho! Ho!" something rumbled.

I stopped and glanced at the sky. "Thunder?"

"Worse!" Gilbert cried. "Flee, Wizard!"

Hands as wide as bread boxes slapped onto the railing. Something huge and smelly swung itself up in an arc and landed with a shock that made the bridge sway. I held tight to the railing and stared, totally dumfounded.

It was about eight feet tall and shaped like a turnip, with legs as thick as kegs coming out of the narrow end. The wide end tapered down into two tentacles with the huge hands on the ends, and two eyes the size of dinner plates stared down at me from its chest. Beneath them, a knob of nose twitched over a vast slice of mouth, which opened in a grin set with shark's teeth.

"What the hell is *that*?" I yelped.

"'Tis a troll!" Gilbert howled. "Not from Hell, but vile enough! Stand aside, Wizard Saul, and let me have at him!"

"How?" I looked frantically to left and right, but there was no place to jump to. Then I remembered that I knew how to swim. I turned to dive over the rail, but Gilbert called, "Nay! He'll leap in after you and catch you in a trice!"

I wondered crazily if a trice was anything like a net, as I turned back to watch the troll slobbering toward me. I backed away, blurting, "But you can't be real—you're a fugitive from a fairy tale! So I can't be your meal!"

The monster jerked to a halt and glanced about him, and I could have sworn he was looking nervous. So help me, one huge finger came up over his mouth, looking for all the world as if he were trying to shush me!

"I will not be silenced!" I cried. "The word is my weapon!"

The troll shrank back, hands coming up to fend me off, and

Gilbert cried, "A deft stroke! Oh, bravely done! Smite him again, Wizard!"

"How?" I cried.

The troll relaxed, straightening up with a slobbering grin, and came slavering toward me again.

I backed away fast, wondering what had spooked it. "What's a matter, big guy? You worried about fairies?"

The troll jerked to a stop again, making frantic shushing motions and glancing about him.

"You are!" I cried in triumph. "You're afraid of the word itself! Okay, Gruesome, try this one on for size!

> " 'Rushing down the mountain
> And trooping through the glen,
> We dare not go a-hunting
> For fear of little men!' "

The troll gave a moan of fear and jumped.

He landed on top of me, and I slammed a punch in sheer reflex—and howled; it had felt like hitting rock. The howl was a mistake, because then I had to inhale, just as that huge midriff slammed me back against the wood. Something cracked under me; I saw stars, and my whole universe was filled with the incredible stench of that monster. I couldn't believe it—that close to water, and he didn't bathe?

Dimly, I heard Gilbert yelling, and heard something that sounded like ringing.

Then, suddenly, there was light, and the hideous smell was gone. I gasped, pushing myself up as quickly as I could—and there, so help me, were a dozen little guys scarcely as tall as my knee, in red caps and brown outfits, kicking at that troll and pinching him. How their pinches could make any progress against that granite skin, I didn't know—but I wasn't about to object.

"You have summoned them!" Gilbert shouted. "Oh, bravely done, Master Wizard!"

Master? I wasn't even a journeyman!

The yelping troll was caught between two packs of little men now. He couldn't even jump off the bridge, because there was a batch of them on each side, pinching and kicking if he came near them. He huddled down into a miserable, wailing bundle, tentacle-arms curled to protect his face. Somehow, I almost felt sorry for him.

"Your charity does you credit, but is sadly misplaced."

"Huh?" I looked up to see a bigger-than-average elf standing on the railing by my shoulder. Instead of a red cap, this one wore a coronet—your basic, minimal crown.

"Yet 'tis foolishness, also," the little guy went on, "for this monster has no mercy within his flinten skin, no heart, no compassion; he would have devoured you as soon as looked at you."

"I believe it." I glanced at the huddled, moaning granite turnip, then back to the guy with the crown. "Lucky for me you were in the neighborhood. Thanks for the save, Your Majesty."

"Highness," he corrected. "I am a prince of Wee Folk, not a king. And 'tis a hobnailed jest to speak of luck, when 'twas your spell that summoned us."

He glanced at his corps, while I stared. Spell?

Then he turned back with a severe frown. " 'Twas unwise of you to venture to cross a bridge without having taken precaution 'gainst that which might dwell beneath it. You know the signs of bridges that were built by trolls to tempt mortals to their doom."

"Uh—no, to tell you the truth, I don't. I'm, uh, kinda new in this country, you see."

"New?" He stared at me. "Have you no trolls whence you come?"

"Not like this," I assured him. "I admit I know some people who could qualify, but they're really human underneath it all."

"This one is not!" He turned on Gilbert, who had come onto the bridge behind me. "You, squire! Assuredly you must know this land—you wear the badge of the Moncaireans! Did you not warn him of his danger?"

"I did not speak quickly enough," Gilbert said contritely.

"Did you not know he was a stranger?"

"I confess I did not realize the depth of his strangeness."

I'd heard that before, from other jocks—but I decided not to take offense, this time.

The elfin prince turned back to me. "Do you henceforth survey most closely every bridge that you may come to! If 'tis rudely made, and the ends of the logs show the marks of teeth, not axes, be sure to recite a spell for the banishing of trolls ere you cross."

I looked and, sure enough, the ends of the logs did look as if they'd been chewed through. "I didn't think to look," I admitted. "Even if I had, though, I probably wouldn't have thought anything of it."

"Not thought!" the elf prince and Gilbert cried together.

"Yeah," I admitted ruefully. "I probably would have just thought somebody had used logs that beavers had cut down."

The prince and the squire exchanged a glance, then turned back to me. "What are beavers?"

Then I remembered that the flat-tailed rodents with the buck teeth were American fauna only. "Uh, small animals, where I come from, who like to chew on things."

"Most amazing," Gilbert muttered. The elf prince said firmly, "I would not offend you, squire, but you alone are not protection enough for this ignorant man."

"Hey," I objected.

"Not a word!" The prince held up a hand, then turned to snap his fingers at his retinue. "Stand back, and let him rise!"

They looked up, startled. "But, Highness . . ."

"Do as I bid!"

Reluctantly, they stepped back.

"Rise, troll," the elf prince said, with a tone that hinted at dire tortures.

Slowly, the troll uncurled itself and stood up to a shaky eight feet, whining at the back of its throat.

"What is thy name?"

The troll shrank back, but a hail of kicks and pinches made it straighten up with a howl.

"Your name," the prince intoned, in a pitch that wavered like the pattern on a Damascus blade.

The troll croaked some incomprehensible pattern of gutturals and rachetings—but it was unmistakably language, if one I couldn't understand.

I stared, amazed that the monster could talk, but the elf prince held up both hands and began to chant something dire. I could tell it rhymed and had meter, but I couldn't have made the first guess as to what the words meant. I only know that it made the troll cower away, hands up to fend off the words, and I caught the grinding and grating of his name in there a couple of times. Then I got a real shock, because the verse ended in my name, "Saul!"

The elf prince clapped his hands, and the troll straightened up, moaning, his huge mitts dropping to his sides.

The prince nodded, satisfied, and turned back to me, fists on his hips. "He is tamed now. I have laid a geas upon him, bind-

ing him to go wherever you go and protect you from any
thing, beast or man or spirit, that does seek to hurt you."

My mouth dropped open; I stared at the troll, appalled. Then
I turned back to the prince to protest that I didn't really want
such a gruesome traveling companion, but the prince only held
up a hand, palm out. "Nay, do not thank me. I know you wish
to protest that I am too kind, but it is our great amusement to
protect good mortal folk from such depraved creatures as this."

I wanted to protest, all right, but not about his kindness.

"Your Highness is exceedingly gracious," Gilbert said
gravely. I turned to ask him if he was out of his mind, but he
was bowing his head to the prince, and I realized anything else
might get me in worse trouble than I was in already. No matter
what, I didn't want these little guys for enemies. I swallowed
my protest and turned around to bow, too—after all, we could
always find a way to lose the monster when the elves were out
of sight. He didn't look to have too high an IQ. In fact, he
didn't look to have an IQ at all.

The prince pointed off toward the east. "The gorge will narrow a league or so farther on, and you will find there has been
a rock slide that will provide a bridge for you."

Something rumbled in the distance, in the direction he was
pointing. I wondered how long that rock slide had been there.
No, I definitely didn't want these little guys to take a dislike
to me.

"Henceforth," he said, with a very severe stare at me, "if
you realize that you shall need our help, summon us at once.
There is an aura about you that tells me that you shall be vital
to the casting out of the rule of evil which we so hate for the
trouble and grief it has caused my people; so summon if you
so much as think you may have need of us; and be sure, we
shall come."

"I'm not really that important." Why did everybody here
think I was the solution to all their troubles? I admit I was
used to that attitude from the women I met, but supernatural
beings were another matter.

"You are," he said, with a steely glare that allowed no argument. "Call at the slightest need. Till then, farewell! Men of
mine! All flit!"

Sunlight got in my eyes; I blinked, and they were gone. There
was no one there but Gilbert, his horse, me—and the troll.

I braced myself, ready to run—I didn't think fighting would
do much good.

But a very dejected troll came mincing up to me, hanging his head—or the whole top half of his body, at least—and fell to his knees.

I backed away, horrified. "All right, all right! I'll have to put up with you—but no kneeling! I *hate* that!"

The troll scrabbled to his feet, staring down at me expectantly.

"Do you remember my saying anything about agreeing to take this lunk along?" I asked Squire Gilbert.

"Why—you have no choice in the matter, Wizard," he said in surprise. "Neither has the troll."

"Oh, yeah?" I started out across the bridge. "Just watch me."

There was a loud groan from below.

I froze. I hadn't stopped to think that Huge-and-Gruesome might have had company. I backed away in a hurry; whatever was under there just might have brains enough to realize that the easy way to get rid of Gruesome's geas was to get rid of me.

On the other hand, if it tried, Gruesome would have to fight it—and it might not be smart enough to realize that. I decided I didn't want to find out. I retreated back to Gilbert's side with alacrity and turned away east. "On the other hand, maybe a one-mile detour wouldn't be so bad after all. Let's go, Gilbert—fast!"

"If you say so, Wizard." He mounted and paced alongside me on his horse, trying not to let his smile show.

I tried to ignore it—and tried harder to ignore the slap of huge flat feet behind me. I'd had experience with that, too, but it wasn't working any better this time than it had before.

Gilbert didn't seem to mind it, but every now and then, I caught him glancing back out of the corner of his eye. All in all, it was a very nervous-making mile, though he and I tried to cover up with light conversation.

"So you were born a peasant, but within the order you can become a knight?"

"Aye. Even so, 'tis not likely, mind you—but I may attain glory enough to cover me with honor."

Interesting metaphor. I was tempted to try to figure out if it was mixed, but resisted in favor of gaining information. "Any chance you can change your mind then, leave the order, and get married?"

"Oh, nay!" He turned to me, shocked. "I would never wish to leave the order!"

"Eighteen is young," I said, from the airy height of twenty-

five. "Twelve years from now, you might be tempted to recon-
sider."

"Heaven forfend! May the angels protect me from such!"

"I hope so," I agreed. "But could you, if you wanted to?"

He started to object again, then closed his mouth, frowning,
and thought it over.

"Purely hypothetically, mind you," I said.

"Nay, I could not," he said. "In the Order of Saint
Moncaire, we do not take our final vows until we are accorded
the accolade of knighthood."

"So." I nodded. "Once you become a knight, you can't quit."

"Aye," he agreed. "Before that time, whilst I am still a
squire, I could leave the order, if I wished—but I do not wish."

I hoped he wouldn't get the quick exit that would no doubt
be the most honorable. I'm sure he would have wanted it,
though. These medieval Christians were crazy for martyrdom.

Well, there went my notion of social mobility. In my own
feudal Europe, the only two ways for a young man to rise in
socioeconomic status were through the army, and through the
Church. In the army, there was an extremely long shot that a
peasant might be knighted on the battlefield for services above
and beyond the call of sanity. In the Church, native ability
alone might push him up to the rank of bishop, or pope if he
were Italian—but he wouldn't have any heirs to leave it to. So,
okay, the Order of Saint Moncaire was giving Gilbert a chance
to improve himself—but only just himself. Well, that was all
he asked, anyway.

So far.

The slapping of big flat feet was coming closer. I glanced
back over my shoulder and saw that the troll was gaining, and
he had a big wide grin. Okay, it was an eager, puppy-dog, ingratiating grin—but it didn't exactly fill me with enthusiasm.
"Uh, Squire Gilbert—should we do anything about our hungry
friend back there?"

"Feed him, do you mean?" Gilbert looked back, then
thought better of the idea. "With meat of beasts, that is."

"Assuming we're not beasts." I gave the troll a jaundiced
eye—glance, I mean. "I'm not sure he knows the distinction—
and he's definitely getting closer."

"But of course! How can he protect us if he is not with us?"

"By being far away." I turned back to the front and hurried.
"Come on. Let's find that rock slide."

CHAPTER 6

It was just a little farther along. A chunk of the hillside was raw and ragged, and the gully was filled with weed-tufted dirt, heavily interspersed with boulders. I eyed it with trepidation. "We're supposed to cross on *that*?"

"It does look infirm," Gilbert agreed, "but the weeds show that it has been here long enough for the rains to settle it somewhat."

"Yeah, too much—it's at least two feet lower in the center." I decided I must have heard another landslide happening.

"I shall essay it first." Gilbert swung down from his horse's back. "Yet let Thorn carry only his own weight, that his hooves may not sink lower than they must."

I glanced over my shoulder at what was coming up behind and said, "No, I'm the leader of this expedition—or at least, you're here because of me. I'll go first." I stepped out onto the dirt bridge before he could stop me.

"Nay, Wizard Saul! 'Tis my place!" he cried, but I waded on with determination.

And I do mean "waded"—the dirt gave beneath my feet with every step. My stomach started fluttering, and I began to envision a mini-landslide with me in the middle. It was almost enough to make me believe in the magic the people here kept talking about. I tried to remember some stabilizing verses.

"We come," Gilbert called behind me. I took his word for it; my eyes were on the path ahead, if you could call it that. I tried stepping on the larger stones, and that was better; they sank in a little farther, but at least my feet didn't. I was glad I wore boots.

71

Finally I reached the other side. I grabbed hold of the nearest tree and let myself sag against it. Then I turned around so I could watch Gilbert finishing the trek.

He was doing better than I had, possibly because he was walking in my footsteps—had to shorten his stride to do it, but it gave him a firmer surface. His horse followed on the reins, with a lot of snorting, head tossing, and rolling of the eyes—but whenever they rolled back far enough, he saw the troll wallowing along behind him and decided the dirt was the lesser of two evils.

Gilbert guided him up onto firm land, then looked back at the laboring troll with a frown. "Mayhap we ought to help him."

"Are you crazy?" I protested. "The monster that would have gleefully had us for lunch—even without ketchup? Besides, we're trying to get away from him, remember?"

" 'Tis so," Gilbert conceded, but his open, honest face looked unhappy about it. "I hate to leave even an adversary so beset."

"You'll get the hang of it," I assured him. "Look, any chance your horse could carry double for a little while? I hate to ask it of him, but I'd feel a lot better if we could put a few miles between Gruesome, there, and us."

"As you wish," Gilbert sighed, "though 'twill do no good. Once under a geas, a living creature will ever press after his duty." He held the horse steady while I mounted. Fortunately, I'd learned a little bit about riding in my one trip to summer camp, so I knew how to get aboard, at least. I hiked myself back behind the saddle, though.

"Nay, Master Wizard! Do you take the saddle!"

"You don't think I'm dumb enough to try to steer this thing, do you? No, you can have the front seat!"

Gilbert gave me a funny look, but he climbed aboard, bending his knee so his foot missed my face—but not by much—then turning the horse's head inland and shaking the reins. The beast started trotting, and I held on for dear life. "Aren't there . . . any . . . shock absorbers . . . on this bus?"

"I do not follow your meaning, Master Wizard, but I'll essay a faster gait." He knocked his heels into the horse's sides. I was about to protest when the ride smoothed out amazingly. I remembered that a canter is less jouncy than a trot—but only by comparison; it was still pretty rough. On top of that, I was discovering why the army adopted the McClellan saddle. I held tight to Gilbert's midriff and glanced back. Sure enough, Gruesome was still wallowing through the dirt and was growing smaller behind us. I relaxed a little, set my teeth, and turned to the front, determined to last it out.

After about fifteen minutes of this—just a guess; my watch seemed to have stopped—I said, "That ought to do it. Must have been a couple of miles, at least."

"Aye." Gilbert reined in. "Will that suffice, Master Wizard?"

"Just fine," I said through clenched teeth. I made it through the deceleration trot, then gratefully slid off the rump. "Maybe he'll lose us now."

"I fear not." Gilbert started to dismount.

"Hey, what're you doing? No reason you should walk!"

"But you are my leader . . ."

"Not your superior, though, only your senior! You just keep riding. After all, you're the one with the armor."

" 'Tis only a mail coat." But he seemed relieved. "Even so, Wizard Saul, 'tis my duty to advise you that distance will not stop a troll, nay, even if he did not labor under a geas."

That was doubly less than reassuring. It didn't exactly guarantee that Gruesome *was* under a geas. Compulsions I could understand, but greed was even more comprehensible.

We strolled along, exchanging biographical notes, and I switched the topic to future aspirations. Gilbert practically glowed as he recounted the glories of knighthood and the potential glories of martyrdom. You can't help liking a guy with that much zeal, but I couldn't help feeling that somebody was playing him for a real sucker. On the other hand, I think Jonah felt that way, too.

The sun was almost overhead, and I was just beginning to think of calling a halt for lunch, when Gilbert looked back and said, "Yonder he comes."

I spun about, staring. Sure enough, there he came, snowshoe feet and turnip shape, grinning from ear to ear with pathetic eagerness. I had to remind myself that I was the one who was likely to be pathetic, not him.

"No help for it," I decided. "Time for lunch, anyway. Let's relax and rest a while—and if he attacks, he attacks, and we'll deal with it then." I was nowhere nearly as nonchalant as I pretended. The presence of an actual, me-eating troll was incentive enough to get me to working up some good verses, not that I really thought they'd help any.

On the other hand, if my hallucination included trolls and

elves, why not magic? Though a troll was hardly the kind of opponent you would expect to start slinging rhymes.

"He will not attack," Gilbert said with blithe unconcern as he dismounted. "He goes under a geas."

Obsessive-compulsive disorders, I could understand—it was just the object of the obsession that worried me. Nonetheless, I let Gilbert lay the fire while I waited, arms akimbo, looking a lot more certain than I felt—but as Huge-and-Ugly came closer, I felt the old, familiar chill within me that seems to come whenever danger looms. I didn't feel fear, because I didn't feel anything. *After* the crisis was over, I'd turn to jelly—but there'd be time, then.

"Running behind schedule, I see," I commented, as he came up.

The troll looked surprised. "Ske-dool?"

That's right—I remembered he'd demonstrated a limited vocabulary.

"Took you a while to catch up with us." I braced myself and said, "I'd really rather you didn't."

It stared down at me with blank incomprehension.

"Don't catch up with us," I explained. "I don't want you near me. Go. Away. Shoo!"

He stared, grin fading, mouth loosening. "Go?" And, so help me, a huge, fat tear welled up in one eye.

My inner chill almost warmed into remorse for a second, but I focused on the shark teeth inside that woebegone lip and said, "You tried to eat me. I can't trust you. I don't want you along."

"Me come!" he protested, in a voice like a basso chain saw. "Fairies see! Fairies say! Want only ward you!"

"He speaks truth, Master Wizard," Gilbert said, his voice low and completely calm. "He cannot turn his heart against you now, not under the elf prince's geas."

He sounded very confident, and it occurred to me to wonder how the troll would react if I really did drive him away. If this was anything like a love-hate relationship, I could find myself with a real nemesis on my trail. "Well ... if you're sure ..."

The troll's grin came back, and he nodded eagerly. At least, I think it was nodding; it might have been bowing. But Gilbert assured me, "He is your guard and servant now, till the Wee Folk remove the geas."

That was the other thing that bothered me. If some enemy magician came along and counteracted this artificial compulsion, I could find myself on the inside real fast, in small pieces. But I didn't really see that I had much choice. I sighed and said, "Okay, Gruesome, you can join us."

The troll looked hugely delighted, then frowned, puzzled. "Goosum?"

"Gruesome," I amplified. "That's my name for you." Then one of my few moral principles kicked in—I hated infringing on anybody's identity; I knew what it felt like to have people try. "But I'll drop it if you have a name of your own."

"Name?"

So much for that idea. "What do other trolls call you?"

"Odder trolls?"

"They are solitary beings, Master Wizard," Gilbert explained. "They are never seen together."

I frowned. "They have to now and then, or there would never be any little trolls."

Gilbert blushed. So help me, he blushed. I tried to remind myself he was an adolescent, and a very sheltered one, in some respects.

"All right," I sighed. "If they don't have a social structure, they don't have any need for names."

"Well, there is the secret name," Gilbert said slowly. "Every creature takes the first sound of its own kind that it hears after birth, as the designation for itself. It is this the elf prince used to compel the troll."

"But it's secret?"

Gilbert nodded.

I'd heard of it. Almost every primitive culture believed that identity was so intimately linked with name that your enemy could use it to work magic against you—so the true name was secret. Everybody had a public name for communication, and a private name for identity. I turned to the troll again. "What is the sound that means you?"

"No say!" Gruesome almost looked panicked—and I wasn't an elf prince, with a host of little accomplices that could pinch hard enough to be felt through that igneous hide. So, "No se, indeed," I muttered.

I fell back on primitive communication, pointing to the troll's granite chest. "You. Gruesome." Then I pointed at myself. "Me—Saul." Then I jabbed a finger at the squire. "Him—Gilbert." I frowned up at the dinner-plate eyes. "Understand?"

"Unner . . . ?"

He didn't have the concept of understanding. "Gruesome, go to Gilbert."

His face cleared, and he turned to trot over to the squire. Gilbert braced himself, but he didn't need to—he was still kneeling by the campfire, and the troll shied away at the sight of flame.

"Gruesome!" I called. "Come to Saul!"

"Gruesome come," he said brightly, and shambled back to me.

I nodded, satisfied. "Good. Now, eat."

The troll stared, unbelieving.

I suddenly realized what he thought I meant he should eat. "Gilbert, food! Quickly!"

"Here, Wizard." A round, hard loaf came flying through the air.

I caught it and presented it to the troll. "Gruesome eat."

The troll frowned down at the loaf, then took it from me between thumb and finger. His lump of nose wrinkled.

"All right, let it go if you want," I said. "But it's all we've got—isn't it?"

"There is a little dried beef." Gilbert held out something that looked like a collection of buckskin thongs. I took them and held them out to Gruesome, but he backed away, shaking his top.

"Well, sorry." I went to sit down by Gilbert. "But we have to eat." I took another loaf, broke it, handed half to Gilbert, and started munching. He handed me a wineskin; I took a sparing sip, then handed it back.

Three bites later, I happened to notice Gruesome. He was sitting down now, with his hands on his knees, eyeing us hungrily. I told myself it was the food he was eyeing, but I didn't believe me.

"I mistrust his gaze," Gilbert muttered.

"I mistrust this whole geas thing." I frowned at Gruesome. "I'd feel a little safer if it had been my idea."

"An excellent notion!"

"Say what?" I looked up blankly.

"Make a spell of your own! That will hold him doubly!"

He looked at me with such total trust that I figured I at least had to go through the motions. "If you say so," I sighed, and turned back toward Gruesome, trying to remember a verse having to do with loyalty. I found it among my boyhood Kipling collection, and tapped my own chest as I recited,

"Now here is your master—understand!
Now you must be my guide,
To walk and stand at my left hand,
As shields on shoulders ride.

Till Death or I cut loose the tie,
At camp and board and bed,
Your life is mine—your life's design
Is to guard me with your head."

The troll sat bolt-upright, looking very surprised. Its eyes glazed, then cleared, and it turned to me and said, "Saul master of Gruesome. Gruesome guard Saul with life."

He said it with such total conviction that I just couldn't doubt him. I decided that trolls were very suggestible.

Behind me, Gilbert let out a hiss of breath. I turned back, surprised, and the kid was staring at me almost with reverence. "You have done it indeed! Ah, fortunate am I, to see such spells worked so hard by me!"

"It's pretty hard by me, too," I grunted, "and speaking of hard, let's finish this journey bread."

But Gilbert was looking past me at the troll. "He is your creature now, and woe betide any who seek to hurt you—but he still hungers."

It occurred to me that Gilbert might be feeling less than secure. "Guard Gilbert, too," I ordered Gruesome.

"Gilbert safe from hurt!" the troll assured me, but he still looked hungry.

"He must be fed, with something," Gilbert said, his voice low.

"I'd rather be a little more definite about the 'something,' " I said, and raised my voice. "Gruesome! Go gobble up a billy goat!"

The troll looked very surprised for a minute, then grinned, gratified, and scrambled off.

Not believing my luck, I stared after him, then turned to start stuffing the rations back into Gilbert's sack. "Quick! Now's our chance!"

"Chance for what?" Gilbert said blankly.

"To lose that monster! Come on, let's go!"

"It will avail naught," Gilbert protested, but he gathered his gear and mounted up.

We were only a hundred yards down the road when I stopped dead in my tracks. "What's the matter with me!"

"Naught, that I can see," Gilbert said, surprised.

"Nice of you—especially considering what some other people I know might have said for an answer." I turned about and started hiking back, double-quick. "I just realized what I told that fool troll to do!"

"Aye—to dine upon a goat."

"Right! And where do you find goats in a country like this?"

"Why, upon . . ." Suddenly, Gilbert's eyes filled with foreboding. "Upon a farm!"

"Right! And I only told him to guard you—I didn't say anything about any other humans! Come on, let's go!"

"Ride," Gilbert snapped.

His tone riled me, but I had to admit there was no time to debate the issue now. I scrambled up behind him and held on for all I was worth. He kicked the horse into a gallop and went pounding up the hillside.

"There he is!" I pointed.

Gilbert swerved, and the horse leapt the fence.

I wasn't expecting it—I almost went flying. But I managed to hold on tighter, and Gilbert grunted as I gave him an impromptu Heimlich maneuver. Then we were pounding over the meadow grass and swung about in front of a slavering troll just as the goatherd boy yelled in fright.

"No, Gruesome!" I held up a hand. "Mustn't eat any people."

"Not eat?" Gruesome protested, wounded.

"Not eat people!" I said with conviction. "Only goats! And wolves and bear and deer," I modified, and turned to the goatherd. "It's okay—he's only after your goats, not you."

"But—but I shall be whipped!" Trembling, he faced us all, crook held slantwise across his body, ready to strike.

I almost invited him to come along right there, he was so brave. I would have, too, if I'd known where I was going. As it was, I just reached in my pocket and fished out a quarter. "I'll buy one goat from you."

He caught the quarter, then held it up, staring at it. " 'Tis silver!"

"Will it . . ." I remembered the principles of bargaining and changed the wording. "How big a goat will it buy?"

"The biggest in my herd! But 'tis a most strange coin, gentleman!"

"I'm a foreigner," I explained. "Make it a billy goat, all right?" I glanced at the troll and said, "A gruff one."

"My worst," he said eagerly. In thirty seconds, he had driven out the most ornery billy goat I'd ever seen, who kept turning and trying to butt him. I didn't blame it—if I'd been being driven toward a troll, I would have tried to run, too.

But Gruesome solved the issue by pouncing. There was a startled bleat that ended abruptly. White-faced, the goatherd backed away.

"Gruesome! Come to Saul!" I said sternly, and to Gilbert, "Walk away."

We turned and started walking. I glanced back; Gruesome was following, taking large bites. I winced and turned away. "Crisis over. Do we have to go through this every mealtime?"

"You will find a way," Gilbert said with total confidence. I wished I'd shared it.

I didn't make the same mistake when we set camp for the night—I made a different one. Well, no, maybe not a mistake, really—as soon as I realized Gruesome was eyeing us hungrily, I said, "Hungry enough to eat a bear?"

Gruesome nodded, a huge slab of tongue coming out to slurp over his lips, what there were of them.

"Then go catch one," I said. "If you can catch it, you can eat it."

He nodded brightly, surged up to his feet, and trotted off into the trees.

Gilbert stared after him open-mouthed, then turned to me. "Will he find one?"

I shrugged. "Whether he does or not, we'll get an hour or so of worry-free sleep."

Gilbert smiled, a slow grin. "Ingenious, Master Wizard! Nay, let us dine quickly and seek sleep faster! I'll take the first watch."

I realized I was dog-tired, so I didn't object. Right after we finished, I rolled up in the cloak Gilbert's commander had sent with the squire.

"Will you not pray first?" Gilbert asked, scandalized.

"No, I don't think so," I told him, then thought better fast. "I meditate while I'm going to sleep."

His face cleared; where he came from, "meditate" meant the

same as "pray." He nodded and turned away to watch the night.

He woke me some time around midnight and said, "Wake me for the third watch." I bit back a gripe and nodded, rolling up to my knees, watching the landscape, and wishing heartily that this universe had discovered coffee. Much better for my health, I'm sure, but no more pleasant than healthful things usually are. Gilbert was snoring within five minutes. I'd heard that soldiers developed that ability.

As my head cleared, I looked around and realized what was missing—the troll. My spirits picked up—maybe the bear had won.

I was really getting to be hopeful when I woke Gilbert about six hours later—my watch had gone on the fritz, so I was going by the Little Dipper. He came awake instantly, took one glance at the stars, and said, "Master Wizard! You should have waked me sooner! Nay, I've slept through two watches!"

"Six hours for you, six hours for me," I told him. "Comes out even." I didn't mention that mine had been two and two. I decided that the next night, I'd take the first watch.

"Natheless, a knight should be able to keep a vigil!"

"How about we talk about it tomorrow evening?" I suggested.

He brightened surprisingly. "Aye, assuredly. Good sleep to you, Wizard!"

"Good night to you, squire," I said, puzzled. I was almost asleep before I realized why he'd been so pleased—saying we'd talk about it tomorrow night implied that I was accepting his company. I broke out in cold sweat as I felt the clammy tendrils of commitment gluing themselves onto me. I was going to have to find some way to send Gilbert back to his buddies.

It took me a while to get to sleep.

I woke in the false dawn, to hear a sound like a chain saw eating its way through a stack of garbage cans. I sat bolt upright to see Gilbert standing guard, hand on his sword, casting nervous glances at a huge, gently heaving hulk. I realized it was my pet troll come home, snoring like a railroad car full of scrap steel, swaying on loose tracks. Next to him lay a collection of bones and hide, all of them sizable.

I stared. So the bear *hadn't* won. I repressed a surge of guilt—better it than me. Or Gilbert.

Then I relaxed—the fact that Gruesome had done as I told

him was very reassuring. So was the fact that he could handily defeat a full-grown bear.

Muscles like that might come in useful for a stranger in a mighty strange land. I decided I'd keep him for a while. All things considered, I might be safer with him than without him.

Unless some enemy sorcerer decided to remove the restraint spell, anyway.

That thought, combined with the dawn's early light, pretty much guaranteed that I wasn't going to get any more sleep. I got up, waved Gilbert to silence, and started rousting up breakfast. If there was one thing I didn't need, it was an ornery, fresh-wakened troll.

I took a chance on nudging him with my boot an hour later and told him we were taking off. He rolled up to his feet right away, eager as a puppy dog.

So we set off south, heading into what I hoped was Switzerland, with a squire looking for enough trouble to win him a knighthood, and a half-tame troll eager to find something to protect me from.

Understandably, I was nervous.

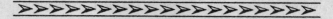

CHAPTER 7

Late that day I looked around, frowning and footsore. "Notice anything strange?"

"Aye," Gilbert said. "We have come into a barren waste."

"Yeah, but there used to be a lot of trees here—at least, little ones." I pointed at the expanse of four-inch stumps, lopped off so cleanly that you could see the rings. "What was it, a lumber crisis?"

"I ken not." Gilbert looked around nervously. " 'Tis uncanny, though. I would we did not have to stay the night here."

"Yeah," I said, "but it's getting dark. Think we ought to pitch camp pretty soon?"

"It would seem likely," Gilbert said grudgingly.

A distant, bloodthirsty moan stopped us in our tracks.

"But not right here," I qualified.

"Mayhap not." Gilbert nudged his horse ahead and drew his sword.

"Hold on!" I protested. "Where do you think you're going?"

"To discover what made that sound," he said, in a tone that brooked no argument. "If 'tis our enemy, 'tis better that we come upon it, than that it come upon us."

"Now, hold on!" I protested. "If it's going to be that dangerous, you can't go in there alone!"

"I am a squire," he said simply, "a man of arms."

"That's what I mean." I stumbled on ahead. "Whatever it is, it's a long ways off yet."

"We must be silent," he protested. "You should stay here."

"Of course," I said, "not."

"Yuh, not." Gruesome flexed his huge hands, grinning, and

padded forward. For all his bulk, he moved more quietly than I did—but then, he wasn't wearing boots.

"See?" I said. "We're coming along, Gilbert. Gilbert?"

"Up here," a voice whispered ahead of me. "For Heaven's sake, be still!"

"Still. Yuh." Gruesome turned to hiss at me. "Still!" Then he turned back without waiting for an answer.

I followed along, wondering what had happened to my usual common sense.

But it was my party—these two were here because of me. I rushed the pace a little, passed Gruesome, and came up level with Gilbert as his horse groped its way along a stony path in the gathering darkness. Gilbert started to protest, but just then the moan burst out again, and I saw a glowing shape drifting toward us through the gloom, its mouth an impossibly wide circle of slavering emptiness, eyes staring and covetous, and its fingers hooked like talons, poised to grab.

Then some stranger jumped out of the dimness, dove past me, and cowered behind a boulder, trembling.

That seemed to be okay with the ghost. It shifted its attentions to me, zooming toward me with a gloating howl.

The fugitive leapt to his feet, turned, ran—and slammed right into the only tree on an otherwise barren hillside. He slumped down, beneath a huge spiderweb with a very large spider in it. The ghost, shifting back to its original quarry, fluttered after its victim, then hesitated, apparently repelled by the spider. I could sympathize, but I knew the specter wouldn't be halted long.

"Hold it right there!" I shouted. I jumped in front of a big boulder, yanking my belt out of the loops and swinging the buckle. "Cold iron, remember?"

The ghost yelled something that sounded suspiciously like "Yum!" and threw itself on the buckle. I dropped the belt and yanked my hand out of the way just in time, and the ghost bored on into the rock, sinking out of sight. Of my belt, there was no trace. There was also a large hole in the boulder.

Then the ghost veered out of the rock face, swooped out in a circle, and headed back toward me, smacking its lips and drooling. Whatever kind of spook this was, it was a virtual flying appetite. It reminded me of a shark—but it also reminded me of my Kipling. I shouted,

"We come to fight and triumph in
The savage wars of peace,

To fill full the mouth of Hunger,
And bid the Famine cease!"

The ghost jolted to a halt with a look of startled shock as its
mouth snapped shut and sealed itself. Its cheeks bulged, and its
body ballooned with a huge flapping sound.

"Wizard Saul!" Gilbert pounded up to me, panting. "Beware! 'Tis a hunger ghost!"

"Yuh," Gruesome grunted, scrabbling up behind the squire.
"Get 'way! Ghost eat all!"

"It will indeed," Gilbert corroborated. "It will eat anything
it encounters—and it is never full!"

"Then I think I've created a first," I said, picking up a stone,
"but get ready with some rocks anyway, will you? If it opens
its mouth, pitch for the breadbasket."

Gilbert turned to the ghost, then stared. "Opens? But a hunger ghost's mouth is never shut!"

"This one's is," I said. "It's full."

Full, and getting fuller—its belly was still stretching, turning
it into a perfect globe with stubby limbs sticking out and a
bulge of head on top.

"It doth depart," a wondering voice breathed somewhere
around my kneecap. I looked down and saw a patched hat with
a gaunt face beneath it, all eyes and pointed nose and jawbone,
with hollows for cheeks, and more hollows at the back of
which eyes glittered.

Well, at least whatever I'd saved was human.

I looked up again just in time to see the ghost drift high
enough to catch an updraft and shoot away to the west,
shrinking until it was lost in the twilight.

"It must have sped most quickly indeed," Gilbert said, "for
'twas still swelling with thy spell, Wizard Saul."

"Spell?" the man I had saved cried. He looked up at me
with a feverish hunger of his own. "Are you a wizard, then?"

"Well, I wouldn't say that," I demurred—but I saw the scandalized look on Gilbert's face and said quickly, "but everybody
else here seems to. Why do you ask?"

"If you are a wizard, you can cure me."

Gruesome looked away, humming. That made me uneasy. I
stalled. "How do you know I'm a good guy? Just because I
worked, um, a"—I swallowed heavily and forced it out—"a
spell, doesn't say which side I'm on. I could have been an evil
sorcerer."

Gilbert stared, appalled, but the famine case shook his head firmly and said, "If you had been a sorcerer, you would have let the ghost have me, and welcome."

"Good thinking," I approved, but I frowned up into the sky. "Do you suppose that thing will burst when it's had too much?"

"Nay, surely," Gilbert said, and the other added, "A hunger ghost can never have had too much."

I was again seized with the unhappy reminder that everybody else in this country seemed to know more about what was going on than I did. To cover it, I said to the man cowering at my feet, "Come on, bucko, up with you!" I caught his arm and helped him stand. "How'd you get that ghost sicced on you, anyway?"

"I think his appearance tells us that," Gilbert said softly.

Yes, it was pretty obvious, now that I looked—the tattered coat, the patched leggings, the holes in the shoes, and, above all, the general emaciation. The arm I was clinging to felt like a bone wrapped by a rag, and the man's whole face was pinched with hunger.

I remembered a college lecture on the Minnesota Starvation Experiment. "Gilbert, could you get a piece of beef jerky out of your saddlebag? And the water skin."

In a second, Gilbert was holding out the tough, leathery strip, and the water skin.

The vagabond snatched the pemmican from him and bit into it—then forced his molars down onto it, pulled his jaw open, and bit down again, and again.

"That's it," I soothed. "Don't bite, chew. That meat is so dried that you *can't* gulp it."

The man gave it a valiant try, I had to admit, but beef jerky takes an awful lot of chewing just to get a bite off the stick, let alone soften it enough to swallow.

"Not much else to eat, I'm afraid," I apologized, and was glad I didn't have to lie. "One swallow of water when you get that bite down, okay? Just one swallow—then another bite of jerky. By the time you finish that strip, maybe we'll have some stew on." I turned to Gilbert. "*Now* I'll take the first campsite you can find."

Fifty yards farther down, the path broadened out onto a twenty-foot-wide terrace. Gilbert pronounced it fit, so I arranged a ring of stones and looked around for firewood. "Seen any kindling, Gilbert?"

"Aye." The squire held out an armload of sticks. "I gathered what I found, as we did come down the slope."

"Ah, to have Gilbert's forethought!" I dumped the sticks into my fire ring. "Good thing this path wasn't *always* above the timberline."

"Aye," our mystery guest said. "This slope bore a few scrub trees, till the Spirit of Famine began to chase me."

I swallowed, hard, at the thought of the hunger ghost planing every living thing off the side of the mountain, and put the thought resolutely behind me. "Gilbert, will you do the honors?"

The squire stepped up and struck flint against steel. A spark fell, and he breathed it into a small flame. Seconds later, fire bloomed from the kindling.

I looked around for something to skewer the provisions Gilbert had collected along the way.

"Will this serve?" Gilbert held up a three-foot splinter of rock.

"Yeah, just fine." I poked the spear through the three pheasants, rested the ends on the highest two rocks, and sat back to watch. I thought of asking how Gilbert had come by the rock spit, but decided I didn't want to know.

Our guest watched them hungrily, but he didn't leap on the raw flesh. The pemmican had filled him up a bit, especially with the water swelling it in his stomach—and it had taken him so long to chew and swallow it that he'd begun to feel full before he could gobble enough to hurt himself.

"A sword would come in handy for this sort of thing," I said. "Remind me to make one right after dinner."

Gilbert looked scandalized at the idea, but our hungry guest said obligingly, "Make a sword right after dinner; are they done yet?"

"They've just barely started cooking." I rummaged in Gilbert's saddlebag, pulled out another strip of jerky, and pressed it into the man's hand. "Chew on that while you're waiting, Pavlov. Say, what *is* your name, anyway?"

"Frisson," the man mumbled through his pemmican.

I nodded. "How'd you get into this fix, anyway? No, I don't mean attracting the hunger ghost—I mean getting so close to starvation in the first place?"

"Why," Frisson said, "I am a poet."

I just sat still for a minute.

Then I nodded. "Yeah, that explains it, all right. But, I mean, you could have gone after a job. Woodcutter, for instance."

"The very thing," Frisson muttered, nodding as he chewed. "I have been a woodcutter, a plowman, a cooper's prentice, and a chandler's prentice."

I frowned. "Then why were you starving?"

"I could not cease chanting poetry."

Gilbert gasped, covering his mouth in alarm, and Gruesome edged frantically away from our guest.

I frowned around at them. "All right, so maybe his verses weren't the best, but they couldn't have been *that* bad. Does everybody have to be a critic?"

"'Tis not that, Wizard Saul," Gilbert said. "For all we know, his verses may have been most excellent. True poetry, mayhap—yet he is not a wizard."

"What difference does that . . . ? Oh!"

Frisson watched me, nodding as he chewed, and Gilbert said softly, "Aye, Wizard Saul. A poet's concern is for the words themselves, for the excellence of the verses and the manner in which they fit together to form a whole—not for their effects."

The poet turned to him in surprised, though masticating, approval.

I nodded. "And if he doesn't worry about their effects, the images he creates in his verses may come to life as he chants, and—"

"Do untold damage," Gilbert finished for me. He turned to Frisson. "What hazards did you unfold, poet? A juggernaut of doom rushing down upon the heads of the men in your master's shop? A corpse come to life in the coffin you were building? Wood nymphs slipping out to seduce the passersby, in the wood you had gleaned?"

Frisson hung his head, but he didn't stop chewing.

"The man's a walking catastrophe," I muttered.

"Oh, poor fellow!" Gilbert burst out, showing an unexpectedly sympathetic side to his nature that got the better of his healthy dread. "You have been cast out to roam the wilds alone!"

The poet nodded; a tear trembled in his eye. "I have sought to prevent it, good squire. I have broken the meter into odd phrases with the accents reversed; I have used slant rhymes, broken rhymes, and no rhymes—yet all to no avail!"

"Of course not." I groaned. "You concocted new kinds of verse, and just made the magic stronger!"

The poet looked up at me, frightened. "Aye, my lord. The mayor's house did fly apart on the instant; my words did breach the baron's wall. I foreswore my verses; I bit my tongue; I ground my teeth against the words—yet all to no avail! I could not help myself; anon I shouted words aloud! They chased me from the town, they chased me from the parish, they chased me from the province—and anon they chased me from my native land of Merovence, to live or die in this wilderness of Allustria."

"But," I said. "But—but—"

Gilbert looked up at me with a frown. "We have only two pheasant and a partridge, Wizard Saul."

"But!" I shouted in exasperation. "But you don't *have* to chant your verses out loud!"

Frisson's jaw gelled, and he stared up, appalled. "I'd as lief stop eating, milord." Then he set to work chewing again.

"Write them!" I exploded. "Why don't you just write them down? Your verses, I mean! Then read them over, and just don't recite anything that looks dangerous!"

Frisson stared up at me; his jaw dropped.

"He has never thought of it," Gilbert murmured.

"Aye, never!" Frisson burst out. "So *that* is why men learned to write!"

"Well, there were some other little things," I said uncomfortably, "such as grain inventories, and bills of sale, and laws, and history. But it works for poetry, too, yes."

"Can ... can you teach me?" Frisson begged.

I just stared at him.

Then I said, "You're a poet—and you don't know how to read and write?"

"I had never thought of a need for it," Frisson confessed.

"Well! I've heard of the oral tradition—but I've also heard of departures." I wondered, uneasily, if I was witnessing the downfall of poetry, or the beginning of its glory. "Sure, I'll teach you to write." After all, if I could handle two dozen freshmen, surely I could manage one starving poet.

Well, it helped. He understood it instinctively, took to it like a goose quill to ink. More likely, like graphite to paper; fortunately, I carried a pocket notepad and a stub of pencil. I showed him how to draw the letters, and the sound each one made. His eyes went wide with wonder; he snatched the pencil and pad from me, and in half an hour, he was sitting cross-legged by the fire, scribbling frantically in an impossibly small hand. From then on, as long as I knew him, he would be constantly writing in that book—he filled it in a day, but fortunately, one of his first poems was a wish for an endless supply of parchment—he didn't know the word for paper—and my little pocket notebook never ran out. On the other hand, after the first fifty poems, it started producing a much higher quality of writing material.

Nonetheless, sometimes some of his magic leaked out. Writing it down seemed to channel it safely, since he didn't speak it aloud—but when he didn't have time to write and suppressed too much poetry, he thought about it so intensely that the magic started working without his having to say it aloud. Sometimes we'd be hiking down the road, and his eyes would start bulging, and a bat would materialize by the roadside in bright daylight, or a gushing fountain would spring up right smack-dab in the middle of the path, or we would suddenly find ourselves walking on gemstones, and let me tell you, when the soles of your boots get thin, that's no picnic.

The first time it happened, I reined in my temper and turned to him with a sigh. "Frisson, you've got to stop and write it down."

"Eh?" He looked up at me, startled, then saw the glitter on the road. "Oh! My apologies, Master Saul!"

"No problem, no problem. Never can tell when we're going to need a little hard currency. Just sit down and write it out, okay?"

So Frisson sat down by the roadside and filled his parchment, while I knelt down and started filling my pockets. As I'd told him, you never could tell.

After a while, though, it got to be a nuisance, especially since I never knew when he was going to start using dragons as poetic images. He never did, fortunately, but the door that appeared right in front of us, too quickly for me to keep from smacking into it nose-first, was almost as bad as the wolf I saw when I opened it. I slammed it fast. "Frisson! Write it down!"

He did, and I showed him how to write as he walked. That helped—but hey, nobody's perfect.

I developed a streak of prudence, though, and I took to going through his day's output every evening, around the campfire; he was pathetically eager to have me read them and tell him how much I liked them—I was careful never to criticize, partly because I knew how hard beginners take it, and partly because I just flat out didn't understand what he was trying to do. But I knew from experience that it worked, so I figured he had to be doing something right.

I always enthused as I handed them back to him—but I kept the ones that I thought might be particularly useful. With his permission, of course—I had a notion that infringing copyright could have bad results, in this particular hallucination. I even memorized the ones that looked to have the most potential. As I'd told him, you never know . . .

But that first evening, I needed a distraction; the first dozen verses he turned out, and proudly showed me, filled my head with such a clamor of acoustics and clashing of images, that I needed some mental soothing.

Of course, a philosophy student always has a distraction to hand—reasoning out arguments. It's risky, because sometimes you get so caught up in it that it keys you up even more, but under the circumstances, I figured it was worth a try. So I spent a half hour or so trying to rationalize my way out of having to believe in trolls or fairies, or magical spells that could have anything to do with either. It wasn't much use, of course—I kept coming back to the conclusion that either the evidence of my senses was unreliable, or what I had seen and heard was real.

Of course, it didn't take much to discredit sensory evidence, for a man of my generation. I seriously considered the possibility that I was simply stoned out of my mind, and all this was happening in a fantastic hallucinogenic trip—but I couldn't help remembering that I had sworn off all drugs for final exams—years ago.

Fortunately, there was an alternative. Bishop Berkeley had pretty much discredited the senses for us all, way back in the 1700s, by pointing out that if we don't actually see something, we can't really know it exists—and that even if we do, we could be wrong, because even if our minds perceive it, all they have to go on is the sensory impulses from our eyes and ears and nose and tongue and hands, all of which can be very easily deceived. Optical illusions are the most obvious example, of course, which is why science insists on measurement—but how're you going to prove, logically and completely, that the ruler itself isn't an illusion? He managed all this without knowing about LSD, too.

Of course, to Berkeley, the fact that we can't really know

anything was just proof that we had to have faith—but to the rest of us, the idea that things don't exist if they're not perceived, and the corollary, which is that we can't know what's real because of the fallibility of our senses, just means that we have to live in the world as we perceive it, while we're trying to stretch the limits of our perceptions—and raises the distinct possibility that hallucinations may just be the perception of an alternate reality, or two, or three. "Heaven lies about us in our infancy," as the poet says, and there may be a lot more to the universe than we see, as Hamlet was kind enough to point out to Horatio.

I was faced with the unfortunate conclusion that both ideas applied to my current situation. The world I was perceiving was certainly real to all intents and purposes, and I had to deal with it as if it were, because it was certainly going to deal with me as if *I* were. Dr. Johnson claimed he disproved Berkeley by kicking a cobblestone, presumably meaning that if the cobblestone flew away, he did interact with it, and therefore he and the cobble were both in the same frame of reference; what he failed to mention was that his toe hurt.

So did mine—metaphorically, at least. Gruesome would eat me if my spell slipped, and there might be a monster around the next hill who would sneak up on me in the night if Squire Gilbert nodded off while he was on guard duty. It might be an illusion, but it would hurt just as much as if it were real—so I was going to have to treat it as if it were totally authentic, or it might kill me just the same.

But I wasn't going to believe in magic. Okay, some unexplainable things had happened, and they did seem to coincide with verses I'd spoken aloud—but coincidence was no doubt what it was, and the events were unexplainable only because I didn't know enough. I made a firm resolution to learn more about this strange-but-familiar world, and not to delude myself into thinking I was practicing magic.

But I decided to save Frisson's verses, just in case.

I remember thinking, just before I drifted off to sleep, that I had stubbed my own toe.

CHAPTER 8

Guardsmen were shoving me roughly, trying to push me into a cell, and one of them was saying something about things being wrong. I turned to him with sullen resentment, and was surprised to see that he had a troll's head.

I stared at the troll, then looked quickly about me and saw the campfire with Gilbert lying on his side asleep, soles of his feet toward the coals, Frisson across from him, curled around the warmth. I realized I'd been dreaming. I looked up and, sure enough, the troll's head was still there—but now I recognized it. "Time for my watch again?"

Gruesome shook his head, looking agitated. "Wrong! Wrong!" He pointed out toward the darkness in several different directions.

I frowned. "What's the problem, then?"

"Dunno." The troll twitched, raising his head to look out into the night. "Feel wrong, wrong!"

"Just a hunch?"

Gruesome nodded and held up his huge mitts. I backed off in alarm, but he only wiggled his inside talons. "Feel pinches! Trouble, trouble!"

" 'By the pricking of my thumbs,' " I quoted, but remembered, in the nick of time, not to finish the verse: "something wicked this way comes." I rolled up to my feet. "I'm never one to scoff at intuition—at least, not in this world. Want to wake up the . . ." I broke off, staring.

With my usual paranoia, I had decided to set up a barrier against supernatural attackers—there had been too many things that had gone bump last night, though that could have just

92

been Frisson dreaming in verse. We hadn't gone very fast today, out of deference to his weakened condition, and we were still in pretty open country, though there were a lot of scrub trees about.

So I had conjured up some talcum powder, sprinkled it around our campsite in a circle, and chanted the tail end of Shakespeare's dirge from *Cymbeline*, with a few adjustments:

> "No sorcerer shall harm thee!
> Nor no witchcraft charm thee!
> Evil ghosts forbear thee!
> Nothing ill come near thee!
> Safe shall we be within this sign,
> For nothing ill shall cross this line!"

I'd figured if anything spooky had tried to get too close, that verse ought to keep it outside our perimeter—and it seemed I'd been right. Just outside the circle of white powder, a blob of formless mist was rising from the ground, thickening and coalescing into a human form—but a mangled human form. Its face was bruised and swollen, one eye socket empty, thumbs dangling, one foot twisted almost backward, and its tunic ripped open to show dark smudges against its chest and abdomen.

"It is a ghost," Gilbert murmured from his place by the fire. Apparently, Gruesome and I hadn't been as quiet as we'd thought. The squire sounded excited, fascinated. "It is the shade of one who died by torture."

I was glad he could take such a detached interest in it. For myself, I felt rather queasy and thoroughly sickened in my heart.

The specter flitted from point to point about the circle, moaning. Chains, attached to the fetters on its wrists, clanked and rattled. "Bewa-a-a-re!" it cried. "Oh, foolish mortals, bewa-a-a-re! Flee! Hide yourselves away!"

I summoned my courage and called out, "Having you hang around just outside the perimeter doesn't exactly imbue me with a great desire to go exploring!"

"Heart of stone, who would mock a soul in torment!" the ghost cried. "O kindred of my fate, arise! Up, all ye who died by torture! Spirits bound to this world in unquiet slavery to a sorcerer's will, come now to school this foolish mortal!"

I had to turn to follow its progress, and I muttered out of the corner of my mouth, "Keep an eye on the place it came from, Gruesome."

The troll moaned in answer—but I figured he'd fight all the harder if he were scared. Either that, or run.

I wished I could.

Moans began to fill the night in horrendous discord, faint, but growing louder; and dim forms, drifting here and there, swam out of the darkness.

"Abandon your ill-advised escape!" the ghost cried. "Return whence you came! For know that, if you do persist in opposing Queen Suettay, you shall become as I—a shadow of a soul who died in agony unspeakable!"

I felt the blood draining from my face. I remembered Gilbert's commander warning me about the evil sorceress-queen of this country. How the Hell had I attracted her attention?

How the Hell?

No. Couldn't be. Just a figure of speech.

But I spoke up bravely. Unfortunately, it sounded more like a croak. "So I'm to be deterred by the thought of a horrible death, a punishment for even *thinking* about leaving Allustria, or raising my hand against the queen?" Not that I had . . .

"Even that!" the spirit cried over the chorus of moans and wails behind it. "I gave the queen my fullest measure of obedience—yet she had me rent apart, while still alive, for her mere pleasure! Chortled with delight at all my screams! And as I died, despairing, she seized my soul, to chain it in eternal slavery to her will!"

Now I began to tremble inside. I scolded myself harshly, if silently, and reminded myself this was all impossible.

"It is true." Gilbert came to his feet. "Suettay tortures folk for mere amusement, daily."

A sadist. I was being pitted against a sadist of the worst kind—and for what?

To get home. Preferably, alive.

I steeled myself to the piteous cries around me and called out, "Go! The afterworld is huge—you don't have to stay around here! The queen loses power over you when you die!"

"Foolish mortal, how little you know!" Another specter swam up beside the first, a ghost like an illustration from an anatomy text, muscles and ligaments naked to the night. "She whose power comes from Satan can petition her master for dominion over others who have turned their hearts toward the Evil One!"

"But you only fall into the Devil's power through your own fault!"

"And so we did," the phantom sneered. "I myself sought power—always power. While yet a boy, I swore to do whatever deed the Devil wished, if he would give me power—and I gained dominion over peasant folk, then over soldiers. Yet Suettay plucked me out for her fell mirth, and I died in agony, crying to my master Satan for power against this corrupted sorceress—and as I cried out to evil, Suettay wove her spell about me to capture my soul! At the last instant, I cried out in despairing repentance, but it was too late. Suettay had claimed me, and I am bound to her!"

I suppressed nausea. I mean, I really felt sorry for them, even if they had been total vipers when they'd been alive. If ever I'd heard a sound reason for being good, this was it. Unfortunately, I was aware of my own enormous failings and knew I wasn't in the world's greatest shape for combatting evil.

"Be of good heart, Wizard Saul," Gilbert counseled. "They cannot touch you here, within your enchanted circle."

I turned, welcoming the change of topic with zeal. "You're right. So why did Suettay sic them on us? Just to make sure we don't sleep and are so weak tomorrow that we'll fall into her hands? I can't really believe that!"

"I doubt it, also," Gilbert answered. "It may be that they seek to frighten you into joining their foul cause."

"That's crazy." I turned back to the spooks, debating within myself. I could only wonder how Suettay had come to know I was here. Crystal balls? Ink pools?

It didn't matter. "Go tell your mistress that it will take worse than you to scare me!"

The ghosts' moans turned into roars, and they came swooping against the invisible barrier like moths to the chimney of a hurricane lamp, anger and outrage in their faces.

I turned back to the squire. "Has to be more than just a try at scaring me."

"It must," Gilbert agreed. "Otherwise, when they saw you were not daunted, they would have fled."

"Yeah." I gestured to the barrier of specters. "You'd swear they were trying to attack us, but it's obvious they can't get in."

"Obvious indeed," the squire said, turning toward the perimeter, but not looking all that sure, himself. "Yet there's this, too—if they cannot come in, it is equally true that we cannot go out."

I could feel my eyes widen. "But that means somebody's trying to keep us here, to make sure we haven't gone anywhere until . . ."

A gout of greenish flame ripped the night, lighting all the hillside with an eerie light. The ghosts moaned in terror as the light dwindled. The residual chartreuse glow flickered on a dozen hooded forms, and lighted from below the face of the huge, grossly fat woman who stood before them, swathed in brocaded robes, rings glittering on her fingers, an elaborate crown on her head.

"So, then." She smiled, and her eyes almost disappeared in folds of fat. "You have the audacity to trespass in my Allustria."

"It is not yours, gross mockery of a woman," Gilbert cried, and I had to stifle an impulse to shush him. "The land belongs unto the people!"

"Then it cannot, of a certainty, belong to you, who come from Merovence." Suettay laughed, a sound like frying bacon. "You are not yet a man—only a beardless youth."

Gilbert flushed; blond beards don't show much.

The queen turned to the row of men behind her. "Counselors, behold a marvel! A boy that speaks like a man! Yet an he were, he would feel desire!"

The hooded forms dutifully laughed, but there was little humor in the sound.

Suettay turned back to me. "The more fool you, to be so cozened into taking a mere boy for to ward you!"

"Oh, he's man enough," I assured her. Bitches always make me mad, and she wasn't the first one I'd run into who'd thought she was a queen. Gilbert looked up at me with surprised gratitude, but it was as much for myself I'd said it as for him—I felt anger growing, just enough to begin countering the fear. "You twisted the facts," I told Suettay. "But then, you twist everything that's true within your domain, don't you? Or try to leach the life from it, if it won't twist!"

"Indeed, as my dunce of a country sorcerer will yet bleed your troll." Suettay's lip curled. "What a vile thing is he, that's neither gnome nor rock! What a catastrophe of nature, nay, a perversion of life! Yet you should thank me, corrupted monster, for you owe your life to me."

"Wozzat?" Gruesome's grunt had a dangerous edge.

"Your father was a gnome who strayed out of his hole!" the queen chortled. "I saw, and cast a glamour over a boulder, to make it seem a woman of his own kind, wondrously beautiful in his eyes! For my own amusement, I inflamed him with lust for it! Then, in my crystal, I watched what did ensue, and oh! what delightful—"

Gruesome's roar drowned out the rest of her words, as he lunged.

"No, Gruesome!" I cried in panic. "If she can get you mad enough to break the circle—"

The monster stopped with a jolt, his head poking out above the white line. I wondered what could have stopped him, then saw Gilbert down below, ramrod straight, shoulder against Gruesome's chest, straining against Gruesome's bulk—but his feet were plowing up the ground as Gruesome pushed steadily toward the witch, and Gruesome's top had made a hole in my defense screen.

The troll roared, almost managing to make words—but anything he was saying was drowned in a mass shriek, as all the ghosts dove at the hole he'd made in the magical wall.

I leapt up to shout at the monster. "It couldn't be true, Gruesome! Rocks can't have children! Only a mommy troll and a daddy troll can make little trolls!"

The troll's eyes suddenly lost focus, and his brow creased with effort as he tried to figure out the facts of life. He wasn't long on brain power—but the distraction was enough for the squire.

"Back, brave being!" Gilbert shoved harder, and the troll rocked back just enough for its head to clear the white line.

The ghosts' noise rose to a howl as they all tried to jam into the hole, but I shouted out,

> "If these shadows have offended,
>   Be but brave, and all is mended!"

The ghosts groaned in disappointment, then roared in rage and began to dash themselves against the invisible circle again.

I called out to Gruesome,

> "Let your hide of flint
>   Deflect all hint
>   Of insults dire!
>   Come to the fire!"

He looked up, blinking his huge, glowing, saucer eyes, totally dumfounded, then turned slowly and came hulking back to the campfire.

Gilbert breathed a long and shaky sigh of relief.

But Suettay and her boys were laughing themselves silly. 'Oh, skillfully done! Skillfully done!" the queen wheezed, between giggles. "Why not march upon my kingdom, mortal! Do! For you should be mired in your own muddle ere the day is out!"

"Oh, yeah, sure!" I strode up to the circle, anger getting the better of common sense. "We're such total klutzes that you bring yourself and your top twelve henchmen out to try to scare us? Meanwhile, of course, you can't even breach this simple little guarding circle I've set up!"

The queen's laughter chopped off on the instant, and her eyes narrowed to slits with glowing coals behind them. "Enough! Show this foolish impostor what awaits him!"

A scream rent the air—but one that was very much alive, not like the ghosts' mourning wails. This one was filled with terror and was definitely feminine.

The hooded ones threw her sprawling onto the grass between Suettay and the guarding circle. She was young, with long blonde hair and an enchanting figure; I could see it through the rips in her tunic. She scrabbled in the dirt, turning toward Gilbert and Frisson and Gruesome and me, her face filled with horror—a face bruised and battered, with a swollen nose, marks of burns on her breasts and belly, blood still dripping from triple gouges in her skin. "Help me! Please, I beg of you, before I—"

Then she broke off into a scream as four hooded forms surrounded her, two of them falling on their hands and knees side by side, the other two catching her thrashing limbs to lift her and swing her up onto the backs of the first two.

I almost went right through the guarding circle. All that restrained me was Gilbert's arm—but it had about as much give as granite. "You cannot help her now, Wizard Saul—you can but break your warding circle!"

"Besides, 'tis like enough that she did put herself into Suettay's power, in hope of preferment," Frisson quavered, staring at the scene in loathing. "The most you can give her now is a quick death, and the queen will do that herself."

The woman cried, "I did not—" but her sentence ended in a scream, as one of the hooded forms twisted something.

My mind raced as I stared. The poor victim had been trying to say she hadn't done anything wrong. How could I save her? Without breaking the guarding circle, of course—that was what Suettay wanted. She was lumbering forward, hitching at her robes and pulling out a long, twisted knife. She held it up in both hands, gloating gaze fixed on the woman's body as she droned out a long chant, overriding the screams.

"It is an invocation," Gilbert told me, "an invocation in the Old Tongue!"

It must have been very old indeed—it didn't sound a bit like Latin, or even Greek. I felt a chill prickling outward from my spine—how could I fight spells in a language I couldn't understand?

"She calls on the Devil." Apparently, Gilbert didn't labor under that handicap. "If the woman, in her terror, despairs of salvation and is damned, the queen dedicates the woman's soul to Satan, but asks that her ghost be the queen's slave as long as Suettay endures."

I felt my scalp prickle; the woman's screams filled my ears, maddening me. I fought to control myself, to keep from charging out to try to save her, knowing that I couldn't win, that Suettay had chosen the time and the conditions. The knife soared high in Suettay's fists, beginning to glow with the chant as the hooded acolytes joined in.

I fought back with the only thing I could think of—a chant of my own. I sang it, of course—that's how I'd learned it.

> "Tell her to make me a cambric shirt,
> Parsley, sage, rosemary, and thyme!
> Without a seam, or belt to be girt,
> Then she'll be a true love of mine!"

The girl stared up at me, and Suettay flushed with anger and jerked a nod at one of her acolytes. He reached down and twisted, and the girl screamed.

I fought down the urge to leap out of the circle and start kicking. I couldn't win alone.

Alone?

"All right, angel!" I yelled. "Now's your chance! You want to make me believe? Then give me a hand—or an idea! Nothing physical, mind you, just inspire me! Fill my mind with a way to rescue this poor victim!"

And, confound me, it was there—the knowledge that the

woman didn't deserve this fate and, moreover, was human and worth any help that I could give, and my mouth was moving, a voice booming out of it that didn't seem to have anything to do with my thoughts, but had a very familiar ring. "Woman, pray! Even now, call upon the Lord your God, and He will save your soul from Hell's power! Only repent and pray to be forgiven, and He will snatch you from the jaws of evil, even in the instant of your death!"

But the knife was slashing down, and the woman was screaming—

Screaming, "My God, forgive me my sins and save—"

Then there was only a gurgle, for her throat had been cut, and the knife slashed downward through her heart. Her whole body convulsed once and was still.

"Rise and obey!" Suettay thundered.

She didn't.

Well, she rose, all right—at least a shred of her, a wraith. It was her ghost, and it floated over toward the white chalk line of my guarding circle as if a breeze were blowing it.

Suettay screamed like a spoiled brat seeing a box of candy being snatched away. "Vile interloper! Ball of slime, thatch of dung! She should have despaired in that last instant and been bound for Hell, whereupon my master would have given her soul into my power! But you have interfered, curse you, and her soul is lost to me! She was innocent of all but the smallest sins, and her spirit will flee to Heaven!"

Then, suddenly, she fell silent, eyes bulging, a depraved grin spreading over her face. "Not yet! Not if I act quickly!" She whirled to the corpse, hands spread wide and going through gestures whose meanings I shuddered to consider while she chanted some racheting verse in a language I didn't understand. A glow sprang up around the body, like the phosphorescence around decaying vegetable matter in a swamp, then died away, and Suettay spun about to me with a crow of triumph. "I have bound her to Earth! As long as her body lives, her soul is bound here, for I have cast a spell that has preserved her mortal coil."

"Why, you filthy bitch!" I swore.

"How dare you!" she shrieked, and her hands clutched something unseen and threw it at me while she snapped out a quick, incomprehensible rhyme. Energy lanced from her fingertips in purple streamers—and dashed itself to sparks on my shield.

This time, though, the queen didn't scream. She only glared at me, her eyes gleaming malevolently in the midst of her slab of pitted face. "See to the purifying of your own soul, Wizard, for if you do not, you shall fall into my power—and you shall meet the same fate as the girl. Maiden, come!" she snapped at the wavering spirit.

But the girl's ghost had drifted across the line into my circle, and now she cowered away from the wicked queen, eyes wide and frightened, shaking her head.

"You have stolen her!" Suettay screamed. "You have taken from me my rightful—"

But her voice was drowned out by a long, shuddering moan that filled the air, rebounding from ghost to ghost, the specters' eyes widening and filling with hope.

"I did repent!" one cried.

"I, too, with my last breath!" another answered.

"God forgive my sins!" a third cried.

One by one, they remembered their final moment of repentance, wailed their appeals for salvation—and, one by one, they winked out, like candles snuffed.

I stared. "You mean all that was holding them here was their own belief in the queen's magic?"

"It would seem so," Frisson said, huge-eyed. "They lost faith—but you have restored it."

That hadn't exactly been one of my prime goals in life. On the other hand, it hadn't exactly been me speaking, either.

But a new moan filled the air, a moan of dread, as the hooded acolytes shrank back from the bleeding corpse, huddling together, terror-filled faces turned up to watch the ghosts depart.

And Suettay was turning to me with a gaze filled with more malice and hatred than I had ever seen before, a glare of berserk fury. She strode forward, arms uplifted, striding straight at my guarding circle, intoning a chant in the Old Tongue.

"She summons a devil!" Gilbert cried.

"Angel!" I yelped. "She's breaking the rules! You can protect us!"

Blue sparks leapt at the queen's fingers with crackles like gunshots. She shrank back with one of the foulest curses I had ever heard, then turned to me and my companions, eyes just slits in fat, hands weaving a symbol I didn't know, bellowing,

"Rot their flesh and boil their blood!
Meat slough off and turn to mud!"

Her hands snapped out, all fingers pointing at us.

A coruscation of sparks filled the air over the white line. A wave of nausea swept me, and my knees gave way, but Gilbert held me up, and my legs strengthened again as my stomach settled.

"Cowards!" Suettay screamed. "Pusillanimous pests! Come out to battle!"

"We . . . we battled," I managed.

"You shall, you must, soon or late! Then shall I be revenged upon you! Then shall I see your flesh fry from your bones, your eyes drop from their sockets!"

I was feeling a little bolder and said the only counterspell I could think of.

> "I'm rubber, and you're glue.
> Whatever you say
> Bounces off me
> And sticks to—"

With a shriek of frustration, Suettay disappeared. Green fire thundered inward on itself, seeming to consume the huddled, hooded forms. It died away, and the night was quiet and dark again.

And clean. Even the corpse was gone.

For some reason, that bothered me.

But I didn't have long to think about it—my head suddenly swam, and my knees gave way again.

"Now, now, buck up! You did marvelously!" Frisson assured me.

"Heroes are made of sterner stuff, Wizard Saul!" Gilbert chided. "You must not collapse as soon as the battle's over!"

"It's better than . . . melting while . . . it's still going on," I gasped.

"That is true, and there is no shame in it, so long as he does wait until the battle's over," Frisson allowed. He propped me up against Gruesome's side and began chafing my hands. "Really, you were masterful—you came only moments from death, and a horrible one at that."

"Huh?" I blinked, the thrill of dread pulling my mind back into focus. "You mean I almost blew it when I started to charge out?"

"You did indeed. That whole affair with the poor peasant

lass served one purpose, and one only—to induce you to leave your magic circle in an attempt to save her."

"Yeah." I swallowed thickly. "Yeah, I knew that's what I was doing as soon as I heard her scream. I knew it, but it almost worked on me anyway—and on Gruesome. Thanks, Gilbert. You saved his life—and all of us."

"Surely, Wizard Saul," the squire said, blushing with pleasure at the compliment. "It was little enough I could do."

"It was enough all right. Thanks again, Gilbert."

"My pleasure," he said, then frowned. "Yet there's another you should thank, whose aid was greater than mine."

I frowned, looking around me. "Who . . . ? Oh. Yeah." I remembered my guardian angel. "Well, I'll give him my warmest, next time he shows up."

The night was awfully quiet.

Then Frisson cleared his throat, and Gilbert looked away, abashed. I looked around, frowning. "What's the matter?"

Neither of them answered.

Then Gruesome growled, and my hair rose. "All right, all right! Frisson, what did he mean?"

"I do not speak the troll's language," the poet said with hesitation. "Still, if I did, I would guess he had said . . . that your behavior was rather . . ." He trailed off, looking away.

"Cheap," Gruesome rumbled.

Frisson looked up, startled. "I did not know he knew the word!"

I frowned. "What do you mean? Angels don't want bribes."

"Of course not," Gilbert said slowly, "but it might be polite to at least indicate a willingness to return the favor."

I frowned at him while his meaning percolated in. Then I went hard inside. "Now listen, and understand this well! I am *not* committing myself to either side, or any side! Anybody who does me a favor, I'll do a favor for him, if I can—but aside from that, I'm not promising anything!"

But it seemed to me that the stars winked, and the sounds of the night began again as the land came to life around me.

CHAPTER 9

It gave me a chill, so I turned away, brusque and growling—to see the ghost hovering near the fire, half-invisible because of its light. Her eyes were glowing, though, so I couldn't miss her. In fact, I wasn't sure I was entirely happy about the way those eyes were glowing at me—but I had saved her afterlife, so I supposed I had some responsibility for her. I came over—and she drifted away with a look of alarm, but still with that morbid fascination in her eyes. At least, *I* thought it was morbid. I remembered the blanket rules for making friends with small animals and sat down, waiting. Sure enough, she began to drift closer—then hesitated as Frisson came up behind me. "Why's she looking at me that way?" I asked him.

"Why, because she is in love with you, Master Saul," he answered softly. "Do you not know the signs?"

I felt the chill again. "Yeah, but I was trying to pretend I didn't. Why should she be in love with me? Just because I sort of saved her?"

" 'Tis reason enough," he assured me, "coupled with your face and form—but there is a greater. Did you not know that the verse you sang was a binding spell?"

My stomach sank. "Oh. Was it really?"

"Aye, and a most venerable one."

"What did it bind?"

Frisson stared at me as if I were crazy—or maybe he was seeing through my attempt at self-deception. "It binds her to yourself, Master Saul—or at least, her affections."

That was what I'd been afraid of. "An old one, huh? I take it spells gain power with age."

"Like fine wines, aye."

So that's why each verse ended with, Then she'll be a true love of mine. "But she didn't have time to make me a cambric shirt."

"It worked by intent," Frisson assured me. "She is bound to you now, Wizard, by the spell that most surely binds woman to man."

Which would have been great, if it hadn't been synthetic. Her ghost looked harrowed, but the marks of torture were fading even as I watched, and she was really, rarely beautiful. Her dress had even mended itself. I'd heard that love was healing, but I thought it had to be mutual to have that effect . . .

Nonetheless, it *was* having that effect. I clamped down on the implications. "How did you fall into the queen's hands, lady? You don't look to have sinned enough."

"I have striven not to, Sir Wizard."

"Saul." I held up a hand. "Just 'Saul.' I'm not a knight." I didn't commit myself about the "wizard" part.

"Master Saul," she amended.

I sighed, but told myself it would help keep distance between us. "Okay, that's my name. What's yours?"

"Angelique," she replied.

I frowned. "Given the local rules, a name like that should have helped protect you."

"That was my mother's intent." A tear formed at the corner of her eye. "She died when I was very small, though."

Somehow, that made sense—and seemed ominous. "But if you tried not to commit sins, how come the queen had a hold on you?"

"Because she wrested me from my father, Master Saul, and forced him to yield his authority over me."

My blood ran cold. "What kind of a father would do that to his own daughter?"

"A father in Allustria," Frisson murmured.

The ghost hung her head. " 'Tis so. He is a merchant who panders to the queen, immersing himself in every sort of vice to gain her royal favor—and grants of monopolies."

"To the point of giving her his *daughter*?"

"Not quite so bad as that," she said stoutly. "Nay, he protected and reared me in total innocence, until I had come of woman's years, whereupon . . ." She broke off, with downcast eyes.

"I would not press her," Frisson murmured.

"Right." I slapped my knees. "I didn't mean to get personal—"

"Nay, I must have you know!" She was almost pleading. "No sooner had I come into earliest womanhood than my father attempted to reap the harvest of my innocence himself."

I froze, feeling myself turn very, very cold. "Why, that infernal louse!"

"He did not succeed," she said quickly. "The queen discerned his intentions and stepped in to halt his incestuous advances. I hailed her as my savior—until I discovered that she had taken me only to save as sacrifice to Satan. She told me that fell prince has a great taste for virgin souls, 'tis said, and they are rare indeed, in Allustria."

The inner chill was still there, and getting colder. "I really don't think I like these people at all," I growled. "And *I* was the cue for her to kill you?"

"There was some other cause," she said quickly. "I did not grasp the whole of it—I could spare small attention for her conversation with her henchmen, the pains of the torture devices being so very severe . . ."

"That *would* hinder concentration." The chill had hit absolute zero and was beginning to bounce back up, as anger.

"There was some talk of barons rebellious," she said, "and of the queen of Merovence readying her troops to invade."

I looked up at Frisson sharply. "I caused all that?"

"I would doubt it," he answered.

Gilbert said, "Nay, Wizard Saul. 'Twas all of a piece with the mission of my order—the mill had been grinding before we came upon you."

Which meant I was only one part of a bigger plan—but whose? "So she was saving you up for a doozy of a spell that would have given her the power to blast her enemies—and when the time came, she decided to get double mileage out of it, by using you to decoy me out where she could annihilate me." I shook my head. "What a horrible life you had!"

"Oh, nay! It was pleasant, with many causes for joy—until these last six years. I grew restive at never being able to roam the town or frolic through the fields, as I saw others doing from afar—but my home was spacious and comely, and I thrived in my father's love." Her gaze strayed, then turned brooding. "Until it soured."

Or until she discovered his real intentions. I wondered if he'd thought incest would score points with the queen. "What about the last six?"

"I was a guest of the queen," she said slowly, "though I could not leave my chamber. It was pleasant enough, even luxurious—but it was all the world I saw."

"Then it's a crime that you should have had so little of life! But at least you have Heaven waiting. Don't tarry here, whatever you do—go on to your reward!"

"I cannot," she said simply.

I stared. Then I said, "No! Not just my binding spell!"

" 'Tis not that which holds me to Earth," she said slowly, "though it fends off sorrow and brings rejoicing."

I wanted a change of subject, quick. "What holds you here, then?"

"My body." She moved her hands in aimless seeking. "It has not yet died; there remains some spark of life within it. I can feel it, I can sense it!"

"The queen has preserved her clay," Frisson said softly.

"Of course!" I remembered what Suettay had said when she cast that fox-fire spell over Angelique's body—and it made perfect sense. "She didn't succeed in sacrificing you the first time, so she's saving your body to try again!"

"But would not the soul need to be within the body, in order for the queen to murder it?" Gilbert asked.

"Yeah, I'd say it would—especially if she wants to make Angelique commit the sin of despair, so Hell can have some claim on her. As it is, her soul's still too pure for Satan to have any hold on it. Angelique's goodness doesn't protect her from physical force, of course, but it does make her ghost immune. That was the whole idea of this horror show the queen just put on—the agony and terror were supposed to make her stop believing in God and Heaven!"

"It would have done so." Angelique bowed her head. "I verged on such despair; I had almost come to think that there was no God, or that the queen was right, and the Devil was stronger than the Creator. It was your words that restored my faith, if only for an instant—but in that instant, the knife fell."

"Glad I could do some good," I said lamely. "But if she can cram your soul back into your body and torture you again, it might work this time."

"Nay." She gazed directly into my eyes. "You have restored my faith; I shall never despair again."

How about if I told her I didn't love her? That chilled me, too—it meant I didn't dare be honest, which really rankled. But we were right. I'd read enough medieval literature to know the rules, if not enough to make me sympathize with the spirit. "So she's going to be trying to get your soul!"

The ghost paled—or, in her case, turned almost transparent. "Then I must leave you! Or my presence will bring her down upon you!" And she darted away. I jumped up to call out to her to stay—but she slammed into my unseen barrier and rebounded with a cry.

"Sorry about that," I said quickly, "but we can't let you go roaming off by yourself—she'd swallow you up in an instant, and you'd be back in the torture chamber."

"I must chance it! I will not imperil you!"

I realized, with a sinking heart, that I could really get to like this girl.

Fortunately, Gilbert spoke up, with quiet certainty. "We would never forgive ourselves, lady, if we abandoned a maiden in peril. Indeed, it would weigh on our immortal souls."

The ghost stilled in her frantic dashing.

"You would not wish to send us toward Hell, would you?" Frisson asked.

The ghost seemed to droop. "Nay, I would not."

"You see," I said carefully, "you've become a crucial element in the future of this country. There seems to be some sort of a campaign going on, to kick out the queen and all her ministers, and the evil that they serve. You were apparently her trump card, her ace in the hole, her secret weapon to give her more power to repel the invaders and the rebellious barons. Now that your sacrifice failed, the Devil and the lords will all drop her as having become too weak—too weak to be of any use to the Devil, too weak to defeat her barons if they rebel. That means that all the nobles will be jockeying for power, each one trying to prove to the Devil which of them is most evil and most ruthless, so that the Prince of Bullies will choose him to be the next king."

Angelique's ghost began to grow brighter, then dimmer, then brighter again, throbbing with anxiety. "But I am only a poor, simple maid of the common folk!"

"Maybe that's why you're so important," I said softly. "Re-

ally good people are hard to find, in any age." I should know;
I'd been looking for a good woman for years.

"But you must not endanger yourselves for my sake!" she
wailed.

"We're already nicely endangered, thank you," I told her.
"Why do you think the queen brought you to us? No, I'd already made trouble for her before you came."

Angelique stared, wide-eyed. "Wherefore? 'Tis folly of the
worst sort to antagonize her with no cause!"

"She wants me to leave, if I won't serve her cause," I
grated, "and to me, that's reason enough to go back in. I'm not
about to knuckle under to authority, unless it has won my respect and confidence. I'm going to do what I think is right, no
matter what the rules say! And something tells me that trying
to get your body away from the queen, and back to you, is
right!"

Suddenly the chill within me stabbed all the way to my vitals, accompanying a sudden total sense of the rightness of
what I had said. With a sinking heart, I wondered if I had
played into the hands of somebody else—the angels. Especially mine.

"I shall accompany you, then," Angelique said slowly, "for
there is merit in what you say, and I perceive that you are a
good man."

But the way she was looking at me said more, much more,
and I went into panic. "No, I'm not! I'm a sour old cynic
who's bitter about human nature in general and women in particular! I think religion was invented by priests for their own
self-interest, and I scorn its rules! I'm an agnostic and a secular
humanist, and by the standards of this universe, I'm thoroughly
despicable!"

I ran out of gas and stood glaring around at them all, panting. Angelique shrank back, but not much, and just hovered
there, staring at me out of those huge, worshipful eyes. Frisson
and Gilbert exchanged judicious looks, lips pursed, and finally
nodded.

Gruesome, of course, just sat blandly by the fire, looking
vaguely interested. Why should he care?

Right.

"And what are you two snickering about?" I growled at Gilbert and Frisson.

"That you lack faith may be true, Master Saul," Gilbert said
slowly, "but we have seen your works."

I frowned. "My works?"

"You do not have it within you to turn away from a soul in need," Frisson explained.

I glared at him, but what could I say? It's my biggest failing. It gets me taken for a chump, time and again. Emotional leeches latch onto me like piglets to a sow, and I let them take and take and take before I finally get mad enough to tell them to bug off. I'm a sucker for a hard-luck story and a gloomy face.

Gilbert delivered the final verdict. "You are a good man, and we will follow you to the death."

The chill hit again, and I snapped up a palm like a stop sign. "Now, wait a minute. Who elected me leader?"

"Why," Frisson said, "who else has the slightest idea as to what we should do, or where we should go?"

It was a good question. But *I* sure as heck didn't.

I was still trying to figure it out as I rolled up in my cloak, to try to eke out a little sleep from what was left of the night. But Angelique was right in my line of sight—deliberately, I was sure, the way she was gazing fondly at my battered, hairy face—and just knowing she was there played hob with my concentration. Every few minutes, I found myself opening my eyes just a little, to drink in the sight of all that lush feminine beauty, that lovely face, those wondrous curves that showed as hints through her long, gauzy gown every time she moved a little, and even when she didn't. I might not have been in love with her, but I sure got a charge out of looking.

Unfortunately, she seemed to have the same problem with me; every time I peeked, she was still gazing adoringly at me.

Suddenly, it hit me with a shock, and I went rigid, fighting to keep my eyes shut. That blasted binding song had worked both ways! I was just as much subject to it as she was! Like it or not, reality or illusion, I was in love!

My mind reeled, trying to adjust to the facts, trying to understand romantic love as a magical spell—not just the product of a spell, but the spell itself. My mind went over and over that idea, around and around it like a squirrel in a cage, until insight struck again, and I realized what the literature had always said love was—magic.

I relaxed, just a little. Of course, I'd been hearing that since I was a kid, from every adventure novel with a love interest, and half the popular songs on the radio.

Nonetheless, the reality was something of a shock.

On the other hand, I'd come to believe some time before that love was nothing but an illusion. I remembered that and got back some peace of mind.

But not much.

We were up with the morning star for a cold breakfast. I longed for a cup of coffee and was tempted to believe in magic long enough to conjure some up—but I turned mulish at the last second. Sunlight and morning had put me back into skeptical mode, and I was discounting all the spells I had worked as being part of the hallucination. Besides, nobody else there needed caffeine.

So we were off as the sun rose, following our shadows down the road to the west, not that I really expected to get very far. After about an hour, though, we climbed to the top of a ridge and stopped short, seeing the telltale shingled roof of an official toll station.

"I don't mind paying for the use of the road," I said to Gilbert and Frisson. "Where there's verse, there's gold. But I'm not exactly up for a session of arguing."

"There is no avoiding it," Frisson told me, "and I have wandered far enough to know. Even were we to slip into the high grass or the woods to bypass the hut, the witch within would know of our presence by her spells."

"Magical border alarm system," I grunted, thinking of electric eyes and radar. "Well, if we have to brazen it out, we might as well do it with style." So I strode up to the doorway and knocked.

My friends stared, then ran after me frantically, but they skidded to a stop as I knocked a second time, their faces sinking as they realized there was no help for it now.

But by the third knock, they were beginning to look puzzled.

"Nobody home," Gruesome grunted, disappointed; I think he'd been hoping for a quick snack.

"A border station, unwatched?" Gilbert stared. "Surely not! 'Tis unthinkable!"

"Then how come you just thought of it?" I turned to Angelique. "I hate to take advantage of your special nature, but do you suppose . . . ?"

"Surely, Master Saul." She was only an outline in sunlight,

a gossamer strand or two—but she drifted through the cabin door as if it hadn't been there.

We waited. I tried my best to look impatient and annoyed. Gruesome just looked hungry, and Frisson looked apprehensive. Gilbert, though, stood like stone with his hand on his sword hilt.

Angelique slipped back out, scarcely more substantial than birdsong. "There is no one within."

I stared. "No one?"

"None," she confirmed.

"But that cannot be!" Gilbert protested, and Frisson seconded him. "No witch who was stationed to guard a road would dare leave her post while she lived, mademoiselle."

We fell silent at that, exchanging glances. I put it into words. "But if she's dead, where's the body?"

"There are signs of haste," Angelique said helpfully.

"Let me see." I pushed at the door, but it was locked.

"Lemme." Gruesome hipped me aside—his shoulders were too high—took the door by the handle, and yanked. Wood cracked and splintered; the door came loose, leather hinges flapping. Gruesome grunted and tossed it aside.

"Uh—yes." I eyed the dismembered door and cleared my throat. "Direct, aren't we? Well, let's have a look." I went in.

It wasn't in the world's best condition, that was true, but it wasn't all that bad, either—sort of like somebody had stopped doing the housekeeping a month ago; that rotten smell must have been the dirty dishes in the kitchen. At least, I assumed that was what the curtained doorway in the back wall led to; this part of the house just had a central fire pit under a hole in the roof, shielded by a louver, and a desk with a huge book beside an inkwell with a quill in it. I stepped closer and peered in; there was still liquid in the pot, but you could see the thick line above that showed it had evaporated. There was a fine coating of dust on the book, not all that obvious unless you looked; I guessed it had been a week or so since it had been used.

I looked up at that curtain hanging across the doorway. Something inside me balked and protested, wanting to leave well enough alone, but curiosity drew me on. Had to be curiosity, right? Couldn't have been anything else.

I pushed the curtain aside and looked in. The smell got a lot worse, and I wrinkled my nose. I couldn't pretend it was just rotting food anymore—it was the stench that goes with sickness, bad sickness. Angelique had been right, though—there was no one there, certainly not in the bed. It wasn't made, though, and the dishes were piled up on the table. This was where the toll-witch lived—but where was she now?

I went back out, shaking my head. "You called it, Angelique. No one home."

Frisson clapped his hands with a smile of delight. "Most excellent! Let us go on past!"

"Yeah," I said slowly, "let's."

But it nagged at me, as we went by the tollhouse. I didn't like unsolved puzzles and I liked even less the idea that somebody might be lying around sick, with nobody to take care of him. However, there was every chance that the duty-witch had been taken in for an overhaul, and that her replacement just hadn't arrived yet, so I pushed my misgivings aside and followed Gilbert into the woods.

Then I heard the moan from the other side of the trail.

CHAPTER 10

It was hard to say whether that moan was of pain or terror—maybe both. But I couldn't ignore it. I stopped. That meant Frisson and Gruesome had to stop, too, or bump into me—but they had stopped already and were frowning into the shadows under the leaves.

"What moves, Master Saul?" Frisson asked.

"Probably nothing," I answered. "From the sound, I'd say whatever made it is too sick to do more than lie there."

Gilbert heard and looked back. He stopped, frowning. " 'Tis not our affair, Master Saul."

"Anybody hurt is my affair," I snapped. " 'No man is an island.' I thought you were a Christian, Gilbert."

"I am indeed!" he cried, offended.

"Then remember the parable of the Good Samaritan."

"The Samaritan," Frisson said nervously, "was in no peril."

"He speaks wisely, Master Saul." Angelique's voice seemed to come from thin air. "There may be danger."

"Can't let a little thing like that stop us." I stepped into the shadows, pushing the branches aside with my quarterstaff—and just incidentally keeping it near the guard position. "Let's see what we'll find."

Leaves rustled as we moved in—then Angelique recoiled. "Evil!"

I could smell it, too—or maybe it was just the aroma of illness. I reminded myself that this massive hallucination included a guardian angel, and kept going.

The underbrush opened out, and there, hovering near a sheer rock face, were two of the ugliest creatures I had ever seen, with multiple fangs and tusks sticking out of their snouts, under baleful yellow eyes set in red, leathery skin that turned into black as it stretched out into bat wings. Their fingernails were claws, and their feet were cloven hooves. I froze; the mere sight of them struck fear through my vitals—or maybe it was their sulfurous smell, or the aura of evil that hung about them.

They were chuckling and gibbering, jabbing long-nailed fingers at the poor bundle of rags and quivering flesh that huddled against the rock face. I took a deep breath, reminding myself that they were just hallucinations.

The deep breath was a bad idea, though; I caught a whiff of her stench and was almost glad the demons' sulfur smell drowned it out—but it was definitely the same as the trace lingering in the back room of the toll cabin.

She saw me and stretched out a hand in supplication. "Aid! Good traveler, aid!"

The devils turned in instant suspicion, saw me, and dove for me, howling.

Terror damn near immobilized me, but trained reflexes made me leap aside and slam a kick at the nearest one. I yelped; he was hard! And hot; pain seared through my toes. My boot was charred.

The devil snarled and turned, gloating—but Gilbert leapt in front of it, holding his sword up like a cross and crying, "Avaunt! Leave off, in the name of the Christ!"

They actually hesitated, and I knew with a sick certainty that the only thing that protected Gilbert right then was his total, idiotic purity and the massiveness of his unquestioning faith. If I had tried it, they'd have torn me limb from limb.

Even Gruesome was cowering back, and Frisson was hiding behind him—but Angelique's ghost drifted to Gilbert, glowing with righteous indignation and purity. "Get thee hence, in the holy name! Avaunt, and begone!"

Now the devils did cower back—but they didn't go. I figured they'd work up their nerve eventually—this was their prey, after all.

Which reminded me about the sick one.

I stepped over to the whimpering bundle. "What's the matter?"

A claw pulled the hood open enough so that two rheumy eyes blinked out at me. "Oh, the pain!" She pressed one hand to her belly. "It tears me apart from within! I have cast spells against it, but it eats through even that power! I die!"

The devils surged forward, cackling with glee.

"Avaunt!" Gilbert shoved his cross-hilt in their faces, and I swear he didn't show the slightest trace of fear. Angelique glowed with wrath behind him, and the devils bellowed with anger, but retreated.

"They will take me," the old woman whimpered. "They will haul me to Hell!"

Sympathetic fear wracked me, but I hung on to my composure and said, "No they're not! Not according to the rules! All you have to do is repent! I remember that, because it always seemed like such a cheat to me, that a man could live his whole life making other people miserable and still go to Heaven if he just repented at the last second!"

"With eons in Purgatory," the witch moaned, "but even as thou sayest . . . The tortures would end, someday . . ."

The devils howled with rage and sprang, vaulting around Gilbert and Angelique in two jumps. One of them slammed me back into the dirt, and pain tore through me where his huge hand pressed. His monstrous face was an inch from mine as his jaws gaped wide, and terror jellied my insides—but I heard the old witch scream in horror, and the sound galvanized me.

"Angel!" I cried. "I'm trying to do your work now! It's in your own interest! Get rid of these monsters!"

Thunder cracked, and searing light filled the little clearing. "Even so!" the angel's voice snapped, echoing all about me. "I am entreated by a mortal who seeks to do God's work! Begone, loathsome fiends!" The light shrank in on itself just enough to be an anthropoid form, and glowing hands reached out to yank the two devils aside. " 'Tis the power of God that flows through me to brand you! Get hence, in His name!"

The two demons howled; the angel hurled them away, and they shrank, diminishing, until they were just two black dots that disappeared with a double pop.

I stared, awed, and muttered, "Dealer wins all draws."

The shining form waved a hand at me. "Let thy pain be gone! Now aid the woman!"

And he disappeared. Just like that.

Gilbert looked up at me, awed. "What manner of man are you, Wizard, that even angels will come when you call?"

"A do-gooder busybody," I snapped. I was too busy being amazed to be polite; the burning pain in my chest was gone.

I took a quick peek down inside my shirt and didn't see the slightest scar, just a bright pinkness in the shape of a huge clawed hand. It was enough to give me a bad case of the shakes, until the poor lump of rags moaned.

I turned to it, trying to remember that this "poor thing" had probably burned peasants and gloated at their pain, in her time, and practiced the rest of the catalog of medieval minor witchcraft, such as making cows go dry and women barren. But I couldn't resist trying to help when she looked so pitiful. "Apologize," I advised. "You know you're going to die—but if you repent, the devils can't have you. Maybe a long, long time in Purgatory, as you said, but not Hell."

"I dare not," the old woman whispered. "The pain is held at bay only by the spells I've cast—and even with their aid, 'tis like to drive me from my senses!"

"And if you repent, you lose your magic powers, so the pain will rip you apart? But remember . . ." I tried to recall the rules, as I'd learned them from Dante. "If you suffer the agony patiently here on Earth for the few days you have left, it will take centuries off your tortures in Purgatory."

"I fear the pain too much," she gasped in despair. "I am too far sunk in cowardice!"

I bit back the urge to tell her she deserved what she was getting, then—I'm sure it wouldn't have seemed that way to me, if I'd been the one that was in agony. I frowned; what to do? If she couldn't repent because she was in pain, but the only thing that made her *want* to repent was that same pain . . .

No, it wasn't. It was fear of eternal pain, in Hell.

"If I can make the pain go away," I asked her, "would you still want to repent?"

"Aye, assuredly!" she gasped. "Anything to save me from an eternity of agonies as I've felt now!"

"Probably worse," I reminded her. "Well, let's see what we can do. What kind of pain?"

"A gnawing, a hideous gnawing!" She pointed to her belly. "Here!"

"Not a burning pain, like a hot coal?"

"Nay! 'Tis as if something did eat me from the inside, with terribly sharp teeth!"

Not appendicitis, I guessed—but it did sound like abdominal cancer, and she was sure old enough.

I sat back on my heels, frowning. How do you use magic to cure cancer?

Then I remembered that "cancer" is Latin for "crab," and that the disease was named that way because it felt as if a crab were digging you out inside with its pincers.

So how do you fight an inside crab?

Obviously, bring it outside.

"Gilbert," I called, "come over here with your sword."

"Nay!" the witch shrieked.

"Oh, it's not for you," I said impatiently. "No mercy killing—I'm not about to end your mortal agony by sending you to everlasting torture."

Gilbert came up, sword ready, frowning. "What moves, Wizard?"

"A crab," I told him. "I'm expecting a giant crab, or something very much like it. If it shows up, stab it. Frisson?"

"Aye, Master Saul." The poet edged up, trembling.

"See if you can't cook up a verse for killing shellfish. Okay, folks." I took a deep breath, tried to ignore the gnawing in my own middle, and reached out for the scrap of parchment Frisson handed me. I read it, chanting,

> "Get you gone up-channel
>> With the sea crust on your plates,
> And get out of that body
>> With the burden of your freights!"

Nothing happened.

Frisson's face stretched so long I thought it was rubber. "I have failed!"

"No, I don't think it was you." The rules again. "She's in the power of evil now, and our spells are based on goodness, so they can't touch her." Except for spells inducing remorse—I'd found that out with Sobaka.

I wondered if I would have to use them again. "Woman! I cannot cure you unless you repent! You have to open your soul to God's grace, or all the goodwill in the world can't touch you!"

She was still a moment, rigid. Then she convulsed around the agony in her middle again, screaming and crying out, "I repent me! *Aiiee*, even if I die in agony, I will not suffer thus for eternity! I forsake Satan and all his lies!"

Then she screamed, as the king of all pains racked her body again—a souvenir from her boss, no doubt. But the woman had amazing grit; she held on, and when the spasm passed, she

went right on where she'd left off, though in a husky whisper.
"May God forgive my sins! I forswear my pact with the
Devil!"

Then she screamed again.

I started chanting on the instant, repeating the verse:

"Come forth from salty bloodstream
        With your pain that cramps and grates!
Get you gone up-channel
        With the sea crust on your plates,
And get out of that body
        With the burden of your freights!"

The witch gave one last shriek, then fell silent, panting
hoarsely as, between Gilbert, Gruesome, myself, and the huddled witch, the air seemed to thicken, growing darker and
darker. Then, all of a sudden, it snapped into sharp, clear
detail—and a crab three feet wide, with yard-long claws a foot
thick, was scuttling straight toward me, its pincers aiming for
my throat.

I yelled and jumped back, just as Gilbert shouted, "For Saint
Moncaire and for right!" and leapt in, stabbing down. His
sword skewered right through the whole crab, pinning it to the
forest floor—and he had the sense to jump back. A high-
pitched keening pierced my ears, and I fell away, hands
pressed over them. Gilbert was staggering, too, fingers in his
ears, while the crab scuttled, thrashing about—until it pulled
the sword free from the earth and came straight at the squire.

With a bellow that shook the trees, Gruesome leapt.

He landed on the monster with both feet; its shell gave with
a sickening crunch. Pincers waved wildly, snaking back to snip
at Gruesome's feet—but he reached down, catching the claws
in huge hands, and straightened up, wrenching them loose. The
monster screamed—I heard it even through my hands—then
went limp.

The clearing was very quiet.

I looked around and saw Frisson, over at the base of a tree
trunk, his lips moving silently.

I sat up, dazed, taking my hands away from my ears, but
keeping them close, just in case.

The only sound I heard was the roar of triumph as Gruesome jumped up and down on the shell, then tore open the
claw and thrust it toward his mouth . . .

"Gruesome, no!" I shouted.

His fangs clashed together but held back, as if he'd just bitten down on a spare auto fender. Then he held off on the claw, looking down at me resentfully. "Hungry!"

"And you certainly deserve a ten-course banquet," I said quickly, stumbling over to him. "I'll conjure one up for you, as soon as we're done helping this poor old lady! But not that meat, Gruesome! Bad for you! Shellfish has parasites! Very bad! Especially since the pieces of this one might pull themselves together inside you and start trying to eat their way out!"

Gruesome stared at the claw as if he'd never seen it before.

" 'Tis well spoken," Angelique said. "The monster weakened outside a host's body, and quickly—but would it not regain strength, once within?"

Gruesome hurled the claw away with a howl of frustration—but even as he did, it was fading, fading . . . and was gone. So was the huge plastron he was standing on, and all the little legs, and the other big claw. Gruesome stared down, dismayed; the lower edge of his huge lipless mouth quivered.

"Shellfish never did stay with me long," I sighed. "Always hungry again in an hour. Don't worry about it, big fella—we'll get you a whole steer, in just a few minutes."

"The witch," Gilbert said softly.

Something in his tone reminded me that without the lash of pain, our witch might not be feeling so remorseful. In fact, there was no guarantee that she wouldn't go back on her repentance.

She was sitting up, staring down at her midriff wide-eyed, pressing experimentally here and there. " 'Tis . . . 'tis gone! I am well! No more hurt!"

"I'd still take it easy for a while, if I were you," I said. "Just because we've got it licked for the time being, doesn't mean it won't come back."

"Nay, it will not, for I saw it torn apart by your huge troll! Amazing, most amazing! Who would have thought there was a crab within? Who would have thought to have conjured it out to fight it with steel?"

"It faded away," I reminded her. "It could reappear inside you—or another one just like it."

"Even if it does not, I may find myself beset by another illness, right quickly." The old woman looked up with tears in her eyes. "Alas! How comes it, good stranger, that you would help me, who have been so cruel to so many and torn the life from no few?"

"I can't resist a call for help," I said, with some self-disgust. "I know that makes me a chump, but—"

"Then a 'chump' must be a most excellent thing! Oh, I will sing your praises wherever I go!"

"Mayhap," Gilbert put in, "it would become you more to sing God's praises."

"Aye, indeed!" The witch sank down on her knees, clasped hands upraised. "I repent me of all my sins! I would that I could atone for each and every wrong I have done! Dear Father, forgive me!"

Nothing happened, no thunderclap . . . but a look of peace swept over her face, and her eyes widened in surprise. "Why . . . is it thus?" she whispered.

"The peace of God." Gilbert nodded. "Yet you must seek out a priest, poor woman, as quickly as you may, that your sins may be shriven."

"Even so! That I shall!" The ex-witch pushed herself to her feet, gathering the rags of her robes about her. "And I must go quickly, for if the queen should discover my betrayal, I shall die quite quickly!"

"And in agony." Gilbert nodded. "Therefore tarry not."

The old woman shrugged. "The agony matters naught; I deserve far worse than ever she could wreak upon me, for all the wrongs I've done. Nay, almost would I welcome it now, that it might ease my burden of guilt. Yet I would not have it for eternity, and therefore will I go hotfoot." She whirled to me, hands upraised in gratitude. "Oh, stranger, I cannot thank you enough for your pity and aid! You have behaved as a true Christian, nay, as a saint would have! May you be blessed forever!"

"Glad I could help," I said, uncomfortably aware of everyone's eyes on me. "Now go your way and try to help others as I've helped you."

"I shall! Oh, I shall! And shall praise your name every night, in my prayers! Farewell!" She turned and hobbled into the woods, and was gone from sight.

"You have wrought well for God this day, Master Saul," Gilbert said softly.

I shrugged impatiently. "I did something good for a human being, out of entirely selfish motives."

"Selfish?" Gilbert frowned. "How so?"

"Because it made me feel good inside." I raised my voice. "Hear that, angel? I'm grateful for your help—but I had it coming, because what I wanted to do was also what you wanted done! I'm not on your side! But I'm not on their side either! Got that?"

But I felt a strange, vagrant wave of amusement that almost seemed to blow through me like a breeze, and I had to turn away fast to escape Frisson's long and thoughtful gaze. "Come on, troops. We've still got a long day's hiking ahead of us."

But we couldn't have been hiking down that trail for more than ten minutes before the roadway exploded in front of us.

The explosion kicked up a geyser of dust, and there stood the wicked queen herself, shrieking pure venom, her rolls of fat shaking with rage. "Vile invader! Your meddling has cost me five minutes' agony, hot irons searing all through my body! My master has punished me shrewdly for letting another soul escape damnation—and has commanded me to obliterate you and your friends! Yet first, I shall see you suffer as I have suffered!"

But it wasn't me she threw the first whammy at, it was Frisson, stiff-arming a gesture that twisted as it stabbed while she bellowed something I couldn't understand.

Frisson screamed and fell, writhing.

I shouted,

"For the unquiet heart and brain,
        A use in measured language lies;
    The sad mechanic exercise,
        Like dull narcotics, numbing pain."

Frisson relaxed with a groan of relief.

"Meddler!" Suettay yelled. "Rogue! Villain!" Yes, I did detect a note of panic there, a note of fear.

Of me?

No. Of her master.

"Mendacious mendicant!" she screeched, then added some syllables in the Latin-like language, winding up to throw me down.

I took a deep breath for a counterspell, hoping I'd think of one in time—but on the inhalation, I felt something pressed into my palm. Looking down, startled, I saw some chicken-track lines scrawled on a scrap of foolscap. The misspellings were horrendous, but they were being viewed by a volunteer tutor who had fought his way through many a Freshman English paper, and I managed to catch the gist of it at a glance. I called out,

"Wicked old queen, come losses or gains,
    Here is the verse to bring you fear:
Go hand, go foot, till naught remains—
    Gone with the snows of yesteryear!"

Suettay began to disappear, from the feet up. She howled in frustration, then lifted her arms to throw another whammy—but they disappeared, too. She screamed in full rage, face darkening and as ugly as I've ever seen, as her hips and abdomen faded. Then, unfortunately, she remembered herself and screamed something in the Old Tongue that made her arms reappear; they wove a quick, unseen symbol as she screamed another verse, and all of her reappeared just as it had gone, but much more quickly. Even as her nether parts were returning, she was winding up another verse that she belted out, hands rolling over and over each other, and a six-foot dragon leapt from them to charge roaring at us.

Gilbert gave a shout of joy and leapt in front of all of us, stabbing in low and jumping back. Ichor spurted from the dragon's chest, and it bellowed in startled pain, swerving to pounce at Gilbert—but the squire leapt aside and chopped horizontally, shearing off a bat wing. The dragon screamed, whirling and lashing out; steel talons cut through Gilbert's mail, and blood slicked the metal. The squire clenched his jaw and chopped again, a roundhouse swing that clipped the beast's head off its sinewy neck.

We all cheered.

But Suettay was chanting again, gesturing wildly, her volume building toward a crescendo.

I gulped. "It's gonna be a big one."

"Can you not hinder her?" Angelique pleaded.

"Frisson!" I snapped. "Any more verses?"

The poet shook his head, huge-eyed. "Naught but an old song comes to mind, Master Saul—a child's bit of nonsense."

"Try it! Anything, right now!"

"As you will." Frisson shrugged and started singing.

"As I went down to Darby town,
'Twas on a summer's day,
There I beheld the biggest ram
That ever was fed on hay!
That ever was fed on hay!
That ever was fed on hay!

When this ram began to bleat, sir,
The thunder, it did break!
When this ram began to walk, sir,
The earth began to shake!"

A deep, dull, thrumming sound boomed through the air, and the earth beneath us heaved and settled. Then the sound and the earth tremor came again, and Suettay shrieked in anger and fear. I risked a peek.

A wall of wool blocked out the sun a hundred yards distant, supported on legs that would've shamed a sequoia. I craned my neck back; up, way up there, a hundred fifty feet up, floated a huge head with magnificent, curled horns the size of a highway cloverleaf—and sure enough, there were eagles circling around them. "Must be nesting season."

But Suettay was still shrieking. "What magic is this, that I've heard naught of?"

"Ethnomusicology," I called back.

But her attention was on the ram, and with good reason—it was ambling toward us, and with legs that size, ambling was high-speed. "What hell-begot monster art thou," Suettay cried, "that comes thundering down on this poor rotted world!"

"Nay, speak not of Hell!" The ram's voice was a rumble in the Earth's crust. "I am begot of the core of the world, a child of magma! What art thou, tedious gnat, that would wake Darby's sleep?" The ram advanced, the earth trembling in sine waves with his footfalls. "For he who'd wake the ram must die, ere I can sleep again!"

Frisson turned pale as milk. It was borne in on me that I had roused an elemental.

"Nay, it was he!" Suettay shrieked, finger spearing toward Frisson. "Pounce on him, jelly him! For he 'tis who waked you!"

"Is it thee?" The ram swerved a fraction of a degree, glowering down at Frisson. "Aye, for I see in thy face that only now dost thou see the danger thou hast waked!"

Damn good eyesight, I noted; there was maybe three inches of Frisson's head showing, from the ram's angle. But, the hell with the risk—I couldn't do anything cowering, and it was my asking that had nudged Frisson to sing the song. I stepped forward, trying to ignore the hollow feeling in my belly and the way my knees wanted to wobble, and claimed the responsibility. "It was I who bade him do it, so it was I who waked you!" I felt a dramatic surge coming on. "Beware, mountain mutton! For I can slay you forever with the breath of a song!"

Hey, it sounded good, right?

"Dost thou threaten *me*?" the ram thundered in enraged disbelief.

I bellowed back at him, "Aye, I do threaten! Therefore beware, and do as I bid thee! Slay this foul witch!"

"Eh, would you dare?" Suettay shrieked. "Heed him not, mighty ram, but turn to slay him! For know that I, too, can slay you!" And her hands began to weave an invisible net, while she chanted,

"Earth, give bellow; fire, blast!
Vomit molten rock and ash!"

I didn't wait to hear any more. Queen or not, if that witch was going to be fool enough to open up a volcano under the ram, it could kill all of us. I grabbed Gilbert and Frisson and threw them to the ground, yelling at Gruesome, "Duck! And after the boom is over, run for your life!" I was only glad Angelique had no body to hurt.

A flue opened, and a jet of ash shot out—but the ram stepped on it. The earth shook a little, and he set another foot down; the earth quieted.

Suettay just stared. Then she let out a screech that had some syllables in it, arms windmilling madly. A sudden whirlwind kicked up a lot of dust and stray ash, then dispersed and settled—and she had disappeared.

"Can we rise now?" Frisson asked around a mouthful of grass blades.

"Uh—yeah! Sure." I stood up slowly, staring at the spot of meadow where Suettay had been.

"Why—she is gone!" Gilbert said, amazed, as he stood up again.

"Yet I remain!" the ram thundered, still quaking toward us.

"Once I am waked, I cannot sleep again till my waker lies buried!"

"Wait a minute!" I barked. "Remember that spell I told you about!"

"Wherefore ought I chance it?" The ram was fifty yards off now, and coming fast. "I shall crush thee ere thy lips can form the words!"

"I wasn't kidding." But I backed up as fast as I could. "I know just the verse for the occasion." But my blood ran cold; I was bluffing.

Frisson stared at me, amazed. "How so, Master Saul? I know the same verse!"

"Then sing it!" I yelled.

"Aye, do so," the ram thundered, only a dozen yards off.

"I *hate* people who call my bluff." Actually, the verse was "Didn't He Ramble": ". . . he rambled till the butchers cut him down." But when it came down to it, I just couldn't stand to see something as majestic as that sheep converted into a mountain of ram chops—not if there was a choice, anyway. So I passed the buck and hoped like fury that Frisson hadn't been bluffing, too. "Frisson! Sing it! Quick!"

The poet started chanting,

"You who were waked from a century's sleep,
In a place dark and timeless, unfathomably deep,
Return to the slumber from which you were waked!
Return, and go quickly! Your blood-thirst is slaked!"

It was working. The ram towered closer, only twenty feet away, and he filled the world—but his outlines were wavering, and the curls of his wool were blurring together.

He covered ten feet with each stride, though.

Somehow, Frisson kept it soft and lulling.

"Sleep, for your great eyes do close!
Sleep, as the years and the centuries go!
Lulled in the magma that rocks you so slow,
Sleep where only the All-Father knows!"

The ram was a mountain, a McKinley, an Everest—but it faded off into the sunlight at the edges, and its body was growing translucent. And it yawned.

I added my two cents' worth.

"Golden slumbers kiss your eyes,
    Smile while sleeping, never rise.
    Sleep, mighty ram, and make no cry.
    Rock him, rock him, lullaby!"

Frisson and Gilbert joined me for a chorus: "Rock him, rock him, lullaby!"

The great hoof swung up for the last ten feet, growing thinner as it came. It lifted high over my head. I held fast with every thread of determination I had, frantically singing, petrified, rooted to the spot, staring up at the great dark circle that seemed to fill the sky. It poised, then slowly came lower—but I could see the clouds through it quite clearly, it faded to barely an outline as it dropped down, an outline that encircled our heads—

And was gone.

And a vast, distant thunder echoed, fading away, half angry bellow, half yawn. It reverberated over the land for what seemed a thousand miles, and was gone.

I let out a very long and very shaky breath, then turned to Frisson. "Fantastic job, Frisson!"

He was still gazing at the place where the ram had been. "It was, was it not? 'Twas truly my verses that effected this!"

"It sure was." I turned to Gilbert. "How bad is it?"

"Naught but a scratch." He looked very happy, eyes glowing with pride. "I have slain a dragon, Master Saul! A small one, but a dragon natheless! I have actually slain a dragon!"

"You sure did, and we're your witnesses," I affirmed. "You didn't hesitate for a second. If that doesn't prove your worth, what could?" I turned back to Frisson. "But where'd you ever learn that word, 'magma'?"

"Why, the ram himself did say it," the poet answered, "did say he was a 'child of Magma.' Who is she, Wizard?"

CHAPTER 11

The day passed without any further incidents, thank Heaven, and we set up camp in a nice, wide-open river meadow. The most menacing wildlife in sight was a convention of spiders, and I was getting used to them. They seemed to be more and more abundant the farther we went back into Allustria—sort of a comment on Suettay's housekeeping, I supposed. In fact, there was a web on every bush around the campsite, flickering with the reflections of our firelight. There were circular webs, triangular, strands of gossamer between branches—every sort any arachnid architect ever thought of trying. Their builders ran the gamut, too, from humble little brown things, up through the medium-sized spotted ones, to the huge, wide-as-a-quarter specimens like the one that had gotten me into this mess in the first place. I glowered at them with transferred resentment, but I couldn't really blame them for what one of their mates had done. On the other hand, I didn't have to let them inside my guarding circle, either.

I suddenly realized that I was beginning to regard them as good company and decided I had definitely been here too long.

Not that I could do much about it. If this was an LSD trip, it wasn't wearing off—besides, I hadn't been dropping any lately—and if it was a dream, I couldn't figure out how to wake up. I had pretty much decided to take the pragmatic approach to the whole problem of being in a world that couldn't exist. Illusion, dream, hallucination, or altered state of consciousness coming from my maybe being hit by a car and lying in a coma—it didn't matter; I was going to have to treat it as if it were real. Magic might have been only another part of this dreamworld, but within the context of the illusion, it worked, and it could hurt me just as badly as a revolver in my own world. I was going to have to treat it as if it were real.

Not that I was going to have to work any magic myself, of course. I didn't have to admit its existence *that* thoroughly—not as long as I had Frisson. Let *him* write up the spells, let *him* be the magician. So what if I was the one who read them aloud? That was just oral interpretation.

Hypocrite? Who, me? I was simply making an emotional adjustment necessary for psychological survival.

I took first watch, since I didn't feel much like sleeping with all that speculation going through my head. It didn't keep buzzing around very long, though, because Angelique was sitting there, unsleeping, just outside the range of the firelight, her form glowing in the night, her eyes glowing at me. I smiled in return, then closed my eyes, pretending to go to sleep.

I couldn't, of course. My favorite fantasy had come true; a beautiful young woman was head over heels in love with me, and I couldn't exactly be indifferent to that—couldn't just dismiss it and yawn, even if she wasn't anything more than a part of a very detailed hallucination—even if she was just a ghost. Of course, pure love shouldn't care about bodies, but I'm afraid mine wasn't all that pure.

It also wasn't love. At least, I wasn't in love with her—or so I was trying to persuade myself. At least, I knew it wasn't real, just the result of a slip of the tongue, so to speak, a rhyme snapped out without due forethought, in a place where verse had a far more potent effect than it had any right to. And I knew da— darn well that Angelique wouldn't have been in love with me if I hadn't accidentally come up with the wrong spell.

But what could I do? Tell her that to her face? I couldn't quite summon that much cruelty—besides which, she probably knew already, but was still in love with me; knowing it was just the result of a binding spell didn't make any difference to the way she felt. No, all I could do was to try to spare her the pain of a phony romance by not letting her know how I felt—but that was definitely becoming harder, with Angelique sitting there watching me adoringly, looking almost mortal in the darkness.

Then all of a sudden, she wasn't.

I mean, she was still watching me—but she was coming

apart at the seams. Then even the pieces were coming apart, shredding into a hundred tatters, and her eyes had glazed, no longer seeing, no longer aware.

It didn't take much to figure out what was happening. I sat bolt upright, calling, "Angelique! Baby! Pull yourself together!" Then I snarled at myself for losing my poise and forgetting to make it rhyme. I racked my brains for an integral verse, but all I could come up with was a variation on "Danny Boy":

"But come ye back, all bits of ectoplasm!
Reintegrate, all shreds of lady fair!
Remain you here, in firelight and shadow,
One integrated whole, with those who for you care!"

Okay, so it was doggerel. What do you expect, on the spur of the moment? But it helped—a little, at least. The tatters and shreds stopped moving. They hung suspended in midair, so that it seemed as if Angelique had just expanded to take in a bit more volume. I racked my brains again, trying to think of a verse that stressed reintegration and harmony of disparate elements—but a voice behind me called out,

"Oh, come back together,
All bits of my bonny lass,
Pull all together, rejoin and tether!
Be all of one, in mind and in body!
Go not to pieces, go not so early!
Stay!
With those who care for thee,
    Care for thee rarely!"

Well, Frisson certainly had learned how to do odd things to rhymes and meters—but it worked; the tatters that were Angelique began to pull themselves back together.

Astonished, I whirled and saw Frisson sitting up in his blanket roll, sorting frantically through the scraps of verse he'd been scribbling since we pitched camp. I felt stunned—but I forced the feeling down and turned back to the rope in my magical tug-of-war.

She was looking a little more solid than before—but even as I watched, she was shredding again. Grasping at straws, I called,

> "Tarry, rash lady!
> Am I not thy lord?"

No, I wasn't—and Angelique wasn't growing any firmer, either. The bits and pieces of her ectoplasm were still drifting away from one another, their form only vaguely resembling a woman's now. After all, the couplet hadn't rhymed—but at least she held steady for a minute.

Long enough for Frisson to thrust another verse into my hand. I gave it a quick glance, then read it aloud:

> "Thou art too long awaited, for
> Thy presence to be 'bated!
> Tarry, lady—stay awhile,
> Till the sun returns to smile!"

That bought us some time, at least. Angelique's pieces began to pull together remarkably quickly; she was almost an integrated whole again. Frisson really didn't know his own strength. She became so whole that I could see she had wakened from whatever long-distance trance the enemy sorcerer had put her in; she was staring about her in horror.

I preferred something without a time limit.

> "Oh, mistress mine,
> Where are you roaming?
> Oh, stay and hear—
> Your true love's coming,
> That can sing both high and low,
> That can sing both high and low."

I was stretching the truth a bit, but I was sure her true love was coming *some*time—I just hoped she'd recognize him when he showed up. But it had worked; her shape was almost complete again, as Frisson found another scrap of parchment and held it out. I caught it up, gave it a glance and frowned, but read it anyway:

> "Oh, lady fair, never be so wroth
> As to part the strong friendships thou hast wrought!
> When the spoiler pulls, as now she doth,
> Bear in mind the loyalties thou wast taught,
> And stay to bind thyself fast to us!"

The verse worked with overdrive; Angelique's form pulled together so fast I could have sworn I'd heard it click.

And was just as quickly shredded again. The enemy sorcerer must have been putting every ounce of his—or her—energy into that spell. I was amazed. I actually began to feel tension in the air around me, growing stronger and stronger, like strands of unseen force, pulling tighter and tighter, and I was the fly caught in the web. The fleeting thought went through my mind, that this must have been what an electromagnet felt like as you boosted the voltage—and I began to feel an intangible pushing, too, as if another field of force was fighting at my own. Was this how an electron felt, inside a transistor?

The webs of magical force intensified around me; I felt the unbearable tension of another magic field repelling my own, trying to pull Angelique apart. My mind reeled; I felt as if it were being stretched thin between two enormous engines, each pulling away from the other with enough force to bend an I-beam—and, in panic, I felt that Angelique's ghost must be annihilated even if its semblance stayed with Gilbert and Frisson, destroyed by the sheer stress of being stretched between two such huge forces.

In desperation, I bellowed the first verse that came into my mind:

> "What can a tired heart say,
>   Which the wise of the world have made dumb?
>   Save to the lonely dreams of a child,
>   'Return again, come!' "

Angelique's tatters began to pull together one more time, becoming more and more integral. Before I could even think about the implications, Frisson thrust another scrap of verse into my hand, and I called it out without even stopping to think:

> "Begone, dull tear-
>   ing of the fair!
>   Away, false rend-
>   er of the pure!
>   Abductor vile,
>   By thine own bile,
>   Be stunned, and fade,
>   And loose the maid!"

Something snapped all about us, something we couldn't hear, something that slammed us all to the ground with its recoil. Dazed, I scrambled to my feet, but the tension was gone, the two vast magical fields dispelled, and Angelique was whipping up, arrowing straight toward me to bury her face in my doublet—and into my chest—arms winding about me in a desperate effort to cling, sobbing in terror and fear.

Automatically, I folded my arms about her, trying to hold them just outside her form while I murmured soothing sounds, but I was really too shaken to appreciate the contact; I felt some interesting prickling, but thrust it out of my mind. I looked up over her translucent head at Frisson and gasped, "Thanks."

Frisson only nodded, though with shining eyes. The look on his face gave me a chill, but Angelique was beginning to gasp out syllables. I turned my attention back to her. "You're safe now," I assured her with more confidence than I felt. "It's gone."

"Aye," she gasped, "yet it was so evil! I feel soiled by its touch, whate'er it was—it was so vile!"

"It was," I muttered. "The magic in this land is of the most depraved sort, all right." Over Angelique's head, I saw Gilbert standing in front of Gruesome, looking at me with outrage. Because he hadn't been able to get in on the fighting, no doubt. I asked, "What sorcerer was *that* we fought?"

"It could have been none other than Queen Suettay herself," Frisson assured me. "Without doubt, she was humiliated by the lady's escape, and again by your countering of her spells."

"Yes." I nodded. "Since she planned on adding Angelique to her retinue of ectoplasmic slaves—it does reflect on her, having Angelique saved at the last stab."

"And to lose all the rest of them to Heaven, too," Gilbert assured me. "It lowers the esteem in which her barons hold her—lowers it drastically; and several may dare to take arms against her, attempting to seize the throne for themselves. We weaken her by protecting the maiden, Wizard Saul."

"And thereby make it vital for Suettay to recover her," I inferred. "She has to save face, or risk a rebellion."

"A nice little uprising would rather help us," Frisson noted.

"So the queen must slay you, to prevent that revolt," Gilbert summarized.

Angelique looked up, horrified, then stepped away from me,

hands warding me off. "Nay, I must leave you, then—for by protecting me, you have made yourself a marked man!"

I felt my stomach sink, but managed to answer gamely, "Don't let it worry you—I've been a marked man for a while now." To keep myself from wondering how much I'd meant by that, I turned back to Frisson and said, "I really appreciate your help."

"I did aid, then?" Frisson asked, eyes glowing. "I truly did aid?"

"Oh, yes," I assured him. "You aided fantastically." But I said it with a feeling of awe verging on fear, and couldn't help wondering if Frisson should be classified as a secret weapon.

Apparently so, from the look on his face. His eyes were lit with joy, and his whole emaciated countenance was suffused with the look of a man yanked back from the grave. "I think," Frisson said, "that I have found my métier."

I knew we weren't going to get off that lightly—Suettay may have lost the skirmish, but she was bound to come back for the rest of the battle. After all, we hadn't eradicated her, just sent her away from us, presumably back to her castle—and once on her own territory, she'd be able to start plotting again. She didn't strike me as the kind of person who would give up. Considering that she had sold her soul and promised her boss a sacrifice, she *couldn't* give up, or she'd end up in Hellfire, permanently. Extremely permanently.

It made me uneasy, wondering what deviltry she was going to hit me with next. After all, she knew my weak point—I glanced over at my weak point, but she was only a heat shimmer in the sunlight. That wouldn't keep Suettay from being able to find her, though. I resolved to keep an eye on Angelique, even if I couldn't see her.

About midafternoon, we came to a village that definitely looked as if it had seen better days. The thatches on the cottages were ragged and moldering; patches of daub were missing on the walls, letting the wattle show through. There was garbage in the streets, as if the people were too tired to take it as far as the garden patches to dig under for compost. The people themselves were ragged and gaunt, walking with a shuffling gait, hunched over, as if the weight of the world were on their shoulders. They darted us quick, suspicious looks out of narrowed eyes, and as quickly looked away, speeding up to get away from us. Within five minutes, we were walking down a street that showed not a single sign of life; there wasn't even a dog or a pig to go snuffling among the garbage.

Too bad; I would have bought it for roasting. The pig, that is, not the dog. I was that hungry, and I shuddered to think how Gruesome must have been feeling. But I noticed a larger-than-average hut with a pole sticking out above the door, and from the pole hung a bunch of broom corn—dry enough to use for sweeping, but still a "bush," which meant the place was a tavern.

"Let's see if they have anything to eat." I angled toward the house.

"If they do, I am not sure I would care to dine upon it." Frisson gave the dried broom a jaundiced eye.

But Gruesome perked up and rumbled, "Food!" so Frisson decided it would be a good idea, after all. At least, they followed me in, and so did Gilbert. Angelique's form brightened as she came into the gloom of the hut, but she disappeared instantly, leaving behind only a murmured, "I must not affright the landlord."

We sat down at a table. It was quiet as a tomb. I waited restlessly, watching Gilbert fidget and Gruesome drool, until my impatience got the best of me. Finally, I cried out, "Ho! Landlord!"

A formerly portly individual—at least I assumed he must have been fat once, because his apron was wrapped completely around him, and the strings were cinched three times—came out, frowning. "What the devil do ye . . ." Then he saw Gruesome, and blanched.

The troll rumbled, "Foooood!"

"But—but there is no food!" the tavernkeeper stammered. "At the least, there is little enough so that only my wife and bairns may dine, and that poorly. All else has been taken by the queen's bailiff!"

I sat rigid for a moment, then forced myself to relax and said, "That sounds like pretty high taxes."

"Tax? There is no question of tax—'tis a question of what the queen will let us keep! 'Tis simply that the crown takes all but the smallest quantity that will keep us alive to raise another crop! Every year they have taken more, and it has been two years since I had hops enough to brew my ale! We live by a small patch of garden, my wife and I, and poorly at that, for three-fifths of it goes to the queen, and on two-fifths must we dine!"

I felt instantly sorry for the guy, but Gruesome had started growling, and Gilbert was standing up, loosening his sword in his scabbard and saying, "If that be so, 'tis my duty as a squire to—"

Just then, the door crashed down.

Yes, down, not open—and half a dozen men in steel caps and leather jerkins burst in, waving halberds and shouting, "Out! Out, one and all! Into the square with you all!"

"What!" one shouted, seeing Gilbert's hand on his sword. "Would you strike 'gainst the men of the queen's bailiff? Nay, Beiner, slay him!"

Gruesome bellowed, surging to his feet.

The soldiers stared for about one second. Then they slammed back against one another, scrambling for the door.

"They are strangers! They burst in without asking leave!" The innkeeper ran over to the soldiers' side fast. "I told them I have no food to sell, and they—"

His fawning restored some measure of poise to the lead bully. He grabbed the man and threw him back to his mates, snarling, "Aye, like enough! We have naught to do with travelers—we have been bidden only to bring the townsfolk! Out with you, now!" And he made a hurried exit, leading his men out with the tavernkeeper in their midst—and Frisson and me right behind him.

In the middle of the press of bodies, Frisson hissed, "Master Saul, why have we come with the soldiers?"

"Because I'm curious," I hissed back. "But they might spot me for a ringer, because of my clothes. If they chase me out, you stick with it and come back and tell me what's going on."

"If I can," Frisson muttered, glancing about him fearfully.

That struck me as amusing. Frisson was probably the most dangerous man there, but he was scared! Somehow, though, I managed to restrain my boundless mirth.

The soldiers herded us out into the village square, along with a hundred other souls of both sexes and all ages. Another dozen soldiers were drawn up there around a roaring fire, and in front of them strutted a little, stocky man in a long black robe embroidered with astrological symbols. He grinned as the villagers were herded up, as if savoring the sight. When they were all there, he snapped, "You have not paid your taxes!"

A moan of dread swept through the crowd—but the tavernkeeper stepped forward. "Nay, Bailiff Klout—we have paid, we have all paid!"

"You know that we have!" an old woman wailed. "Why, you were young among us, yourself—"

"Aye, and the most despised and shamed of any!" Klout snapped back, eyes glittering. "Fools! You could not see my inner greatness! But the shire reeve did, and has given you all into my power!"

"And every year you have made our taxes higher!" a woman groaned.

"The queen is never satisfied," Klout retorted. "Yes, you have paid your taxes for each person, each household—but you have not paid the tax for your village!"

"A tax for the village!" A man with a long white beard stepped forward. "Never have I heard of such a thing!"

"You hear of it now! The shire reeve has given me leave to take as much from you as I will, the better to serve the queen . . ."

"He keeps a share for himself, right?" I hissed to Frisson.

"It is the custom," Frisson acknowledged.

". . . and I have deemed it fit to levy a tax for the village as a whole, due to the shire reeve and the queen! Ten pieces of gold! Pay! Pay now what you owe!"

"But we have no more money!" a woman wailed. "All our coins you took long ago!"

"Then I will take cattle or pigs, grain or fruit! But you will pay, you will pay, or I will burn this village down!"

The people gasped with horror.

Klout surveyed them, gloating. "You laughed at me when I was a small, clumsy runt of a child! There is not a woman of my own age who did not mock me for an ugly gnome when I was a youth! Well, mock now! Laugh now! For by the queen, I surely shall!"

A low moan rose and swelled among the villagers.

I could sympathize with Klout, but only just so far. Revenge I could understand, but this was way too much.

"No coin?" Klout cried. "Why, then, burn!" And he gestured to his men, who yanked torches from the bonfire and whirled them around their heads, setting the flames to roaring.

But another roar answered them—Gruesome, waddling out of the tavern, and beside him strode Gilbert, bright sword drawn.

Klout recoiled. "What monster is that!"

"Just a friend of mine." I stepped forward. "We're all from out of town, you see."

Klout swung around, staring at me wildly. "You! Who are you?"

"Just travelers." I worked at being way too casual about it. "Stopped at the tavern for lunch, but it seems they've gone out of business—no food to sell. So I got interested in the situation. Think I'd like to check on the details."

"The queen has sent you!" Klout cried.

"I never said any such thing!" But I wasn't about to stop him if he wanted to believe it. "I would like to see your books."

"Books?" Klout turned ashen, and a murmur of gratification went through the crowd.

"Your ledgers, your accounts! So we can all see whether or not the village has paid the tax due! Come on, trot them out!"

"You have no authority to demand this!" Klout said.

Gruesome stepped up beside me, grumbling with his mouth and rumbling in his stomach.

"Just an interested bystander," I agreed. "Call me a visiting magician, asking for a professional courtesy."

Klout took another glance at Gruesome and didn't seem disposed to dispute my claim. He only turned a lighter shade of ashen and snapped to one of the soldiers, "The ledger!"

"Cook the books!" I whispered at Frisson.

He stared at me as if I'd gone crazy. "What, Master Saul?"

"Give me a verse to make his accounts show he's lying! Quick!"

Frisson formed an O with his lips and turned away, pulling out his charcoal pencil and a scrap of parchment.

The soldiers were collecting their nerves and themselves, pulling together into a knot in front of Gruesome, who grinned and licked his chops. The soldiers faltered, and the ones standing guard at the back and sides of the crowd began to pull together into clumps. That left some unguarded peasants, who began to sneak away between the huts.

The soldier brought the book from a saddlebag and set it in Klout's hands. He opened it and held it out before me. "There! You shall see every penny that each of these villagers has paid, and shall see that each has rendered no more than the levy set for him!"

Beside me, Frisson was muttering.

I paged backward, frowning. "Where does your tenure in this office begin?"

"On page thirty-one," he said.

I found it, and saw the change of handwriting—but I also saw the handwriting change. Nothing obvious, just a few Roman numerals transforming, two *I*s close together turning into *V*s, two *V*s merging into an *X*, and so on.

Now, I'm not exactly skilled at Roman numerals, so it took me a while to puzzle it out. It certainly turned out to be cumbersome—I had never realized what a blessing the Arabs had given us when they invented the zero, and the decimal system that went with it. Double-entry bookkeeping would have helped, too—this was just a list of figures, and I began to appreciate the layout of the checkbook I never kept up.

I took my time turning the pages, checking out all three of the years Klout had been in office, and he began to get nervous—I could tell by his fidgeting, while the crowd eroded at the edges. Finally, he snapped, "Will you study it all day?"

"No," I said. "I'm up to date. Each person in the village has paid more than he owed, by anywhere from one penny to ten—and the extra more than covers the town tax."

He stared, then whipped the book around and started doing his sums. His eyes grew wider and wider as he paged backward through the book, growing more and more frantic.

"In fact," I said, "it looks as if you owe the village some money."

"Witchcraft!" he bawled, and hurled the book away from him. "Liar and thief! I know what I wrote there!"

I was sure he did—always less than the person had really paid. I looked up at Frisson. "You saw the figures?"

"Well enough," Frisson agreed nervously.

"Do those figures show anything more than any of the peasants really paid?"

"Not a penny," he assured me, and he sounded much more certain about it.

" 'Twas the foulest of magics!" Klout was turning hysterical. "Vile twisting of ink stains and marks! You cannot come from the queen, or you would not seek to make taxes less!"

Any peasants who hadn't taken to the tall timber were tiptoeing away now. The soldiers let them go, gripping their weapons tightly and edging around to surround Gruesome, with Gilbert, Frisson, and me around him.

"Smite them!" Klout pointed at us. "The queen shall not shield them, but my magic shall shield you!"

I pulled out my sheaf of Frisson's verses.

The soldiers roared with delight and pounced.

Gilbert knocked aside a sword and sheared through the
leather jerkin behind it in one blow. The soldier screamed
and fell back, as Gruesome reached over the squire's head and
picked up another soldier in each hand. They screamed and
struck at him with their halberds, but he only laughed as the
steel glanced off his hide. Then he squeezed, and the men
screamed even louder. Gruesome threw them away and
reached for two more.

Klout shouted something in the Old Tongue, pointing at
Gruesome with both forefingers. Gruesome froze. So did Gilbert, in midswing—for a split second.

Just long enough for me to yell out,

> "The sun beat down upon us,
>   And we gasped for cooler air,
> But the sunrays melted all the ice
>   That held us frozen there!"

The soldiers roared with vindictive rage and swung, but Gilbert came alive again, parrying two cuts with one swing, then
chopping back to shear through two halberd handles. Gruesome came alive, snatching up soldiers and hurling them. Their
mates yelped and leapt back.

Klout turned purple. He pointed at me and screamed,

> "As a lying embezzler, *I hearby indict you*!
> Let all of these numbers rise up and bite you!"

They did. They really did.

Like a fool, I was holding the book again, open—and I saw
the Roman numerals pry themselves off the page. That was
enough; I threw it away with a shout, but the *X*s and *V*s were
arrowing through the air to stab at me, and the *L*s and *C*s were
growing diminutive jaws and biting. Sharp little pains shot
through my skin, none more than a mild nuisance by itself—
but they were all over my face, my arms, and my hands! I had
never been so glad that I wore denim and boots! I flailed at
them, trying to swat them, and shouted, "Frisson! Take over!
Don't worry about me, just knock out the soldiers!"

Frisson stared, taken aback, then shook himself and yanked
the sheaf of poems out of my pocket.

Fortunately, Gruesome and Gilbert were keeping the troops
too busy for them to take advantage of my being out of the ac-

tion. The troll gathered up two more soldiers in each hand, knocked their heads together, and threw them at the five who were charging him. They went down in a tangle of steel and limbs, and Gruesome waded in, stony talons stabbing.

Klout wasn't idle, though. He was making mystic passes and chanting in the Old Tongue.

Frisson flipped frantically through the sheaf of poems, found the one he wanted, and chanted,

"Letters and numbers are toys for the playing,
    Able to hurt only when saying
    The vituperative injuries formed by a man's mind.
    Freed now from that bondage, numbers assigned
    For forays of truth, wound the men of deception!
    Stab them and bite them, in justice's reception!"

The numbers froze in midair, then turned and arrowed toward Klout and his soldiers.

"Flee!" the lead soldier bellowed, and suddenly the remaining soldiers were scrambling to their feet and running in panic.

Gruesome yodeled with joy and ran after them.

They looked back, saw him, yelped, and ran faster. They pulled away—they were much quicker than he was—but he kept it up for a while, having fun, shouting and blubbering and chortling like a whole chorus of haunts.

Klout leapt on a mule and dashed away down the road. But at the village limit, he reined in, turned back, and faced me, weaving complicated symbols in the air while he chanted something inarticulate.

Frisson took the next verse from the stack and called out,

"Mule, you have labored right,
    Therefore of sleep you have great need,
    So vanish instantly from sight,
    And rest you from your worthy deed!"

The mule disappeared, and Klout slammed down, hard, on his tailbone. His verse broke off into a yell of agony—and the numbers caught up with him. He leapt to his feet with a howl, then ran hobbling away, hand pressed over his tailbone. The numerals shot after him, buzzing like mosquitoes, catching up with him, and away he went, surrounded by a cloud of the figures of his own deception, bleating in pain until his shouts faded away.

All of a sudden, the village was awfully quiet.

Then yells of joy burst out all around us, and the peasants came charging out to hoist Frisson, me, and Gilbert up on their shoulders. They paraded us all around the square, singing our praises in terms that would have made Roland and Arthur blush.

"Did I do well, then?" Frisson called anxiously to me from his seat on the neighboring pair of shoulders.

"What do you think they're praising you for?" I shouted. "You did great! And thanks, Frisson—for saving my hide! What's left of it, anyway!"

He took the hint and got busy crafting a verse that would get rid of my integer rash.

The peasants had just about gotten the celebrating out of their systems by the time Gruesome came waddling back, grinning, whereupon they put us down, backed away, and got down to the serious business of trying to find something for the troll to eat.

They fed us, too, as it turned out—with their usual peasant shrewdness, they had managed to salt away a few staples that not even Klout and his soldiers had found. As darkness fell, full and replete, Frisson and I rolled up in our blankets with Gruesome already a snoring hill and Gilbert standing watch.

They fed us again in the morning, and we were hard put to refuse any of it. We managed to set off without being totally foundered, but the only one who had really avoided over-stuffing was Angelique, and I could have sworn that, if they'd been able to see her clearly, they would have found a way.

Our breakfast was beginning to settle, and we were beginning to pick up speed, when we came to the circle. The road met another at right angles, but instead of the two crossing at your average plus-sign–shaped intersection, they all ended in a ring-shaped track, for all the world like a traffic circle. I stopped, frowning. "Awfully advanced traffic engineering, for a one-horsepower culture. How come they don't just let the two roads intersect?"

"Because," said Frisson, "that would make a cross, like to that on which our Savior was hanged."

I seemed to feel the air thicken at the mere mention of words that were forbidden here, but I did my best to ignore it.

"It was a crossroads once." Gilbert pointed. "The newer grass, growing where there once was beaten earth, is some small part browner than the old. Look closely, and you can still see the sacred sign."

The air seemed to thicken even more with foreboding. I looked closely, and sure enough, I could just barely make out where the old intersection had been. "Getting a little fanatical, aren't they?"

"I assure you, it would have inhibited the power of the queen and her henchmen," Angelique's voice murmured, though I could scarcely see her.

"Well, we do need to get across it, if we're going to keep going," I said. "Let's go, folks." I stepped out onto the circle, turning to my left.

Just then, a man wearing black velvet with a dull silver chain rode out of the woods and into the traffic circle. There were a dozen armed men behind him, so I could just barely hear him shout, "Halt!"

He shouldn't have bothered; I'd stopped already and was feeling in my pocket for the sheaf of Frisson's latest poems.

"Fool, turn!" the man in black barked. "Would you break the queen's law by going with the sun?"

I stared at him. " 'With the sun'? What are you talking about?"

"He speaks of the direction in which you were walking, Master Saul," Frisson said in a low voice.

The head honcho barked, "Go widdershins! Against the sun! Thus is it commanded of all who come to a road-circle!"

I stared at him for a long moment, then shrugged and turned around. "Okay, so I'll go from west to east—counterclockwise, if you insist. Big deal!"

"Hold!" he shouted again. "I like not your manner of speech."

"Well, you've got a pretty lousy accent yourself." I looked up, frowning.

He narrowed his eyes and moved his horse closer, glaring down at me. I stood my ground, beginning to feel mulish.

"Odd clothes, odd speech, insolent manner." He looked up at my companions. "And accompanied by a troll." Back down at me. "You are he who has been curing witches of their deadly ills, are you not?"

"Only two." I definitely did not like the way this was going, especially since his men were making a lot of noise rattling their sabers as they drew them. "What's the big deal?"

"Know that I am the reeve of this shire!" the man snapped. "Word has come to me that you bilked the queen of tax money yesterday, and raised your hand against a bailiff into the bargain!"

"Self-defense," I snapped, "and what's so bad about curing the sick?"

"Have you a permit for it?" he returned.

I stared. "A permit saying I can cure people? What is this, the AMA?"

"The queen has ever banned the curing of a witch on her deathbed! None who had her license to cure would ever dream of doing so! Nay, and worse—you have encouraged them to repent, to break their bonds with Satan!"

"Breaking bondage is definitely what I had in mind."

His sword whipped out. "You had no right, nor license! You shall cast a spell this instant, revoking those cures you have worked—or you shall die!"

CHAPTER 12

Gruesome rumbled, and the soldiers had to quiet their horses. They started looking nervous.

I waved my group to be still and said to the reeve, "Can I see your license for breathing?"

He stared. "What license?"

"For breathing," I said, impatiently. "If you have to have a license to get well, you must have to have a license to breathe! Hasn't the queen gotten around to informing you about it? Show me your license!"

"There is no such thing!" he snapped.

"Ah-ha, you don't have it!" I waved an admonishing finger at him. "Everybody who lives in this country lives at the queen's pleasure, right?"

"Well ... aye ..."

"Any heart that's beating, is beating because the queen lets it beat, right?"

"Well ... aye, but ..."

"Then anybody who's breathing is only breathing because the queen lets them! Because the queen gives them license! So where's your license to breathe?"

"I ... I have not any ..."

"No license to breathe? And you trying to lay down the law! Where do you get off telling me to stop curing people just because I don't have a license? If you really think that makes sense, then you stop breathing—because *you* don't have a license!"

That shut him up, and I thought he was just staring at me,

145

until his face got red. Then I realized, all of a sudden, that his chest wasn't moving.

"Master!" the soldiers cried, and started forward.

Gilbert drew his sword with an entirely unnecessary clatter, and Gruesome growled loudly as he stepped up.

The reeve fell off his horse.

I leapt forward and caught him just as the soldiers shouted. They started forward again, but hesitated, seeing him in my hands.

"This is ridiculous!" I snapped. "Don't you know satire when you hear it? Now stop this silliness this instant, and start breathing again!"

He turned blue instead.

"You don't have to obey the queen!" I shouted. "Besides, she never said anybody had to have a license to breathe! I made it up!"

His face grew darker, and I realized with a shock that it wasn't just that he *wouldn't* breathe—he *couldn't* breathe. I had made the argument sound too sensible, and he had something like a posthypnotic command going that compelled him to obey the queen's will—or whatever he even thought of as her will!

But that was impossible—hypnotism couldn't make people do something they were dead set against, I knew that.

It followed that the reeve wasn't set against being dead.

It hit me like a ton of bricks. She had linked a posthypnotic command to his death wish! "Frisson! Praise life!"

The poet held up a scrap of paper in front of my eyes. I read it aloud, and quickly.

> "You find yourself in love with Death,
>   Yet be assured, she
>   Is a damsel most distressing,
>   And confers no blessing.
>   Turn from her, and gain some longer breath!"

I remembered a Drayton couplet, and added it in:

> "Now if thou wouldst, when all have given him over,
>   From death to life,
>   thou might'st him yet recover."

And, just so Tennyson wouldn't feel left out—but I made a few modifications:

"Drink life
To the lees; all times you shall enjoy
Greatly, as you've suffered greatly, both with those
You'll find to love you, and alone!"

The reeve's body convulsed with a huge, shuddering breath, and his complexion lightened. I went almost as limp as he did.

"You ... you have saved me!" He looked up at me, staring, wide-eyed.

"Darn right I have! Another minute, and you would have been at Hell's door!" I suddenly realized an implication. "That's right—being a civil servant to a sorceress-queen, you must have sold your soul to the Devil, too, didn't you?"

"Aye! Yet I have gazed at the fiery portal! 'Tis no children's tale, but truth!" He looked shaken, but even so, his eyes were narrowing, and he was beginning to look at me as if estimating how much torture I could take before dying. I decided the view of Hell hadn't been enough for him. "Frisson, do you have a verse for empathy—feeling what other people feel?"

There was a quick riffle of papers behind me, and the reeve shook himself, glaring over my shoulder. "Is he your scribe?"

"With his handwriting? Not a chance!" I reached for the slip of parchment Frisson was handing me—but the reeve started to chant in that confounded ancient language, so I snapped out a Shakespeare verse that had been tugging at my memory:

"My conscience hath a thousand several tongues,
   And every tongue brings in a several tale,
   And every tale condemns me for a villain.
   All several sins, all used in each degree,
   Throng to the bar, crying all, 'Guilty! Guilty!'
   Oh no! I rather hate myself,
   For hateful deeds committed by myself!"

The reeve froze in midsyllable, a stricken look on his face. So far, so good. I held up Frisson's verse and read it.

"There is no creature but I should love,
   And all that I have wronged, should feel my pity.
   For hateful deeds that I have done to others
   Should each and all be visited upon my heart,
   That I myself should feel the pain
   That I have done to others!"

The gathering malice in the reeve's face suddenly dissipated. His eyes widened, then turned into pools of misery. He bent over, as if there were a pain inside him. "*Aiiee!* What have you done! I remember every cruelty I've wrought; I feel the pain of those I've injured! How have you done this thing to me!"

"By poetry," I answered. "That's one of the things it's supposed to do—make you aware of what someone else is feeling."

"I ache, I burn! Oh, how could I have done such vile things! Curse you for having given me a conscience! Never again shall I be able to smite down an innocent!" A single large tear formed at the inside corner of his eye. "How can I ever make amends for those I have wronged?"

"Well," I said gently, "you could start by repenting."

"I do, I do! I repent me of my sins! Alas the day that ever I swore allegiance to the Devil, and banished my conscience! Ah, I ken not who to hate the more—he for having taken it, or you for having given it back!" The reeve groaned. "Oh, where is there a priest? For I must confess my sins, I must be shriven!"

I stared at him a long minute; then I said, "I have a notion you know better than I do—if there are any priests hiding out in your shire, you've got a strong suspicion where they are. You just haven't gotten around to hanging them yet—too many other things to do, like whipping peasants into paying another tax."

" 'Tis even so." He managed to get his feet under him and stood, bracing himself against his saddle. "I shall find such a one, I shall confess! I must know that G . . . that Go . . . that I am forgiven by the Most High!" But his body convulsed like a whiplash as he said it, as if the mere attempt to speak of something sacred had resulted in intense pain. He set his teeth and pressed on in spite of it. "I forswear my pact with Satan! I shall turn to G . . . to Go . . ."

"Keep trying," I urged. "You'll get it out eventually."

One of the soldiers screamed and charged his mount at the reeve, his sword swinging.

Gruesome took two steps and picked them up, both horse and rider, gave them a hard shake, and threw them away. The man struck his head against a stone and lay still. The horse scrambled to its feet and bolted.

The other soldiers backed away with a moan.

"I take it that was your second-in-command?" I asked.

The reeve nodded. "He would have become reeve in my place, if he had smitten me down for treachery to the Devil and the queen. Another will do so soon enough, I doubt not, but I shall have made some amends for the harm I've done."

I looked at his glossy black hair and realized it was no longer glossy. In fact, I was definitely seeing a gray hair or two. "Uh . . . if you don't mind my asking, how old are you?"

"Ninety-seven," he answered. "I have preserved life and youth by black magic—and *ahhh*!" He almost screamed, back arching in pain. "What I did to bring about that spell, the number of those I bled! Nay, 'tis only justice if all my years come upon me now!"

They were doing just that—he was aging even as I watched. The black magic that had kept him alive and relatively youthful was gone, now that he had rejected his bargain with Satan, and his debt of years was pressing to be paid.

"Find that priest," I suggested, "and quickly, while you still can."

"I shall!" He scrambled back onto his horse and clutched at the pommel grimly. To his men, he said, "Get thee back to my castle, with word that I shall never return! Say also that even *my* witchcraft succumbed to that of this stranger! I bid thee repent, for the hegemony of evil is passing!"

Frisson, pale-faced, pressed another slip of parchment into my hand. Surprised, I gave it a quick once-over, then nodded emphatic approval and muttered,

> "He is a sinner, I know full well,
> > And yet his death is not God's will.
> But his return to live and dwell
> > Until a priest has seen him, still
> Bitten by sin and doing ill.
>
> One thing is certain, that life flies—
> Yet can be slowed for he who tries
> To seek the solace of his faith,
> And find the peace repentance buys!"

That last one sounded like something out of *The Rubaiyat*, but I wasn't about to criticize.

The reeve looked up, startled. "What did you say?"

"Nothing to worry you," I answered. "Better get on your way. Who knows? Suettay might appoint a new reeve before the day's out."

The erstwhile reeve shuddered at the thought and turned his

horse away. "Aye, 'tis even as you've said! Farewell, stranger! I withdraw my curse on you; I bless you instead, for the agony of conscience you have wrought will save my soul. But beware the queen, for she never had a conscience, ever, so no spell can give her one!"

"Thanks for the warning." I exchanged a worried glance with Frisson. "Hope your trip is smooth."

"If it were rough as rapids, I could not complain of injustice. Farewell!" He rode away into the woods—but I noticed that he went clockwise around the circle.

His men groaned and turned back the way they had come, riding fast.

I turned back to my friends. "Let's just cut across the circle—what do you say? And get under the trees fast. I don't think we want to linger."

The trees petered out in late afternoon, and we found ourselves on an open tableland with occasional straggling lines of undernourished scrub to show where there was a watercourse. We camped by one of them just as the sun was sinking, ate a meal of journey rations that tasted like cardboard and hot water, then turned in. At least, Gilbert and Frisson did, and Gruesome curled himself up into a very large ball. But Angelique didn't sleep, of course, and I took first watch; I was too restless to doze.

So were Angelique and Frisson, to judge by all the whispering that went on for the next hour—but Gilbert corked right off like the seasoned campaigner he was, so I woke him up for the second watch, sometime in the wee hours.

I couldn't sleep, of course. Suettay's threats were too much on my mind.

Gilbert looked up in surprise to see me wrapped in my cloak against the night's chill, but still sitting by the campfire, staring into the glowing coals. He came over to say, very softly so as not to wake Frisson, "Will you not sleep, Master Saul? You shall need your rest on the morrow."

"I don't doubt it—but I've got much on my mind. I'm trying to meditate, Gilbert."

He frowned. "Do you speak of prayer?"

"It's like praying," I hedged. "In fact, prayer can lead to meditation, and vice versa. Either way, it's a good way to relax and get the worries of the day off your mind."

"Ah." He nodded, satisfied, and stood. "Then I shall leave you to your holy thoughts, Master Saul. Good night."

"Good night," I answered, and went back to gazing at the coals, reciting a mantra.

At first I thought it was doing no good—the coals just reminded me of Hell, which reminded me of Suettay, which reminded me of danger. So I gazed down at my cupped palms instead, trying to imagine the sound of one hand clapping, and it was just beginning to work when there was the faintest of whispers beside me, and Angelique murmured almost in my ear, "Why are you so sad, Master Saul? Can I aid?"

Now, that was exactly what she was not doing. Maybe she didn't have a body, but she certainly still looked as if she did, especially at night, when her form glowed its brightest, complete with all her curves, which certainly were not in the slightest conducive to a tranquil state of mind, and definitely not the holy one Gilbert was hoping I'd have.

"I'm not sad." My voice was more gruff than I intended it to be, and she drew back a little, hurt—so I amended my statement and tried to soften my tone. "I'm troubled, yes—worried about the queen's being after us. But I'm trying to calm down and put her out of my mind."

"Mayhap I can aid." She reached up to touch my forehead with her hand, and insubstantial though it was, a breath of coolness seemed to touch my skin. I shivered, but not with the chill, and reached up to push her hand away with what I hoped was gentleness. "Your touch would inspire anything but tranquility. Might distract me from thoughts of the queen, maybe, but it sure wouldn't put me to sleep."

She frowned. "I do not understand."

I just stared at her, then nodded. "Good. I think it's better that way."

Then I unwound myself to my feet. "You'll have to pardon me. Just sitting isn't doing any good, so I think I'm going to have to take a walk."

"Oh, beware!" Concern replaced the hurt that had been briefly in her face. "The world is not safe for good folk, at night!"

"Then I shouldn't be in any trouble." I turned and went away quickly, before the sight of her made me feel any less good. I glanced back briefly as I restored the guarding circle, behind me, and saw that she was looking hurt, which made me feel wretched—but what could I do? And don't give me any guff about spiritual union—under these circumstances, it would have been highly unsatisfying.

I strode out into the long grass, walking fast, trying to work out the sudden spurt of energy her presence had given me. I kept telling my hormones that ghosts can't emit pheromones, but my glands weren't listening.

There were too many longings in my body to let me relax enough to put the witch-queen out of my mind. Besides, Angelique's presence reminded me that Suettay knew my weakness, and that weakness was entirely too beautiful, even as a wraith, for my peace of mind—and far more appealing than she knew. I hoped.

But Suettay knew it, I was sure. I wondered if Angelique was safe back there, with only Gilbert and Frisson to protect her if the queen tried anything again—but I decided that, at the least, they'd manage to call me if anything went wrong. I turned back to see just how far I had come, then stared, shocked—the coals of the campfire were only a glow in the distance, and I couldn't even see any of the bodies around it. I had come entirely too far. I started back.

A cloud of green smoke erupted ten yards ahead, a silent explosion in moonlight.

I dropped into a defensive crouch, whipping out my clasp knife. Adrenaline slammed through my veins.

The green smoke thinned and drifted away in the night breeze. A squat, bulging shadow stood black against the moonlight, a floor-length robe blending its outline into a monolith. A low, mocking laugh came from the silhouette. "Come, novice! Do you truly think you can defend yourself from me by force of arms?"

I recognized the voice: Suettay, gilded by moonlight.

I straightened slowly, folding the clasp knife and putting it away. "No ... but then, I don't really need weapons, do I?"

But my heart was hammering, and the adrenaline of fear was flowing. I had faced Suettay and won, yes—but that had been with friends beside me, including a squire who was as skilled as any knight, and a poet whose talent verged on genius. How could I stand against her alone?

Not that I was about to let her know it, of course.

"Ahhhhhh, insolence!" the sorceress breathed. "You have gained arrogance since our last meeting, Wizard Saul!"

"Oh, so now I'm a wizard, am I?"

Suettay laughed, a noise like a nut grinder. "Certes! 'Tis

what the common folk call you. Did you not know? I assure you, *I* did. Naught could happen in my kingdom that I would know not of—for if anything transpires, my ministers and their clerks tell me of it! Though there was no need for such offices in this instance; yourself was enough."

"Enough?" I frowned. "You mean just by living, I give myself away?"

"There is something to that." Suettay wheezed; I think she meant it for a laugh. "You should not think so hard about magic—it makes you quite conspicuous, to those with the Sight."

"True—but you've been watching me all along anyway. How come you didn't just send another of your minions tonight? Figure you're ready to take me on personally now?"

"The audacity of the slave!" Suettay breathed, almost in admiration. "Indeed, I have your measure—and you'll be like a child's toy to my power! I am sure of your strengths and weaknesses and know best how to use them!"

Illogically, I felt a flow of confidence that spread a grin across my face. "Sure of yourself, eh? Is that why you've bushwhacked me out here in the middle of nowhere, away from Gilbert and Frisson?"

"Perhaps," Suettay sneered. "They are, indeed, part of your strength—and you are shorn of them now. You are quite at my mercy."

"Oh?" I raised an eyebrow in polite skepticism. "Mercy? Do you have any?"

"None to mention," Suettay snapped, and her arm swung down like the arm of a catapult, a fireball leaping from her fingertips.

I dodged, but the fireball swerved to follow me and exploded against my chest in a soft fountain of sparks. A huge, mushrooming pain answered from inside my chest, an instant of unbearable agony, then . . .

Nothing. No sensation at all.

The night seemed to darken about me, and strength ebbed from my legs. As I fell to my knees, I realized, with horror, that my heart had stopped. Panic thundered in, but I threw it back with a wrench. *Think fast, or die!*

And my mind chilled into total clarity, with an icy lack of emotion that almost frightened me in itself. There was, after all, no time for panic—scarcely time for a single sentence. I rasped it out with what breath was left in my lungs:

"Life ebbs now in full retreat,
    Till once again begins the beat—
Heavy, steady, short, and hard,
    Beats the never-ending heart!"

Pain wrenched my chest again, but blood roared in my ears and a jackhammer yammered inside my ribs. I breathed in against its beat thankfully. As the haze cleared from my eyes, it cleared from my mind, too: This wasn't going to be a trial of strength, or any other limited form of conflict—Suettay was playing for keeps. If she could kill me, she would.

Could I bring myself to try to kill her?

The sorceress came into focus as my heart slowed and steadied. Suettay's hands were weaving, her lips moving. Then the sorceress froze, and I realized she'd finished another spell while I was trying to restart my pump.

Suddenly, the air was filled with darting, whirling streaks of silver—a thousand knives spinning toward me. I threw myself to the side, but the knives followed me, swooping. I whipped out my pocket knife, swinging it in a frantic figure eight as if it were a rapier, chanting,

"I, the spirit master,
    Can fend off all disaster.
Multiply my slight stiletto
    A thousandfold, by whirling ditto!"

There was one slant rhyme, and the meter wasn't exactly constant, but it worked—the air was suddenly filled with a thousand whirling clasp knives. They buzzed out at Suettay's daggers, and I grinned as I watched each of the poniards collide with one of the pocket knives and fall to the ground.

Then the grin slipped as I caught sight of Suettay; I realized I shouldn't have taken time out to watch the show. The sorceress' hands were weaving air again, stringing a pattern of forces. My face tightened grimly, as I realized the nature of the fight. Working a spell took time—so, while I was chanting my counterspell, Suettay was working up her next attack. That meant that I was going to stay on the defensive, unless I could figure out how to jump a spell.

I had to, or I was dead. Sooner or later, I'd tire—and if I was late on just one counterspell, I was had.

Dust writhed, and a hundred serpentine heads lifted up around me, spreading cobra hoods.

It threw me back to my childhood, and Kipling's stories.

> "Let us have a mongoose plural
> From an Indian village rural,
> Skilled at fighting snakes, and glad to—
> A hundred mongeese, fighting mad, too!"

I carefully did not watch as the dust boiled alive about me; I didn't have time. Suettay's arms were weaving, and I took the offensive:

> "Let a dust storm boil up from the plains of the thirties,
> Filling the sky; and before the next word she's
> Trying to speak, let it blow in and under—
> A real Kansas dust storm, sudden as thunder!"

I didn't even get to the chorus before the tableland was filled with a howling wind, laden with dust. It swept between the sorceress and me, blocking us from each other. Far off, I heard a roar that just barely penetrated the thunder of the churning dust wind—Gruesome, letting out an unbelieving, horrified bellow.

Yes—my mascot was out in this, too. He must have waked, seen I was gone, and realized I was in danger. I felt an instant panic—had he broken the guarding circle as he came waddling out to search for me?

I whipped a fold of my cloak over my nose and mouth, but Gruesome wouldn't know he should do that. Besides, he didn't have a cloak. The storm would kill him as quickly as Suettay's spells.

And maybe not just Gruesome; my chest heaved with a huge, wracking cough. Some of the dust was getting in through the cloth.

But I only needed a few seconds to rank the priorities in my mind:

One: Get rid of whatever it was that Suettay was whipping up for her next spell;

Two: Throw another spell of my own at her, and keep on throwing; and

Three: Get rid of the dust.

Right. Get going on number one.

> "Still more fool shall she appear
> By the time she lingers here.
> With one fool's head she came to war,
> But she'll go away with more!"

Actually, now that I thought about it, that took care of point two, too; Suettay couldn't do much of a spell with an IQ suddenly lowered to slightly better than an onion's.

If she hadn't deflected my spell in time. The dust was thinning, and the wind was dying down. So Suettay had wasted time lessening the loess?

Then I heard a rumble of thunder and realized I was wasting time, myself.

Too late. With a sound like a breaking sieve, the rain drenched down. The dust settled, fast; and through the curtain of water, I saw Suettay—or something that had been Suettay.

It still wore the queen's robes, but it had small eyes under a very low forehead, and a wide, gaping grin—on one of its heads. The other two were similar, and maybe worse. I stared, appalled—was this what happened when you practiced magic without a license?

Certainly without really knowing what you were doing. I was disgusted with myself. A clean death would have been infinitely better!

Until I realized the loose grins were forming themselves into words. Sure—two heads are better than one, and three idiots add up to a modicum of sense. Whatever spell it was going to be, it wouldn't be too effective—committee work never is—but I didn't feel like waiting around to find out. I grabbed for another verse:

> "This monarch will be hanged
> With a silver chain—
> 'Tis not the chain of many!
> Stole the lives of serf and peer,
> And must be hanged for any!"

A silver chain lashed down out of the rain, snaked around the center head, and snapped taut. Suettay's body jerked upward a good three feet and dangled, kicking and writhing, from a chain that wasn't attached to anything.

But the other two heads were still forming words, slowly and painfully . . .

Alarm sizzled through me. I'd only solved one-third of the problem! Quickly, I started muttering,

> "Triad, by the rule of three,
> Multiply this spell for . . ."

Too late. The other two heads were fading, disappearing, and the loose grin on the one in the noose was tightening as intelligence came back into the eyes. The forehead moved up—and it was Suettay's normal face again! The lips writhed in a snarl as she hoisted her hands up to grab the chain above her head. She pulled, got her throat clear of the links, and took a deep breath.

I grabbed for another verse.

> "They plucked the entrails of an offering forth,
> And could not find a heart within her breast!"

Suettay looked up, grinned, and started chanting.

I froze. It hadn't worked! Okay, it was only a couplet, and it didn't rhyme—but it was Shakespeare! It should've shown *some* result!

Then I remembered an old medieval tale, transformed into a modern fairy story, about sorcerers who, afraid of death, put their hearts outside their bodies for safekeeping—say, in an egg, which was inside a duck. Or an amulet. How that could work, I couldn't see, unless . . . yes . . . wait a minute . . . Assume a hyperspatial link, so that blood could flow from the sorceress to the heart in another dimension, and back . . .

I came to myself with a jolt. Too much thinking! Suettay was spitting out the last phrase, and I had lost the initiative. Suddenly my whole body went rigid. I couldn't move! And the paralysis was creeping over my chest to seize heart and lungs, then trickling up over my shoulders toward my neck. If I didn't get a quick spell out, I'd have lockjaw! Plus death.

And Suettay was spell-weaving again!

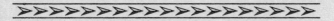

CHAPTER 13

I took as deep a breath as I could and spat out:

"Can't freeze my bones or rot my spleen,
'Cause I've been shot with Salk vaccine!
So I'll hang loose from stern to prow—
Paralysis can't touch me now!"

My knees suddenly flexed, and my hands relaxed at my sides. I tried a step and managed it—but slowly and painfully. Well, you couldn't expect a cheap spell like that to work wonders . . .

But Suettay hadn't wasted the time. She was back on the ground, the silver noose still hanging above her head, and was finishing up another chant, her hands pantomiming yanking something up from the earth.

And four lions leapt out of nowhere, straight at me, roars shaking the plain.

But a greater roar drowned theirs out, blasting from behind me—and Gruesome thudded past me, straight at the lions!

They hit the brakes, plowing up sod with iron claws and terrified howls—or three out of four did. The fourth bellowed all the louder and leapt straight at the troll. I couldn't help thinking that this was how evolution put an upward limit on courage.

Gruesome was very direct; he slammed in an uppercut. His timing was just right; he caught the lion under the jaw. It went flipping up over his head and down in an arc, its head flopping at an unnatural angle.

The other three decided their initial instinct had been right, and fled out across the plain with howling yips of fright.

Suettay's hands flew; crooked syllables clanked off her tongue.

Gruesome turned slowly toward me, a hungry glint in his eye.

"What's the matter?" I backed away. "Look, I didn't *mean* to get you into this!"

"Juicy." Gruesome's slab of tongue came out and smacked around his chops. "Taste good."

I yelped and whirled to run; Suettay had canceled the fairies' anti–human-eating spell.

Gruesome's feet pounded behind me, coming closer, and I knew that, though his legs were much shorter in relation to his body, they were longer than mine, since he was so much bigger—and he could move them faster, no matter what he looked like. I wasn't going to get out of this by running—just by talking. Or rhyming, rather. I swerved around behind the biggest boulder I could find in that barren land and started chanting,

> "You cannot eat but little meat—
>   For your stomach, I'm not good.
> Obey elf-prince and wizard friend,
>   Not sorceress in hood!
>
> Why then should you seek quarry more,
>   And still seek friends anew,
> When change itself can give no more—
>   'tis easy to be true!"

A huge fist came down and smashed the boulder to smithereens. Gruesome loomed up, huge eyes lit with glee, mouth spread in a horrible, drooling grin, upraised hands hooked to pounce, and I turned to run. Huge nails clawed my back, and I howled with pain, tripping and falling. I rolled to my feet—

And I was just in time to see the glee dim from his eyes as his mouth puckered in confusion. "Wizard? What I do?"

"Nothing." I went limp with relief. "You chased away some lions for me, Gruesome. Thanks."

But beyond his bulk, I saw Suettay, hunkered down on her knees, bent over diagrams she was drawing in the dirt, and intoning a long, droning chant.

My heart sank. Whatever she was whopping up, it was

big—if symbolic gestures increased magical power, symbolic drawing would be even worse!

Then full inspiration hit me, and I realized that a sword can cut both ways, no matter how clumsy. "Gruesome!" I cried. "There's another one!" I pointed at Suettay.

" 'Nother one what?" the troll rumbled, turning to look. I chanted quickly,

> "What you see amid the waste,
>   See as something you would taste!
>   Be it horse, or cat, or bear,
>   Or a sorc'ress, kneeling there.
>   In your eye it shall appear
>   As a morsel sweet and rare!"

Slant rhyme again, but I hoped it would work.

It did. Gruesome let out one gusty "Yum!" and started running—straight at Suettay.

The sorceress looked up, startled. Then she sprang aside with a howl of fear, in the nick of time—Gruesome thundered by, plowing up her diagrams with his great taloned toes. Suettay howled in rage and frustration—and I seized the moment, my mind shifting into high gear. I knew better than to waste a single second by this time. While she was on the run, I chanted,

> "Be reversed from Galatea;
>   May your limbs and joints betray ya!"

I ripped a thread loose from my shirt, frantically tying knots in it as I went on:

> "Knot the stomach, bind the head—
>   Let your limbs go weak with dread!"

The sorceress collapsed, falling back on the ground with a howl of anger and fear.

Gruesome bellowed victory and stooped for the kill.

"Be as thou wast wont to be!" I shouted. "See as thou wast wont to see!"

Gruesome froze.

Then his face wrinkled, and he turned away in disgust. "Yugh! Sorceress! Tough! Sour!"

Suettay stared, not knowing whether to be insulted or relieved. The fear spell was still on her, but she started muttering anyway.

Gruesome whipped about, looking from side to side in total bewilderment. "Where goody? Where juicy piglet?"

So that was what he had seen, instead of Suettay. "It got away," I said quickly. "Why don't you go back to the campfire and see if Gilbert has any leftovers from dinner?"

"Deer haunch." Gruesome nodded sagely and turned away. "Yum!"

I pulled out my clasp knife, snapped it open, and stepped up to touch the point against Suettay's throat. "Cut it," I snapped, "or I will!"

The last syllables of the chant died in the sorceress' throat as she read the conditional sentence in my eyes.

But she saw something else, too, and a slow, mocking smile spread over her face. "You believe you have beaten me, then?"

"I did sort of have that impression, yes." Privately, I wondered how long I could hold the knife still.

"Slay me, then." Suettay smiled, showing teeth.

I stared.

I clamped my jaw, narrowed my eyes. She was mocking me, riding a bluff. She should have known better; it only made sense for me to kill her. I braced myself for the thrust—and stayed braced.

Suettay's eyes danced, mocking me.

I ground my teeth and tried to summon up the resolution for the fatal blow. "Start a spell."

Suettay shook her head, grin widening.

"Damn!" I whirled away, plunging the knife into the earth.

Suettay laughed, a mocking bray. "I congratulate you on your . . . honor, Wizard."

I swung about, fuming.

"Aye, slay the helpless old woman," the sorceress jeered. "When you rendered me defenseless, Wizard, you bound your own hands."

"Nothing," I ground out, "gripes me more than someone who takes advantage of someone else's good nature."

"I could not be more pleased with your . . . virtue." Suettay made the word an insult.

I spun away, burning, taking a deliberate step away from the woman so I wouldn't do something I'd feel sorry for in the morning.

Behind me, the sorceress sang out a rhyme in that ancient language I didn't know. I spun about in alarm. She was stretching luxuriously. "Thank you for affording me a moment to recite my counterspell, Wizard. Be assured, I'll not return the favor." Her hands started weaving.

I snatched up the knife and turned back to her, shifting from side to side, coming in low. Of course, she could have blocked that with three words, so I chanted,

> "Her freedom is gained,
> Her malice unfeigned!
> The blow need not hold,
> For blood's no longer . . ."

Suettay stared, alarmed, then broke off her chant to cry, "Hist!" She held up a hand, turning her head a little to the side and frowning, as if listening to a distant sound.

Then she turned back to me, snarling, "How you have worked your vile spells, Wizard, I do not know—but I grant you've been far more formidable than I had thought you would be."

A truce? I wondered if it was wrong of me to feel relieved.

"I would I could stay and finish what we've so lately begun," Suettay spat, "but sudden, urgent affairs have arisen, which require my personal attention—blast that monk and his obstinancy! We shall meet again, be certain—yet I must own, I've gained some respect for you. When next I see you, 'twill be with an army at my back."

Yes, I decided, wanting a truce *was* wrong. I screwed down my mercy and began reciting,

> "Fear no more the heat o' the sun,
> Nor the furious winter's rages . . ."

Suettay looked up in amused surprise. I set my teeth and went on:

> "Thou thy worldly task hast done;
> Home art gone, and ta'en thy wages."

Suettay cocked her head to the side suddenly, as if she were again listening for something.

Trying to distract me, I thought. I focused tightly on her face, chanting:

"Golden lads and girls all must ..."

Suettay turned back to me with a long, gloating laugh that ended abruptly in a shouted, unintelligible phrase as she swung her arms in opposing circles.

"As chimney sweepers!" I shouted.

Suettay disappeared.

". . . come to dust," I finished. "Damn! And I had a good excuse, too!"

Then I started wondering what she had been laughing about. Probably just trying to distract me, as I'd thought . . . but . . .

How about if she had seen some trouble coming for me and my companions?

On a wide-open plain? In the dead of night? Ridiculous! After an act like that, what trouble could make any difference?

Then I heard the clank of arms, Gilbert's shouting, and Frisson's howl, faint but clear across the plain. Gruesome roared, and a crowd of voices answered him. Metal clashed on metal.

"She sent an ambush party while she had me out of the way!" I cried. But I didn't answer; I was already running, and trying to figure out how I could get there faster.

Faster? I skidded to a halt. I was a wizard, wasn't I? At least, that's what they kept telling me. I could get to any place I wanted, instantly—at least, within this hallucination. All it took was the right spell.

"The trouble's fast-moving, and so must move I,
   Till I'm set by the fire
   'Neath this bright midnight sky.
   Let me, in an instant, a league or more gain,
   In the bat of an eye, far out 'cross this plain!"

There was a sudden rush of giddiness—then my head stopped swimming, and I looked up at mud-and-thatch walls, crude plank furniture, and dirty, unkempt people in ragged, dun-colored homespun.

The man of the house looked up, startled, from his place at the table. He had a long beard and a large axe.

I stared. What had gone wrong?

Terminology. I'd said "by the fire," but I hadn't specified

which one. And I had said "across the plain"—so here I was, in a peasant hut presumably on the far side of the plain.

I gave the denizens a toothy grin and tipped an imaginary hat. "Sorry about the intrusion, folks. Just semantics, that's all."

The man's lips writhed back in a snarl as he came up from the table, hefting his axe.

Obviously a grammarian. I ad-libbed,

"The lure missed the fish, and wound up in a shack.
I return to the world, 'cross the plain. I go back!"

The axe swung down—and I was suddenly in the midst of bright moonlight again. I turned around, totally confused—and saw a bright spot on the horizon. Dimly, I heard clashing and yelling.

I sighed. Overshot again! Well, I hadn't exactly had time to get specific.

But my friends were in a jam. I had to come up with a spell while I made it to them.

"The starry welkin cover thou anon
With gloomy fog as black as Acheron
And lead these treach'rous soldiers so astray
As each come quickly in the other's way!"

Suddenly, fog rose up from the ground, getting thicker and thicker as it climbed. In two minutes, it had hidden the stars—and the distant clash of arms was liberally interspersed now with shouts of surprised and angry pain, and cursing.

That would hold them for a while. I dredged up an orientation verse:

"Take me back to my new friends
At the campsite where they fend
And guard themselves with might and care
From the foes attacking there!"

There was that moment of disorientation again—then things steadied, and I found myself staring at the coals of our campfire. I whirled about to see Gruesome tossing soldiers like Indian clubs. Gilbert was laying them about him with his broadsword, and Frisson crouched by the fire, reading scraps of paper aloud. Angelique flitted here and there, trying to scare enemy soldiers, and not terribly worried by their weapons.

But I was—because the fog suddenly lifted. Only ten feet or so, but that was enough for the soldiers to see where we were and turn to center on us with some very nasty oaths.

If their field sorcerer could disperse my fog, he might be able to trap Angelique! I had to find some way to bust up his party.

"Like the leaves of the forest when summer is green,
 That host with their banners at sunset were seen.
 Like the leaves of the forest when autumn hath blown
 That host in the morning lay withered and strown."

A huge unseen hand seemed to slap back and forth in the middle of the raiding party, and troopers went flying. That left only a man in a gray robe and pointed cap, frantically dodging the unseen force. He was going to be confused for a few minutes, and I decided to make it worse.

"I'll chant to him in summertime,
    And in the winter, too!
 But the only, only thing
    That I'll sing for his song
 Is to shroud him in the foggy, foggy dew!"

The fog came down again, all the way to the ground—and among the moans of the soldiers, I heard a tenor cursing. I grinned; that should keep this junior sorcerer confused for a few minutes.

But he'd pick up the pieces pretty quickly. I needed something a little more enduring, that would scare the symbols off his robe—and his soldiers, too.

And I knew just the thing. I grinned with anticipation as I took a deep breath and recited, with my best attempt at the original pronunciation,

"The fierce spirit painfully endured hardship for a time,
 He who dwelt in darkness . . .
 The grim spirit was called Grendel, a rover of the borders,
 One who held the plains, fen and fastness . . .
 There came gliding in the black night the walker in darkness,
 From the plain under the mist-hills Grendel came walking,
 Wearing God's anger!"

Night thickened around them, and I took off, following the crashing Gruesome was making. On my third step, I slammed into something hard and furry. A roar resounded around me, and a huge, clawed hand reached down through the darkness toward me. Far above, two little red eyes gleamed. I howled, ducked around the giant shin, and ran.

Grendel apparently wasn't about to change course for so small an irritation, because the crashing of boulders being ground into pebbles was going away behind me, and I didn't think that was just because he was running so fast. A yell of horror confirmed it, followed by the rattle and clash of suits of armor being jumbled together. I slowed and looked back, but all I could see was a black cloud with a horse arcing above it and a sorcerer beyond, sawing the air frantically with his hands. The horse landed on its hooves, by some miracle, and streaked off in a panic—but the sorcerer had to stand his ground and keep trying. I didn't think he'd have much luck when he couldn't even tell what the monster was—especially since I didn't think the man knew Middle English. Too bad the Dark Age bards hadn't left a few verses with a wider range of applications—but their interests had seemed to be rather narrow.

Wide enough for current purposes, however. I noticed that the crashing seemed to have stopped. So did the sorcerer—he was frozen with his arms half-raised, looking uncommonly as if he were surrendering to a Wild West sheriff. Then he whipped about and disappeared back into the pass. The black cloud drifted after him, leaving huge, clawed, vaguely anthropoid footprints.

I didn't really care about the sorcerer, but I couldn't leave a scourge like that to prowl the countryside. I tried to remember how the fight had gone, decided to be a little more humane, and improvised a different ending:

"Grendel must flee from there, mortally sick,
  Seek his joyless home in the fen-slopes.
  He knew the more surely that his life's end had come,
  The full number of his days."

The black cloud kept moving up toward the pass—but as it moved, it thinned until, by the time it reached the top, it was almost gone. A vague outline hung in the air for a second, huge and gross, like a monstrous parody of the human form—or was it reptilian?—then was gone, so quickly that I wondered if I'd really seen it. I sighed and turned away—there had been something heroic about the monster, after all.

Gilbert was glancing warily up toward the hilltop, then back to the place where his opponents had been. There was only a dust cloud there now.

I looked at it, surprised. "What did you do—knock them all the way back to the mountains?"

"Nay. They saw that black fog you raised, and turned tail. They fled, and I came near to fleeing after them."

"Near! If I'd had a clear field, I would've been flying out of here so fast, my backwash would have knocked you over!"

"Me, too!" The troll actually looked shaken. "Goosum go, fast!"

I looked up at Gruesome, frowning. "I thought trolls weren't scared of anything."

"One." Gruesome nodded vigorously. "Found it."

"And you banished it, Wizard." Gilbert looked up at me, the whites still showing all around his eyes. "Nay, you have certainly cleared our pathway! Have you disbanded them so quickly, then?"

" 'Dismembered' may be more like it," I answered. "You'll pardon me if I don't go back to check."

"Aye, certes." Angelique looked down from where she wafted around Gruesome's shoulders, eyes huge. "And what monstrous apparition was that which you did raise against them, Wizard Saul?" Being a ghost, she had a professional interest in the question.

"That's a long story." I sighed. "And a very old one. I'll tell it to you sometime—but right now, I think we'd better reset the guarding circle that Gruesome broke when he came out to help me—thanks, old monster . . ."

"Help you?" Angelique looked up, ready to fibrillate.

"That's another story," I said quickly. "I thought you wanted to hear the one about the monster while we wait for daylight."

"Aye, but . . ."

"Then we'd better get busy." I pulled out my can of talcum powder and stepped over to the break in the circle. Angelique drifted after me anxiously, but by the time she caught up, I was deep in, mumbling the spell. When I finished, I looked up brightly and said, "Okay. Anybody want to hear?"

Angelique's protest was drowned out by noisy concurrence from Frisson and Gilbert. I glanced around and saw that even the troll was looking mildly interested. I relaxed and took a deep breath. "Okay. Now, once, long ago and *very* far away, a hero named Hrothgar built him a hall, hight Heorot . . ."

And they sat up around the campfire listening for what was left of the night, eyes growing larger and larger as they listened to the wondrous tale of the hero Beowulf.

What with one thing and another, we weren't in the world's greatest shape for traveling when we broke camp and buried our fire the next morning. We made it until noon, but when we saw the gleaming castle in the distance, sitting on top of its mound in the middle of the plain with bright banners flying from its turrets and the midday light glistening off the white stone of its curtain wall, I couldn't resist it.

"Just a little farther," I coaxed my friends. "We'll ask for hospitality there, and if they say yes, we'll be able to rest in peace and security."

"Aye," Angelique said, "for surely no one evil could live in so fair a fortress!"

But Gilbert didn't look convinced, and Frisson said, "Can any who are not evil hold a castle in Allustria?"

But Gruesome grinned from one side of his face to the other and chortled, "Food!"

"Yeah, but just grain, okay?" I looked up at him nervously. "No gobbling up the castle horses, now—we don't want to eat out our welcome."

"Goosum be good," he promised, and we pressed on to our new short-term goal with renewed vigor.

As we came up the slope, though, I frowned. "Odd. Drawbridge down, banners flying—but not a soul in sight."

"Mayhap they are all gathered in the bailey for some purpose," Frisson ventured.

"Surely they would have left sentries at the walls!" Gilbert expostulated.

"Well, we'll find out soon enough." We had come up to the drawbridge's edge. I called out to the little slit windows in the gatehouse, "Is anybody home?"

A face with a steel cap showed at one of the windows. "What wish you?"

I let out a breath that I hadn't realized I'd been holding. "Hospitality. We are wayfarers who seek a night's lodging— and we are of gentle blood."

The face looked up a little above my head. "*He* is not."

I looked around. "Who, Gruesome? No, he's a troll, but he's friendly."

"I doubt the castellan would countenance his entrance," the porter called back. "He must stay without until the lord of the castle has spoken—but the rest of you may enter."

I stood rigid for a moment, then hissed to my friends, "Maybe we'd better look for a different campground."

"Mayhap," Gilbert said. But Angelique, unseen, said, "You could do well with a soft bed and a strong wall about you for a night, gentlemen, and the troll will not fret."

"Goosum hunt!" the troll averred.

"Well . . ."

Frisson's eyes were feverish. "A real kitchen, with true food! A dinner of any other thing but journey rations!" He turned to Gruesome. "Surely you would not feel neglected, would you, good monster?"

Gruesome shook his head—or the whole top half of his body, whichever way you wanted to look at it. "Goosum no trouble!"

Well now, that could have meant that he wouldn't be any trouble if we took him into the castle, or it could have meant that it wouldn't trouble him to be left outside, but I chose the latter interpretation. "Okay, Gruesome, you wait out here. Go hunt a boar or something. We'll see you in the morning— sooner, if the lord of the castle has a change of heart."

Gruesome nodded affably and turned away toward the nearest woods.

Somehow it bothered me, having him out of sight, but I reminded myself that I was probably safer that way, anyway. "Okay, he's taking a hike," I called up to the soldier in the little window. "Can we come in now?"

"Aye! The drawbridge is down, and the keep awaits you!" he called back, and disappeared.

I turned to my companions. "Shall we, friends?"

We went through the gatehouse, Angelique glowing visibly in its shadow—and the skin on the back of my neck prickled, expecting a volley from the little windows all along both sides of the passage. But nothing happened, and we came into the bailey.

" 'Tis fair enough," Frisson said.

It was. The courtyard was bare in the center but with a broad fringe of grass, where a few horses were grazing contentedly. They wore only bridles, but they were big—knights' mounts. Smoke came from some of the buildings against the wall, with cooking odors from the kitchen range and the steady clang of metal from the smithy. Both of them relaxed me a little more, though it still seemed odd not to see anybody around.

"No doubt they are all inside." Frisson sniffed the delicious aromas and smacked his lips. "Come, friends! To the keep! Must we not present our compliments to the lord and his lady?"

"Yeah, I guess that's the correct protocol." But this time, I let Frisson take the lead.

We walked across the courtyard to the tall, round building that was the keep and went through the doors at its base—into total gloom, in which Angelique shone brightly again. Frisson stopped with an exclamation, and Gilbert came through last, looked about him, and growled.

" 'Tis a ruin!" Frisson cried.

"Well, I wouldn't go that far." I prowled past him, looking around. "Structurally, it's in good shape."

"But 'tis filthy, with the dust and dirt of a century at least!" Angelique protested.

It was. A little light came in from two small windows high up on the walls, enough illumination to show us a huge round room with fat pillars holding up the ceiling—and huge cobwebs that stretched everywhere there was a right angle. A few of them were new, with active spinners busily mending tears or rolling flies, but the others were lank and ropy, thick with dust. The floor wasn't much better, coated with humus that had once been moldering straw. Broken benches and tables poked up here and there, and I could see the remains of a few campfires, where wanderers had spent the night.

"But how could it be?" Frisson protested, visions of a good supper fleeting away. "The outside is so fair, so well kept and well tended!"

"Wherefore would they neglect the keep?" Gilbert looked about him, frowning. "Do not the lord and lady live here?"

The answer hit me like a thunderbolt. "No, they don't, and they haven't for fifty years or more! The place is deserted! Somebody just tidied up the outside to lure us in!"

"But who would go to such great labor?" Gilbert cried.

"*What* great labor? It just took a little magic! And I'll give you three guesses who uses magic on that scale! Out of here, folks!" I turned and headed for the door.

Just a second too late. A howling war cry cut loose all around us, waking echoes that the old hall hadn't even known it had.

CHAPTER 14

Soldiers came charging out from behind the pillars. Around
the edges of the room, knights stepped out from doorways,
clanking down on our little group.

Gilbert's sword was out before I'd noticed. He swung it with
a bloodthirsty howl, as I snapped my staff up to guard. The
squire chopped into a helmet, used the rebound to slash at a
belly, and snapped the sword straight ahead to fend off the oncoming soldier. But a huge net fell from the rafters to enshroud
him. Gilbert roared and flailed at the net with his sword. He
managed to cut a few strands, but more of them entangled
the sword.

I howled in anger, yanked out my knife, and sawed at the
mesh, trying to free my friend—but soldiers crowded me from
either side, and I had to turn to dodge a halberd and lunge at
its owner. The soldier yelled with pain and went down under
the feet of his comrades, and a pike head jabbed at me from
the side. I managed to parry, then remembered I was supposed
to be a wizard and frantically tried to think of a verse. Difficult, because I was also dancing around the guardsmen, trying
to leap in to cut at them and get out before a sword or halberd
hit me. Worse, I was distracted by the sight of Angelique, almost a whirlwind of gauze, swishing across a trooper's eyes
long enough for Frisson to thwack him with his staff.

Angelique undulated in front of another trooper long enough
to make him stop in his tracks. The man behind him jarred into
him, and the two of them turned to fighting each other with
shouts of anger. Angelique sped away, flitting through the attackers, causing havoc.

171

Frisson fought gamely with a staff, though he was clearly
getting the worst of it.

A bellow split the air, and the soldiers drew back in fright,
for a behemoth strode into the fight with teeth and claws.
"Gruesome!" I shouted with relief. The monster must have
heard the sounds of the fight and come running back to get in
on the pounding.

Then some sixth sense warned me, and I spun around.
Someone had managed to get behind me, and a weighted club
was swinging down toward my sinuses with a fully armored
knight behind it. I took a breath to rattle off a verse, but the
club swooped down to fill the world, a huge pain exploded at
the side of my head, and I didn't get to see how the fight came
out.

The murk cleared enough for me to see something gleaming.
I blinked, focused, and saw shining, pale-yellow teeth curving
upward in a grin. I squeezed my eyes shut and shook my
head—and immediately regretted it; pain wreathed my brain in
fire. I groaned, clutching my poor fevered pate and squeezing
my eyes shut.

Something nudged my shoulder, none too gently. "Look up,
Wizard! Ere I cut your lids from your eyes!"

There was a certain gloating quality to the words, one that
made me think the speaker would just love an excuse to carry
out her threat. I gritted my teeth and forced my eyes open. The
murk, mercilessly, had fled, forcing me to see the smile in
context—and the context was pretty repulsive. In fact, it was
Suettay's face.

I winced and turned away, hoping for a better alternative.

There was an alternative, all right, but whether it was better
or not was decidedly moot. We were in a dank stone chamber, filled with wicked-looking instruments that I vaguely
recognized—an iron maiden; thumbscrews; and, beside me,
several racks. On one lay Frisson, bound hand and foot—and
beside him, Gilbert, who was awake but groggy, and sitting up.
Gruesome was missing. Oddly, I felt a spurt of relief—at least
one of us had escaped the ambush. Then anxiety reawakened
in the wake of the thought, and I hoped the troll wouldn't be
so fanatically loyal as to try to rescue us. After all, what could
he do?

On the other hand, I was a bit more anxious about Angelique.

In fact, she was my prime worry, because she was here, too—in the flesh! Although now that I looked at it, the body's chest was still, none of the gashes were bleeding, and it was deathly pale.

Deathly . . .

Suettay had put her corpse in with us.

Outrage hit me. How dare Suettay save Angelique's mortal clay like a trophy?

Or was it for some other purpose?

Suddenly, I remembered what the witch-queen had said about preserving Angelique's body, and why. I found myself really hoping my favorite ghost wasn't in that room with us—but I was very much afraid she was, and in some condition I couldn't detect.

No way around it—I decided I'd have to recognize that we were in a real, genuine, bona fide predicament, and no matter how ugly it was, I was going to have to face it. I turned back to Suettay.

The queen saw my resignation and laughed, a sound like a truck trying to roll with a broken bearing. I sighted and reevaluated her—when you got right down to it, the queen was a very ordinary-looking fat woman, if you didn't count the cruel glint in her eye or the gloating, eager smile on her glistening lips.

A scream scoured the air. I turned frantically to my companions—and was hugely relieved to see that none of them had made the noise. It did, however, jerk Frisson rudely back to consciousness, staring about in instant panic. Suettay laughed again.

I turned to look at her and was amazed to see that the queen wasn't looking back. In fact, she was looking off to my right with rapt fascination, nodding slowly and grunting. "Good, good. Again, again!"

Sure enough, the scream split the air once more, and Suettay's eyes glistened like a connoisseur's regarding a Picasso—or, I revised it, like a voyeur's watching a pornographic movie. I turned to follow Suettay's gaze, puzzled.

I turned away again, as quickly as I could. I could tell from the sounds that my companions had made the same mistake.

Suettay, apparently, watched torture for fun.

Fortunately, the victim wasn't anybody I knew. I wondered if the poor man had done anything to deserve torture, or if Suettay's soldiers had just grabbed the nearest passerby.

The queen turned toward me, grinning from ear to ear. "Do you not find this pastime amusing, Wizard?" She said the last two words with so much sarcasm that they might have cracked under the load.

But I was in no condition to notice; I was fighting a rising gorge. "Uh, no thanks, Your Majesty—that's more like my idea of work."

The torturer giggled as he turned some minuscule device, and the prisoner screamed again.

Suettay's face reddened on the instant, engorging with rage. "Do you think yourself so much better than me, then? Torturer!" She waved at the official. "Release the prisoner! We will save the rest of his agony for a time of proper leisure!" Then, to two apprentices standing by in leather loincloths and black masks, "Seize this churl and lay him on the table!"

In the middle of the apprentices' giggles and my friends' cries of outrage, all I could think, as they unstrapped me and hustled me over to the table, was that at least I'd spared the poor peasant some pain.

"Fight, Wizard Saul!" Gilbert shouted. "Do not let them doom you without a struggle!"

But I didn't have any time to fight—I was too busy thinking up verses.

The torturers slapped me down on the table. Very effective —it knocked the breath out of me long enough for them to put the shackles on. Then the main torturer advanced, grinning over a glowing branding iron. I tried to forget it was for me and started to mutter—but the torturer nodded at an apprentice, who stabbed the ball of my thumb with a fat pin. I yelped, the verse going completely out of my mind. But it reminded me of another one:

> "By the pricking of my thumbs
>   Something wicked this way comes!
>   Open locks, whoever knocks!"

The shackles sprang loose with a clatter, and I bounded up, stiff-arming the torturer as I passed. "Sorry, but I don't really have time today, I have an appointment with—"

Gilbert and Frisson shouted approval, but the queen stared, appalled; whatever she'd been expecting from me, that hadn't been it. Her face darkened then, and she barked, "Seize him!"

Two guards jumped me and slammed me back down on the

table. Suettay gave a curt nod toward the rest of the captives, and other guards backhanded them both across the mouths. Frisson reeled back down, and Gilbert recoiled.

Anger filled me, for which I was thankful. I glared at the queen, who laughed with vindictive pleasure as the torturer came back with the heated iron, its glow dulled to a sullen red. He moved it slowly toward my forehead, his gloating grin growing again.

I stared at the horrid, glowing pentacle, as fascinated as I was horrified, trying for the life of me to think of a verse—and I did.

> " 'Tears are for the craven,
> Pleading for the clown,
> Halters for the silly neck
> That cannot keep a crown.'
> He was taken prisoner,
> He was cast in thrall,
> Iron, cold iron, is master of them all!"

The iron star cooled amazingly, its glow dimming to blackness as it neared. The torturer cried out—was that fear, or just disappointment?—but Suettay's hands moved in some odd pattern while she snarled something with a heavy meter in a tongue I didn't know, and the star glowed into brightness again—not just red, but white-hot. The torturer's grin grew back with it, and I just had time to realize that Suettay had been expecting some sort of cooling spell before the heat of the iron seared my whole face, then passed beyond my sight, and pain, bright liquid pain, worse than any I had ever known, shot outward from the center of my forehead, drowning out all other sensations—my friends' shouts of horror, Suettay's victorious crowing, my own scream.

Gradually, the pain diminished until the things I saw could register again, though my whole head was still wrapped in agony, and my whole spirit quailed in total, abject, gibbering fear. I could hear Suettay soothing, "Softly, softly. Pain on pain will yield no gain; he will not feel the pins, while he's curled in agony from the iron."

Good advice, and I realized the smart thing would be to keep screaming and pretending I was delirious—but I saw Angelique's bruised corpse; Gilbert, a bruise darkening on his cheek; and Frisson, crumpled against his rack, blood trickling from the hand cupped over his mouth.

There was no room for anger now; my whole being was filled with fear, horrible fear that the torturer would do that again, and I whimpered, "Please ... please ..."

"Yes, it does please me." Suettay chuckled. "And will please me for all of this day, and part of this night, I doubt not." Suddenly, her eyes blazed, and her whole countenance contorted. "Fool! To defy my will! Now will you learn the fate that befalls those who oppose Suettay! Now will you learn what it is, to die in torment!"

She motioned, and pain lanced through my hands. I screamed; then, as the pain dimmed, the thought fleeted through my mind that at least I didn't have any major sins on my conscience at the moment, so I'd die Heaven-bound ...

The realization blossomed like a flower, even through the pain, and I had no doubts as to where it had come from. By myself, I wouldn't even have thought of those terms, and if I had, I would have thought that because I wasn't holier-than-thou, I couldn't have been good. But the inspiration came, and I realized that, yes, I was in a state of grace at the moment—not perfect, but I'd been doing more good works than bad—enough so that Satan had no power over me. That meant Suettay could only control me with physical force; as far as magic went, her spells were by no means unbeatable.

If I could only find the right one. And if I could just get it out of my mouth.

But Suettay saw the hope rising in my face, and screamed, "Lance him!"

Pain bit through my thumbs again. This time, though, I knew it was coming, and I could grit my teeth and ride it out. I held tight to the thought of defense. My mind searched frantically through the verses I knew, rejecting anything the queen might expect, seizing the least likely:

"You get a good spadesman
To plant a small tradesman
(First take off his boots with a boot tree),
And his feet will take root,
And his fingers will shoot,
And they'll blossom and bud like a fruit tree!"

The torturer cried out in alarm as invisible hands wrenched off his boots. A block of stone flipped itself out of the floor, and the unseen hands jammed the torturer into the dirt beneath. Then he howled with pain and fright as his arms stretched out like tree limbs. His fingers elongated like little branches, the tips bulging into buds that sprang open into flowers.

My friends shouted with delight, and the apprentices shrank back with a moan.

"Mercy!" the torturer cried. "Mercy!"

"You're welcome," I muttered. I wasn't thinking too clearly, what with all the pain.

Suettay paled, falling back a pace. I started to flounder up off the torture table, though, and the queen snapped out of her shock. "Guards! Seize him!"

But all of a sudden, the guards were reluctant, and it gave me time to climb to my feet, searching frantically for another verse.

"Will you not seize him?" the queen ranted. "Must I turn you all into flaming brands?"

The soldiers paled and started forward.

I decided to stay with Gilbert and Sullivan.

"If you want a proud foe to make tracks,
    If you'd melt a cruel monarch in wax,
    You've but to call in the old resident jinn,
    From Seventy Simmery Axe!"

An explosion of expanding air rocked the chamber, and there it was, a full-fledged Arabian jinn, complete with turban and beard. "Your command, master?"

The companions and guards both stared, and somebody made a sick moan—maybe it was Suettay.

"More like a client, actually," I clarified, remembering what one tradition said happened to jinn's masters. "I'd like you to clear the guards and torturers out of this chamber, banish them to some oasis in the nearest desert. But not too lush an oasis," I added, remembering what the torturers had done to me.

"Your wish is my command." The jinn raised his hands . . .

And Suettay got her mouth working. Her hands twitched through the air as she recited some incomprehensible syllables— incomprehensible to me, but apparently something understood them somewhere, because when the jinn cried aloud some an-

cient syllables of his own and threw his hands up, the whirlwind
that sprang up just as quickly died down.

The jinn stared, unbelieving, then suddenly gasped and spat
out a string of words, making mystic passes all around himself.
His form wavered and thinned, then solidified again.

Suettay grinned, chanting again as her hands stirred the air.

"I cannot," the jinn gasped. "The sorceress moves against
me! 'Tis all I can do to fend off her magics!"

But I had taken time for a thinking break, and chanted,

"And the might of the Gentile, unsmote by the sword,
Hath melted like snow in the glance of the Lord!"

The guards cried out as a huge, invisible hand slammed
them against the wall. They crumpled to the floor, out cold.

"I cannot prevail," the jinn gasped. "I can at best withhold
her might!"

"You're doing just fine," I assured him. "While you're holding her off, I'm free to work on her henchmen. Now, let's see
. . . a verse about torturers . . ."

Suettay's face twisted, and she snarled, "Seize her!"

The apprentice torturers leapt to Angelique's body.

Frisson and Gilbert struggled against their bonds, but
Suettay snapped, "Hold! Move, and her spirit dies!"

I whirled to her, staring. She was holding a corked bottle
over her head—and it looked to be made of very thin glass.

One of the torturers, hearing, whisked out a knife and held
it to the throat of Angelique's body.

"So," I said. "When your men knocked me out, you managed to compel her ghost into a bottle."

"Why, how quickly you understand!" Suettay crooned.

"So break it." I frowned. "All you'll do is free her ghost
again."

"Nay, for I'll scream the spell as I do—and as the lady
comes out from the flask, her ghost will leap to her body. Look
at it! The boot is on!"

I whirled to look. Sure enough, the iron boot was clamped
around one of Angelique's feet, and there were thumbscrews
on each hand. I knew, with a sick certainty, that they had
been there ever since she'd died. If her ghost went back in
there, and the body came alive again, it would be in instant
agony.

But the explanation had taken time from Suettay's spells,

and the jinn shouted what sounded like an oath. A huge scimitar appeared in midair, slicing down at Suettay. The queen answered with a curse, and the huge blade winked out just before it hit her. She broke out in a sweat and snapped, "Banish him, Wizard, or the woman lives!"

I was in no shape to appreciate the irony.

Neither was the jinn; he was chanting again. Suettay's face reddened, and her hands sawed the air furiously; she managed to croak a verse . . .

The torturer pricked, and a drop of blood welled up on Angelique's pale throat. Frisson groaned, and Gilbert cried out in dismay.

I capitulated. "Thanks, O Jinn—but I'm afraid we're outflanked. Back to the place of your people, now."

The jinn cried out in relief and delight, and disappeared.

Suettay wiped her forehead with a shaking hand, drew a deep breath, and forced a grin. "Now, Wizard. I believe we understand our positions."

"Not quite." My eyes narrowed. "If that slab of beef harms a hair on her head, I'll turn him into a turnip."

The torturer looked up, appalled.

"I think not," Suettay purred, "while I can prevent it."

"True. First, I'll turn you into a pig. Not that it will take much."

Frisson crowed his approval, then caught himself, eyeing the queen fearfully.

Suettay reddened, and her eyes narrowed. "Attempt it, and she will wake into agony while you chant."

"Not if the torturer knows you'll gobble him up the next minute—or do you really think you'd be able to resist the temptation? You're not too good at that, you know."

"I think I shall still be as I am, and you shall be a toad!"

I raised my hands, ready to gesture. "Ready to try it? On the count of three . . ."

"Be still!" Suettay watched me with narrowed eyes. Beyond her, I saw Frisson's abstracted gaze, and knew I could count on magical help from an unexpected quarter. On the other hand, I wasn't sure what the effects of that help would be—if inspiration struck, he was apt to forget practicalities.

"You prevaricate," the sorceress guessed, "for you would not chance the woman's life."

I said slowly, "Not if there's a way to guarantee her safety, and that of my friends, no. Trouble is, I don't see any such way."

"There is one," Suettay said, with a leer. "Ally yourself with myself and with evil, and the maid shall go free."

I lay rigid with shock—but beside me, Gilbert called out, "Nay, Master Saul! She would smite the lass nonetheless!"

"I would not," Suettay retorted, "for if I did, the wizard might turn against me."

"That . . . makes sense," I said slowly.

"Surely you are not tempted!" Frisson cried.

"Tempted, sure." I shrugged. "Anybody can be tempted, right? Can't avoid that. Giving in to it is another matter—but yes, I am tempted."

"Tempted most shrewdly." Suettay's leer broadened. "Come, Wizard! Swear allegiance to me and to Satan, and the soul of the lass shall go free. Nay, further—I'll remove the spell that keeps her body alive, so that her soul may fly to Heaven."

It was a good deal, and it was very tempting; I loved Angelique dearly, and sending her to eternal bliss would have made her very happy. Unfortunately, it would have made me very sad—I finally admitted to myself just how thoroughly I'd fallen in love with her, and how much I wanted her with me. With me, in body as well as spirit, I might add—I might have been substantially in a state of grace, but I was no plaster saint. I wanted Angelique and I wanted her alive, well, and corporeal.

But that was selfish.

"No, Master Saul!" Gilbert cried. "You must not! Without you, we should all be—"

Suettay nodded at a guard, who slapped Gilbert hard across the mouth, then stuffed a gag in.

But he'd said enough. Without me, this whole complex of forces that was gathering to oust Suettay and clean up Allustria might falter and fail. I know that sounds conceited, but I didn't really know what my part in the whole scheme was—only that I was definitely a part of it, and if one part failed, all the rest probably would, too.

But more importantly, Suettay still needed Angelique for that virgin sacrifice—and once I committed myself to the power of evil, I would be under her authority, and powerless to stop her.

"He hesitates," Suettay snapped. "He is a fool, and will do us no good."

The torturers rumbled agreement—of course—and Suettay stepped up to Angelique's body. She handed the flask to one of her henchmen. "Pull the cork when I bid you, and the spirit shall be sucked back into the clay." Then she began to weave a pattern of strange, vaguely obscene gestures over the corpse, chanting in that strange, eerie language.

I had a sudden vision of that poor, gentle body coming alive, convulsing in pain, screaming in agony. "No, wait!"

"Will you join me?"

My heart twisted within me, and my whole body twisted with it. All the fears and horrors of the evil I'd seen flitted through my memory, and an intuitive impulse such as I'd never had surged through me, adding up to a panic of denial— but there lay Angelique's body, with her ghost ready to hand . . . "No."

"Curses!" Suettay spat. "How strong is your love, then, if you will not sell your soul to save the maiden from pain?"

That suddenly made everything clear, and I felt the peace of certainty flow back through me—for I realized that selling my soul would be the denial of love. Love is healing, love pulls the soul toward Heaven, because it's a tiny taste of Heaven—so if I sold my soul, dedicated it completely to evil, I'd be locking myself away from love. If I signed up with Suettay, I would no longer really be able to love Angelique.

But I would still desire her—and what might I do to her then, with no conscience and no empathy?

"No," I said. "If I sold my soul, then I'd be placing her completely in your power—there would be no one left to shield her."

"A curse upon the spirit that has told you that!" Suettay snarled.

I suddenly realized where all these inspirations had been coming from. "Won't work. He's curse-proof."

Suettay's eyes narrowed. "Then I'll proffer you another bargain. Cease your hold on this world, and I shall let the girl's ghost go free."

Panic again, at the thought of leaving Angelique—but the logic of it made me hesitate. Sure, if Suettay could augment her power by converting a wild card of a wizard to her side, it would make her that much stronger, and her enemies that much weaker—but if she couldn't subvert me, she could at least get rid of me. That would give her one less thing to worry about.

A return to my own world was what I wanted anyway, right? Except that I was trying to find Matt—but I'd sure found out where he had gone, and there was no particular reason to think he wasn't alive and well. If I really wanted to find out, all I had to do was go back to my own world, find the parchment he had used, and read whatever spell it contained—it would take me to him. Nice double cross for Suettay, too.

But what would happen to my friends in the meantime?

I summoned all my nerve and said, "No."

"That was my final kindness, fool!" Suettay screamed. "Why do you disdain it?"

"Because," I said, "as soon as I'm out of the way, you'll go ahead and sacrifice Angelique, then start in on my friends."

"But you would have no knowledge of that! You would not care!"

"Oh, I would care," I assured her, "very much."

Her eyes narrowed to glitters of malice. "Then we shall remove all the sources of that care—by simple murder! I am loath to waste objects of pleasure in quick killing—but if it will speed you hence, I shall do it! Guards! Slay—"

"No!" I shouted. "You kill them, and I'll hang on in this universe just to get revenge on you!"

She broke off, looking up at me with a strange, malicious smile. " 'Tis tempting—for revenge is sinful, and in letting yourself be consumed with hatred and the desire for vengeance, you would succumb to the lure of evil, and be subsumed in it."

My heart sank.

"Sweet though that would be," she said regretfully, "it would be of no aid to me, myself—and might hinder me, in your rebellion."

I saw my chance. "Yeah! And the sinfulness of my revenge might even be balanced by the good I did in getting rid of you!"

" 'Tis even so." Her eyes were back to the nasty glitters again. "So it would seem that you must join me, or die."

I felt my stomach drop down to the bottom of the shaft, but I set my jaw and said, "Death. Definitely death." And I tried to sneak in one more spell:

> "He took the Wine and blessed it,
> He blessed and broke the Bread . . ."

"Enough!" Suettay screamed. "Silence him!"

A hard hand backhanded me across the mouth. I saw stars, and wondered if I'd need a dentist or an orthodontist.

"To the dungeons with them!" Suettay ranted. "The wench shall remain imprisoned in this flask, till I incorporate her to watch his final agonies! Let them rot in my most dreary cell, while I begin preparations for a revenge dealt in a manner that will most please my master!"

Then I was running to try to keep from falling as the apprentice torturers hustled the three of us down the hallway and into a cell. My skin crawled with apprehension. Somehow, I didn't think the "master" Suettay had referred to was anyone human. I had a nasty, sneaking suspicion that I knew how high up in the nonhuman hierarchy that individual was—and what kind of revenge he would find most pleasing.

CHAPTER 15

We landed sitting down—hard, and it hurt. The door boomed shut behind us.

Oddly, my initial impression was one of peace. It was so nice and cool after the heat of the torture chamber, and the darkness was soothing, especially since it was relieved by the dim glow through the little barred window in the door.

My second impression was one of amazing satisfaction. I had put a long-term crimp in Suettay's plans; there was no telling how long the queen would be tied up trying to figure out a way to cancel my existence. Apparently I was an odd enough customer that she would have to do it carefully. For a moment, I was tempted to believe it was the overwhelming strength of my "spells," the legacy of my nearly completed English major—but skepticism got the better of ego, and I realized that it probably had more to do with who had brought me into this cockamamy universe, than with me, myself.

If I ever met that guy . . .

I chopped off that line of thought as a new suspicion dawned. If I was such a delicate article, no wonder Suettay had tried to deal! Which raised the possibility that she might try to bargain again; I decided I'd better get busy figuring out a new set of counterspells. If she had any brains, she'd gag Frisson at the outset.

Or kill him . . .

I mumbled a quick charm to clear my head; I knew I couldn't concentrate through the pain. Then Gilbert swore, with loathing.

"What's the matter?" All other concerns were instantly forgotten.

"Something with warmth and fur did brush my thigh!"

"Don't try to hit it if you can't see it!" I had a sinking certainty that I knew what it was.

Then I heard a dry, high-pitched chuckle from the depths of the lightless hole.

I froze and hissed, "Everybody stay still!" Then, aloud, "Who's there?"

The chuckle came again, with a nasty edge to it.

It made the hairs on the back of my neck stand up. "I warn you, I'm a wizard—and the queen herself has just found out to her sorrow that I'm not without power even here, within the realm of evil! Answer! Who are you?"

The chuckler was still. Then a rasping voice came out of the darkness. "Have you hurt the queen, then?"

"Not really," I said, "but I do seem to have snafued her system."

"I do not know that spell," the voice said. "Tell me, does it cause her humiliation?"

"Because she can't fix it? Yeah, I'd say so—and frustration. But nothing compared to what I'm feeling! Are you going to tell me who you are, or do I have to come over there and drag it out of you?" The day's woes suddenly boiled over. I shoved myself to my feet and strode toward the voice.

There was a scrabbling in the darkness ahead of me, and the voice hissed, "Beware! Or my pets shall have you!"

There was something sinister in the way he said "pets" that made me halt, in spite of the loss of pride it entailed. "Blast! We need some light in here!"

"Nay!" the voice cried, but I chanted,

"Oh, light was the world that he held in his hands,
And light shall bloom here, to show us this man!"

A torch flame flared in the darkness, and I saw a fat, bald man with a wrinkled, chinless face, deathly pale from being too long in darkness. His clothes were filthy rags, but they had once been fine robes. He flinched back from the light, baring long, yellow teeth. Half a dozen huge rats scrabbled back with him, lips writhing in snarls, long, stained incisors bared. A couple of them burrowed into his robes.

I swallowed. "I see your point." I cleared my throat and said, "Odd choice of associates, don't you think?"

"There's little enough else by me here," the bald man snarled, "and they are better company than most folk I have known."

That was a signal, if I had ever heard one. I stilled inside, and inquired, "People done you wrong?"

The bald man laughed, a hissing series of expelled breaths. "Who among them has not? Yet I must own there was a rightness to it—for I did them harm, as oft as I might. Is not this the way of the world?"

"Nay," Gilbert croaked.

"Aye," Frisson contradicted. "Yet that's not to say it should be."

"Should be!" the bald man spit. "A pox upon your 'should be'! I will abide with what *is*, not with what 'should be'!"

"As you always have?" I murmured.

"Aye! There's at least some slight honesty to it! Your 'should be' is hypocrisy!"

"Not if we look for the better world," Frisson said softly.

"If all could behave as they *should*, look you, the *world* would become a far better place," Gilbert insisted.

"Yet your 'all' will not do so, not even a moiety!" the bald man declared. "Nay, I shall abide by my 'is'!"

"After all," I said, "it's done so well for you."

The glare the bald man gave me was pure hate. "It did well indeed for me, young man, for three dozen years! Ever did I rise higher through the ranks of the queen's clerks, till I stood above them all as chancellor, with a dozen desks 'neath my sway, and twenty scriptoriums to each! Directly below the queen's privy chamber I stood, and would have risen to a post within it, had not misfortune intervened!"

"The queen's privy?" Frisson murmured. "I should think that an unfortunate position."

The bald man's eyes narrowed again. "Mock if you will! But those who are the queen's most senior servants have power indeed, because they are privy to her counsel!"

"So you were the top man in the second level of the bureaucracy," I interpreted.

The bald man frowned, peering keenly at me. " 'Bureaucracy'? What is that?"

"Literally, 'government by desks,' " I answered. "It's the organization of clerks who actually run the country."

The bald man held my gaze for a moment, then slowly nodded. "Aye. 'Tis oddly said, but 'tis how Suettay doth govern."

"And," I inferred, "you made a little mistake in your climb to the top?"

"Aye, a small mistake only," the bald man grated, "and one that I should have seen would be so—for I did bethink me of a means toward greater power for the queen, believing she would create a new chancellery for it and for me, and raise me to the privy chamber. Yet she saw, and clearly, that such power might give me some chance to move against her, and therefore sent me here."

I nodded. "You did your job just a little too well. She realized the true scope of your ability, so she made haste to put you where you couldn't do her any harm."

"Would she had slain me instead!" the bald man hissed.

"That would have been nicer," I agreed. "Trouble is, it might not have made you enough of an example for ambitious young men who show too much initiative and do more than they're told. How many times has she pulled you out to parade before her clerks?"

The bald man frowned. "Twice, o'er the years—and, as you say, 'twas before her clerks assembled. Yet 'twas to demand of me the scope of my chancellery, matters which my successor had forgotten."

I nodded. "And, conveniently, on the inauguration of the new chancellor, each time—just as a little warning to him."

The bald man's eyes widened, burning. " 'Tis even as you say! What a fool was I not to have seen it!"

"Understandable." I shrugged. "You fell victim to the bureaucrat's big weakness—you started caring about the job itself and forgot it was just supposed to be a means of personal advancement."

The glittering gaze held for a minute, before the bald head nodded slowly. "Aye. Fool that I was, I thought that excellence of work would raise me up by itself."

" 'The race is not always to the swift,' " I quoted, "nor advancement to the most able—at his job, at least. It *is* to the most able at currying favor and influence. Of course, if he can't do the job, he gets fired."

Gilbert shuddered. "Woe to Allustria! If it is to be governed by such willful incompetence!"

"No, it *is* competence," I corrected, "but *only* competence."

I turned to the bald man. "And you let the queen see that you could actually excel."

The long teeth bared in a mirthless smile. "Aye, fool that I was."

"Then you hit the midlife crisis." I lifted an eyebrow. "I take it your chancellery had something to do with the fall of Allustria?"

The bald man grinned. "You may say that if you will. Certain it is, that Queen Graftus, the queen unseated by Suettay's grandmother, became greedy and boosted the taxes—but then, at the recommendation of her chief adviser, began to try to be sure the taxes were collected. First she had a complete list of all possessions made up, then verified the taxes each person owed and, when they were paid, checked them against the record—all under the direction of her chief adviser, of course. In cases of underpayment, she dispatched a squad or more of royal knights with a clerk, to collect. When recalcitrant dukes managed to resist, her adviser recommended magic, and went herself, with a small army, to work sorcery against the reluctant dukes."

"Let me guess," I said softly. "The chief adviser was Suettay."

The bald man frowned. "Nay, her grandmother, the Chancellor Reiziv. We speak of events two hundred years gone, young man. How old do you think the queen to be?"

I exchanged a quick glance with Frisson, but only said, "Sorry. I guess I'm just overly impressed by Her Majesty. I take it Queen Graftus was happy with her sorceress-adviser?"

"Aye; the stratagem was so successful that the queen allowed Reiziv to recruit junior sorcerers, and no baron dared to resist again. Queen Graftus thus became very wealthy and very powerful."

"Very," I agreed. "How long did it take her to realize her chief adviser Reiziv really held the reins of power?"

"Never, till she waked in the middle of the night with a knife in her throat, and the sorceress' laugh of glee ringing in her ears, all the way down to Hell. Then did the sorceress become queen, and all the people did witness the power of sorcery."

"Yes, of course—after all, it had won, hadn't it? So you grew up wanting to become a sorcerer."

"Aye." A shadow crossed the bald man's face. "Yet I was

found wanting in talent. Therefore did I turn with zeal to becoming a clerk."

"Next most profitable career, I guess. What was your dazzling improvement on the system?"

The bald man's gaze darkened with self-contempt. "Oh,
'twas a marvelous scheme, to be sure, and so simple! 'Twas
only the posting of a junior clerk to each town, to oversee all
transactions and judgments, and to undertake whatever actions
the queen would think good!"

"With a junior sorcerer to guard him, of course," I murmured.

"Aye. Being of the royal household, the clerk would pay no
heed to the wishes of the townsfolk, or their mayor and reeve.
He would be answerable only to the queen."

"Which meant, of course, to his bureau chief," I murmured,
"which would have been you."

"Aye," the bald man spat. "Fool that I was, I did not realize
the extent of the power this would have given me."

"But the queen did."

"Oh, aye! Therefore did she set out the clerks as I had
suggested—but kept their governance to herself."

"And threw you into the dungeon."

The bald man nodded, bitter as a London pint.

"The reward of the capable man," I sympathized, "but of
the man who is more capable of doing the work than of currying favor."

"I was a fool," the bald man spat. "A talented fool, mayhap,
but a fool nonetheless."

"Quite talented," I agreed, "though not at the sorcery you
wished for."

"Aye." The bald man's eyes brightened with bitter satisfaction. "Yet here, at the end of my course, I have discovered that
I did have some modicum of a true and most singular talent—
much good may it do me in this place!"

"Oh?" I asked softly. "What's that?"

"I have befriended the rats," the bald man hissed, "so well
that they come when I call. Nay, I could raise up a hundred of
them now and tell them to overwhelm you!"

Gilbert growled with menace, but Frisson asked, "Would
they do what you bade them?"

"They would." The bald man showed his long yellow teeth.
"Aught that I told them, even to running headlong into death,
so long as they could do it in a body."

"Lord of the rat pack," I mused. "Frisson, do you 'remember' that verse about cats?"

"Nay, but I will bring it to mind most quickly."

"And I know one about terriers." I gazed thoughtfully at the Rat Raiser. "A very considerable power. With them at your command, why do you languish here?"

"What should I gain by their use?" the Rat Raiser countered. "It would appear that even you, at a thought, can summon up creatures to oppose them! What, then, could my sovereign Suettay do?"

"Annihilate them," I answered, "probably by calling up a demon or two."

"And would annihilate myself with them," the Rat Raiser answered. "Nay, I've no wish to die, or to see my pets fry. An I wished it, I could have bade them slay me long ago."

"And you've thought about it, eh?"

"Who would not?" the Rat Raiser returned. "Yet I abide. Why, I know not—but I abide."

"No doubt just waiting for us to come help you out," I said breezily, and turned to Gilbert. "How long do you think those locks can hold you?" Out of the corner of my eye, I noticed the Rat Raiser sit up straight—but he slumped again, glowering. Of course, I realized. Who knows better than a bureaucrat, to distrust promises?

"I have tried them," Gilbert answered. "There is a spell to hold us here; the locks will not budge, nor the bars bend, and the wood is like armor. 'Tis you who must take us forth from here, Wizard, or we will rot with the rats and their friend! Nay, bend thy talent to its utmost and bring us forth from here quickly! For with every moment that passes, the lovely maiden comes closer to torment!"

The Rat Raiser laughed, a shrill, high stuttering of breath. "Fool! Do you think you can prevail 'gainst the vile, twisted power of the queen?"

"It's possible," I said slowly. "I seem to be in a state of grace, at the moment." More thanks to my guardian angel than to myself, I had a notion. "Let's start by trying to get out of this cellar." Not easy, for a guy who claimed not to believe in magic—so I relayed it to one who did. "Frisson, if I sing you a couple of songs, can you craft them into a spell that will get us back to the torture chamber?"

"Why would you wish to go there?" the Rat Raiser gasped.

"Because the queen is about to visit a friend of ours with a

fate worse than death—it must be worse, because she's going
to bring her back to life just for the occasion. How about it,
Frisson?"

"If you wish it, Master Wizard, I shall essay it," the vagabond said slowly.

Before they could talk, I recited,

> "Over his parchment the musing bard,
> Beginning doubtfully and far away,
> First lets his quill wander afar,
> As he draws on his muse for his lay—
> Then as his point drinks up sable ink,
> So his heart takes fervor, feeling his theme,
> Rising in flashes, in darkness to sink,
> To make realize that are as they seem."

I shuddered to think what I'd done to Lowell's verse, then
consoled myself with the thought that there was so little of it
left, he'd never have noticed.

A pen, an inkwell, and a sheet of foolscap appeared, hovering in the air. I took them and handed them to Frisson. "Write
it down—I taught you how! That way, I can check to make
sure it'll work before it gets said aloud."

Frisson took the pen with a show of reluctance, which I
didn't believe for a moment. "If you say to, Lord Wizard.
Natheless, I am yet slow to form my letters."

I had to admire how well he took a cue. "Try," I urged. "Do
you know an old song called 'The Castle of Dramouye'?"

"From the Isle of Doctors and Saints? Aye, I have heard it."

"You might try a variation on that, to get us into her dungeon. Then we'll need one to get us out of this castle; have
you ever heard a song that goes like this?" I hummed the first
eight bars of "Greensleeves."

The poet nodded. "I have heard them. Must I hold to their
limits, though?"

"Of course not! If the muse visits, wear her out! Write what
comes to you; I'm just giving you a starting point—call it
muse bait."

But Frisson was already sitting down cross-legged, gazing
off into space. After a moment, he dipped his quill and
scratched a few words, gazed off into space again, then dipped
his quill once more and started scribbling furiously.

Slow to form his letters. Right. Well, I had known the man was a genius—I wasn't surprised that he'd learned so quickly.

The Rat Raiser was, though. He was staring, though the rest of his face was immobile. He didn't say a word, of course—too experienced a bureaucrat to give anything away—but from the way he watched, I knew he was reassessing our skill as wizards. Admittedly, Frisson was too ragged to look like much, and my clothing was too outlandish—but if the "spells" we used were so potent that we had to write them down and check them before we read them aloud to cast them, we must be mighty indeed.

I didn't argue.

Frisson looked up and held out the page, looking very anxious. "Will it sail, Lord Wizard?"

I took the parchment and studied it. My eyes widened. Could this really be as excellent an adaptation of a folk verse as I thought it was?

It could. After all, I had just finished reminding myself that Frisson was a genius. "This is very good, Frisson," I said slowly. "Almost too good to be used as a spell."

Disappointment shadowed the poet's face.

" 'Almost,' I said! If I weaken it a bit, it should work stronger magic than anything I've ever made up. Brace yourselves, men—and join hands."

Gilbert seized my right hand, and Frisson seized my left as I closed my eyes, took a deep breath, and began to recite,

> "Summer winds turn chill around
> The Royal Keep of Doom.
> Cries of pain and fear resound
> Within its torture room.
> There let us be transported all,
> Its anguish to subsume!"

The cell darkened, the light went out, and the Rat Raiser cried in the darkness. A wave of nausea swept through me and was gone; then the light came back, and I saw Angelique, still stretched out on the torture bench, eyes wide and unseeing, chest still.

Beyond her, Suettay was just taking the cork out of the bottle, intoning a chant. The torturer, restored, was chuckling as he tightened the thumbscrews on the corpse.

The ghost rose from the bottle, trembling with apprehension. Then Suettay saw us, and stared at us in amazement and alarm.

The assistant torturer held the corpse's leg, stroking it lasciviously, as the chief torturer paused to make a last adjustment to the iron boot. He looked up, saw the expression on his queen's face, spun about, and smashed a fist into my face.

I saw it coming just in time to roll with the punch—but I saw stars, and pain racked my head, stirring up anger. I was too slow, though—the squire beat me to it.

Gilbert roared and leapt forward; the torturer was just beginning to turn when the squire's fist caught him under the jaw. I heard something snap, but all I saw was the torturer sailing over the table in a perfect parabola. He crashed into the wall just above the floor, but by that time, his first assistant was in midair heading for the south wall, and Gilbert's fist was in the second apprentice's midriff. Then he picked up the man like a javelin and sent him after the first; he almost had all three in midair at the same time. I hadn't known the squire was a juggler—or such a strong one, either.

It only took him a few seconds, but that was long enough. Suettay whirled about, teeth bared in a snarl, and began to shout a verse.

I rose up from the floor, trying to forget that my momma had taught me never to hit a lady, and slammed a fist into her jawbone. She slumped, out cold, and the bottle hit the floor, shattering. The ghost drifted free with a cry of relief.

Two guardsmen shook off their stupors and stepped forward. One drew a sword; the other hefted his pike, then realized it wasn't there.

I leapt forward, shouting, "Go down!"

The guard looked up, startled, just long enough for Gilbert's fist to connect with his cheekbone. As he was crumpling, his mate was looking around for his pike when he tripped over its butt, fell sprawling, rolled over, and found himself staring at its blade. Gilbert spared him confusion by clouting him neatly on the crown, and he lapsed into unconsciousness.

Then Frisson whirled and stabbed down with the pike he'd used to trip the guard. He plunged it straight into the queen's chest.

It was a good move, and one Gilbert couldn't have forced himself to do, since it was in cold blood, and therefore without honor—but Frisson wasn't a knight, or a squire. I just didn't have the heart to tell the poor vagabond it wouldn't do any good.

Gilbert whirled to Angelique's body, unscrewing the boot. "Be consoled, maiden! It shall not hurt you any longer, even if you are reincorporated! Nay, fear not—your tormentors shall harry you no more!"

He wasn't even panting.

I turned to Frisson. "Thought you were a poor, law-abiding victim."

"What—this?" The poet looked at the pike as if he'd never seen it before. "Well, I have learned some knack of separating people from objects, aye."

"Valuable objects, right? And without their ever noticing it."

Frisson shrugged. "The mammon of wickedness can be turned to a good purpose, Lord Wizard."

"Oh, I don't dispute your use of the techniques—just wondering how'd you'd learned them."

Then Angelique's ghost gave a cry of horror.

Gilbert was at her side in an instant. "Be assured, fair maid, 'tis only us, who are your friends."

"But who is *he*?" Angelique gasped.

Frisson followed her glance and said quietly, "We came accompanied, gentles."

"Aye," Angelique said. "Who is yonder old coil?"

"Old coil!" a voice behind me cried. "I'll have you know, lady, that I am scarcely into the middle of my years."

I turned slowly. "That's right. It's just that a lot of those years passed while you were in a dark dungeon. That aged you a bit." Then, to Angelique, "Milady, may I present to you a former star of Suettay's administration, fallen upon evil days— the Rat Raiser."

"A henchman of Suettay's?" she cried. "How came he to accompany you?"

"Why, by seizing hold of the wizard's hand, when he bethought him 'twas that of one of his comrades," the Rat Raiser cackled.

I turned to Frisson. "I thought it was you holding my left hand."

"Nay," the vagabond said, "I did seize the squire's fist."

I turned back to the Rat Raiser with a face like an iceberg. "You definitely were not invited."

The bureaucrat glared up at me with vindictive malice. "You

would have gone off and left me no better than you had found me, would you not?"

I cocked my head to the side, considering. "Maybe not, if you had asked. But of course, if you were going to continue working for Suettay . . ."

"Wherefore should I do that?" The Rat Raiser stared, appalled.

"To try to get back into her good graces."

"Wherefore? So that she might turn me out again? Faugh!" The Rat Raiser glared at the unconscious queen, gloating. "Let her look to her own!"

"She cannot look to anything!" Frisson stared, frightened at his own accomplishment. "She is dead!"

"I fear so small a stroke as steel through the chest will not kill so puissant a witch," the Rat Raiser said bitterly. "We should have some few minutes ere she wakes—but waken she shall."

Frisson backed away from Suettay, trembling.

"Would she would not," the Rat Raiser said, lips tight. "Nay, if I find any way to injure her at no risk to myself, I shall do it!"

"Even if it means repenting your sins and adhering to God?"

The cell was very quiet as the two of us stared at each other across a gulf of tension.

"Aye," the Rat Raiser breathed. "Even that."

"Even if it means devoting yourself to the good of your fellow man? Becoming the servant of the poor and weak?"

The silence was even longer this time, but I saw the Rat Raiser's countenance begin to lighten, eyes widening at a new concept. "Aye, even that," he breathed. " 'Twould hurt the queen grievously, would it not? So that is the meaning of the 'coals of fire upon his head'!"

"I can think of better motives for taking up a life of goodness," I said, "but I'll take what I can get. Who knows? Maybe it'll grow on you, after a while."

"You do not mean he shall accompany us!" Gilbert protested. Angelique touched his arm and said, "Aye, he must. Ask me not why, but I feel the rightness of it."

Gilbert opened his mouth to protest further, but saw her face and fell silent.

"Shall I swear?" the Rat Raiser demanded.

"What good would that do? If you're secretly holding fast to a life of evil, you'll break an oath without even thinking. No,

I can feel the 'rightness' Angelique is speaking of. I'll take a chance on you, Rat Raiser."

The bureaucrat cracked a smile. "I thank you, Wizard. You shall not regret it."

"I hope not—because if I do, you will, too." I gazed into his yellowed eyes a moment longer, then turned back to my friends. "Okay, time to leave, before the posse arrives."

"But who can know? . . ."

"Suettay's second-in-command. I'll bet she had six kinds of magic alarms rigged to our cell. When they find us gone, they're bound to try here. No, don't try to kill her by magic— you'll just trigger some kind of ectoplasmic guardian that will be *really* rough to handle."

" 'Tis even as he says," Angelique quavered. "I ken not what they may be, but I sense some dark and lingering presence that awaits any threat to her body."

"But I slew her!" Frisson cried.

"Nothing fatal, I'm afraid," I sighed, "which is why the guardian didn't respond. She doesn't keep her heart within her chest. Don't let it worry you, Frisson—you'll get another chance. Remember, the idea right now is to escape—we'll figure out a way to kill her some other day."

The poet looked crestfallen, but he squared his shoulders— and his chin.

"Okay," I said, "everybody hold hands, now." I took the Rat Raiser's paw myself—after all, I already had once, hadn't I? Knowingly or not. Everybody else linked up on my right hand. "Here we go, folks! Frisson, the parchment, please?"

The poet held up the sheet of foolscap, and I read it, chanting,

> "Alas, foul witch, you do us wrong
> To chain us so unjustly,
> Where folk have suffered oh, so long,
> Amusing your foul cruelty.
> Green grass is my delight,
> Blue skies are all my joy!
> I yearn for freedom with all my heart,
> In a place of great security!"

The door was opening, and soldiers were bursting into the torture chamber, just as it faded and sank into the void.

CHAPTER 16

There was no world and no time, and no sight but light. There were colors swirling about me, but mostly what there was, was Angelique.

I wasn't alone in the mist this time. I was a separate identity, but I was also integrated with Angelique. Somehow, her soul was interleaved with mine, touching me far more intimately than any embrace of bodies could achieve, in contact with me at every point, and the thrill of her touch was ecstasy. I couldn't see her, but I could perceive her, perceive the memories of horror, the aftershocks of agony, but all of it was muted now, numbed and faded, far less important than her joy at having found a man who loved her deeply.

Because I couldn't hide that from her, now—our souls were open to each other. The only way I could have hidden my feelings was to have locked her out entirely, and to do that I would have had to become catatonic, completely cutting off perception of everything but myself.

But I didn't *want* to hide my feelings, somehow.

Maybe it was because she couldn't hide anything from me, either, and I could perceive her love for me, ardent and deep. I realized that the spell had only made her see my good qualities before—but now she saw all my faults, too—the temper, the mulishness, the hypocrisy, the sprees, the sordid little affairs, the chip on my shoulder. But my virtues were so important to her, so much of what she needed and admired, so much like her own ideas of what was good and right, that my harshness and abrasiveness seemed unimportant to her. She knew them for the front, the shield, that they were, and knew also that they didn't really matter—but that what they protected, did.

As for me, I was a total goner. I'd been able to see beneath the bruises and see in her glowing ghost that her face and body were beautiful, the most beautiful I had ever seen—but I began to realize now that her beauty was only partly physical, that what raised her above every other woman I'd ever known was the sweetness and steadfastness of her soul. Her spirit was far more beautiful than her body could ever have been, than any woman's body could ever have been.

My own lack of purity saddened but did not repel her. I could feel, through the beating of her energy field against mine, her urge to heal my soul of the rifts made by the women who had hurt me, the men who had ground at me until I had learned to strike back. Her touch, if the contact of spirit with spirit can be called that, was cool and soothing, then heating, inflaming. It crossed my mind that this beat sex all hollow, until I realized that this *was* sex, in the ultimate—or rather, that this intimacy was what we poor, fumbling men of clay are trying to achieve, through the use of our physical extensions.

That's when I really began to believe in the soul—and with it, I began to suspect that there might be an afterlife.

Then, suddenly, there was a rude pain—or no, not a pain, really, but a jolting shock that made Angelique cry out soundlessly and made me grapple her to me more tightly, trying to surround her, to shield her, anger kindling against the being who had disrupted our idyll, defaced our Eden. But the anger did no good; a stern voice was echoing all about us, commanding,

> "Maiden, leave that body!
> Depart, and leave him breath!
> Separate, if you do love!
> Would you make him yearn for death?"

With a soundless cry, Angelique disengaged herself from me, breaking apart at the horror of the thought. Raging with anger, I surged up, snapping to alertness, body in fighting stance, eyes open . . .

I saw Frisson's face, staring right into mine not six inches away, with a grimness that I hadn't even suspected he had in him.

Then the room spun, and so did I, with a dizzy spell unlike

anything I'd ever had before. A hand caught me, a hard arm braced me, and as the stars faded from my vision, I saw that Frisson and Gilbert had propped me up between them.

"What ... what happened?" I croaked.

"You did blend your soul with Angelique's ghost," Frisson explained. "In our journey through that realm that is and is not, from one place to another, your soul loosed itself from your body, as it ever does, and clasped Angelique's soul, as your hand did hers—for that was the only way in which you could carry her from one place to another."

"Thank Heaven for small duties," I breathed, "and Heaven it was!"

"Only a small taste of Heaven, if what I suspect of that state of bliss has any truth in it."

"You mean it gets *better*?" I shuddered in anticipation of unguessable ecstasy. "I'd be glad to spend a whole lifetime being good, if it got me into that state again after I die! In fact, now that I think of it, why bother waiting?"

"There, maiden, is the peril in which you have placed his soul," Frisson said severely.

Angelique lowered her gaze, abashed.

"For shame, maiden!" the poet went on. "Moments more, and you would have made him yearn for death before his time—and the fruit of that yearning is suicide, which would have reft him from you for eternity! You have tempted him into ending his life before his worldly tasks were done—and how many would have suffered because of the work he did not do? How many would have perished because he was not there to save them?"

"Hey, that's low and dirty!" I stood up straight, glaring at him. "Emotional extortion!"

"A new term, but perhaps an apt one," Frisson acknowledged. "Yet the words I've said are true. Bear this in mind—if she did tempt you to take your own life, that would be a great sin upon her soul. How then could you be joined after death?"

"Well ... maybe not in Heaven, but—"

"There is no joining in any other realm." Frisson chopped his hand sideways, in total denial. "Each suffers alone in Hell; there is no companionship of any kind. The greatest torture there is the total absence of God, and of even the small reminders of his presence that are other souls."

Now, that kind of stubbornness always gets me angry. "How would *you* know?" I demanded.

"Why, how think you I would?" For the first time, Frisson showed a flash of anger. Only a flash; it was gone in melancholy a moment later as he said, brooding, "I have sought early death more than once, Wizard Saul. A maiden whom I loved with ardent passion spurned me, and in the misery of love unrequited, I yearned for death so greatly that I tied a noose about my neck and hanged myself from a tree. I live to speak only because a wandering monk happened by and cut me down ere I had quite strangled. He spake with me long and earnestly, showing me that lovers' despair is like any other despair, and to give up hope of love is to cease to strive for the touching of souls—which is to say, to cease in striving for Heaven." He turned to me alone. "I have great cause to be thankful to you, Wizard Saul, even though death by hunger would have satisfied my hunger for death—thankful because, in staying alive, I have come to know friendship and the caring of those for whom I care. Though it is not love, it is enough to live for, and to give me hope of greater worth."

"Why . . . uh . . . thanks, Frisson." I felt outraged and humbled all at once. "I'm glad I did some good. I mean, it would have been ridiculous for a nice guy like you to let himself die, just because he didn't think anybody could ever like him!"

"Yet so would I still believe, had you not taught me how to shift this curse of poetry, by the gift of writing."

"Then you've just paid me back." I sighed. "Well, if it's too soon for the real thing, let's get back to trying to make Heaven on Earth, shall we? Or at least to get rid of Hell." I looked around me, regretfully shouldering the burden of life again.

Sunlight beamed down upon us from some high window, showing us a pool of thick dust over rock. I looked around and saw a large room, a hundred feet across, ceiling just barely visible in the shadows. An old, faded tapestry hung on one wall, showing a maiden in Norse garb gathering golden apples from a tree. There were only a few trestle tables and benches over by the huge, cold black fireplace—but there was nonetheless a feeling of peace to the place, even of coziness. Over at the bottom of the stair was a dark archway, with more steps going downward—but strangely, it didn't seem threatening.

" 'Tis a castle long vacant," Gilbert said. "Praise Heaven! We are free!"

"Be not too quick with your thanks," the Rat Raiser said, but even he was having trouble restraining a smile. "I know this place; 'tis a castle taken from Lord Brace, who could not pay the fullness of his taxes. The queen hath said she will someday set a court here, for we are in her capital of Todenburg."

"The queen take up residence?" Frisson looked about him, wide-eyed and smiling. "Nay, how could she? For the peace of this house doth fill my soul, and the traces of laughter and kindness that emanate from its walls do exalt my spirit!"

"Even so," the Rat Raiser said sourly. " 'Twill be easy enough to desecrate, look you—but until she does that, she cannot bring herself to reside here for any length of time. Therefore has this castle stood thus abandoned these ten years. I came with a troop of clerks to list all goods within, then remove them—and I was sorely tempted to cease my sinning." His face twisted. "As I am now." He turned squarely to me. "What you would do, I advise you, do quickly, for we are still in Todenburg, not a mile from the queen's stronghold, and she will surely be working divination, even now, to detect our presence!"

I looked up in surprise. "That's right, she will, won't she? Quick! Everybody down to the dungeons!" I turned away toward the dark doorway at the foot of the stairs.

The Rat Raiser started, astonished, and Angelique gasped. "Wherefore the dungeons?"

"Do not ask, milady," Frisson answered. "He knows what he is about—and there is small time to explain." He set off after me.

"Belike we would not comprehend, even if he did lay it all before us." Gilbert offered his arm. "Come! Have faith in the Wizard Saul."

Reluctantly, Angelique came with him, though it was an open question whether her hand was *on* his arm, or in it. They were last in line; the Rat Raiser was scurrying ahead of us.

Fortunately, there were torch butts in the sconces, and Frisson turned out to be carrying flint and steel.

"Wherefore do you not make light with a spell again?" the Rat Raiser fairly howled. "Quickly! The queen will be upon us!"

"That's why I don't want to use magic," I said evenly. "It'd be like a flame in the night, showing her where we are. Besides, the wood's old and dry. See?" I held up a lighted torch. "Thanks, Frisson."

"Oh, 'tis my delight." The poet rose and stamped out his pile of tinder. "May we go, Wizard?"

202   Christopher Stasheff

"Right this way." I led down the curving steps. I stayed close to the wall; there wasn't any guard rail.

Angelique looked about, frowning, as we came out into the middle of a huge underground chamber. "Even here, there is peace, and no aura of misery."

"What would you expect?" The Rat Raiser spat. "Lord Brace kept no prisoners, nor did any of his forebears, and I doubt he even thought of torture! That is why there are no cells!"

"But there is water." I frowned, listening.

My companions quieted, and heard the sound of dripping.

"Yon." Gilbert pointed toward an archway.

"Just fine." I headed for the portal.

"Hold, Wizard!" the Rat Raiser rasped. "That way leads to a vault 'neath the courtyard!"

"Even better for my purposes." I looked back over my shoulder. "Come on! Believe me, it's important!"

My friends exchanged baffled glances. Then Frisson shrugged and turned away. "We have followed him thus far; why not farther?"

"Is there peril yon?" Gilbert asked the Rat Raiser.

"None to speak of." The bureaucrat frowned. "Only rats, who will do my bidding. Yet wherefore would he wish a parade ground over him, not a castle?"

"We shall learn, I doubt not." The squire turned toward the archway. "Milady, will you walk?"

"Willingly, good sir."

The Rat Raiser shrugged and followed us.

As they came up to the torchlight, they found me standing by a large puddle, fed by a drip near the wall. The drops had worn a little channel to the center of the vault and formed a small pool. But I wasn't looking at the water; I was frowning around. "Wood . . . wood . . ." My eye lit on Frisson. "You're wearing wooden shoes!"

Frisson looked down at his feet. "Sabots, we call them."

"Then let's try a little sabot-age! Lend me a foot, will you?"

The poet stared at me as if I were mad, but he passed over his shoe.

"Okay, everybody grab hold." I knelt and poked the toe of the shoe in the pool underneath the drip from the ceiling.

Gilbert looked at Angelique, then at Frisson. The poet shrugged and knelt, hooking a finger into the sabot. The ghost and the squire sighed, knelt, and took hold. Grumbling, the Rat Raiser knelt at my left and touched the shoe.

"And now?" Gilbert asked.

"Ground the torch," I grated.

"We must not be without light!" Angelique cried.

"Have to. Be brave, folks—it's vital. No, don't drown it! We'll need it later. Just grind it out."

Gilbert looked up, startled, the torch poised over the pool. Then he shrugged and jammed the flame against the stone.

It was totally dark, except for the glow from Angelique. Personally, I couldn't have found a more lovely light, but the darkness bothered her—reminiscent of the grave, no doubt; but it had to be. She was brave, though, and only gave a half sob, then was silent.

I reached out to push my hand into an overlap with hers. Her touch was cold, very cold, but she seemed to gain reassurance from mine.

"What do we do now?" Gilbert asked.

"Now we wait," I answered. "Get comfortable, folks. This could take a while."

They waited. Time passed even more slowly than the drips from the ceiling.

Claws clicked on stone, and something furry brushed my calf. Angelique cried out.

The Rat Raiser's voice crooned, "Peace, little one. We shall not disturb thy silence long."

The chamber was silent for a moment. Then the claws sounded again, fading away.

"Be of good heart," the bureaucrat's voice advised us. "They shall not trouble you."

"Thanks," I breathed. "Kind of glad you came along for the ride."

"We are ever pleased to be of service," the Rat Raiser said dryly.

A sudden chill touched my spine, and I felt a strange sort of tingling along my scalp. Frisson's head snapped up, eyes widening.

"Hist!" the Rat Raiser rasped. "She comes!"

Interesting that he could feel it, too.

"Just hang on," I said, voice low and calm. "As long as you keep touching the shoe, we'll be all right."

Angelique was trembling, and white showed all around Gilbert's irises.

Then the feeling of "presence" was gone, abruptly, totally.

I relaxed with a sigh. "Okay, folks. It's over—and she won't be back." I stared straight ahead, murmuring,

> "Suns that set may rise in glare—
> So if we lose this torch's light,
> We won't be in perpetual night.
> Our brand once more will flare!"

The torch burst into flame again.

"How can you be certain?" the Rat Raiser demanded.

"Because I jammed her radar." I straightened up, holding the shoe out to Frisson. "She couldn't see us, because it was dark—so she had to go by feel. She could tell we were here—but she was going by clues, indirect evidence. She knew we were under earth, under stone, and touching wood which was touching water."

"A coffin!" Frisson cried.

"You're quick, mate. Yes, she figured I had somehow transported us all into our graves."

"Then she shall not trouble us further!" Angelique cried. "She will think us dead!" Then she remembered her own state and blushed, which is no mean feat for a ghost.

Gallantly, I affected not to notice—I only nodded.

But the Rat Raiser cautioned us, "She will nonetheless seek us now and again, in case she might have guessed wrongly. Yet, all in all, she will cease to concern herself with us."

"It gives us some time, anyway," I said.

Slowly, the poet took the wooden shoe and put it back on. "I will ne'er question you, Wizard, after the manner in which you freed us."

"Uh, thanks, I guess." I didn't feel entirely comfortable with such faith.

"Praise Heaven she is beguiled!" Frisson sighed, leaning back to look up at the ceiling. "Ought we not to fly, Wizard? You have bought us time by your subterfuge, but it is not by any means the eternity which the queen thinks it to be. We cannot stay in any one place, or Suettay will find us again."

"No, we don't want that," I mused. "I want to find her, instead—but only after I've gathered enough force to restore Angelique to her body, then free that body."

Gilbert glanced at me, troubled. "Beware covetousness!"

I shrugged. "Look at it this way—if I can bring her back to life, I can ask her to marry me."

"True," Gilbert allowed, and looked much more comfortable—but Angelique was staring at me, huge-eyed.

"Just ask," I hastened to reassure her. "Nobody's going to force you to say yes."

That brought her out of it. "Wherefore would I need force!" Her insubstantial hand brushed through mine.

"Beware the death wish!" Frisson scolded.

"Aye, and beware the queen," the Rat Raiser said sarcastically. "To free the maiden's body, you must first slay Her Majesty."

I shrugged. "Okay by me."

"Nay, Saul!" Angelique cried. "Must you afright me so? To wish to murder another is to imperil your immortal soul!"

"Not in this instance," Frisson demurred.

I nodded. "Wishing to kill a woman who is corrupting a whole kingdom isn't a sin. In fact, if I were able to do it, the amount of good I'd achieve would balance out the evil of the murder."

Somehow, when I put it that way, it didn't sound hypocritical. Maybe it was because it was me who was saying it.

Gilbert, of course, looked very happy about the whole thing. The Rat Raiser, though, just stared at me as if I were insane.

"However," I said, "on a more practical level, how could I find enough force to go up against the queen?"

"A telling point," Frisson said, relieved. "We were best to use this time the wizard has bought us to find a deep hole in which to hide."

"Or a vast enough space in which to run." The Rat Raiser looked relieved, too.

"Aye," Gilbert agreed. "Where shall we go to escape her wrath, Wizard?"

"Nice question." I pursed my lips. "Anybody have an idea?"

They were all silent, looking at one another in alarm. If the wizard had no idea where to hide, how could any of them know?

Light glinted off a thread of silk. Looking up, I saw a spider, stretching a fan between two layers of the barrel vault.

The Rat Raiser followed my gaze. He saw, and his eyes glinted. "There is a legend, Wizard—one told by prisoners, who know no other life but rats and spiders . . ."

"Aye," Frisson said, with the ring of one who knew the subject, "a tale told of a King of Spiders, who dwells in a land no mortal can discover."

I felt a sudden prickling up the spine and across the scalp, very much like the one Suettay's surveillance had just given me.

Angelique shuddered. "What a loathsome thought! To dwell with a vasty spider!"

Frisson grinned. "Nay, milady. He is not himself a spider, but a man, though one in a weird."

"As I am not a rat," the Rat Raiser grunted, and glared at me as if to contradict him.

I didn't answer, because the feeling was stronger than ever, and the spider was one of those big round-as-a-quarter jobs. Who was watching me now?

"And are we, then, to seek him, this Spider King, and walk into his weird, never to return?" Angelique demanded.

The dungeon was silent. Nobody answered her—but they all turned to me, and the look on my face must have been answer enough.

Angelique's eyes began to grow wide and frightened. "You cannot truly think it!"

"Why not?" I shrugged. "We're in the dungeon already; we can't go much lower."

"But you can! Are we to step into the underworld, then?"

"Nay," Gilbert said slowly, "for therein dwell Suettay's masters. Yet I, too, have heard of this Spider King, and his kingdom is a realm apart, neither underworld nor afterworld."

I recognized an allusion to an alternate universe. I frowned. "You're talking about going through another dimension to gain access there. How do we do that?"

They were quiet again. Then Gilbert said, with deference, " 'Tis you are the wizard. If you cannot say how to come to this Spider King, which one of us can?"

"But I've never heard of him before!"

"You had not heard of Suettay, either," Angelique reminded me, "yet you countered her."

I glanced at her in annoyance. "When did you switch to pushing for this travelogue? All right, I suppose I could work up a long-distance projection spell using this Spider King as the focus . . ."

Frisson took on a faraway look.

"Write it down," I said quickly.

The poet sighed, coming back down to earth. "If I must—

yet 'tis such labor, to carve words with a pen when they are so easily spoken aloud."

"Yeah, but it takes us so long to clean up the mess afterward!"

"As you say," Frisson said, with rue. "Yet we cannot simply spell ourselves a long way to this enchanted realm, Wizard."

"Aye," the Rat Raiser agreed. "The Spider King's realm is said to be everywhere, but nowhere."

"Overlaid on ours like an egg on a flapjack." I nodded. "That's a description of an alternate universe if I've ever heard one!"

Gilbert frowned. "Then how can we come there, Wizard, if 'tis all around us, yet beyond our ken?"

"Through another dimension," I explained. "No, don't ask me what a dimension is—you already know. Length, breadth, and depth—those are the three dimensions, and they're all at right angles to one another."

The squire frowned. "But there is no other!"

"Yes there is, though we can't perceive it—and not just one, but many. How we go through the fifth dimension in order to come back to the third, though, is a problem I haven't tackled before."

"Then do," the Rat Raiser urged.

I pursed my lips. "Other dimension or not, we won't get there by standing still. We have to start walking somewhere."

Gilbert, Angelique, and Frisson glanced around us, perplexed, but the Rat Raiser said slowly, "There do be sewers underlying all this town—huge old drains, small tunnels, left to us from the empire great Reme spread throughout this middle earth."

I nodded. "That'll do. Do you know your way around them?"

"No," the Rat Raiser said, "yet I have friends who do." He made a peculiar kind of squeaking noise, and Angelique let out a very funny, throaty noise, like the sound of a scream being stifled. We men stiffened, hackles rising, as a troop of huge gray rats scampered into the pool of torchlight, coats filthy, fangs gleaming.

The Rat Raiser knelt, holding out a hand and crooning. The rats came up to him, nuzzling his fingers. "Nay, I've no food for you now, little friends," he said with regret, "but there shall be feasting, if you can bring us where we wish to go. Lead us down below ground, yet through tunnels high enough for us to walk without stooping. Lead us down, and bid all like you withdraw, to let us pass."

Angelique shuddered.

"Not the most salubrious notion in the world," I agreed, "but it's better than staying here and waiting for Suettay to catch us, isn't it?"

Angelique swallowed and nodded. Gilbert murmured, "Be brave, lass. However long it may be, we shall pass through; it shall end."

"All right, we're ready now," I said to the Rat Raiser, softly.

"Off, little ones!" the bureaucrat commanded with a wave of his hand. He rose as the rats scampered away. "Follow," he said over his shoulder, and stepped off after his pets.

"Ready?" I asked. "Well, we're going, anyway." And I followed the Rat Raiser.

Off we went into the gloom, the poet and squire bunched protectively around the lady's ghost, leading onward and downward, following the wizard—me—who was mumbling some very strange verses indeed as we descended into the lower depths.

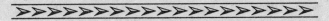

CHAPTER 17

I wasn't entirely sure where the cave in the dungeon wall had come from—I could have sworn it hadn't been there when we had come down—but I wasn't about to object. If the rats knew where it was, it had to be real—at least, assuming the rats themselves were real; which made me begin to wonder about the Rat Raiser.

While I was wondering, we were going downhill; I couldn't help but think of Hellmouth in the old mystery plays, and wonder if this was its throat. It was certainly dark enough—and growing warmer; and the aromas rising were anything but life-giving. Trickles of water glittered in the torchlight here and there, becoming broader as we descended deeper.

Time to start the active part. I took a deep breath—and regretted it—and began to recite:

> "Where Alph, the sacred river ran
> Through caverns measureless to man
> Down to a sunless sea.
>
> Turn, to where there's naught but rest!
> Turn, to find the spider's nest!
> Through all the worlds his web he spins,
> Catching prey by hidden sins!
> Turn, to pierce his secret ring!
> Turn, to find the Spider King!"

We moved down, our pool of torchlight coming with us, until water glistened below, black water, and the Rat Raiser whispered, "We have come into the sewers. Carefully, now, children—the water is deep, and the way is narrow."

He turned to the left, following his pets. I saw a spark off to the side and frowned, glancing at it; then I glanced again. There were two sparks, a pair, and, as I watched, another pair appeared, and another.

"We are regarded," Gilbert said, indicating a bank of little jewel-eyes glowing at the edge of our torchlight.

Angelique gave a strangled gasp, but the Rat Raiser crooned, "Gently, children, gently. 'Tis only the small ones who dwell here—and, no matter what you think of them, they will not hurt you while I am here."

It was a gentle reminder of who held the power at the moment, and I didn't trust it. I thought up a protecting verse and held it ready on my tongue. I also glanced at Angelique, to make sure she was okay—then glanced again.

She was solid!

Apparently, her incorporeality was right in phase with whatever nonexistent realm of nonreality we were in.

My lord, that woman was beautiful! None of the bruises or wounds showed on her ghost—only a hollowness of the cheek, a darkness around the eye, that spoke of the harrowing experience she had been through. Even that enhanced her beauty, rather than diminished it—or was I so much the captive of my own binding spell, so much in love with her, that nothing could lessen her beauty in my eyes?

I shook off the notion with a shudder and turned away. Women were for enjoying, nothing more—and since you couldn't just enjoy them without hurting their hearts, I was determined not to notice them. Never mind that Angelique already knew my true feelings for her—that didn't mean I had to let them show. I resolutely turned my back and followed the Rat Raiser into the unknown—and surely that couldn't have been a small, very self-satisfied smile I had glimpsed on her lips as I had turned away, could it?

We paced the narrow path, scraping the stone wall on our left, with a host of bright beady eyes watching us. To our right, torchlight reflected off thickened, tainted water. The aroma had become almost unbearable; we breathed through our mouths, but I could have sworn I was tasting the air.

The surface heaved, and a huge clawed hand broke through with a long, scaly, tooth-filled snout behind it. The hand groped toward us, and the Rat Raiser shrank back with a

squeal that had the ring of command—but also of fright; and
his pets answered him with a squealing and skittering as they
disappeared into the darkness.

But I was already chanting,

> "Room for our shadows on the path—
> Let us pass!
> To the left and right, stay clear!
> Or we shall call the Buyer of the Blade—
> Be afraid!
> Call upon the great god Tyr!"

The questing talons paused, wavered, then withdrew, slowly
sinking out of sight.

"I thank you, Wizard." The Rat Raiser sighed. "I had not
known such a monstrous being might rise from this stew."

"Always pays to be ready." I didn't tell him what I'd been
ready for. "Frisson, do you think you could hold that verse
ready to chant? And no improvements, mind you! I have another spell to recite."

"Aye, Master Saul," the poet said grudgingly. "But be mindful, I am no wizard."

"Don't worry, I am." Okay, so it was a little white lie—but
they needed the reassurance, just then. "I'll join in and chant
with you, as soon as I can drop the other verse. But my reac-
tion time will be slow, and I think yours will be fast."

"Be sure of it," Gilbert muttered.

"I shall." The poet sighed.

"Well enough." The Rat Raiser pulled himself together and
stepped forth, making little squeaking noises interspersed with
words. "Where have you gone, sweetings? Nay, come back,
little friends—the monster has fled, and we have need of your
guidance."

Slowly, a couple of huge, ragged rats appeared at the edge
of the torchlight.

The Rat Raiser nodded with satisfaction. "Lead on,
then—we shall follow."

We did—not that we had much choice.

I watched the Rat Raiser's back, gauging him. The man
hadn't been quite the abject coward I had expected him to
be—but then, he couldn't have been short on nerve, to have
dared the climb within Suettay's organization. Sense, maybe,
but not nerve.

I started reciting my navigation spell again, with a touch of
the frantic. At the end, I repeated, "Turn, turn, turn!" with perhaps excessive force.

Excessive, because the Rat Raiser was just warning us,
"Slowly, now, and warily—for this ledge was made only for
guardsmen from the castle, who knew its ways. Strongholds
have been taken by parties raiding through the sewers, look
you, and—"

He broke off with a gasp—because the water was dwind-
ling, showing blank stone to either side.

"Keep walking," I grated, and went back to mumbling my
verse.

The Rat Raiser stumbled as the walkway disappeared, and
he cried out. His rats echoed him, squealing with horror and
fleeing away; but the sludge had dwindled to a mere trickle,
and I demanded, "Go on!"

"Nay, I am no longer master here," the Rat Raiser panted,
white showing all around his eyes. " 'Tis you must lead now."

I shoved past him with a mutter of impatience. The Rat
Raiser fell in behind me, staring incredulously at the stone underfoot. It was completely dry now, but curved, in the middle
as much as at the sides. "We are no longer in the sewers!"

"Praise Heaven!" Angelique sighed. "I may breathe again!"

"Yet where are we, then?" Gilbert demanded.

"In the wizard's realm," Frisson answered. "Be patient, my
friends, and trust our guide; surely he knows where he goes!"

"Then he must know where we are." The squire had to shift
his gait as the tunnel curved to our right. "Ho, Wizard! What
place is this?"

"A torus." My voice sounded remote even to me, uncon-
cerned with this mundane reality; but the roof rolled over us,
and the tunnel's curve had become permanent. We were walking inside a granite doughnut.

Yet not granite either, for it was seamless, and slightly resilient underfoot. What it was, I couldn't have said. My friends
muttered behind me, afraid of the unknown—but they followed.

I wasn't really perceiving my surroundings all that well—I
was busy muttering, concentrating on what the next develop-
ment should be, so intent on where I was going that I wasn't
really aware of where I was.

Shadows loomed about us, just outside the circle of torchlight. Then the shadows parted ahead, and I saw two tubes,

branching in a fork. I bore to the left with complete assurance, not even thinking about it—almost as if I hadn't even noticed the split—and my companions followed me, mute with astonishment.

After a few minutes, the way branched again, then again.

"Are you sure of your course?" the Rat Raiser husked, but I only nodded once briefly and paced ahead, mumbling.

Then, suddenly, the tunnel ended. We halted, facing a blank, curving wall. My companions muttered with overtones of fear, but I just frowned at the wall, shaking my head, irritated, and turned back, retracing my steps. My companions made way for me, then hurried to fall in behind again—but Gilbert demanded, "Wizard, where are we?"

"In a maze," I answered.

They fell silent again, and I could almost feel their dread. I didn't want to—I had enough of my own. My skin was trying to raise hair where there wasn't any.

"Do you know the way?" the Rat Raiser whispered.

I came to a halt, head cocked at a thought. Slowly, I turned back to the Rat Raiser. "Maybe *you* should take the lead again, come to think of it. Rats are very good at running mazes."

"I am not a rat!" the ex-bureaucrat stammered. "And none of my little friends are here!"

I just gazed at him with an abstracted frown, then sighed and turned away. "Guess it's up to me, all right. Come on, folks."

They did.

The tunnel branched, and I chose a way. It branched again, and I took the arm that curved back the way we'd come. Another fork, and I turned to my right, but muttered to the Rat Raiser, "Try and call your pets, will you?"

The Rat Raiser sighed and let out a series of squeaks.

We waited.

Finally, the Rat Raiser shook his head. "There are none near us, Wizard. Whatever place this may be that you have taken us to, it has no rats."

Gilbert frowned. "What manner of human place is this, that it has none?"

My attention caught on the word "human"; it sent prickles down my spine. "Good question. Should we maybe ask, instead—what *does* live here?"

My friends exchanged quick, apprehensive glances.

"Saul," Angelique said, "if you can lead us through this maze, I pray you, do so quickly!"

"You can, can you not?" Gilbert asked with a worried frown.

"Given enough time, yes," I said slowly. "I was always pretty good at solving mazes when I was a kid, sick in bed. But I think we may need faster action than that, right now."

"Indeed!" Gilbert agreed. "Bring us out, Wizard!"

"Patience, friend," Frisson counseled. "He is only human, after all, as lost as any among us."

"We could wander here till we die of thirst!" the Rat Raiser cried, appalled.

"Oh, come on!" I protested. "I can always conjure up a good meal, you know."

The tunnel was silent.

Then Frisson said, delicately, "That is not entirely reassuring, Wizard Saul."

"What, because you think it's really going to take that long?" I shrugged. "Look—you knew this wasn't a morning's jaunt. Even without the maze, this could be a long journey."

They looked at one another, and I could feel the apprehension growing. Finally I capitulated. "All right, all right! I'll see if I can't summon a guide who can take us out of this mess!"

"What manner of spirit would that be?" Gilbert still looked wary.

"One good at figuring out mazes, of course." I frowned. "Which means one who could understand how a straight, direct path could become twisted and convoluted."

"Why, I am able to ken that," the Rat Raiser said.

"Yes, you would be, wouldn't you? Any good bureaucrat would. But I had in mind the one who's good at *coping* with bureaucrats—one who knows how to weave in and out of the red tape, how to go around the runaround, how to keep from losing his way in a paper storm." I frowned, rubbing my chin. "Let's see . . .

> "We need a one who can discover
> The tortured track that turns and runs
> Through forest dark and hidden bower,
> Past concrete towers and Stone Age duns,
> A spirit who can comprehend
> The twists and turns it finds inside,

And so can lead us past blind ends
To where the monarch hides!"

There was a flash of light, so bright as to dazzle us all with afterimages—but a gravelly voice was calling, "What? Where? How came I here?"

In a panic, I blinked and rubbed, trying to clear my eyes before the creature I had summoned could turn on us.

Too late—it was howling, "What benighted son of a sorcerer and a witch has brought me into so bleak a place as this?"

"Guilty!" I shouted. "It's my fault, not theirs! But have the courage to wait until I can see you, you . . ."

"Then clear your eyes!" the newcomer snorted; and suddenly, I could see again.

I blinked, asking, "What kind of creature can . . . Oh."

My friends gasped with shock. The "creature" looked up from the neighborhood of my belt buckle, arms akimbo and his other two arms folded under his shoulder blades, tapping the forward-facing foot while he balanced on the backward-facing one and took aim at my shin with the third. His noseless face glowered up at me in indignation, huge saucer eyes glowing an angry yellow while he twiddled the tentacles on top of his head. Overall, he looked like a mauve cucumber whose vines had decided to turn into legs and arms and prehensile hair. He wore pointed shoes with curling toes and a wide belt loaded with every sort of tool imaginable, plus a few that I couldn't.

And he wasn't happy.

I swallowed. "Hi! I'm Saul, um, a wizard. And who are you?"

"Who did you expect?" the gravelly voice growled. Yes, its lips moved.

"Just somebody who understands the illogical well enough to get us out of here. Uh—who are you?"

"I," said the little monster, "am the Gremlin."

I stared.

"Saul," Angelique quavered, "what is a Gremlin?"

"An imaginary creature whose goal in life is making things go wrong," I told her. "If anybody can understand the kind of realm we're in, he can."

"But will he aid us?" Frisson breathed.

"Unlikely," the little monster grated. "I delight in foiling and frustrating, not aiding—especially to folk who yank me unceremoniously from my home!"

"My apologies," I said, "but there really wasn't any way I could ask you ahead of time."

The Gremlin unlimbered an arcane tool from his belt. "I'm minded to send you back in that time you speak of, to give you space to learn your manners."

"No, please! We really do need your help. We're stuck in this maze, see, and we need to get through it fast. There's a whole kingdom that needs our help."

"What's your kingdom to me, or I to it?"

"You could be its rescuer," I said, "and it's a goodly land that's being laid waste by black sorcery. Forests are being blighted—trees and animals are being twisted out of their natural forms . . ."

"How foul!" the Gremlin cried, outraged. "That is my work—though I would rather work it through machinery, and the more complicated, the better. What bastard of spirits usurps my prerogative in such fashion?"

"Her name is Suettay," I explained, "and her grandmother seized the throne three generations ago. They've been ruining the land ever since."

The Gremlin shook his fists, hopping mad—literally. "So many years? Have my tasks been usurped for so long as that? Why has no one told me of it before?"

I sensed an opening. "Because they didn't know how. I mean, even with me, it was as much accident as intention."

"But you did at least bring word!" The Gremlin stilled, scowling. "Surely I shall help you, if it will bring me a chance to annihilate this usurper! What do you wish of me?"

"Well, we're trying to get to the Spider King, see—we're hoping that maybe he—"

"The Good Bourgeois King?" The Gremlin stared. "Aye, most surely he could aid you! But how think you to come to *him*?"

"That's why we're trying to get through this maze, see. I recited a spell that should take us to the Spider King."

"A spell?" The Gremlin rounded on me, looking me up and down. "Art a sorcerer, or a warlock?"

"Neither, really—I think I'm a wizard. But I don't believe in magic, see, and the spell didn't take us right to him, so . . ."

"A wizard who works magic that he does not believe in!" the Gremlin crowed. "Why, this is too delightful! How shall I bollix work for you, mortal? By making your spells all work aright? Oh, this is priceless!"

I exhaled a shaky breath. "Surely you wouldn't do anything so perverse."

The Gremlin eyed me shrewdly. "I think you know me by repute, and too well to think there is anything too perverse for me. So you wish to come to the Spider King, eh?"

"Yeah, but my spells haven't been working, and—"

"Nay, I should think not! His realm is too closely guarded, to come at him unawares!"

"Unawares?" I looked at the tunnel about me. "You mean this whole thing is his early warning system?"

"He will know of you when you arrive, aye." The Gremlin tilted his head to the side, looking me up and down. "This much I will do for you—I will lead you back through this maze, whence you've come."

"Nay!" Angelique cried. "We must go on!"

The Gremlin looked up, surprised.

" 'Tis the salvation of the land we speak of," Gilbert explained.

"Besides," I said, "you don't know what's waiting for us back there."

"Tell me," the Gremlin coaxed.

"Oh, all right." I sighed. "An evil queen and a torture chamber, not to mention a dungeon."

"You have reason to wish to go on," the Gremlin admitted. "Yet 'tis not so simply done as that. There are greater dangers than this maze, look you."

"If you think they're bad, you should see what we left behind us."

"I have." The monster leered. "Or ones much like them. So you think, then, that you are on the road to his palace, this Spider King?"

"Well, to his kingdom, maybe."

The Gremlin shook what passed for his head, with certainty. "His kingdom runs throughout the heart of the continent between the Northern and the Middle seas; it overlies your own, like a saucer on a plate. You seek his palace, not his kingdom alone. I will take you there, for I'll need his aid against this woman who usurps my prerogatives." He grinned. "And, too, I'm minded of the mischief you will wreak in Allustria, if the Spider King lends his strength to your cause."

I didn't remember mentioning a cause—and I certainly

didn't remember mentioning Allustria. The prickling feeling moved over my shoulders and the back of my head again, as I began to feel the tendrils of a conspiracy waft around me. The worst of it was that I suspected that I might be part of the conspiracy, not just its object—but I wasn't exactly in a position to be picky. "Then you will help us?"

"And gain a chance to help confound the self-important and harsh-ruling ones? Aye, and gladly!" The Gremlin leapt to the fore. "Follow me!" He strode off into the darkness. "Do you follow close!"

I hurried after him, and the gang followed, but I don't think any of us was convinced that it was entirely a good idea.

Lead us the Gremlin did. How, I couldn't have said—but every time my sense of direction told me I should zig, the Gremlin zagged, and every time I thought we should turn left, the Gremlin turned right. Archways and corners swooped past us in dizzying array, for the little monster never faltered. How he could tell where to go, I couldn't guess, but I wasn't about to argue.

Then, finally, the tunnel opened out. I looked up, with a notion of what I might see—and I was halfway right, at least. I saw a convex wall curving up and away from me, continuing onward in a great circle. It was as if we stood in the center of a doughnut.

But what was above that doughnut was a surprise.

"Wizard," Angelique said softly, "what is that darkness all about?"

It was dead black, flat, total darkness, without the slightest hint of light. It seemed to dim everything near it.

"The void," I answered. "That's what lies outside of space and time."

"Then what," Frisson said, "is that great curve that rises above us?"

It was like a huge corkscrew, rising up over the rim of the doughnut, slanting upward into the void and out of sight.

"Yonder lies your path," the Gremlin informed him.

Angelique frowned. "Yet how are we to come to there?"

"Through yonder gate." The Gremlin pointed. On the far side of the circle, the wall curved inward, forming the mouth of another tunnel.

"If we must, we must," Gilbert growled. "Lead on."

"Even so," the monster murmured; but he had taken

scarcely one step when a huge roar sounded, a roar that shook the very walls, a roar that pained our ears and hit us with almost physical force.

"There are impediments," the Gremlin murmured.

Forth it came from the darkness of the tunnel mouth—a monster who stood upright on hooves and switched an oxtail, whose body swelled into the deep, muscular chest of a bull, merging into huge, human arms and shoulders. The mouth opened and loosed another roar; I thought, at first, that it was a lion's head. Then, looking more closely, I realized there was no muzzle, but only a great russet beard and mustache, and that the face was human, though with a huge mane of tawny hair.

But those were fangs inside that human mouth—fantastically elongated canines.

Angelique moaned and shrank back against me; I reached out a protective arm.

"Wizard," Gilbert said, "what manner of creature is that?"

"He is the Bull," the Gremlin answered, "and he is set to slay any who come herein."

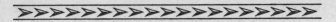

CHAPTER 18

The Bull charged, arms reaching out for easy meat.

"Scatter!" I shouted, leaping away to my left, Angelique darting with me. Gilbert dashed off to the right, and Frisson leapt out ahead, then veered around in a circle.

The Bull turned to follow him.

But the Rat Raiser popped up in front of the monster, crying, "Hold! Show me your permit!"

The Bull screeched to a halt, forgetting Frisson in its amazement at the sheer arrogance of this overweening human. Then it lowered its head, shoulders rising, and let out a bellow of tripled rage, lunging toward the bureaucrat.

The Rat Raiser turned and fled, crying, "Summon the men-at-arms!"

"Why, then, here am I!" Gilbert cried, and threw himself at the Bull's hocks in a perfect flying tackle. The monster slammed down like a tidal wave hitting shore, letting out a roar like an earthquake. I winced, and hoped there'd be enough of Gilbert left to hold a ceremony over.

One way or another, the squire had bought us some time, enough for me to search my memory.

But Frisson got in there before me:

> "Gazing down from Olympian heights,
> Zeus beheld the Phoenician maid,
> Whose face and form with beauty bright
> Awoke desire in the Jovian blade.

He changed himself into a Bull;
He mingled with her father's herd
With gentle mien, and hide all white,
His breast with ardent passion stirred
As he watched the maid; his heart was full.
Europa saw, and in delight,

Plaited a garland of blossoms while
Each graceful movement made him sigh—
Her beauteous face, her glowing smile,
Sweet curves of breast and cheek and thigh,
And thresh of limbs as she came nigh!"

Something glimmered in the center of the circle, glimmered and took form, that of a tall, voluptuous woman in a chiton, blonde hair piled high, with a face of pure innocence. She whirled and ran, revealing smooth ivory thighs.

Of course, if you looked closely, she *was* a little translucent.

Maybe transparent—the Bull saw right through her, anyway. He stampeded straight past the illusion, shaking the whole chamber with his bellow, and the Gremlin gibed, "You have mistaken quite, if you wish a female for his taste."

And, suddenly, the illusion-woman wasn't there anymore; in its place was a young and shapely heifer, slender—for a cow— and, even to my eyes, somehow alluring. She sauntered out between the humans and the Bull, who dug in his hooves and jolted to a halt, its eyes fairly bulging. The heifer turned, switching her tail in his face, ambling away from me and my companions.

Bewitched, the Bull followed.

Gathering my wits, I dashed over to Gilbert, but the squire had pulled himself together and was sitting up, shaking his head. I stopped by him with a sigh of relief. "You okay?"

Gilbert looked up with a frown. "What is 'okay'?"

"Uh—sound, in this instance."

"Aye." Gilbert caught my arm and pulled himself up. "Sound, and ready for another round. Where is our foe?"

Another wall-shaking roar answered us. We whirled and saw that the Bull had finally caught the heifer—but she had turned into a Spanish fighting Bull, head lowered and pawing the earth. The half-human Bull bellowed his bafflement and rage, and charged.

Somehow, he missed.

And, somehow, the Spanish Bull was a heifer again, scampering away with a playful moo. But the Bull, fully aroused, roared his wrath and pounded hot-hoof after her.

I saw our chance. "Now! While he's too mad to think at all!"

"Even as you say." Gilbert hurled himself forward again.

"Hey, no!" I cried, appalled; but the squire did even better than before. He landed in a crouch right in front of the Bull and, with its next step, surged upward, arms wrapped around the monster's knees, pitching upward with his full strength, slinging the Bull high and hard. The monster's bellow took on a note of bafflement; it flailed about as it flew, and Gilbert turned with it, hands still on its hooves, then slammed it down with all his might. The Bull hit the ground with an impact that shook the whole cavern, and Frisson yanked off his wooden shoe, leapt in, and swung hard. The *crack!* of wood on bone was almost as loud as the roar, and I winced, hoping the Bull wasn't dead even as I wondered if I'd have to conjure up a new shoe for Frisson.

But the Bull only sagged, pushing itself halfway up, then tilted over and fell heavily again. He lifted his head, looking about, then rolled over to his belly and got his legs under him.

"He has a hard head," Frisson noted, pulling his shoe on again.

"Yet he will recover, and soon." The Gremlin was there by me. "Quickly, Wizard! Conjure tea!"

"Tea?!" I stared, totally taken aback.

"Aye, tea and scones, with a silver service and a linen cloth! Quickly! Lose no time!"

"But what good will tea and . . ."

"Do you not hear me? I tell you, I know this Bull! High tea, and promptly, for even now he regains his senses!"

I gave up trying to make sense out of it, and recited:

"Oh, some are for the red wine, and some are for the white,
    And some for guzzling moonshine by the pale moonlight;
    But I'm for tea and crumpets, for high tea just sets me
        right!"

The air thickened; then light glittered off shiny surfaces, and a linen picnic cloth was there, with cups and saucers next to a bone-china teapot. Hot scones nestled in a linen napkin lining a silver basket; another held crumpets, with butter dish and jam pot close by.

"Maiden, pour!" the Gremlin urged.

Angelique stared, startled to be told to do something for which she'd had no training; but she turned, gamely stepping in with her upbringing as a proper hostess, and sat gracefully by the pot.

"One hand keeps the lid on," I whispered.

Angelique took the cue as if she hadn't even noticed it, pouring tea into a cup and burbling, "How pleasant the weather is! Quite cool for August, do you not think? Lemon, sir, or milk?"

The Bull looked up, staring at the service like a shipwrecked sailor sighting an island.

"Sweetening, perchance?" Angelique prompted. "One lump, or two?"

"She picked up on that awfully fast," I muttered at the Gremlin with a hint of accusation.

The little monster looked up at me with a mischievous twinkle in his eye. "There are more ways than one to put a notion into a body's head, Wizard."

"Two lumps," the Bull rumbled, pulling himself up to sit cross-legged.

Frisson and Gilbert exchanged a look of amazement, but Angelique didn't even bat an eye. She dropped two lumps of sugar into the cup with silver tongs. "Will you take milk, or lemon?"

"Milk, if you please," the Bull answered, with a good public-school accent. "And perhaps a scone?"

"Surely." Angelique presented him with a cup and saucer, then turned to take a bit of scone from the basket. "Butter?"

"Of course."

"So I had thought." Angelique spread butter, set the cake on a plate, and handed it to him, then looked up at me. "Saul?"

"Milk and sugar." I folded myself into a tailor's seat, surprised to find I was hungry. "And a scone, if you please."

"Most certainly." Angelique poured, chattering, "I think we will have an early fall, do you not? And you, Sir Bull, what fine chance brings you our way?"

The Bull frowned. "I might have asked the same."

"Then do, I prithee! And might you have a name?"

"John," the Bull said.

Of course.

Then, obligingly, "And what chance brings you *my* way?"

Slowly, Frisson and Gilbert came up and sat down. Angelique poured tea with milk and sugar for them as she answered, "We flee a wicked tyrant, who would imprison us, abuse each of us in ways as foul as she can imagine, then slay us by slow torture. And yourself?"

"I have been here as long as I may remember," the Bull answered slowly, "and that is long, maiden, very long."

"Centuries," the Gremlin breathed.

"Even so." The Bull bowed his head to the monster in acknowledgment. "I know not who sent me here—only that his voice did echo all around me as I woke, saying, 'Here you stand, and here you must remain, slaying all who seek to pass until fair Chance may send you they who seek to rise for good.' "

Angelique exchanged a glance with me. "Mayhap we are they."

"Mayhap," the Bull said slowly, trying to throttle hope. "Where do you seek to go, and why?"

"To the castle of the Spider King," Angelique answered. "We seek his aid in defeating a foul sorceress who has laid a whole land 'neath a grid of rules and clerks. Indeed, her people scarcely dare to stir out-of-doors without her say-so."

The Bull frowned. "Why should the Spider King aid you?"

"Why," Angelique said, "we have heard that he is a good man, who aids those who seek to help the poor, and yearn for justice."

"He does that, aye, does both. Yet what advantage is there for him in thus aiding you to give aid?"

"I . . . I do not know," Angelique admitted.

"Maybe we could tell, if we knew what he wants," I said slowly. "Do you know?"

"He lacks nothing," the Bull said.

I shook my head. "If that were the case, he'd either help people just for the fun of it, or he'd be getting something out of it. A sense of purpose, maybe?"

"How old is he?" Frisson said.

"Centuries," the Bull said firmly. "As long as I have been here, at the least."

"Mayhap, then," the poet offered, "he has need to justify his continued existence?"

I looked up, startled. Where had this country bumpkin taken his philosophy course?

But the Bull was nodding. "I could think that, aye. Why else does he constantly seek out human misery and invent ways to assuage it?"

"Does he so?" Frisson fastened on the words, his eyes keen.

I wondered at it, but the poet didn't seem inclined to expand upon the point, so I said, "If that's his motivation, why does he have you here to keep people out?"

"I cannot say with any surety that 'twas he who set me here," the Bull said slowly. "As to the 'why' of it, I cannot so much as conjecture."

"Not without knowing the 'who,' no," I said dryly. "Well, let's assume for the moment that we're the ones you're supposed to let through."

"Let us not!" the Bull said sternly. "And let us recall that, when this teatime is ended, we shall war again, you and I."

Inside, I went cold, but my mouth kept going. "But what if we *are* the ones you're supposed to help?"

"If you are, why, you shall defeat me, and I shall go on to the Spider King's palace with you." The Bull sounded angry, and I could imagine the anguish he was feeling at the moment of decision. "If you are not, then you shall die in the attempt."

But Frisson had fastened on the first sentence. "If you are to go with us, can you guide us? Have you been to the palace before?"

"No," the Bull said slowly, "yet I have a memory of the route. 'Tis as if I were made with it in me."

"DNA can do such wonderful things," I murmured. Then, louder, "Trust the inborn hunch—and take a gamble on us. After all, how many other groups have ever come this way?"

"Only three," the Bull admitted.

I felt another chill, trying to imagine what the last questers must have been.

"Yet they were all men," the Bull continued, "and wore the black robes of sorcery. There was a reek of evil about them, which there is not about you."

"We are a force of right," Gilbert said with total conviction.

The Bull gave him the jaundiced eye, but I said, "At least we're fighting evil . . ."

"And each of us has suffered from it," Gilbert stated.

"Well, yes," I said, shifting uncomfortably as I remembered a few of my less glorious deeds, then shifting back with apprehension as I remembered my encounter with my guardian angel. "I have to admit I'm out for my own ends, though."

The Bull's head snapped about to stare at me. "How so?"

"I'm trying to find a friend," I explained, "and after that, I'm out to get back home." But I glanced at Angelique as I said it, and suddenly found the issue much less pressing than it had been. "It just seems that I'm going to have to defeat the evil queen before I can do either."

"His gain will be the people's salvation," Gilbert said quickly.

The Bull ignored him, eyes still on me. "That is not the most noble motive for a quest."

"It's better than a lot of 'em," I answered, reddening, "and its side effects *would* benefit the people of Allustria. Couldn't very well be worse than what they've got."

"There is that," the Bull admitted. "And, mayhap, it would be less of a bore to assist you, than to guard this gate interminably. It would, at the least, be adventure."

My hopes soared. "Oh, I guarantee it wouldn't be boring!"

"Indeed it will not," the Bull admitted, "for we must pass mine enemy. Will *you* aid *me* in fighting him?"

I felt sudden interior brakes slamming on. If this monster felt the need of help confronting the next one, how horrible did *it* have to be? "Just what kind of beastie is this?"

"His name is Ussrus Major," the Bull answered, "and he is the Bear."

The tone in which he said it was enough to chill the blood, but Frisson murmured, "Saul, you are a great wizard, surely."

"Yeah, with your verses." I remembered a poem, took a deep breath, and said, "Okay. Count us in."

"I may indeed," the Bull answered, "for the Bear blocks the way to the Spider King."

Suddenly, he straightened, slapping his knees. " 'Tis done; I am with you. If I am wrong, and mayhem strikes, why, then, let it come!"

"You are noble," Angelique murmured.

"I wish escape from my prison."

"You are brave," Frisson qualified.

The Bull stared at him for a moment, then nodded. "Yet every man fears something, and this is mine, this journey. Still, I long for it, too—so let us be about it."

He rose in one single, lithe, twisting movement and set off toward his cave. We others sprang to our feet and followed. I glanced back; saw the remains of our picnic; and, with a quick, muttered verse, banished the mess. It twinkled and was gone.

The Bull wrenched open the gate, and we followed him into

the cave beyond it—with some trepidation, if truth be known. Me, I was remembering the story of Chicken Little—but the cave extended, going on and on. I realized it was another tunnel.

"What spell you used to seek out the Spider King, use now," the Bull rumbled. The Gremlin nudged me; I took a breath and started chanting, low, almost subvocally.

I had scarcely finished the first recitation when the tunnel started changing. Its roof developed a split; then, as we walked along, the split became wider and wider until the roof was gone. I began to eye the dark space beyond it nervously, especially as the walls of the tunnel began to taper down, lower and lower, until they were scarcely knee-high, and we were walking on a concave pathway.

"Now," the Gremlin said, "one might feel dangerously exposed."

"One might," I agreed, with a nervous glance at the darkness around us—then looked again. "Hey! It's getting lighter!"

"We approach his region—mine enemy." The Bull came to a halt, pointing. "Yonder lies the pit of greatest danger for me—the pit of the Bear! Mark it!"

There he came, shambling through the mist, a huge dark shape in a phosphorescent cavern, and my heart sank down to my boots. But the trail led through that huge cave, a floating pathway with no visible means of support, angling through the ghostly cavern, perhaps six feet off the floor.

"Onward," the Gremlin said, face grim. "We gain naught, if we stand to be prey."

"Why, then, pray we must," Frisson countered, and immediately chanted, loudly,

> "God of pity, God of wrath!
> Save us from the ursine path!"

I looked around in a panic, but there was no visible damage, and I let out a sigh of relief. "Please, Frisson! Write it down!"

"Even a prayer?" the poet cried, amazed.

"Anything," I snapped, "as long as it's original."

But the Bear had heard and reared up on his hind feet, forelegs upraised as if imploring, "Comrades, please! I wish only detente!"

"Keep walking," I said grimly, and we did, though our steps had slowed with dread.

"Surely we are too heavy for so fragile a path," Angelique demurred.

"Forward," I commanded, "or he'll take the hindmost."

"Can you not make our weight less?"

"Oh, all right," I grumped.

> "Afoot and hearted I take to the climbing road,
> Healthy, free,
> The world before me,
> Rising up undismayed—
> Forward the Light Brigade!"

"Volga, mother dear!" the Bear cried, "you have never had such a gift as this!" With that, he swung a huge paw with double eagle's talons at the maiden, to snag her dress. She screamed and shrank back, but the Bull roared in anger and leapt from the pathway, hooves slamming straight toward the Bear.

Ussrus stepped back just in time, and the Bull landed right in front of him, slamming a haymaker into the Bear's jaw. Its head rolled back, and its arms came up. "Comrade, please! I come in peace! A truce, I beseech you!"

"Don't trust him!" I called. "Cry no peace with the Bear who walks like a man!"

The Bull only kept his guard up, glowering.

"Bring him up, quickly!" the Gremlin hissed. "We cannot go on without him!"

The way ahead was luminescent, glowing with distant fires. I called,

> "Up, up and away!
> For he who fights and runs away,
> Will live to fight another day!"

"There is sense in that," the Bull admitted, "yet should I therefore not give him his truce?"

"No!" I bleated.

> "Horrible, hairy, human, with paws like hands in prayer,
> Making his supplications rose Adam-Zad the Bear . . .
> When he stands up as pleading, in wavering, man-brute
>   guise,
> When he veils the hate and cunning of his little swinish eyes,

When he shows as seeking quarter with paws like hands in
      prayer,
That is the time of peril—The time of the Truce of the Bear!
Over and over the story, ending as it began:
There is no truce with Adam-Zad, the Bear that walks like
      a man!"

"Betrayal!" the Bear cried. "Our plan is discovered!" His huge paw scythed toward the Bull's face, but the claws tangled in the Bull's long hair, just long enough for John to beat away the attack and counterpunch. The Bear recoiled, then came back roaring, with scythe-claws flailing. "Transform the imperialist war into civil war!"

Frisson pressed a piece of paper into my hand. I read it without thinking.

> "Raise up our tiring friend!
> That we might rise away with him,
> Up toward our chosen end,
> Clambering dire to meet the arachnid sire
> Spiraling higher in a widening gyre!"

The Bull shot up into the air as if a huge hand had grabbed him, then dropped back onto the pathway—but very lightly, as if that same invisible hand was setting him down with the greatest of care. I began to wonder about Frisson's verse of prayer.

The Bear recovered, its shoulders hunkering down, an ugly gleam coming into its eyes. "Do not set yourself above us! For surely, all history is that of class conflict!"

"The conflict part, I can believe," I said to the Gremlin, "but he totally lacks class."

"Keep walking, Wizard," the monster answered nervously.

"I sense an uprising," Gilbert muttered.

The pathway shuddered under our feet, then pulled itself loose from the ground and drifted upward, curving into a widening spiral that wound up out of sight.

The Bear rose up, both forepaws hammering at the pathway, claws flashing like icicles. "Let us restructure the economy!" He hooked huge talons into the spiral and pulled downward.

The path jolted, and my companions cried out, fighting for balance. Frisson and I fell, but Angelique and Gilbert managed to keep their feet. The Bear dragged the pathway down, roaring, "Scorch the earth and burn the city! Let not a scrap remain to strength the enemy!"

"Too much anachronism is too much," I growled.

"Oh, hear you not the singing of the bugle, wild and free?
  And soon you'll know the ringing of the rifle, from the
      tree!
  Oh, the rifle, yes the rifle,
  In our hands will prove no trifle!"

Light gleamed along a length of blue steel, and I found myself holding a Kentucky flintlock.

Well, one shot was better than none. I tucked it into my shoulder and sighted.

The Bear dropped the pathway and backed away, arms up high again. "Brothers, do not shoot!"

The pathway whipped back up, then sank down, then back up, and even Angelique and Gilbert howled as we tumbled. I squeezed the trigger, and the hammer snapped down—but there wasn't even a flash in the pan. I threw the rifle at the Bear with an oath of disgust.

The butt caught Ussrus right across the chops, and he reeled, head spinning.

"Enough of this!" the Gremlin cried, exasperated, and jumped down into the cave of the Bear.

"No!" I cried in alarm, but the Gremlin was muttering something as he dashed in a circle around Ussrus Major.

The Bear suddenly let out a howl. "What are these leaves? What are these—gooseberries?"

"What ails the beast?" Frisson asked, wide-eyed.

"He supposes he is a bush," the Gremlin answered, hopping back up onto the pathway. "But the spell will not endure forever, Wizard. The Bull must find some way to bring this path up high, where the Bear cannot reach, or he will surely drag us down."

"Right." I pulled myself together, racking my wits for some verse about a rising path. The first thing that came to mind was,

"Up and away, Chingachgook!
  The hunter who follows shall now be shook!"

"I'm out of rhymes!" I shouted. "Take it, Frisson!"

The poet ad-libbed as easily as a stream flows:

"As we go faster, we slow our pursuer!
The pilgrims rise up, and disdain the lure!"

"Walk!" the Gremlin commanded us, and we scrambled to
our feet, swayed a moment in the motion of the rising path,
then managed a sort of bowlegged gait, leaning into a hike that
had suddenly become a climb, as the path rose up at an angle
and kept rising. Below us, the Bear roared in impotent fury,
clawing in vain at a curve that had risen so high that it ex-
ceeded his grasp. He stood below us, flailing away at those
whom he would drag down, until his voice was lost in the
mists that rose up to obscure him, mists that rose even higher
until they were all about us, then hardened—and we found
ourselves walking in an enclosed tunnel once again.

"You have succeeded, Wizard," Frisson whispered.

"Yes, but only because I had a lot of help. The tunnel has
changed a lot, though. Are we still on the right path?"

"Aye," the Bull said, "for we have but discovered the way
to the Spider King, in spite of all the deceptions with which
the Bear sought to enshroud us."

"Yet it seems to differ so," Angelique objected. And it did,
for the curve was much sharper, and rose in an incline. We
toiled upward through a torus that became a hollow expanding
helix, ascending and ascending until it suddenly opened out
into a great room, so vast that its ceiling glowed in an opales-
cent mist, a fabric of gossamer threads. It had no walls, but
columns as numerous as the trunks of a forest, with vistas of
hills and meadows and groves visible between them, bathed in
sunlight and vividly green. We walked out in wonder, across a
floor that was a mosaic of marble so huge that our eyes
couldn't even begin to discern the picture it formed.

Directly before us, in an archway, stood a stocky figure with
a flowing cloak, silhouetted against the sun.

"Gentlemen and lady," the Bull said, in a hushed, almost
reverent tone, "we have attained our goal. We stand in the palace of the Spider King."

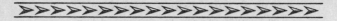

CHAPTER 19

The dark form came forward. As he left the sun-dazzle, his face became visible. At first glance, he wasn't a terribly prepossessing figure—only a man of middle height, wearing tunic and hose of dark gray broadcloth, a hip-length coat with wide sleeves, and a cap encircled by a band of leaden medallions.

Then I saw the face, as rough as if it had been hewn from stone, with fire in the eyes and a grim set to the lips, and I quailed for a moment.

Only a moment, not even long enough for my natural mulishness to arise—because I looked at his eyes again and decided that if this man told me to follow him into a battle we couldn't win, I probably would.

"Be welcome in my palace," the Spider King said. "If you have found the means to come to me here, the stoutness of heart to win through, you must be good folk."

I glanced around, but nobody else seemed inclined to answer, so I cleared my throat.

But Gilbert spoke up first. "You must be sure indeed of your power, Majesty, to greet so unseemly a crew as we, with no guardsmen or knights about you."

The Spider King's lips quirked into a smile, apparently ignoring the element of threat in Gilbert's words—was the squire out of his mind? He started to answer, but before he could get out a single word, a horrifying apparition came dashing from behind a pillar. He was only a man, but incredibly ugly. His eyes and nose were surrounded by a huge tangle of red hair and beard. His tunic and leggings were of good cloth, but irretrievably rumpled. He ran hunched over, a standing cup of

232

dull white metal in his hands. "The cup, Majesty! The antimony cup! You must drink!"

The king glanced at him, irritated. "Away, Oliver. I have affairs in train."

But, "You must drink!" the shaggy man maintained, and he set himself beside the king like a tree that had suddenly taken root.

The king gave him a look of exasperation, but took the cup and drank off the draught. Then he pushed the cup back and said, "Now begone! I shall summon you at need!"

"As Your Majesty pleases." The vagabond bowed and scurried off.

"As you see, I am attended," the Spider King said to Gilbert. The squire had not moved, but somehow gave the impression of having shrunk away in loathing as Angelique had very definitely done, and the rest of us had backed away a pace or two.

"He could repulse a squadron by the mere look of him," Frisson murmured.

"Not that he would have need to." For some odd reason, Gilbert seemed to relax. "We have come in peace, Majesty, to beseech your aid."

"None would come for aught reason else," the king said, with a sardonic smile. "You seek aid against the queen of Allustria, do you not?"

Something clicked in my mind. "Yes, we do," I said slowly, "and I think you know all about it—starting with my being transported to this universe."

"To the universe of Allustria and Merovence," the Spider King corrected me. "We stand between all universes, here. Yet I cannot be certain that I know all your grievances. Therefore, tell me them."

For a moment, Gilbert looked lost. "There is so much . . ."

"I am a poet whose verses wreak evil, Majesty," Frisson said, "even though I intend it not. Yet this wizard . . ." He nodded toward me. ". . . has taught me to write, so that my verses no longer need to be spoken, and no longer wreak havoc."

Gilbert took his cue. "The people of Allustria have suffered at the hands of Queen Suettay, Majesty, and I was of the band of the Order of Saint Moncaire sent to free one good yeoman and his family from her oppression. Yet my general did command me to accompany this Wizard Saul, for he had a vision that showed Saul to be the salvation of Allustria."

I still didn't like the sound of that.

"He wrested me from my prison cell," the Rat Raiser said, "where I had languished for years, since Queen Suettay consigned me there for no crime but fulfilling my function too well."

"And seeking to rise higher?" The Spider King fixed him with a gimlet stare.

The Rat Raiser bore it as long as he could; then he lowered his gaze and muttered, "I was ambitious, aye. Yet I did not seek her throne."

"That would have come," the Spider King assured him. He turned to Angelique. "And yourself, lady? Have you, too, suffered at the hands of this Queen Suettay?"

Angelique straightened, lifting her chin. "She did sacrifice me to evil, Majesty, and did attempt to ensnare my ghost to be her slave—but the Wizard Saul did remind me that I had but to repent my sins, and I would be Heaven-bound. He thus freed me from her power—but she kept my body between life and death, so that I must yet linger on this Earth."

The Spider King nodded slowly, eyes still on her. "And 'tis only the trickle of life in your body that holds you here?"

Angelique blushed and lowered her eyes, and I felt a thrill shoot through every limb and extremity. It surpassed anything that was ever brewed in a test tube.

Then the Spider King turned to me with a skeptical lift of the eyebrow. "What say you, O Hope of the Oppressed?"

"Uh . . ." I swallowed through a suddenly dry throat. "I just want to find my friend Matthew Mantrell, Your Majesty." I was about to add the bit about getting back to my own universe, but I glanced at Angelique, looking so vibrant, alive, and curvaceous, and decided to leave that part out. Honesty, however, compelled me to admit, "I also want to get Angelique's ghost back into her body."

"How shall you do that, with the queen in your way?"

I shrugged. "Take the queen *out* of the way."

"So you are set upon the slaying of a monarch?"

"I hadn't thought of it that way," I admitted, "though I wouldn't mind, now that you mention it—nobody could deserve it more. Besides, her grandmother usurped the throne—she isn't a rightful monarch."

"If she was born to it, it is hers by right," he stated with an air of full authority.

I looked at him narrowly; I've developed this instinct for knowing when a person's trying to snow me. "You don't believe that for a second," I accused. Then pieces pulled themselves together in my mind—the picture of that great fat spider sitting back and laughing at me, after she had just bitten me in Matt's apartment, and all the little arachnids that had been watching me ever since. "You were the one who brought me here in the first place! Maybe you can tell me how I'm going to unseat Suettay! That's what you want, isn't it?"

He stood still for a moment, then smiled. "You are astute, Wizard Saul—and, yes, you are a wizard; your denials are futile. As to deposing the usurper, you are the lodestone to which the forces of opposition will gather, and may have the strongest chance of success—but it is not by any means certain."

I frowned. "Just a minute, there. In the first place, I thought you said Suettay wasn't a usurper."

"Her own actions betray that she is, at least, no rightful monarch," the king said. "Since taking the throne, she has sought for the rightful king; for twenty years she has sought the descendant of the queen her grandmother slew."

I nodded. "So she knows she's trying to impose herself on a land that isn't hers, one that rejects her naturally." I had heard of such a thing, in the comparative lit major that I almost finished. "So if I kick her out, I'm just punishing a would-be regicide. And since she's a sorceress, it will be in the land's best interests for me to overthrow her."

"Even so." The king's face darkened; right or wrong, the killing of a monarch went against his grain. "None but a monarch born may claim a crown—and one who knows her claim to be unrightful must bring chaos upon the land she would rule. To do so is to offend against nature and goodness! To do so is to turn her power to evil!"

His glare was so damned intimidating! I stood against it, though, and said stoutly, "So whether she was evil or not, she certainly would be, once she had decided to keep the crown and kill the rightful claimant—if she could." Privately, I was remembering the long history of European dynasties being established by usurpation, and the Chinese convention of the Mandate of Heaven passing to the successful usurper—but the rules seemed to be different here. Or, no, not different, but lying on a deeper foundation; there was some sort of affinity between the rightful ruler and the land itself. Now that I thought about it, European usurpers usually had been related to the previous dynasty in some way, no matter how tenuous—at least, the usurpers whose families had managed to hold the throne for several generations. I took a deep breath and said, "Majesty, aid us in overthrowing this vile sorceress, and we will seek the legitimate heir!"

Gilbert and Angelique both stared at me, eyes very wide. I didn't blame them; I felt the same way. I had been so determined not to get myself committed! But this was, at least, only a short-term commitment—and it seemed to be the price of the king's help. I guessed that was what he had brought me here for.

Seemed I'd guessed right, too. The Spider King stood in thought, chin sunk on his breast. Finally, he lifted his head and said, "Will you swear?"

I ground my teeth in resentment, even though it meant I'd guessed rightly. But he didn't leave me much choice, now. "Yes. But I want to hear the wording first."

"You shall have it." The king plucked one of the leaden medallions from his hat and held it out in his palm. "Upon Saint Louis! Swear that you will hold the throne only to search for its rightful occupant, and that you will make no attempt to take the crown permanently for yourself or for your line!"

I didn't move, just stood there and looked him eye to eye. "I wasn't planning to take it at all."

"And who will rule the land when the usurper is dead, while you seek out the rightful heir?" the king said impatiently. "Come, swear!"

"I'm tempted. But, actually, I had in mind a ruling council, maybe with representatives from all the different classes—uh, estates."

His mouth twisted in sarcasm. "And who will lead it?"

I just glared back at him while my mind raced like a rat in a maze, searching for a way out. There wasn't one, so I went for the most limited terms I could think up on the spot. "Okay, so I'll call myself prime minister, or president . . ."

He frowned, not understanding.

"The one who presides," I explained, my exasperation beginning to show. "But I won't call myself king."

He glared at me, but the glare was softening a little. Finally, he gave one short, curt nod. "Good enough. Swear!"

I stared for a second longer, then sighed and gave in. I clasped my hand over the king's. "All right. I swear."

"Speak the words!"

I took a deep breath, as much for patience as for a long sentence. "I swear by Saint Louis that, if I come to lead the gov-

ernment of Allustria, I will hold it only for the purpose of . . ."
I broke off, staring at our joined hands.

Beneath my palm, the medallion had grown warm.

"Swear!" the Spider King commanded.

All around me, I felt tension, as if the air itself were
thickening—but I couldn't see anything. I looked up, and the
king's glare seemed to bore into my eyes. "Swear!" he demanded. "Or are you false?"

I reddened and tried to ignore the heat. ". . . for the purpose
of governing its people as well as I can, but only while seeking
its rightful heir . . ."

But the tension in the air was growing physically tangible,
and the medallion had become hot. It was beginning to be
painful. I gritted my teeth and went on. "I swear that I shall
never leave off searching for the heir and will resign as soon
as I have found him—or her! And that—" The medallion was
a searing pain beneath my hand, but I forced myself to ignore
the agony and go on. "—under no circumstances will I seek to
take the throne for myself, or for my heirs! By Saint Louis!"

Then I tried to pull my hand away, but the king still held it,
gaze probing mine, as the heat died away and was gone. Then,
finally, the Spider King released my hand. I snatched it away
with a groan of relief and looked at my palm to make sure I
wasn't burned.

There, tan against the skin, was the image of Saint Louis.

I screamed. "No! I'm nobody's man! I'm not property!"

My friends stared at me, Angelique frightened, Gilbert appalled, and Frisson very interested.

"It will fade when the terms of your vow are completed,"
the Spider King advised me. "But for now, you are committed.
Never forget."

"How can I, when I've got this brand to remind me?" I
shouted.

He nodded slowly, unfazed by my anger. "That is its purpose."

"And to make sure everybody can tell whose side I'm on,"
I yelled, "including my enemies! What chance do I have now
to survive if I'm captured?"

"What chance did you have before?" he returned.

I just stared at him while the blood drained from my face.
He was right—Suettay knew who I was, sure enough, and so
did all her henchmen. A disguise might have worked, but I
doubted it.

I was a marked man—in more ways than one.

The king still held my gaze, then nodded slowly. "Peradventure you will not forget. Yet if ever you are tempted to, you have but to look in your palm."

I stared at the image in my hand.

"As is your body, so be your soul," the Spider King said softly. "May your duty to Saint Louis and the people of Allustria be as a brand upon your spirit."

I lifted my head, staring in surprise and shock. Then finally I remembered how I had come into this mess in the first place and said, "It is. It already was."

But I hadn't realized it before.

So did it matter that I was now locked into it?

Not really. No. But it sure made me feel eerie. I hated being committed, in any way.

I looked up and noticed Angelique eyeing me with a very leery look. I think she was noticing my attitude, too.

Heat . . .

I had felt the force of magic enveloping me, binding me, through the leaden icon of the saint. I was branded, indeed, and I wondered what form the results of that branding would take.

"Now," the king said, "I will hearken to your tale of woe. What moves in this Allustria of yours that is so ruinous to her people?"

"Sorcery!" Gilbert declared.

"Slaughter and rapine!" Angelique cried, appalled.

But I just stared into the eyes of the Spider King and said slowly, "You already know all that, don't you? You have spies everywhere."

"Everywhere," he said, "and too much—for I must winnow amongst my knowledge to find that whereof you speak. Where is *your* Allustria?"

Gilbert frowned, puzzled. "By Merovence, and north of the Middle Sea."

"In which universe?"

The others stared, floored. I felt a chill, even though I had guessed this, and said, "In that universe in which magic works by poetry, Majesty, and in which Hardishane's empire drove out the minions of evil, with the aid of Saint Moncaire."

"Ah! Saint Moncaire." The Spider King nodded. "I know the hundred of which you speak. Tell me more of it."

"Why," Gilbert said, "Alisande has become queen of Merovence, five years past—"

"The only one in which evil has not overwhelmed all of Europe! Aye, I know it! Yet my attention has turned to the other universes near it, which are more in need of my aid."

"Allustria stands in need of your aid, Majesty, too, and desperately," Angelique protested. "We dwell in horror there, as fodder for evil men!"

The king shrugged. "I pity you, lady—yet what may I do? There must be some who wish the rule of right, and one to lead them; else I can do naught."

"Why, we wish such a rule," Gilbert cried, "and here is our leader." He clapped me on the back.

I regained my stability and forced a smile.

The king turned to me, interest whetted. "Is it so? Then tell me summat of this Allustria, and of yourselves."

But I shook my head and said slowly, "It's the Allustria that you brought me to, because you wanted me to fix it."

The king's mouth quirked toward a smile, but he said nothing.

"You have tendrils reaching into all the universes, don't you?" I accused.

"Not all," the king admitted, "only those in which I, or my analog, one very like to me, was born, or will be. I am outside time, as are the saints. In the universe that holds your home, I have been dead for almost five centuries; in life, I was known there as Louis XI of France. In this universe of which you speak, I was the Crown Prince Karl of Allustria—but when Suettay's grandmother slew the rightful queen, she also slew all her heirs, and all her possible heirs. Thereby did I die."

I stared, shocked. Then I gathered the remnants of my wits and said, "But that was a hundred years ago!"

"Two hundred," he said. "These sorcerous monarchs live far past their natural time."

"But why didn't you call me in sooner?" I bleated.

"Because you had not been born," he said simply, "and because the forces that can be gathered to oppose the queen did not yet exist. Now, however, Alisande rules in Merovence and has a most puissant Lord Wizard by her side, who defeated the evil sorcerer that sought to take her kingdom. When I saw how Allustria had fallen and my system of clerks been perverted, I resolved to one day cleanse both—and my chance came when a wizard rose who spearheaded the overthrow of the sorcerer-king of Ibile—Matthew Mantrell, Lord Wizard of Merovence."

I stood galvanized, just staring at him. He knew why, too, the bastard; he just smiled back at me with that small smile and that self-satisfied look in his eyes.

Then I burst out, "Matt? A lord?"

"Aye," he said, "and a royal consort, after three years."

"Married?" I turned away, my brain whirling—and thoughts tumbling. Matt had always had the look of the kind who would get married, mind you—but to a queen?

Well. Good for him. I pulled myself together and turned back to the Spider King. "I'm glad to hear it—he's my best friend—but you knew that, didn't you?"

"The times were right, at last," he answered. "There is a similarity of talents to you two."

"So you just followed his back trail and looked for a man who could do what he had done." I looked at him narrowly. "But you did say three *years*?"

The king nodded. "Time runs at different rates, in your world and mine. I sought a man who had a strong enough sense of self, whose individuality was so certain, that he would not compromise with any group force, but would maintain his integrity in spite of all temptations."

I backed away, staring, shaking my head, harder and harder. "No. Not a chance. That's not me. No."

"Truth," the Spider King insisted, with iron tones. "Yet there was this flaw in the scheme: A man who is so obsessed with becoming his true self is not committed to either evil or good, and his commitment to himself may make him corruptible by self-seeking."

Well. That sounded a bit more like me.

"That's really a minor danger," I said slowly. "Self-aggrandizement would violate my integrity. I'd just like it clearly on the record that I resent being drafted, though."

"Noted," the king said, his eyes glowing, and somehow, I was certain the fact had just been written down, somewhere, by some being that I preferred not to know about. "Noted—but 'drafted' you are."

"Yes, damn it!" I snapped. "You know just what you've done, don't you? Throwing these really solidly good people in my path! You've got me too caught up in this universe, now, to be able to reject it without trying to save it!"

"Therein am I indeed guilty." The bastard sounded proud of it.

"But you don't do anything!" I exploded. "You just sit here and watch! How can you call yourself a force for the good?"

"In your universe, and in many others, I was a force for goodness overall," he qualified, "though I achieved my ends with guile and stealth, which laid a great deal of guilt upon my soul. I thus was able to see to your world and recruit you. Your friend the Lord Wizard would not do for this affair—he is too strongly allied with good and too scrupulous for some of the means we must use to combat Suettay. But you, with your determination not to commit yourself to any larger force, to remain yourself, alone if need be—you may be able to combat this system of Suettay's, that seeks to grind all souls into the same likeness."

"I do have an interest in fighting depersonalization," I admitted. "But with the kind of power you have, I find it difficult to believe that you couldn't have just walked in and kicked out any of these evil monarchs, anytime you wanted."

"The power," he agreed, "but not the right. If these people do not wish to change their queen, what right have I to meddle?"

I stared. My companions stared, too, aghast.

CHAPTER 20

Then the statement suddenly made sense to me. "It's not just the queen, is it? Her successor might not bring better rule, after all. So a new king can't do any good there, unless he changes the system of rule. That country can keep running just as well as it does now without *any* king—or just as poorly!"

"The monarch has appointed clerks and reeves enough," the Spider King said, by way of agreement.

I frowned, trying to pierce the man's emotionless mask by the sheer intensity of my own feelings. "And you think that's good, don't you? A good way to rule."

"If the clerks are mastered, aye. If a capable monarch of good intent commands them, they can strengthen the land immeasurably, preserving the peace and bringing greater wealth to all."

"Like Joseph in Egypt," I murmured, "storing up grain for the famine. That's your goal, isn't it? No one starving, no one wearing rags or sleeping on the streets."

This time, the king nodded as he smiled.

"But that's not enough." I frowned. "No one should have to kneel to someone else, just because that someone else is stronger. No one should have to live in fear of an overlord's cruel whim. No one should have to be locked into doing whatever job someone else assigns him, if he doesn't want it and can find other work that he likes better!"

"None should have to marry where they do not wish," Angelique murmured.

"All should be free to seek their own paths to Heaven," Gilbert added.

242

The Spider King pounced on it. "Freedom for Heaven is in one's soul, squire. Earthly bondage will not hinder it; mundane freedom may not aid it."

"There is some truth in that," Frisson admitted. "Yet how if one dwells in agony of spirit, Majesty, as the peasants do in Allustria? If they seek to live morally, they are sorely beset by the miasma of evil and tortured by its minions. The lives of the common folk need not be Hell on Earth."

The Gremlin just stood by, looking interested.

The king pulled his head down, glowering. "You speak truly," he admitted, "and the reign of sorcery must cease. Yet that is a fault of Suettay's, not of the form of her government. A rightful king, devoted to good, may transform that heap of clerks into a force for virtue."

"The rightful king cannot return!" Frisson protested. "The heir cannot be found! For if he is, Suettay will slay him out of hand!"

"Then seek him out and protect him," the Spider King said, with an air of grim finality. "Bring him to the throne. For the clerks wield the law, look you, and the law preserves the weak against the assaults of the strong."

"Unless the law is made by the strong for their own advantage," I pointed out.

The king cast a quick frown at me, then turned back to Frisson. "Those who are freed to seek their own destiny may ofttimes go astray and find instead their own ruination."

"Free or bound, 'tis they who must answer to God for the prosperity or corruption of their souls," Frisson said evenly. "Their lord cannot speak to God for them, when they are come to Judgment."

"And shall their lord hinder them, if he is unjust and evil?"

"He shall," Frisson said, "if the torments he visits upon them try them unduly."

"All life is the trial of the soul, if the priests speak truly," the Spider King returned. " 'Tis God who allocates tribulation, each to the strength of his soul. The withstanding of it is the winning of Heaven."

"Then isn't it the king's job to make life as pleasant as he can for his people?" I put in. "He can leave it up to God to assign hardships."

The king's lips twitched with impatience. "Should the king, then, ennoble all his peasants?"

"Not a bad idea," I said. "And if he can't do that, he can at least stop preventing them from ennobling themselves."

"They who mislike their lowborn state, may aspire to clerkship," the king returned, "and rise within the king's service."

"Until they do their tasks too well," the Rat Raiser said. "Until the king says, 'Thus far, and no farther.' "

But I addressed the larger issue. "The government of clerks may be led by a strong king, Majesty, true—yet unless he is *extremely* strong, the layers of clerks will choke off his will and govern in his stead."

The king turned to me again, frowning. "Why, how is this?"

"The clerks will begin by serving the government, but end by becoming the government," I explained, "a government that becomes like a living being itself and works to maintain its own interests, disregarding the good of the people."

"Is this an old wives' tale?" the king demanded. "Or have you seen such monstrous growths?"

"Oh, yes," I said softly. "In fact, they're so common where I come from that the law has even made them legal entities, and scholars have stated the rules of their behavior."

"Why, what rules are these?" the king demanded.

"They were deduced by a man named Parkinson," I explained, "and they describe the workings of a form of government called 'bureaucracy.' "

The king frowned. "What is the meaning of that word?"

" 'Government by desks.' The problem is that any request for action has to go from one desk to another, higher and higher up the ladder, until it reaches the one that can actually do something about it."

"What monarch would so ignore his clerks?"

"Any one that doesn't enjoy work." I raised a hand to forestall the king's protest. "I know how scandalous that sounds, Your Majesty, but there have been quite a few of them."

"They cannot have been rightful kings."

I shrugged. "All right, so they were illegitimate. They stayed in power for fifty years and more, though, sometimes, and their sons and grandsons after them. It's all well and good to say they weren't fit to be kings—but no one else was doing the job."

The Spider King gave me a fierce glare, but held his peace.

"Not that it matters," I qualified. "After all, once the bureaucrats take hold, they set up so many layers of desks that the king can't possibly keep in touch with all of them. That's one of Parkinson's laws—that every clerk will try to hire more people to work for him."

"Who will allow him, if he does not need them?"

"Anybody who looks at his situation on paper—and paper is the key word. The ambitious clerk manufactures more and more pieces of paper that need to be filled out for any one decision, until he really can't do them all by himself—never mind that they don't really need to be written. And when each bureaucrat does that, pretty soon you have an immense number of people, and it takes a king's whole reign just to figure out who is really necessary and who isn't."

"It cannot be," the king scoffed, "for naught would ever then be done, and the land would sicken."

I carefully looked elsewhere. Gilbert cleared his throat with a covert glance at Angelique.

The king's gaze darkened. "Speak, then! For I know that Allustria does languish—but can this be why?"

"It is," the Rat Raiser said heavily, "and 'tis some fault of mine. I made a ladder of command from the smallest town to the queen's chancellery, that any command might be executed the next day. 'Twas for this Suettay cast me into the dungeon—yet she kept my ladder to make her will felt on the instant, wheresoe'er she wished. 'Tis even as the wizard says—each reeve chose bailiffs, and each bailiff chose a watch, and each watchman chose—"

"Enough." The king chopped laterally. "I take your point. Yet all will jump to the king's whistle, will they not?"

"They will," Frisson said slowly, "when they hear it, which can take a great deal of time, if they wish—but the peasant who cries to the king for aid will not be heard."

"Why, how is this? Surely these clerks dare not withhold news from the king!"

"Well, not openly," I answered. "But the lower down the ladder they are, the less power each one has to make a decision—so each one thinks it over for a day or two, then passes it up to the man above him. Unless he takes a dislike to the person who made the complaint, of course—then he just loses the piece of paper with the complaint on it. Parkinson called that one, 'Delay is the deadliest form of denial.'"

"And if it does come to the chancellor," the Rat Raiser breathed, "he will have piles of such petitions. He must decide which to show the queen, and which Her Majesty would count a waste of time . . ."

"And which ones might make the chancellor look bad," I added.

"If the king should discover he has suppressed a report . . . !"

"He'll have a good excuse. He 'lost' it, or it was too minor to trouble Her Majesty with, or—"

"Enough." The king closed his eyes, pressing a hand to his forehead. "Can a monarch care so little for his power?"

"No, Majesty, but she can care that little about her people. All Suettay really cares about is whether the taxes come in, and whether the orders she does give are obeyed."

"And her chancellor will always assure her they are," the Rat Raiser finished.

The king lowered his hand and looked up again, eyes burning. "Yet if what you say is true, the land would be near chaos! Bandits would be rife . . ."

"I was beset by armed bands three times, ere I met the wizard," Frisson murmured.

". . . barons would cease to fear the king's peace and would rise against one another in war . . ."

"We've seen it," I said, "and they do it with the queen's blessing."

The king stared, aghast. "And the peasants? Cares she not that they starve?"

"She cares that they be able to farm," Frisson said, "that they grow wool for her to shear. Beyond that? What cares she if they wallow in squalor? If their clothes are rags, and their faces pinched with hunger? When they are too weak to follow the plow, mayhap she will take notice . . ."

"Yet before they come to that," Gilbert put in, "they will have abjured the faith and gone to serve the reeve—or taken to the greenwood, and gone in banditry."

"Her minions set neighbor against neighbor," Frisson added, "by saying that whosoever the village watchman chooses as best plowman shall be accorded extra victuals—meat once a week, a sack of meal each month, and new cloth for his family."

"These are great prizes indeed," the Rat Raiser informed him.

Angelique stared, shocked. "Will they not, then, seek each to plow harder?"

"Aye, and all will excel. Yet the watchman must rank them, as first, second, and third—so each peasant seeks to curry favor with the watchman and to revile his neighbors. They, in turn, seek to take the credit for his work, by claiming 'twas of their doing; and each seeks to make all others believe poorly of his fellows."

"Each bailiff, meanwhile, accepts favors from his watchmen," the Rat Raiser added, "and the plowman is pressed to bring his comely wife, or his blooming daughter, to the bailiff for the night—"

"If those chaste ladies have not come to the watchman themselves," Frisson pointed out, "seeking favor for their husbands—"

"Or for themselves, in *disdain* of their husbands—"

"Anon the husband, discovering he's a cuckold, strikes down his wife—"

"And the plowmen ply the watchman with such gifts as they may discover—"

"Uh, boys, I think that's enough," I said. The king looked ready to explode.

"Enough it is—a surfeit!" The king turned his back, stalking away toward the archway, where he stood looking down. "Alas for Allustria! If matters have come to so foul a pass there, we must find a way to hale down this false queen!"

I breathed a sigh of relief and saw my friends go limp. I, of course, was as sturdy as spaghetti.

"Yet we cannot tear out her whole government, root and branch," the king mused, "or the land will be plunged into chaos absolute—and in that chaos, Satan's minions may well establish themselves anew."

"But you cannot leave these parchment-bound clerks to plunder the people!" Gilbert cried.

"Nor shall I—but 'tis you who must do the work. I can aid you with knowledge, I can tell you where to seek the lever that will topple the tyrant; I may even lend you strength, through the strands of my web. Yet I cannot march with you; I must remain here, in the nexus of the worlds."

The others stared, not understanding, but the Gremlin nodded, and I pursed my lips. "We can't rightly ask for more—and the bureaucrats will be quick to reform, once they see their sorcerer overthrown, and a God-dedicated king on the throne. But how about the system, Majesty? Any bureaucracy has certain inherent tendencies toward corruption."

"Why, so does a man," the king cried, "and 'tis naught but the morality stemming from his sense of self that makes him retain his wholeness, his integrity, to resist the Tempter! And whence, I ask you, comes that morality, that self-warding wisdom?"

"Why—from the priests," I admitted, "and the philosophers. And the poets, and all the wise men who try to guide people away from ruin and toward fulfillment."

"An odd choice of terms." The Spider King frowned. "Yet they are nearly as true as to say that the men of God guide us away from the road to Hell and seek to set our feet on the path to Heaven. And as they do for men and women, so may they do for the government by clerks."

"A spiritual adviser for a bureaucracy?" I frowned. "I'll have to think about that, Your Majesty. I'm not convinced a bureaucracy has a conscience."

"Why, then, 'tis a beast, and not a soul, and may be purged and goaded without compunction! You have but to find your emetic and your prod."

"Now wait a minute!" I held up a hand. "It's made of human beings, after all!"

"Who need to be governed in their own right," the king returned, "and justice meted out, even to those who mete out justice."

"Who shall watch the watchers?" I hazarded.

"Nay," Frisson said. " 'Who shall govern the government?' "

"Be mindful!" The king raised a forefinger. "If they are humans, may not another human be their conscience? For is not a 'conscience,' after all, but the wisdom to preserve one's own soul?"

"Recognizing one's ultimate good, even if it means a temporary or apparent loss?" I frowned. "Interesting notion. But even human consciences need to be made aware of the pain and disaster that befall those who stray."

"Then make them so aware! Find some device that will punish the clerk who strays, and will make his plans of malice go awry!"

"Why," the Gremlin chuckled, "that can I do."

The Spider King bent his frowning gaze upon the monster. "I am sure that you can—but have you the self-denial to withhold your mischief when a clerk does rightly?"

I stared. "You two know each other?"

The king looked up, amused. "Whence did you think he came, Wizard?"

"We are both outside the universes," the Gremlin explained, "and flit from one to another, as need or inclination dictates."

I found myself wondering about the forms of angels—or disguises.

"What is this?" Gilbert demanded. "What shall the monster then do?"

"Why, as I will," the Gremlin answered. "Does a clerk write out a writ of foreclosure? I shall make it go astray. Does a reeve set out a warrant? I'll make sure the writing's changed ere the bailiff comes unto the victim. Does the chancellor seek to withhold reward from one who has toiled long? Does he seek to imprison one whose only fault is aiding those in danger? Does the king himself seek to draw and quarter one who would resist him, or to exile a saint on a desert isle, for no offense but that of lending comfort to souls in misery? In a sieve I'll thither sail!"

"And, like a rat without a tail," Frisson murmured, "he'll do, and he'll do, and he'll do!"

I clapped a hand over the vagabond's mouth. "Hold it, boy! You were coming perilously close to poetry!"

"Let him versify; he cannot cause havoc here, where we are beyond the laws of any universe," the Spider King said.

I took my hand away, and Frisson beamed with glee.

"Yet before he speaks," the king said hastily, "we must confer on ways of confounding your vile tyrant. The Spirit of Disorder will beset his clerks . . ."

"With effects that are comic and tragic," the Gremlin murmured.

"So much the better; you may then make these puffed-up clerks to see their own fallibility, thus restoring to them some measure of humility."

"Mayhap I shall even make them to laugh at the absurdity of their own vanities and strivings after dross!"

"Ah! If you can, if you but can! Then might they see themselves as they are, and see how petty are the goals for which they strive!"

"It would destroy them!" the Rat Raiser said, ashen-faced.

"Mayhap; but out of this crushing of the soul, they may emerge with some truer view of life, and greater inclination to labor for the common weal."

"Yet that cannot be," the Rat Raiser said, frowning, "for each clerk, in the end, labors for himself."

The Spider King wheeled toward him. "We have each the

need to labor for something greater than ourselves, friend, so that we may feel less alone, and feel our lives to have worth."

But the bureaucrat only frowned, not understanding.

I didn't blame him. I couldn't help thinking that this Spider King had an awfully idealistic view of bureaucracy.

The Gremlin clapped his hands and chuckled. "We shall craft a bureaucrat's bane! Ah, what fun! I have not had so grand a time for eons! I have grown rusty, I have grown stale!"

"We're going to pit entropy against perversity, then?" I asked.

The Spider King nodded. "It may not succeed in great measure, since the one is but an aspect of the other . . ."

"Oh, no," I said softly. "That could be very, very effective."

"Devastating." The Gremlin chuckled. "If an enterprising spirit doth move the confrontation."

"And on this kind of issue, you can be very enterprising, right?"

"Just so!"

"So much for Suettay's ministers." The king dismissed them with a wave of his hand. "They may be rendered benign. Yet how shall you deal with the woman herself?"

That brought me up short. I spread my hands. "Confront her and try to match magics with her, I guess—and hope I've got better verses."

The king shook his head with certainty. "That way lies disaster. You must enlist a power greater than your own, that together you may be more than the sorceress-queen."

I frowned, instantly suspicious. "How do I do that? Pray?"

"Nay." The king beckoned, and I came over to the archway with him. Looking down, I saw an azure field ringed with green and tan, and with a fleck or two of green in it. With a shock, I recognized the Mediterranean.

"Yon lies the world of Merovence and Allustria," the Spider King murmured.

I wondered how he had locked in the view of that one universe from this nexus. I began to realize why the man was called "the Spider King."

"There is a man who is bound for sainthood, though he knows it not." The king's arm reached past me, pointing at an island in the Aegean. "There, where Circe beguiled the men of Odysseus, dwells a nymph named 'Thyme'—and the sorceresses of Suettay's guild have kidnapped the saintly man and placed him there, within the bondage of her spell."

"What a way to get to sainthood! I take it he's having a good time?"

"Nay. His spirit's sorely tried, and he is racked with the hot irons of desire—for he will not yield to the nymph's blandishments. He knows that no man can serve two masters, and that love is a most demanding one—but he chose Christ for his master long ago. He seeks to do Christ's work, aiding the poor and friendless, and therefore will not yield unto the nymph."

"Wholeness," I murmured. "Integrity. The unity of his spirit."

"Even so. Yet from his enduring struggle, his soul has gained strength tenfold—and it was a mighty spirit ere he came there. Folk said that he worked miracles of curing, and of producing food, but he denied it. Yet if any man can give you strength 'gainst Suettay, it is he."

"A veritable treasure," Gilbert mused behind him. "How shall we know the man?"

"By his sex—he is the only male on the island—and by his habit."

"Habit?" The squire frowned. "Is he a cleric, then?"

"He is—a monk, of the Order of Saint Louis, one Ignatius by name. And you will find him a source of strength in other conflicts, too; he may even rekindle the ideals of the clerks."

"If he can do that," I murmured, "he *can* work miracles."

"And so, away!" The Spider King clasped my arm, turning me around and propelling me toward another archway. "Yonder lies your path! Together, now, and off upon your quest!"

"Hey, wait a minute!" I tried to backpedal, but the king's grip was surprisingly strong, and I found myself gliding over the smooth marble floor in spite of my efforts. "How are we going to get hold of you if we need help?"

"You will not—I will maintain touch with you! Each separate one of you is now at the end of one of my threads; you are all caught within my web! When you doubt it, find a moment in a place of stillness, and you will feel my power! Now, Godspeed! And may your patron saint stand by you!"

I tried to stop, but I skidded through the archway, and my friends came tumbling after me with shouts of alarm, tumbling after me into a warm, clinging darkness that enveloped us, rocked us, soothed us . . .

And vanished.

CHAPTER 21

The trees crowded in on us, towering up to form a roof overhead, lowering down with an ominous susurrus. I swallowed against a knot of apprehension deep in my throat and glanced back at my companions.

They were feeling it, too—some lurking presence that did not want us there.

Fortunately, we had the Gremlin along to chase the baddies away. "Uh—you sure you know where you're going?"

"Of a certainty, I know!" Then why did the monster look worried? "I am going to the bower of the nymph Thyme!"

"Uh—right." I frowned. "Did you, uh—have any idea what route we were going to take?"

"As I told you, we follow the sun. If it is before us in its course as it arcs dawn to dusk, we go aright."

I glanced back at my friends, noting Angelique's apprehension and the Rat Raiser's angry glower. "Right. Say, uh, Gremlin—we haven't been able to see the sun for six hours now. Not since we got kicked out of the Spider King's palace and found ourselves in this forest."

"Do you doubt me?" the Gremlin challenged. "Could I go astray without wishing it?"

"Just what I was going to ask."

"Mayhap the wood itself wishes to mislead you," Angelique suggested quickly.

The Gremlin halted and heaved a huge sigh. "You have said it, maiden, and I think you may have some hint of truth in that saying. Nay, we have lost our way."

I frowned. "Of course, it couldn't just be that you think it's fun to help travelers get lost."

"Not when I am one of them! I swear, Wizard, 'tis no doing of mine!"

I winced and glanced around me. "Please! You swearing *anything* strikes me as extremely hazardous!"

"We must forge ahead," Gilbert said grimly. "We shall come to naught if we do naught."

"There's a certain sort of sense in that," I agreed. "Onward, *mes amis!*"

"If the way 'onward' doth reveal itself," the Gremlin grumped; but he started forward again.

An hour later, I called a halt again. "Okay—we've been watching the light on the trees, and it has always stayed on their fronts—but I'm sure I recognized that birch tree at least three times!"

"Why," the Gremlin growled, "how can you be sure it is the same tree?"

"Because this is a deciduous forest, mostly oak and ash, and that's the only birch tree I've seen. Also because the markings on its bark have twisted themselves into a gloating leer."

Everybody turned and looked at the birch tree. " 'Tis true," Gilbert said. "In the center of the trunk, the blackbird marks have shrunk into eyes, and the one beneath has widened into a grinning mouth."

The Gremlin stamped up to the tree. "At what do you laugh, white-face? Do you dare?"

It must have been the wind in the branches. The tree couldn't really have been laughing.

"I submit," I said, "that the queen knows where we are and has placed a spell on this forest to keep us going around in circles."

"But she thinks that we are dead!" Angelique protested.

"She must have developed suspicions and looked in her crystal ball."

"Not likely," the Gremlin said, coming back, "for no crystal can see into the palace of the Spider King, unless he wills it. I would as lief believe the forest was enchanted in antiquity, and all who dwell nearby do know to avoid it."

"Could be." But I glanced aside, distracted. "Frisson, what are you doing?"

"Only toying with a stick." Frisson snapped up straight, hands going behind his back.

My scalp prickled. "Why do I get the willies when you start playing around? What's the game, Frisson?"

"Oh . . . naught but this." Frisson took the stick out from behind his back—three sticks, actually. One was a section of a tree trunk, like a flat table; the other was a peg, going through a hole in the center of the long one.

"What does it do?" I asked suspiciously.

"I recited a verse in praise of the Pole Star," Frisson explained. "It will always point to the north, now. Just an idle amusement, of no worth—"

"No worth, he says! He just invented the compass, that's all!" I went around behind the poet. "Lead on, Frisson! As long as that stick is pointing toward us, we're going south!"

Frisson looked up, pleased, then started off into the forest again. The Gremlin followed at the end of the line, grumbling.

Another hour later, I called a halt again. "Okay. No luck. We've gone in a straight line according to Frisson's compass, but here's that blasted birch tree again. I've got half a mind to blast it for real."

A long moan sounded.

I glared at the tree. "That got you, didn't it? Gonna let us go, now?"

The moan came again, drawn out and quavering.

"Saul," Angelique said, "it came from our left, and the tree is to our right."

I looked up, frowning, peering off into the underbrush. Sure enough, the moan came again—but it was coming closer. "Everybody step back!"

The moan came loud and clear, and a gnarled, bent old woman tottered into the clearing, hurrying as fast as she could, glancing over her shoulder in terror.

That bothered me—badly. "What's chasing you?"

"My death!" she cried. "Away, fool! Or would you catch the pox that does infest me? Then Death will dog your footsteps, too!"

Everybody edged back, including me—but the rational part of me took over. "You can't run away from Death, lady—you have to stop and fight him."

"Do you think my master would give me power to fight Death?" she screeched. "Fool, thrice a fool! When Death has taken me, the Devil shall have me! Begone!" And she tottered straight toward me.

Reflex took over. I stepped aside, saying, "If you repent, maybe I can heal you."

She stopped dead—as it were—in front of me, and those old green eyes pierced me to the marrow. "If you can heal me, do so now!"

"You've sold your soul," I pointed out. "I'm not a priest or an exorcist, just a magician." One of us was, anyway. "My magic can't work on you as long as you're in Satan's grasp."

"Then I repent!" The panic suddenly broke through, and the woman sank to her knees, hands uplifted in prayer. "Lord of Heav ... of Hea ... Lord above, save me! I know I am unworthy, for all the evil I have done—but let this foolish magician save my raddled hide, and I shall never work evil again!"

Something rattled in the shadows. I glanced at them apprehensively and held out a hand toward Frisson. "Pox."

"I have searched it." Frisson pushed a piece of parchment into my hand.

I held it up and read it.

"Smallpox, cowpox, all are healed!
French pox, East pox, marks annealed!"

That inspired me; I added a couplet Frisson couldn't have known about:

"Spirochetes be rent asunder!
Germs of raddles, be plowed under!"

Whatever was rattling in the shadows stopped.

The ex-witch looked up, amazement lighting her face—and even as we watched, the hideous marks of the disease were fading. " 'Tis true! I can feel the sickness leave me, feel the fever abate, my strength reviving!"

"It might not last," I said, "if you don't get to confession. You're out of Satan's power, but not very far out."

"Aye! I must seek out a priest without delay!" She scrambled to her feet and headed off into the forest, her thank-you floating behind her. "I cannot bless, for I am too sodden with evil—but I thank you, kind strangers!"

A sudden inspiration hit, and I leapt after her. "Which way to the nearest priest?"

"South! He lives in a village in the plain beyond these woods!"

"Follow that witch!" I shouted to my friends, and we all pelted off through the forest.

The sun was nearing the horizon as we came out of the forest and saw the plain, rolling away under a huge expanse of sky. Even from the edge of the forest, we could see the roofs of three little villages. Between, the flatland was a jigsaw puzzle of small fields, divided by hedges.

The nearest town was maybe half a mile away. Sunlight glistened off whitewashed adobe houses. "The priest lives yon!" The old witch pointed toward the smallest hovel in town. "Oh, how deeply I rejoice that I put off and put off the bearding of him, and the slaying of him for the queen!"

So she had been an official. A nasty thought occurred to me. "You didn't maybe put a spell on that forest so that anybody trying to get through it would get lost, did you?"

"Aye. It protected me from those who sought to hurt me— they could not find my cottage. Farewell, kind strangers! When I am shriven, I shall bless you! I shall sing your praises throughout the land!"

I felt the old familiar chill again. "I'd really rather you didn't. I'm working on a low profile here, you see, and—"

"Ever shall I trumpet your virtues!" she cried. "So wise and merciful a wizard is deserving of glory! And when I'm shriven, I shall bless you with my every breath!" She went tottering off to find a priest, and absolution.

I turned to the Gremlin. "Narrow thing, that. You wouldn't have had anything to do with her catching the pox, would you?"

The monster grinned, showing a lot of snaggled teeth. "I did not happen by here so many years ago as that, Wizard."

"Just wondering. By the way, which way to the nymph's house now?"

"Yon." The Gremlin pointed due south.

"Yon it is." I sighed. "But only until sunset. We're still in hostile territory, and we'll need some time to pitch camp."

"Shall we never leave Suettay's country?" Angelique sighed. "It was so great a blessing to be free of her, in the palace of the Spider King!"

"I'm afraid she knows we're still alive," I said with chagrin. "I shouldn't have cured that last witch."

"Nay, you should have," she said quickly, but her eyes were huge with trepidation in the shadows.

"Mayhap you need not come, milady," Gilbert told her. "Perchance the Spider King would let you remain in his palace. The poet will stay with you—will you not?"

"Aye, if you bid me." Frisson sighed. "Yet I had hoped to witness the end of this sage that unwinds before me."

"You shall," Angelique said quickly. "I shall not be left behind."

I wondered if it was courage, or reluctance to be left alone with Frisson's unharnessed verses. "Okay, then, we're all agreed," I said. "Southward ho!"

"All right, sprite, want to explain this plight?"

We stood between the forest and the seashore, watching the breakers foam up onto the gravel.

"We seek the nymph, Thyme," the Gremlin said stubbornly. "The path to her lies yon." He stood with the setting sun at his right and pointed toward the south—and several hundred miles of waves, sea stretching away to the rim of the world.

"Yeah, I thought it was an island." I sighed. My stomach sank, rehearsing its probable behavior as we crossed the sea. But there was no help for it. We couldn't exactly drive, and though I was tempted to think about flying, I didn't—what would happen if Suettay managed to cancel my spell when we were a thousand feet up over the miles and miles of waves that were all there was between the island of Thyme and this southern border of Suettay's kingdom. I guessed the little port town I saw in the distance would have grown up to be Trieste, in my own world. "At least we get to leave the queen's jurisdiction."

"Then we shall go, and gladly," Gilbert said. "I confess that I, too, rejoice that the nymph does dwell outside Allustria's borders."

The Gremlin shrugged. "For all we know, she may not. Who holds sway over these little islands?"

It was a moot point, and one that hadn't been entirely resolved even in my own universe. "If she lives on an island," I said, "why didn't the Spider King just send us there?"

"Mayhap he has work for us to do on the way," Frisson suggested, "though I could wish he had told us what it was."

"You and me both, brother," I muttered.

"Peace, gentlemen," Gilbert soothed. "He could have sent us into the middle of Allustria, to fight our way free again."

"Praise Heaven he has not!" the Rat Raiser said.

"Yeah," I said, "but after we find this monk Ignatius, we have to come back."

"What must be, must be." The Rat Raiser was surprisingly philosophical. "Yet be assured, companions—if we must return to Suettay's domain, we are better to do it by sea, where there is less chance of meeting with her wardens."

"Yes, now that she has definitely decided to get rid of us," I agreed. "And it will be a lot quicker, in any event. We got through from the mountains last time, but it took a *great* deal of luck."

"Come, then!" The Gremlin turned away. "We must seek out a ship and a captain. Yet I think it best that you be the one to haggle with him, Wizard—he might be shy of my dealings."

"Understandable," I muttered, as I followed the monster. I called back to my friends, "Come on, folks! Gotta hurry!" I forced my tired legs into long strides.

Even so, Gilbert caught up with me. "Wherefore must we hasten, Wizard?"

"Because," I said, "Thyme and tide wait for no man. Let's go."

"I carry only cargo," the captain said stubbornly.

It could have been worse—it could have been night instead of sunset, with Angelique totally visible, instead of being washed out by the sun's orange rays. If he could have seen her, he would no doubt have been pointing out that a woman on a ship is bad luck. Come to think of it, he might have extended that notion to ghosts, too, so it was just as well my beloved could stay hidden.

"We're not asking you to take us any great distance," I argued, "just to some obscure little island out in the middle of nowhere."

"But you have no passports." The captain eyed the gold in my hand. No question about it, he was tempted—but he was balancing the danger of breaking Suettay's emigration laws, against the cash in my hand. So I slipped another gold piece from my pocket and added it to the stack. The captain's eyes fairly bulged, and he drew in a sharp breath.

"Guaranteed," I said. "Just an offshore island. We'll even supply our own local transportation—all you have to do is carry us there and lower us over the side in the longboat."

The captain stared at the stack of gold, teetering on the

brink. Then he cried, "Done!" His hand scooped up the coins and made them disappear.

I gaped, wondering if *I* could make money vanish that quickly. In fact, I hoped his wouldn't. My money never lasted very long, anyway.

"But you must board right now," the captain said, "while my crew is ashore on their last roister. As to the longboat, you shall have mine, for two gold pieces more. I shall buy another in Mycenaea."

He sure would, I reflected as I climbed the gangplank—and for a lot less than even a single gold piece. But I wasn't about to haggle. Besides, I could make more of the stuff whenever I wanted to. I just had.

We clambered down a ladder and stowed ourselves in the hold, under the captain's cabin.

"How may we be sure of his troth?" Frisson asked, wide-eyed.

"By his own peril," the Rat Raiser answered. "We have but to denounce him to the harbormaster, and he is food for the gulls."

"But he need not take us to Thyme's isle! He need but have us thrown into the sea, as soon as we are too far from land to swim!"

"And what sailor-man would raise his hand against us?" Gilbert retorted. "We are not the most mild-seeming of bands, look you."

"We could make short work of his whole crew," I assured the poet. "So you might scribble down a verse for giving sailors heart attacks—and either you or I will be awake at all times."

Frisson nodded slowly, frowning.

"Then, of course, there are the members of the party they haven't seen." I glanced at a row of hogsheads against the wall of our timber dungeon. "Are you in there, Gremlin?"

One of the barrels wavered, waxed, and transformed itself into a monster. "Aye," the Gremlin answered. "Let this trip be quick, Wizard! I mislike so much water!"

"I'll make certain they have a favorable wind," I assured him. I tried to remember what I'd heard about the Finnish recipe for summoning a breeze.

The ship tossed and heaved, and the Gremlin was green from top to toe. On the other hand, that wasn't that far from his natural color. "Wizard, you have given them too much wind!"

I held my hands out, palms up. "Not a bit! They were doing fine without me; I didn't even whistle!"

"Yet mayhap," Angelique gasped, "you could find a way to slacken their progress some little."

Chartreuse was definitely not her color, I decided. How she was managing to be seasick without a body, I didn't know; must have been psychosomatic. "I know it's rough, but try to stick it out. Ships always pitch and heave a lot, especially little ones like this."

Gilbert turned away, his hand over his mouth. I decided that I shouldn't have said "heave."

The Rat Raiser frowned at us, puzzled. "I do not ken it. There is excitement in this, truly, but no cause for discomfort."

"It's all right for *you*," I retorted. "You've got friends here!"

But the Rat Raiser shook his head. "No longer, Wizard. My little furry ones have sought their holes in the keel beam."

I sat bolt-upright. "They *have*? Then something must be *really* wrong!"

A huge blast of thunder answered me from above. I frowned upward; I seemed to hear yelling.

" 'Tis a tempest," Frisson moaned.

The trapdoor overhead wrenched open to show the captain's face, glaring down at us in the light of a lantern. "What ill luck besets my ship?" Then he saw Angelique, and his eyes went wide. "A woman! Know 'ee not 'tis bad luck to bring a woman aboard ship?"

"Not really," I said. "She's a ghost." Then I bit my tongue, but I was just a second too late.

"A woman *and* a ghost!" he howled, wide-eyed with sudden fright. "Small wonder my ship is beset! Now could my bark founder and all my crew drown on her account!"

Gilbert forced himself to his feet and stepped over to stand—or sway—in front of Angelique.

"Don't plan anything rash." I scrambled to my feet. "Here, let me take a look."

But the captain pushed me back, though not before I had seen a couple of hulking sailors behind him, glowering with resentment and trembling with fear. "Are you daft, man?" the captain demanded. "It is hard enough for a seagoing man to hold his feet above decks. A landlubber would certainly be lost to the waves!"

"You can lash me to the nearest mast," I offered. "Believe me, I can help."

"Oh, aye," one of the sailors sneered. "And who do you think you be—the Old Man of the Sea?"

"No, but I'm sure we'd be on speaking terms, if we met. You see, I'm a wizard."

Their eyes widened, and they shied away. Even the captain was startled just long enough for me to push past him. He came back to himself quickly enough to lurch after me, trying for a tackle, but I sidestepped and threw myself toward the mast.

The wind hit me like a sandbag, and thunder blasted my eardrums. Lightning dazzled me; I almost *did* go into the sea. But I managed to grab a rope and haul myself up against the sudden wash of icy water as a wave broke over the little vessel. I came up gasping, shivering, and chilled to the bone, but still aboard, and pulled myself a little farther until I could get an arm around a belaying pin.

"See you not the folly of it?" the captain roared in my ear; I could just barely hear him. "Do you not see you can do naught to aid? Nay, get below!"

"Not ... yet," I gasped, and dredged up Kipling's words, with a few quick adaptations:

"The tempest caught us out at sea, and built its billows high,
 Till we heard as the roar of a rain-fed ford,
 The roar of its wind and sky.
 Till we heard the roar of its wind and sky
 Rise up, die down, and cease—
 And the heaving waves did all subside
 Till we sailed on a sea of peace."

It might have been my imagination, but I thought the wind abated a fraction.

" 'Tis not enough!" the captain called. "It will still drag us under!"

"We must throw the ghost-woman to the waves!" the first mate shouted. "Then will they be appeased!"

Nice to know who was the vice of the piece.

"Give it time," I shouted back. "It didn't fall on you out of a clear blue sky, you know."

The mate and captain exchanged looks. Then the master called out, "Indeed it did! One moment, we sailed in fair weather—the next, the sea heaved, and a gale struck us like a huge hand, with a torrent of rain in it!"

I stood immobile, hanging on to the rope and staring at the sea.

"Wizard?" the captain called, scowling.

"Yeah, I'm here." I turned to look at him. "That means the storm was set on you by a sorcerer."

CHAPTER 22

"Beset by a sorcerer?" the captain cried. "Aye, because of the woman!"

"No—because of me." I turned to scowl out at the waves, muttering, "Now, how the hell did she find out where I was?"

So I missed the startled glance between the mate and captain—but I turned back in time to see the way their faces hardened with purpose as they advanced on me. I was in time to see their fists coming up, too.

I raised *my* hands and started spouting nonsense syllables.

They stared, appalled, then lowered their hands.

I smiled with bitterness. "I may have a better way. It'll take a little time, of course, because I'm battling a sorcerer, not just a storm—but it'll bring back the sun." Then I turned back to the waves and started singing.

> "Peace, we ask of thee, O Ocean,
> Peace, peace, peace!"

The racket began to subside. The mate and captain looked up at the sky, startled—but the wind had already abated enough for them to hear each other without shouting.

"He *is* a wizard," the mate said.

But the captain frowned. "Who is this who has sailed with us?"

Then the wind hit us like an earthquake, and a tsunami towered over us.

They shouted and grabbed at belaying pins as the water fell on them. It drained away as the wave lifted the little ship crazily toward the sky, and the horizon dipped and rolled around us. The captain coughed out some unintelligible remark, and I stopped my singing long enough to call back, "I know—it's going to take more than that!" And it certainly would—I'd almost lost my hold on the rope! A new wave smashed down on me, and I held on for dear life, very close to wishing I would never have to see another drop of water. Then the wave washed by, and there was shouting all around. I gasped for air, searching my memory frantically. I didn't dare take out my packet of Frisson's verses; I had to rely on remembering them.

> "Built straight by a worthy master,
>   Staunch and strong, a goodly vessel,
> That shall laugh at all disaster,
>   And with wave and whirlwind wrestle!
>
> Small showers last long, but
> Sudden storms are short;
> The waves reach high in play,
> And with the winds disport.
>
> Domain of soaring gull and diving pike,
> The winds are wanton, and the sea is like
> A lass flirtatious, whose lover is ginned—
> Oft shifts her passions, like th' inconstant wind,
> Sudden she rages, like the troubled main,
> Now sinks the storm, and all is calm again!"

I chanted through to the end and, when I'd finished, started from the beginning again. As I chanted, the wind slackened and the waves began to subside.

Then a fresh gust hit us, and I knew Suettay was calling in more power from somewhere.

Well, I had reinforcements of my own. "Saint Brendan," I cried out,

> "Patron of they who sail in ships!
> Aid us with the power of prayers from your lips!
> Patron of those who sail on sea and air,
> Aid us now with the power of your prayer!"

Then I sang on.
The storm slackened again—and kept on slackening. As I

chanted the hymn over and over, the wind died down and the waves subsided until the sailors could tell it was raining. Then the rain itself died, and the clouds drifted off to the west. A sunbeam lanced down, and the sailors bellowed a cheer, waving their caps.

I left off singing with a cough. "A drink! I've sung myself dry."

The mate dashed away, still bellowing for joy.

Even the captain grinned, but his eyes were shadowed with concern. "What if the sorcerer strikes again, Wizard?"

"Then I'll have to start singing again," I croaked. "I feel sorry for you. Get me that drink, quick!" Silently, I breathed a quick thank-you to Saint Brendan, the holy Irish sailor who had set out to explore the Atlantic in a cockleshell of a boat, and who may have found North America.

The mate shoved a wooden tankard into my hand, and I drank gratefully. It was warm, bitter beer, but at that point, it tasted heavenly.

A long, triumphant cry split the air above us.

"Land!" cried the sailors who had gone aloft to unfurl the sails again. They pointed off toward the west, crying, "Laaaand!"

"Aye, 'tis land." The captain shaded his eyes, following the sailors' pointing arms. "That storm has lent us wings indeed, if that coast be Crete."

" 'Tis an island!" the lookout cried, but the men cheered anyway.

"Land is land," the captain said, his face closing into a mask. "You paid us to take you to an island off the coast of Allustria, Wizard, no more."

"Yes, I did, and we'll count the contract fulfilled." I couldn't rightly put him and his men into peril again—and after that ride, I was definitely set against sea travel. I'd make a magic carpet, or something. "And, uh, might I suggest that after you drop us off, you go find another island to visit for a week or so? You might want to give Suettay time to forget who brought us this far."

The longboat pitched and tossed—after all, the storm hadn't been over all *that* long—and Gilbert and Angelique were still looking rather green; but they managed to summon up the energy to wave good-bye to the retreating ship. The sailors raised a shout and waved back. I didn't doubt that a sourpuss or two

among them might remember who had gotten them into the
storm in the first place—but to most of them, I was only the
hero who had saved them.

Then the ship slipped below the horizon, and I turned back
to rowing. We didn't even need the sail; the waves were carrying us toward the island on their own. I needed the oars mostly
to steer.

Then the bottom rose up to meet us, and the longboat
ground into the sand. I jumped out, trying to remember that
my jeans would dry out, and threw all my weight against the
bow. Gilbert muttered something about incompetence, dragged
himself over the side, and all but fell into the water. I leapt to
help him up.

"I thank you, Master Saul," the squire gasped. "Aid me to
stay upright, here." With my help, he tottered toward the bow.

"Look," I said, "seasickness is sickness, no matter how you
slice it! You're in no shape to . . ."

Gilbert grunted as he yanked on the bow, and the longboat
slid up the shingle till its forward half was clear of the water.
Gilbert leaned against the side, gasping and swallowing.

". . . exert yourself," I finished. I tried not to stare.

Gilbert slumped, hanging onto the side of the boat and gasping like a beached whale.

Angelique was over the gunwale and at his side in a second,
although she was still looking somewhat bilious herself. "Are
you? . . . Courage, valiant squire! It . . . it will . . . pass."

Gilbert hauled himself upright. "I draw courage indeed,
from your gallant example, maiden." He forced himself to step
away from the side of the boat, but kept a hand on the gunwale. "Into what . . . manner of country are we come, Wizard?"

"Rock and scrub, mostly." I frowned, looking around me.
"Not exactly the most hospitable beach I've ever seen."

The beach itself was gravel, turning quickly into flat, shelv-
ing rock that mounted upward in steps, like the seats of an am-
phitheater, toward a fringe of grass adorned with the occasional
stunted, twisted tree. Its cousins grew here and there about the
rocky shelves, interspersed with boulders and thickets of scrub.

"Are there . . . any folk about?"

"Not that I can see." I cocked my head to the side, listening
for the mewing of the gulls. "Nor hear, for that matter."

Up high, a goat leapt down onto one of the rock ledges and
let out a bleat.

I grinned. "Well, there's life, at least. Come on, folks. Let's see if we can find a spring. We deserve a little R & R before we shove off for Thyme's island."

"Aye ..." Gilbert agreed, "water ..." He pushed himself away from the boat and stumbled after me.

Angelique, whose pride ran in different directions, was quite willing to lean on Gilbert's arm, especially since she wouldn't tax his strength any, not weighing anything.

Jealous? Who, me?

The Rat Raiser brought up the rear, frowning as his eyes flicked from side to side; he didn't trust the outdoors. If the Gremlin was still around, he gave no sign.

Perhaps with good reason; we hadn't clambered up more than three stony shelves before a dozen men stepped out from behind rocks and bushes, gathering silently in an arc before us, arms akimbo.

I stared, totally taken aback.

Then I whirled, thinking about the longboat ...

Another man stood by it, and six more stood along the gravel beach between us and our transportation.

"I think," I said slowly, "we've definitely got the wrong island—and I think we've been trespassing."

The Rat Raiser grunted. "I might have known. Where there are goats, there are people."

"Let us have at them," Gilbert groaned, pulling himself together.

I glanced at the squire. If Gilbert had been in shape, I might have chanced it—but even without him, I could unleash Frisson ...

"Wizard," the poet said, "let me speak—"

"Nay, do not!" the Rat Raiser said sharply. "Work magic so near to Allustria, and Queen Sue—the queen will know our placement to the inch!"

"I think she's already pretty close," I said, "but I hate to shed blood when it isn't necessary."

"It is not," Gilbert said. "Smite them down with a blow; stun them, no more. But if you wait, we may be so beset that you cannot choose your verses with care."

"A point," I admitted, "but I notice none of them is holding weapons."

They weren't. Each of them wore a knife as long as his forearm, but all the knives were still thrust through the peasants' belts—though their hands, clapped to their waists, weren't exactly far from the hilts. They were broad-shouldered, thick-chested men, dressed in belted tunics and loose pantaloons, with brightly colored kerchiefs tied around their heads. Their faces were swarthy and hard, and most of them wore mustaches that drooped down around their mouths. If I had been the kind to judge by looks, I would have thought they were pirates.

"No fighting," I decided. "We're not enemies yet." I pursed my lips, gazing at the man directly in front of me, who stood a little in advance of his comrades, and made up my mind. "You folks stay here." I stepped forward, ignoring Gilbert's shout of alarm, and inclined my head in greeting. "Sorry to intrude—but we didn't have much choice. There was a storm, you see . . ."

"Indeed. We saw." The man's voice sounded like a hacksaw chewing through old iron. Even so, I looked up in surprise. The words were heavily accented, but he spoke the language of Allustria. "We saw, too, that the ship left you in your longboat and sailed away. What plague do you carry, that the sailors should wish to be rid of you?"

I stared at the man. Suspicious, weren't we? I glanced at the hard-faced peasants to either side of him, remembered the ones behind us, and decided on the truth. "We are enemies of Sue . . . of the Queen of Allustria. Are we also enemies of you?"

The man's brow drew down in a scowl, and his whole body tensed, but he said, "Mayhap—though it may also chance you are not." Then he stood still, just glaring at me.

My mind flipped through alternatives and decided I didn't want the ball in my court. I held my best deadpan, looking right back in the man's eye.

It did as much good as anything. Finally, the peasant nodded and turned away. "Come," he said back over his shoulder. "This is a matter for the duke."

The castle he took us to was hundreds of years old, to judge by the weathering and the thickness of the crust of salt spray. It was squat and thick, with Roman arches and thick, Doric columns. If I'd been in my own world, I would have guessed that it had been built by adventurous Normans, and would have called it Romanesque.

For all that, though, it wasn't especially menacing. It was made of some light-colored stone that had a touch of red in it, warm with the stored sun-heat. It might be forbidding, but it wasn't gloomy.

Its owner was very much like it.

The duke, as it turned out, was somewhere in his fifties, grizzled but still powerfully built, looking about as aristocratic as a rugby scrum. Certainly he fitted right in with his men—except that he was wearing a midnight-blue robe decorated with the signs of the zodiac and girded with a belt that held a heavy-looking broadsword. He carried a six-foot staff made of some hard, gleaming wood, so dark as to be almost black, carved into the form of a serpent. Instinctively, I braced myself; the astrological gown was neither black magic nor white, but the staff was definitely tending toward symbols of evil. In European culture, the snake was, if not always a sign of Satan, at least usually a sign of menace.

"I am Syrak, duke of this island," the martial magician said. "Who are you, who come unbidden to my shore?"

I decided on the most general truth. "We are wayfarers, seeking to come to an island near Allustria, milord."

"Vincentio tells me you were cast adrift by the ship that brought you here."

"That was by our own request."

"Request? Why would you request to be set adrift from a ship, hey?" The duke's gaze sharpened. "Did you not tell Vincentio you were enemies of Queen Suettay?"

I winced at his use of the queen's name, but maybe it wouldn't matter—if she noticed him, she might not notice us. I nodded, still carefully deadpan. "We did. We did not wish the captain and crew to suffer for having brought us."

"And you also wished to go secretly from Allustria, did you not? You did not care whether you would bring the queen's wrath down on us, hey?"

"We weren't really planning to land on an island with people on it," I admitted. Out of the corner of my eye, I noticed that Gilbert's scowl had darkened, and that he had noticeably perked up a bit. I did not think that was an entirely favorable sign.

"But you *have* landed on an island with people! And if we let you go free, Suettay's wrath will fall on us! Will it not?"

His men stirred around him, muttering.

"There's a chance of it," I admitted. "But, if we get some fresh water, and a little rest, and food, we can be away before dawn tomorrow. The queen doesn't even have to know we were here." And to Gilbert, "We're outnumbered, you know."

"When has that ever given you pause?" Gilbert asked.

The duke scowled, but decided not to notice him. "There is something in what you say—if you speak truly."

"Oh, I do!" I said, with alacrity. "Believe me—there is absolutely no reason to doubt my veracity!"

"Yes," the duke said. "And surely you would say just that if you lied. In truth, the more false your words, the more you will swear they are true."

I drew myself up with maximum indignation. "Are you saying I'm a liar?"

"I am saying that I wish you to prove the truth of your words."

I stared at him, trying to think of a proof. Finally, I shook my head. "I can't. I *am* telling the truth, mind you—but, prove it? Short of bringing the queen here to testify, I can't think of a way."

"No, and I think she would be a grumbly guest," the duke said, with grim humor. "Yet if you cannot think of a way to prove your truth, be assured that we can."

"And that is?" I asked, with foreboding. Somehow, I had a notion that the duke's idea of proof wouldn't exactly delight Euclid.

"The Ordeal," the duke said, and I could hear the capital. "One of you must undergo the Ordeal, that the others may go free."

"Me," I said, without even stopping to think—which was a good thing, because Gilbert was one syllable behind me.

"I shall!"

The duke nodded, a slight smile curving his lips. "You have said it," he said to me. "It is your portion!"

"But I—" Gilbert started, before Angelique drowned him out.

"Ohhhh, nooooo!" She threw herself between me and the duke, her substance wavering, growing brighter and dimmer as she tried to hold his attention. "You have no way of knowing what manner of horrible things this Ordeal may hold, my love! Oh, nay, Lord Duke, do not submit him to the torture! You cannot, you must not! He is a good man, he is truthful in all he says and does, he is not deserving of such horrid treatment!"

Gilbert stared, flabbergasted.

"Gently, gently," I soothed. I caught her hands, wishing I could feel them, and summoned up every ounce of reassurance I could. "I'll survive, never you fear. And as to pain and torture, why, I expect I've withstood worse. Right, milord?"

The duke stood with a face of flint. "What manner of man are you, that you have won the love of a ghost?"

"A wizard," I answered.

"But one not wise." Nonetheless, the duke nodded. "Still, it speaks well for you that your friends are so quick to leap to your defense."

"There, I knew it," I said quickly. "You see? It'll be all right ... Gilbert, help the lady, will you? There now, darling, don't worry. I've been though tortures before."

"But there is no need! You are an honorable man!" she cried, then collapsed weeping into Gilbert's arms. He held her up and turned her away, his face a study in consternation.

"You will take them to their boat," the duke informed Vincentio. "Bid them sail, and watch till they've gone from sight."

Vincentio nodded, and his band closed around my companions, hiding them from view.

I didn't even get to watch them out of sight, myself; the duke took me by the elbow and turned me away, leading me back across the drawbridge and into the castle. "So, then, you come. And begin your Ordeal, yes?"

"Of course," I said, feeling somewhat numb. At least the duke wasn't gloating about it. I took that to mean he wasn't a sadist—so things could have been worse.

Couldn't they?

As we passed through the huge portal into the keep, a shadow moved, and I thought I recognized the Gremlin's silhouette—but I hoped I was wrong. I'd far rather he was with Angelique and the boys. I didn't think the sprite could do much for me, but he could make the difference between freedom and capture for my friends.

But it would have been nice to know I wasn't completely alone.

Besides, how bad could the Ordeal be? I eyed the duke, again taking in the astrological signs on his gown and the snaky staff. He wasn't completely gone over to black magic, that was obvious. Using some aspects of it, maybe, but not wholly dedicated to it yet—playing the old game, thinking he could take what he wanted of the Devil's power without giving anything of himself.

I halted, shocked. Was that what I was trying to do?

Certainly not. There had to be a distinction. Had to.

That was it—I wasn't trying to use the Devil's power. Or God's, for that matter, though I wasn't doing as well there—I had called on a saint or two, now and then, and even recited a prayer or two directly to the Top. As an equivocator, I wasn't doing so well. Could be the duke was better at the balancing act.

Or maybe he wasn't even the equivocator he seemed to be. Maybe he was a white magician who was only borrowing a few diabolical symbols.

And being tempted. Sorely.

The duke led me up to the battlements so I could watch the longboat put out to sea. I could just barely make out the little black dots that were heads, but the duke was true to his word. My friends, at least, were safe.

"Now you come," the duke said, and led me down the stairs.

And down.

And down.

Somewhere below the dungeons, in a pool of torchlight, we stopped. Before us, a stone slab rose up from the floor, knee-high, six feet long, and four feet wide. I eyed it warily and decided it was too low to be an altar. Which was a definite comfort to me, as the peasants stripped off my shirt and started tying me down.

CHAPTER 23

The duke hit the floor with the heel of his staff. It struck with a huge, booming reverberation, out of all proportion to its size. Then he thrust it up high, swirling its tip above his head in a widening helix and calling out. The call became rhythmical, settling into a chant. I frowned, straining to understand; the language sure wasn't the one I'd been hearing. It seemed older somehow, kind of like Latin.

Latin! Once I realized that, I was able to catch the occasional cognate. "Sun," that word had to be, and "heat," which made sense—and sure as taxes that next one had to be "water," or a near relative. That was a number—five! And was that "days" after it? Wasn't that a negative suffix, though? But why negative? . . .

The duke finished his chant, brandishing his staff again, and the peasants repeated the verse; the cavern boomed with it. Then all of a sudden they went quiet, and the duke shouted out a last sentence, punctuating it by slamming his staff against the floor again . . .

Where the heel struck the rock, an explosion blossomed in silence, a burst of searing white light against the cavern's gloom, swelling, expanding, filling the chamber . . .

It was the sun.

I squeezed my eyes shut against the glare; afterimages danced. I gave my eyes time to adjust to the crimson, then opened them just a little, squinting.

I was still lashed to the rock—but it was surrounded by miles of sand. Heat waves shimmered about me, and the sky was a brazen coin in pitiless blue. There wasn't a cloud in

sight, and the heat baked me as if I were in an oven. I could
have sworn I could feel the rock heating up below me, and I
was already bathed in sweat.

Suddenly, the significance of the duke's "five days" hit
me—I was supposed to stay bound to this stone bed for a hundred and twenty hours! And the negative suffix was about water!

In panic, I realized Frisson had been right—like it or not, I'd
have to try to work magic on my own. Call it working within
the frame of reference of the hallucination, call it selling out,
call it whatever you like—I was going to have to do it, or die.

Preferably without drawing on either the powers of good, or
of evil.

I tried to think of some verse that would stop my sweat
glands—I was going to need every ounce of water my body
held. Then I remembered that without sweat, I would overheat
in an hour.

Decisions, decisions!

It was going to be a long day.

I decided it *had* been a long day already, but the sun was
still ominously close to the zenith. My tongue felt like a piece
of leather, and my skin felt about right for writing. How long
had it really been—an hour? Maybe less?

No matter—I wasn't going to last the day, and I had a notion my body was going to stay there without me for at least
twenty-four hours. I had to have water, fast—or *something* to
drink, anyway. What I wouldn't have given now, for a cola . . .

Inspiration struck. Commercial jingles! Could I remember
one?

Could I ever forget?

Could I talk enough to recite it?

I smacked my lips, or tried to—and found I couldn't get
them to open. In desperation, I worked my cheeks, trying to
pump up some saliva—but nothing came. Panic began to grow,
but I forced it down sternly while I kept working my
cheeks . . .

Pain lanced through my lower lip. Blast! I'd bitten it again.
It hurt, on top of everything else, and I tasted blood . . .

Blood.

Moisture.

I moved the tip of my swelling tongue against the inside of

my lips, pushed hard—and they opened. I took a deep breath . . .

And the blood dried up.

Quickly, before my mouth could seal up again, I cried,

> "Drink Sass-Pa-Rilla, like a man,
>   In the bottle, in the can!
>   Right from the store, into my hand!"

Something slapped into my palm, something cold and wet. I breathed a sigh of relief and started to bring it to my lips . . .

My hand wouldn't move.

It was tied over my head.

I bit down against anger, and called up a verse:

> "Unravel the cord, and untie the knot!
>   Loosen the binding, for bind it shall not!"

I felt a writhing about my wrists and ankles that made my innards twist in revulsion. Sternly, I schooled my stomach; it was only the ropes untying themselves—I hoped. I lifted the arm with the soda in it, experimentally . . .

It lifted. And was instantly filled with a hundred hot needles.

I let the arm fall back, groaning with agony. But I had to get at that soda. I lifted again, but the effort made my body roll, and I finished up scraping the can across the stone toward my mouth. I made it, and my teeth closed on aluminum.

Just aluminum. No soda.

I had forgotten to open the can.

I just lay there a second, marveling at my own stupidity. Then, with another groan and a great deal more stabbing pain, this time in the upper arms, shoulders, and chest, I managed to work my way up onto my elbows and achieve the stupendous feat of hooking a finger through the ring. I pulled; the top popped; I bowed my head and lifted, and a splash of soothing, chilly Sass-Pa-Rilla flowed into my mouth. Most of that first shot ran down my chin and sizzled onto the rock, but enough of it sloshed into my mouth to fill me with the blessed, icy taste, burning the cut where I'd bitten my lip. My throat worked, and I felt the trail of cold all the way down into my stomach. I sighed, lifted the can, and took a real swallow. I had never known a commercial product could taste so good and decided I'd never make a joke about Sass-Pa-Rilla again.

Which was very good because, as I lifted the can, it disappeared.

I stared at my cupped and empty hand as if it had betrayed me. Then I curled it into a fist, feeling the anger rise. Not my hand, but somebody else, some person, had betrayed me—and I had a notion who. The duke had decided he didn't want the rules changed. I didn't feel sorry for him; after all, I'd told him I was a wizard before he tried hanging me out to dry. He shouldn't have been so sure I couldn't survive—even though, come to think of it, I wasn't all that sure of it, myself.

But I was also a wizard who was going to need a little help to fight back—and whatever I was going to do, I was going to have to do it quickly, before the spurt of energy from the cold drink wore off. Already, I could feel the searing heat enveloping me again, and the first tendrils of a headache were rising to meet it. Where could I get reinforcements?

Of course! The local spirits. Every little location had them— the nature spirits, the sprites and dryads and nixies and pixies, the spirits of trees and streams and even grass!

> "Ye elves of desert, rocks, and wind-blown dunes,
> And ye that on the sand with printless foot
> Do chase siroccos, and do fly them,
> Whose aid, weak masters though ye be,
> I now require, to bedim the noontide sun,
> And save my hide from furnace winds!"

Well, Shakespeare would forgive me.

Tendrils of mist started to rise from the ground around me, from the boulders and the sand—mist, where there was no moisture. I breathed a sigh of relief and croaked, "Let's hear it for animism."

Then the spirits finished taking form.

There wasn't much of them—just tenuous, smoky-looking, hulking shapes about knee-high. Behind them was a miniature whirlwind filled with sand—a dust devil?

"You have called," one of the rock-faces croaked. "We have come."

"What manner of spirits are you?"

"You have called for the spirits of the land," another boulder-type grated. "We are they—spirits of rock and sand."

"I should have realized," I groaned. "Mineral spirits."

"We will aid you, if we can," the first rock-ghost growled. "How may we do so?"

"Hanged if I know," I muttered. "You wouldn't have anything cool about you, would you?"

"At midday?" hissed the whirlwind. "Nay! We all are heated through and through."

"I figured as much." The rock under me was getting hot even in my shadow. "And none of you have any moisture, do you?"

"You cannot get water from a stone," a boulder grated.

The whirlwind drifted closer. "Shall I fan you with my breeze?"

The first tendrils of moving air caressed me, and I gasped, drawing back. "Uh, no thanks! I appreciate the intention, but you have all the charm of a furnace!" A horrid notion crossed my mind. "Uh—what do men call your kind of spirit?"

"A dust devil," the whirlwind answered.

"I thought so." I swallowed, painfully. "You, uh—haven't come hot from Hell, have you?"

"Nay!" The tone was indignant. "You asked what men call me, not what I am!"

I nodded. "I thought so. What's in a name? Not much, in this case. You're no more a part of the Hell crew than—"

I broke off, my eyes widening.

"Than what?" the dust devil pressed.

"Than something I learned about in general physics! Of course! If I'm hot and I want to get cool, who *should* I call for but Maxwell's Demon?"

"I know of him," the dust devil hummed. "We dwell in neighboring realms and are much alike in that we are neither evil nor good, but much maligned by men."

"Can you get him here? He's an expert in air-conditioning! If anybody can save me, he can!"

"I shall try," the dust devil said, and whirled faster and faster until it had flung itself to bits, disappearing.

I stared. That was going home?

Then I realized what I had asked for, and waited in dread. Maxwell's Demon was a gimmick James Clerk Maxwell had dreamed up, in an attempt to get around Newton's laws of thermodynamics. Being from the never-never land of scientists' whimsy, he wouldn't be either good or bad—he'd be an impersonal force. So he wouldn't be one that could be ordered around—and might decide not to help me. In fact, there was no guarantee he would be here; he came if he wanted to, and didn't if he didn't.

Maybe I hadn't made the situation clear. I tried again.

> "Entropy personified,
>   I will soon be mummified
>   If your power retrograde
> Comes not eftsoons unto my aid!"

I wasn't sure about the "eftsoons" part; after all, Maxwell had invented his Demon in the nineteenth century, not the—

Air split with the sound of gunshot, and the Demon was there, a point of unbearably intense light, with the dust devil rising from the sand again behind it. The Demon was singing and humming, "What have we here? What other mortal knows of me in this universe of magic?"

"The name's Saul," I said, with my most ingratiating smile. Then the implications of the spark's remark hit me like a ton of books. "*Other* mortal?"

"Aye. I have a friend who knows my name, though he learned of it in another realm within the curves of time and space."

I forced myself not to ask; first things first, and right now, survival was kind of the top priority. "I don't suppose you'd be willing to lend a hand to another know-it-all, would you?"

"Mayhap," the Demon hummed, "if it strikes me as amusing. Know, mortal, that the bane of existence of immortals is tedium. If you can offer me respite in the form of some unusual event, I shall be quite pleased to intervene on your behalf. What diversion can you offer me?"

"How about saving my life?"

"I have saved mortals before." The Demon seemed irritated. "What is new in the fashion in which you would have me save you?"

I began to realize that I was really dealing with an embodiment of physical principles—impersonal, like a computer, and therefore needing explicit instructions that it would follow to the letter. Unlike a computer, though, it wanted to be amused.

I would have to be very careful of what I said.

"I specialize in paradoxes," I told the Demon. "You might have fun watching."

"Paradox?" The Demon sounded interested. "In what fashion?"

"Well, for openers, I contradict myself every five minutes—especially since I came to this universe. Not my own idea, by the way."

"I doubt it not." The Demon's hum deepened to a lower pitch. "In what manner do you contradict yourself?"

"I'm bound and determined not to be committed, you see—not to a woman, not to an idea, not even to myself, if I can help it—but especially not to good or evil."

"Amazing," the Demon murmured. "How have you endured more than thirty seconds in this universe in which all action stems from either good or evil, from God or Satan?"

"By pure dumb luck, I guess, until I found out what was going on. But as soon as an emissary from each side had tried to recruit me, I dug my heels in and turned mule-headed. I was bound and determined not to be a tool for either one—so every time I accidentally did something a little bit good, I tried to follow it with something a little bit bad."

" 'Tis a set of poles, not a continuum," the Demon corrected me in an abstracted tone. "Indeed, you live in contradiction—not in thoughts or words alone, but in deeds. Yet do you dare no more than little bits?"

Indignation hit, along with the age-old alertness that someone was trying to infringe on my identity, to twist me into his own path. "I'm me," I said, "not an extension of somebody else, natural or supernatural. I have to be me; I can't be anybody else. If I go in for big gestures, stupendous feats of nobility, I'm committing myself to good so thoroughly that I become just an extension of it. Worse, I'd have to counteract that by doing something really vile, which would mean I'd have to infringe on someone else's identity, destroy their integrity, and that's just flat-out wrong. No, I'll do little bits of good and evil, thank you, but all I'll go for in a big way is being me."

"Excellently stated!" the Demon hummed. "You have grasped the essence of paradox!"

I had?

"I cannot allow a mind such as this to be wasted and withered," he went on. "What would you of me?"

"Shelter!" I gasped—then, afraid of seeming too eager, I tried nonchalance. "As you can see, I'm in the kind of a bind only you can save me from."

"Save?" The Demon hummed, surveying the situation.

The local spirits groaned and winked out, vanishing into their boulders and sand grains.

"Kin!" the dust devil gusted. "Source and lord!"

"In some measure, mayhap," the Demon hummed, and to me, "Wherefore seek you my aid? Here is one with power enough!"

"Only to make things hot," I groaned, "and my species doesn't do too well at temperatures above ninety degrees Fahrenheit."

"Aye—I had forgotten you were so fragile," the Demon answered. "I ken not how your kind has survived so long, balanced on so fine a line of energy."

"Cultural evolution! Artificial temperature control! Technology! But the duke and his men stranded me out here without any machines, and I'm just not built for it! *Please*, Demon—take me someplace cool! About seventy degrees Fahrenheit," I added quickly. Somehow, I didn't think I wanted to be where it was cool for the Demon.

"Someplace that is neither hot nor cool, rather," the Demon corrected me, "a barrier between heat and cold. Aye, I know of such a place. But 'tis such a realm as would drive a mortal mad."

Ingrained caution welled up. "How so?"

"Why, for that 'tis a realm of paradox incarnate, where a mortal would be lost in confusion ..." The Demon's voice trailed off, then ignited with enthusiasm. "Aye, we shall put you to the test of yourself! Do you think that you are so wholly dedicated to paradox as to withstand the confrontation of it?"

I hesitated—but he was putting me to the test of my self-image. "If I'm not," I said, "I want to know about it." Then the counterimpulse made me say, "Besides, if I can't, you can always drop me back in the real world—preferably at some point a little less extreme in temperature."

The Demon keened with delight. "You contradict yourself indeed! Nay, let us see how you withstand the test that you yourself conceive! Come, mortal, away!"

The landscape tilted and slid—or was it I who was sliding? I didn't know, but suddenly, blessed coolness surrounded me. In fact, I shivered.

"Sixty-eight degrees Fahrenheit," the Demon informed me.

"I'll get used to it," I promised, "fast. Thank you, Demon.

You're a lifesaver." I looked around, and found myself in a realm of formless gray. Mist seemed to fill all the volume about me, and beyond it were only clouds. I looked down and, for all I knew, I could be sitting on another cloud. "Where are we?"

"Where you have wished to be," the Demon said, "the barrier between the cold and the hot."

I looked up, startled, finally recognizing the reference.

"Welcome to my home," the Demon sang.

"Uh—thanks." I looked around, feeling kind of weird—new boy in town, and all. And a town there was; shapes were beginning to show through the mist—houses, or things that my mind was interpreting as houses; it occurred to me that I probably wasn't seeing what was really there—or, rather, that I was seeing it, or my eyes were, but my mind couldn't accept it or comprehend it, so it was giving me familiar analogs. If that was the case, then the mist would be the fog of my own confusion. One way or another, it was thinning as I began to be able to recognize forms, and I was feeling a bit better at being able to see houses—in the shapes of geometric solids, and with polygons for windows and doors, but definitely houses. And a street—though it looped about in a funny way, and I couldn't see anything supporting it. And some strange, amorphous masses of greenery that kept fluxing and flowing and changing shape, like vegetable amoebas; I figured they had to be analogous to trees and bushes.

And there were animals.

Or should I say, "creatures"? The first ones to come ambling up were a pair of cats that hadn't quite made it into twins—there were two of them from the middle forward, but at the end of the rib cage, they joined, and only had one set of hindquarters. A single tail snaked around and tickled the ear of the head that had its eyes shut; they opened, and the other head's eyelids closed.

That unnerved me, not to mention its offending me—how would you feel if someone sauntered up to you and fell asleep? "What's the matter?" I asked the wide-awake head. "Early morning last night?"

"Nay," the cat answered, which somehow didn't surprise me. "He has died—and I have come alive."

I stared.

Then I said, "Is *he* going to come alive again, too?"

"Aye, at some odd moment. We can never know when,

though. We know that when he lives, I die, for the two of us cannot both be alive at one time."

Something connected. "I thought that only applied when you were in your box," I said.

"Nay," he contradicted me. "When we go home to our box, both become comatose—neither alive nor dead."

"Till someone opens the lid," I said. "You're Schrödinger's Cat." Which explained the joined hindquarters—only the front part had split into two time lines yet.

The cat turned to the Demon with a look of surprised approval. "You have found a mortal with some modicum of sense."

"No," I said, "just a little knowledge."

"Then you are very dangerous."

"More than you know," the Demon sang. "I did not find him—he called for *me*!"

The cat looked at me and shuddered. "You could visit chaos upon us all!"

"I could?" I said blankly, then realized that I was throwing away a bargaining chip. "Oh, yeah, I could! I wouldn't, of course—especially since your friend Maxwell's Demon has helped me out of a tight spot."

"A hot spot, rather," the Demon explained. " 'Twas like to fry his brains."

The cat looked at me as if that might be an improvement. "Can you not send him back?"

"Aye, when the night has come, and coolness with it."

I glanced around at the alien setting, feeling kind of nervous. "If you don't mind the waiting." I wasn't sure I didn't.

"Oh, we need not wait!" the Demon sang. "From this space-time, we may project you to any point within your own."

"Oh," I said, feeling stupid. "You mean I'm not even in the same universe?"

"Nay. This realm lies between universes."

"Then it's a universe of its own."

"Mayhap, though I would be reluctant to term it so, when 'tis so small."

I sat bolt-upright, galvanized by a sudden revelation. "Then you could just as easily send me back to my home universe!"

"I could," the Demon agreed. "Do you wish it?"

That brought me up short. I frowned, considering alternatives—Angelique, and the fun I'd been having not working magic, and Angelique, and the adventure, and Angelique, and the friends I'd gained—or companions, at least—and Angelique, and the fact that I felt as if I was worth something. Especially to Angelique. Okay, there was danger in it, too, but at least it wasn't boring. "No," I said slowly, "not just yet."

After all, I couldn't commit myself to not committing myself, could I?

"Then to the universe of Allustria, whence you came," the cat urged.

But the Demon asked, "Are there many like you, in your home universe?"

"Not enough for comfort." I frowned; a long horizontal plane was coming into focus, looking like a fence made out of a continuous sheet of plywood. "Like me in what way?"

"In believing in Maxwell's Demon."

"Oh." I relaxed, shaking my head. "No, not many. Maybe a million."

"A million!"

"Out of three billion," I said quickly. "Even out of the ones who know about you, most of them think you're just a scientific fable."

"But we are," the Demon and the cat sang together, and the Demon went on, "This is the home of all such fables—and of those of logic and reason, too."

But I was distracted by the big eyeballs and the long nose peeking over the fence. When I glanced directly at them, though, they disappeared. "What's *he* doing here?"

The Demon didn't even look. " 'Tis as much his home as Yehudi's."

"Yehudi?" I glanced around, noting a series of level planes rising away off to my left, like a staircase—but it was empty. "I don't see him."

"Of course not; the little man is not there," the cat said contemptuously. Behind him, I noticed two guys with saffron robes and bald heads, sitting in lotus position facing each other; each was holding a lightbulb, but one was so dark it must have been burned out.

"I suppose that makes sense," I said. "Then the Gremlin is here, too?"

"Shh!" The cat glanced about with apprehension. "Speak not of him, for if he comes, he will make all go awry."

"I don't think so; we've been getting to know each other." I felt better, knowing the Gremlin still wasn't home—and even better, from the cat's look of surprise. I noticed a guy with medium-length hair and a very bland face, in a powder-blue oxford-cloth shirt, blue jeans, and running sneakers, strolling along the row of polygons. "Who's he?"

"The Norm," the Demon sang.

"I thought he didn't really exist."

"Be still!" the cat spat, but he was too late. The Norm faded away and disappeared. "Now you have done it." The cat sighed. "It will take him many days to believe in himself strongly enough to manifest again."

"Sorry," I said, feeling very guilty, so I whispered the next one. "Who's the anorexic over there?" I was talking about the guy who was a stick figure, like the ones kids draw—a featureless circle on top, with straight lines for arms and legs and torso.

"The Statistical Abstract," the Demon hummed softly. "You need not fear; he will not go away."

A robot came clanking up and ground to a halt.

I stepped back, ready for trouble. "He doesn't belong here! Where I come from, he's real—these days!"

"Only my body," a voice said, but the robot's mouth just opened once, and a wispy form drifted out of it to float in midair before us. "I had wondered how long 'twould be ere you came amongst us!"

"Hey, I know you!" I said. "You're the philosophy assignment I really resented!"

"The Ghost in the Machine," the breezy voice agreed. "Wherefore did you resent me?"

"Not you," I said, "just having to prove that you didn't exist, when something inside me told me you did!"

"Indeed I do, but only in this realm that defies all logic," the ghost agreed.

"Oh," I said. "So that's why you thought I'd come here some day."

"Indeed," the ghost agreed. "Do you still rail against reason, even as you practice it?"

"Not really," I said with a smile. "Kant got me out of that."

"Even so," said the large, egg-shaped guy who came strolling up. I looked closer and realized he really was an egg. " 'Tis even as I've said about words—only a matter of whether they will master you, or you will master them."

"Right." I nodded. "Logic's just a tool. You can't let it run your life by itself." But I was bothered by the implication of his knowing my inner thoughts so well—was I really as much of a fence sitter as he was?

Yes. I had that sense of balance.

In the distance, I heard a long and mournful whistle, and a locomotive chuffed by drawing a train around a circular track, with so many cars that the engine was both pulling the tender and pushing the caboose, which was pulling it. I didn't have to look; I knew it had no driver. It was going faster and faster the longer it ran, and I looked away. "Say, you wouldn't know where I can find the Dinganzich, would you?"

"It is not here," the ghost lamented.

"We have only its shadow among us," the Demon said.

"No," I said with regret, "I was looking for the real thing. Next dimension, huh?"

"Nay; beyond them," the Demon commiserated. "I fear, mortal, that what you truly seek is not here."

"And probably not anywhere," I sighed, "except inside me after all."

"Or in Heaven," one of the monks spoke up.

I frowned, looking up at him. "Thought you guys didn't believe in that state."

"It has many names," the monk explained.

"Look, I gave up on trying to find God a long time ago."

The monk shook his head. "Foolish. You must seek while you live, if you would find Him after death."

But that had a false ring to it. "Next thing I know, you'll be telling me the Ultimate Buddha is in Heaven along with Jehovah."

"Nay," the monk contradicted. "They are Heaven, and they are one."

"One what?" I asked, then felt a chill pass over my back and into my vitals. I tried to chase it by saying, "You would think that way," but I shivered and turned to the Demon. "I think maybe I'd better get out of here. I'm not ready for this."

"Will you ever be?" the cat mocked, but the ghost said, "He may be, if he never leaves off seeking."

"Yet for now, you have the right of it," the Demon told me. "Back to your Ordeal, mortal. Are you refreshed?"

"Enough to last," I told him. "Could you send me back to just before sunrise at the end of the fifth night after you found me?"

"Gladly," the Demon said. "Prepare yourself."

"Hey, just a minute!" I said. "I almost forgot. This other guy in that universe—the one that you said knew about you, too. Who is he?"

"He is Matthew Mantrell, Lord Wizard of Merovence. Do you wish to go to him?"

It was tempting—but there was Angelique, and the need to get her body back. "No," I said slowly, "I'm just glad to know he's alive and well."

"He is," the Demon assured me. "Now let us see to yourself. Lie back and relax, mortal."

I did, closing my eyes.

"Awake," the Demon's hum said right next to my ear. I opened my eyes and sat up—and realized I *could* sit up. Of course—I had spelled away the ropes. No reason to think they would have come back, was there?

"Thanks, Demon," I said. "I won't forget you for this."

I could feel an impulse to laughter somewhere around me, and the Demon's voice hummed, "I am rewarded in your mere existence, mortal, so long as you seek to remain poised on the cusp of paradox. Farewell, for the sun is rising."

I looked toward the east just as the first ray pierced the lightened sky. "Good-bye, Demon," I said into the roseate glory of the new morning. "And thanks."

CHAPTER 24

They appeared as black dots on the face of the rising sun, then expanded hugely, seeming to zoom out of the ruddy disk—the duke, with a dozen of his men behind him. Most of the men carried shovels, but one of them was nice enough to be carrying a big water skin—probably for them, not for me.

I debated whether I should play dessicated semicorpse, or just be sitting up obviously alive, well, and nonchalant. That last sounded suspiciously like bragging, but what the Hell, it was the truth, so I went with it.

They loomed dark and darker until they were close enough to begin seeing features. That's when I sat up.

They shied off like elephants confronting a lemming, and the duke took time for some loudly intoned verses in his archaic language, with a few mystic passes. I just sat there and watched, studying his technique—but I didn't feel anything, so he must have been working on de-ghosting a risen corpse. Wouldn't have any effect on me, of course, since I was still alive and in my body . . .

The duke finished his gestures and chants, and his eyes widened when I didn't disappear or even waver. He came closer, very carefully, as if I were a rattlesnake that might strike any minute, the whites showing all around his irises. He edged up near enough for a close inspection, reached out toward me as if he were going to prod me to make sure I was really there, but said instead, "You live!"

"That's my main occupation," I agreed.

"He should be dried!" one of the boys in the back row muttered, with a quaver that would have done credit to a vibraphone. "He should be leather!"

"I'm not feeling too chipper," I admitted. "But I'm still juicy."

" 'Tis not unknown." You could see the duke was doing a quick revision on his estimates. "Yet those few who have endured till the second morn were feverish, seeing sights that mortal eyes seldom view . . ."

I felt a chill; that sounded uncomfortably like the Demon's home. "They told you about that, did they?"

"Some one or two who endured to reclaim life," the duke admitted. "Most have not lived to see a third dawn, no matter how gently we tend them, for they are the chattels of the god, look you . . ."

The god? Suddenly I realized why this man's magic seemed to be halfway between good and evil—he was a pagan and didn't realize the source of the powers he was drawing on!

". . . and surely none can speak of the holy sights they have seen, when we find them, for their tongues are swollen." A look of foreboding came over his face. "How is it yours is not?"

I didn't see any reason to lie. "I conjured up something to drink."

"That, I did sense—and did seek to block! How is it you were able to go around my wall, and without my knowing of it?"

I wondered where he thought I'd brought that drink from— and I began to see what he was afraid I'd been doing. "I went away. I called up some friendly spirits, and one of them took me to one of those places your victims see, but can't tell you about. He and his friends took care of me and sent me back as you see me." I didn't figure I needed to tell him about the time shift—that would just have complicated matters.

The man in the back row spoke up again, his voice trembling. "What spirits are these he can call upon?"

"Be silent!" the duke snapped, so viciously that I knew he must be scared—and overawed, or he would have thrown a whammy at me. "In truth," he said to me, "you must be a far more puissant wizard than I had thought."

I caught the subtext—that he was afraid I was more powerful than he was. Maybe I could play on that. "I guess so," I agreed. "Things being as they are, maybe you'll go a step further than just letting me live, the way you promised."

"What step is that?" He was braced for the worst.

"A boat," I said. "Nothing elaborate—just a one-man craft, with a sail and a rudder. Say, about twenty feet long."

He looked startled, and another anonymous voice from the ranks muttered, "What will he conjure up to sail it for him?"

Now, that was a thought. For a moment, I toyed with asking Sir Francis Drake or Christopher Columbus in for an excursion, but I decided they might be otherwise occupied. "I'll manage," I assured the duke. "You might put in a few goodies, too—say, a week's worth of journey rations. And water."

"Oh, aye!" He nodded his head, most emphatically. "For one who has survived the Ordeal? Oh, most surely."

You bet he thought it was a good idea. Get me out of his hair, for only a longboat and a week's worth of rations? Cheap at the price. For all he knew, I might have been sore enough to turn against him. Which wasn't that bad an idea, now that I thought of it—but I didn't have time; I had bigger fish to spear.

"And speaking of water . . ." I glanced suggestively at the water skin.

The duke snapped his fingers, and the water carrier hurried to the front with the skin. He started to hand it to me, then thought better of it and shoved it at his boss. Let *him* take the risks.

"All praise to he who has survived the Ordeal," the duke said, presenting the skin as if it were a trophy.

By extreme self-control, I managed not to snatch it; I only took it from his hands slowly, popped the cork, and shot a jet from it into my mouth, reflecting on the irony of cool wetness tasting so good, so soon after I had almost hoped I would never have to see another drop of it. I was going to have to be careful what I wished for.

A couple of men-at-arms were very willing to push the boat into the waves for me, saving my legs from wetness at the cost of their own dousing. I could have done it myself easily enough, but if they wanted to honor me, I was willing to let them. I was beginning to realize the value of status and prestige in a world like this one. Besides, it helped them feel as if they were doing something to get rid of me. I let go of an oar long enough to wave bye-bye, then managed to catch it again before it had quite slipped away into the next wave. It was going to take me a while to get used to having just a couple of pegs for an oarlock.

Nonetheless, I did manage to get the boat through the breakers and out beyond the bar—I could almost hear the soldiers snickering at my lack of seamanship, all the way out here. After all, on a little island like this, every able-bodied man must have started out as a fisherman or a sailor, even if he later became a soldier. They'd make fantastic marines.

Out into the swells, I shipped the oars and hoisted canvas. I'd learned to sail in the summers, out of sheer boredom—when you grow up near the Great Lakes, you have all sorts of opportunities for water sports. So I managed to get the sail up and catch a breeze without capsizing. My wake began to foam, and I was off.

Very quickly the wind picked up. I frowned, shivering and wishing I'd thought to ask the duke for a cloak, then glanced up at the sun.

There wasn't much of it there.

I glared up at the clouds, willing them away—but I felt a sinking feeling in my stomach. The day had dawned clear and sunny—very sunny. If it was clouding up so soon, it could just be a storm front moving in—or it could be Suettay, out to have another try at drowning me. If I had another storm blow up, there wouldn't be any Frisson around to hand me magic verses. I'd have to try to lull it by myself—and I hated working magic on my own. It felt like surrender, somehow. Besides, I wasn't all that sure I could succeed.

None of that! I reminded myself sternly. Defeatist attitudes wouldn't help. Besides, I didn't really need to make the storm go away—just manage to get safely to shore.

Safely?

A nasty suspicion budded in my head and blossomed into the full-grown conviction that the storm dying down just where it did hadn't been completely my doing. Suettay could have seen that I was going to win that round and kept wrestling just long enough to drive us onto the island, hoping that its xenophobic duke would do her dirty work for her, conveniently killing us off before we could do her any more damage. Maybe I hadn't won such a great victory, after all. Maybe it had really been a very deliberate conjuration by a very nasty sorceress.

Of course, she might have been doing me a favor—as a ghost, I could no doubt have had a much better time with Angelique than I could as a—

I clamped down on that thought, hard. That way lay suicide, and losing all hope of getting Angelique completely free of Suettay's machinations.

Careful, there, boy, I warned myself. You're coming perilously close to admitting that magic works in the here-and-now.

No. Absolutely impossible. A philosophical absurdity. Which, of course, was the point—magic was completely illogical.

Completely?

I reined in my thoughts, exasperated. When would I ever learn to stop making sweeping generalizations? They always had exceptions.

Okay—so maybe this universe was one of the exceptions?

I backed up against that one like a Missouri mule against an overloaded wagon. Somehow, I was constitutionally unable to accept the notion that magic might work, outside of a massively detailed hallucination. Possibly because if I allowed that it did, I would find it very hard to come up with a reason to avoid committing myself to one side or the other.

Or to Angelique?

Well, now, that was the advantage to being in love with a ghost. The vow, after all, reads, "Till death do us part," and death already *had* parted us—before we even got together.

Somehow, that sounded pretty thin, but I held on to it.

All right. Try something else then. And hurry, stupid—those clouds have grown awfully thick and awfully low, and that breeze has a definite taste of rain to it.

Okay. I decided to suppose, just suppose, magic really did work in this world. How would I work my way out of this storm?

All right, so I was cheating. I put that issue aside and decided to deal with it when I had time.

Actually, I wasn't all that sure I wanted to get rid of the storm. Drifting without any wind at all wasn't exactly my idea of a picnic, either. If I could throttle it down, maybe, or direct it . . .

Or both. After all, the nymph Thyme was supposedly nearby, on one of these Mediterranean islands. I decided to work from that.

> "So blow, ye winds, heigh-ho!
> To Thyme I wish to go!
> I've stayed no more on the Ordeal's shore,

> So let the music play!
> I'm off with the morning's gain,
> To cross the raging main!
> I'm off to see Thyme
> With a pack of rhyme,
> So many miles away!"

The wind veered. I knew, because my sail swung about almost ninety degrees. It creaked as the strength of the wind bellied it out to its limit, and the wind sang in the stays—sure enough, the music played! I noticed that, just as a burst of spray drenched my back and shoulders. I yelped—it was *cold*! But that didn't matter, because just then a giant kettledrum boomed overhead and rolled all about me, and its owner pulled the plug. Rain sluiced down, not bothering with individual drops, and I was soaked to the skin. Shivering, too, and my canvas sail groaned. I hitched around, alarmed, to lower it—and my feet sloshed through a few inches of water. I stared down, feeling the first faint fingers of fear take hold as I realized I might ship enough water to sink.

All of a sudden, I was in favor of half measures. A little thunderstorm can be a blast, when you can revel in the wildness of the wind and the power of the storm—but when it's all directed right at you, it can be a little unnerving. Scaled down, mind you, I would probably have loved it—if I'd had a sou'wester.

What harm could it do? I tried.

> "So blow, ye winds, heigh-how,
> But not so hard as now!
> I've need of speed, but less, indeed,
> So slacken your gale-force blasts!
> My sail can't stand the strain!
> Slow down your wind and rain!
> I can wait for the tide,
> And Thyme can bide.
> Be a good stiff breeze that lasts!"

The thunder cracked and growled, and I could have sworn it cursed. But it faded even as it snarled, and the wind slackened. My sail groaned with relief, and the rain toned down to a heavy soaker with headstrong winds. I shivered and sneezed. Landing near Thyme's hideout wouldn't do me much good if

I was dead of pneumonia when I got there, or even just delirious with fever. I thought of trying for that sou'wester, then rebuked myself for being greedy, not to say soft. What was a little rain, anyway? After all, yesterday I would have given anything for this. I gritted my teeth and held on.

Over the waves that gale blew me. I lashed the line around a thwart and held on to the tiller for dear life. It wasn't too bad for the first hour, but then I began to get tired. It didn't help that I couldn't see too far in front of me, either—but after the second hour, my eyelids were drooping so much that it didn't matter terribly, either. How far could it be to Thyme's island, anyway? I thought these Mediterranean mountaintops came in archipelagoes.

Finally, the sky lightened. The last thunderclap sounded far behind me, and the rain lightened to a drizzle. Not that I stopped shivering, though. Fortunately, the wind was still strong enough to keep my boat going into the waves, instead of veering crosswise; unfortunately, it was also hard enough to keep my teeth from chattering.

Then I realized there was a dark blob on the skyline ahead of me.

My spirits lifted amazingly. I tightened my weary grip on the tiller and grinned into the salt spray that doused me in the face. Relief was in sight.

Relief swelled up mighty fast, too, the blob growing into something that filled most of the horizon. Almost too late, I realized that the wind behind the boat was going to keep driving me until I was right up on the shore—which would be just fine if there weren't any rocks in the way, but I heard a suspicious booming, dead ahead. I managed to pry my fingers loose, pulled my right hand off the tiller, and just barely got the knot loose in time. Then I hung on as the rope sizzled through my fingers so that the sail would collapse, not blow away. I yelped as the rough hemp burned me, then reflected that it was the first heat I'd had in hours. First too much heat and dryness, then too much heat and coldness—I longed for a happy medium.

The boat slowed down just in time for me to notice rocks rising up to left and right, but I could see a narrow gap between them. I heaved and pushed at the tiller, just barely managing to slip the boat through without shoaling. Then I realized that there was a pole in the bottom of the boat. I caught it up and fended off the rocks on either side until, amazingly, they were gone.

I turned and looked ahead to see the beach heaving toward

me. I figured it was my boat that was doing the heaving, not the shore, and held on to try to enjoy the ride. Okay, after those rocks took out the worst of it, the surf wasn't anything you'd find on Malibu, but it was still enough to drive my long-boat ashore.

It jammed into sand, and I barely had enough presence of mind left to jump out, wade to the bow, and haul it onto the beach before the backwash could pull it out to sea again. Then another wave came along and pushed, and I gained another yard or two, enough to keep the boat secure from the next tug of receding water. I waited for the next wave. It came, I closed my eyes and threw my weight back against the boat—and it came. Easily.

Too easily.

I had to run backward to keep from being bowled over. I opened my eyes to see what had happened and saw a huge pair of hands clamped onto the far side of the boat, pulling. I kept pulling, too, as I followed the hands up arms like hawsers, to a huge and hairy chest with eyes like saucers at the top, looking down at me while a huge mouth curved open into a grin set with shark teeth.

I stared up as my heart dropped down, trying to hide in my boot tops.

Then I recognized him—I hoped. "Gruesome!"

The grin widened even further, and his top half nodded eagerly. "Yuh! Yuh! Goosum!" And the huge arms crunched me up against his stony hide while his basso voice chirped, "Goosum so happy see Saw!"

It was more of a croak than a chirp, actually, and he stank abominably. I made a mental note to teach him about bathing and squirmed around enough to gasp, "I'm glad to see you, too, Gruesome." And I was, surprisingly—after that stint in the desert and all that ocean, anything familiar looked good. Besides, he had saved my life once or twice, or had at least helped out.

But that clinch was inching me uncomfortably close to those shark teeth. "Yeah, glad to see you. Uh—how about putting me down, Gruesome?"

He started to, but hesitated with both huge mitts wrapped around my ribs, holding me up, and I could have sworn I saw a hungry glint in his eye. I was sure about the drops of drool glinting on his canines. They made him swallow, and it sure sounded as if he smacked his lips.

"Down, Gruesome!"

"Yuh, yuh! Down!" He finally lowered me till my feet touched sand, and loosened his hold. I twisted the rest of the way out of his grip with a sigh of relief, telling myself that I really hadn't had anything to worry about—but myself wasn't listening too well. "You won't believe this, but I'm really glad to see you. What're you doing here, though? I thought you were still on the mainland!"

"Mainland?" He scowled.

I decided that was better than the grin—it showed fewer teeth. "You know—Allustria? The place where I met you? Where we fought Sue . . . uh, the wicked queen?"

"Queen! Uh-h-h-h!" He shrank away. "Queen found us! Shell men! Sharp!"

Us? Had Gruesome somehow found the others? If so, I gathered that they had made it back to the mainland, but Suettay had ambushed them with a dozen or so knights—and panic stirred in my depths, assuming I had any. "Couldn't Frisson make them disappear?"

"Yuh, yuh!" He nodded. "Got two! But shell men had spell man!"

"The war party had a sorcerer?"

"Yuh, yuh! Bad, bad! Stopped Fish-un's spells! Shell men hit him—boom!" He slammed one huge fist into the other for emphasis.

I braced myself against the shock wave, then said, "You mean a couple of the knights knocked him out?"

"Yuh, Yuh! Sleep! More shell men hit Gibbet! And me!"

"I was wondering if you'd done any fighting." Frankly, I had difficulty imagining that he hadn't. I hoped he'd remembered that just because something's in a shell doesn't mean it's fair game for eating. "How many of them did you knock out?"

"Two! T'ree! Five!" Gruesome held up one combination of fingers after another, and his brow furrowed at the immense task of counting.

I decided to spare him the trouble. "You knocked out a lot of them, anyway. How come that didn't stop them?"

"Spell man! Threw fire! Fire sticks! Hurt, hurt!"

I got the message. The party's sorcerer had thrown lighted torches at Gruesome, thick enough and fast enough to drive him away. But that didn't sound like your garden-variety sorcerer to me. Alarm thrilled through me. "So they captured all of them?"

"No, no!" Gruesome shook his head most emphatically. "On'y Angel!"

"Angelique!" I yelped. "How could they capture her? She's a ghost!"

"Bad spell! Bad, bad spell!" Gruesome shook his head to show how thoroughly he disapproved, scrunching up his whole face. "Held up jug! Skinny jug! Angel go skinny, too, and go in jug ... *Thhhhhwpp!*" He made a sucking noise through pursed lips. "Shriek! Loud!" He clapped his hand over his ears, remembering. "Bad, bad!"

Now the anger started. "Into a bottle?" I howled. "He said a spell that sucked her into a bottle? And it hurt her?"

"Yuh, yuh!" Gruesome nodded. "Shriek!"

Of course, she might have just been scared, but either way, I was mad enough to go turn that sorcerer inside out, even if I did have to work magic to do it—and even if he was more powerful than the average spell-caster. "Which way did he go? Where did he take her?"

"No, 'he'!" Gruesome waved his spread hands back and forth. "Changed! Like lizard skin! Not magic man, magic *woman!*"

My heart sank. "Once Angelique's ghost was in the bottle, the sorcerer changed into Sue ... into the *queen?*"

"Yuh, yuh!" Gruesome nodded vigorously. "Wanted Saw! Mad, mad!"

"I'll just bet she was," I growled.

It all made sense. Suettay had come out in disguise, expecting me to be with the party and knowing that once I saw her, I'd forget about everything else and just get Frisson working on immobilizing her spells. But with your ordinary infantry sorcerer, I would have put him on the back burner and set Frisson to knocking over the knights. Once she saw I wasn't there, she changed herself back into Suettay—especially since, by then, Gilbert and Frisson had been knocked out, and she'd driven Gruesome away.

Which raised another issue. "You hung around close enough to see all this?"

"All!" Gruesome nodded. "But couldn't stay watch! Queen tell shell men kill friends! Couldn't watch! Shriek, run back, hit!"

"Good troll!" I could just picture Gruesome thundering down on the knights again, bellowing in rage. "I'll bet they pulled back!"

"Yuh, yuh! Shell men run! Goosum put Gibbet and Fish-un in boat! Queen shout, shell men run back! Hit, hurt! Gibbet and Fish-un wake up! Fish-un make spell, wind come, blow boat into water!"

For him, that was a major soliloquy. It wasn't all that bad a job of reporting, either—I'd heard worse on the ten o'clock news. "They left without you?"

"No, no! Queen throw fire, Goosum run into water!" He shuddered at the memory, and I could only think that there must have been a lot of fire, considering the troll's fear of water. "Gibbet pull Goosum into boat!"

That must have darn near swamped it, but it sounded like the kind of foolish, gallant thing Gilbert would do. The incongruity struck me.

So. They had reached the mainland right enough, but as soon as they had, they'd walked into an ambush. Suettay had looked in her crystal ball, or pool of ink, or whatever, and seen where they were going to land. She'd taken a band of knights and waited for my buddies to show up. When they had, the knights had descended on them, four overwhelming Gilbert while a dozen or so harried Gruesome, who harried them back—but then Suettay, in disguise, threw fireballs at him until he had to run, while a half dozen attacked Frisson. He got two of them with his spells, but the "sorcerer" knocked him out with a magic verse, then recited another one that pulled Angelique's ghost, screaming, into a bottle. No wonder—the sorcerer was Suettay, disguised enough so they wouldn't be able to detect her. She was no doubt outraged to discover that I wasn't with the party, and headed back to her castle with Angelique locked up in the bottle. On the way out, though, she had thoughtfully ordered her soldiers to kill Gilbert and Frisson. That was when Gruesome had flown into a rage and charged from his hiding place, holding off the soldiers just long enough to drag Frisson and Gilbert back to the boat. Apparently the dragging brought Frisson around, reviving him just in time to call up a wind that blew them out to sea. Suettay had come back and thrown fireballs at Gruesome, driving him into his hated enemy element, water—but Gilbert had pulled the troll in at the last second, nearly swamping the boat.

"Wait a minute," I said. "If that all happened on the mainland—what're you doing here?"

"Big wind!" Gruesome made whirling motions with his paws. "Fish-un say queen send! Blew back toward land!"

"The queen conjured up a gale to blow you back to her." I nodded.

So did Gruesome, apparently delighted that I'd understood him so easily. I wished he weren't delighted so often—all those shark teeth made me nervous. "But Fish-un make spell! Wind change, blow from land! Goosum look back, see boat sink!" He shuddered. "Goosum see Goosum go into water!"

"It was just an illusion," I said quickly, "like a dream."

Gruesome frowned, puzzled; apparently trolls didn't dream.

"Pretend." I struggled to explain a concept. "Something that wasn't real. Like a story, only you could see it happen."

His eyes widened, and his mouth formed a saw-toothed *O*.

"You know it didn't really happen," I pressed the point, "because you're really here. It was just a fake Gruesome that drowned—like a picture."

He nodded, faster and faster, *O* turning back into a grin. "Then wind blow, land go away. Then wind go away, too. Gilbert push boat."

I had a sudden vivid vision of Gilbert getting out to walk on the water, pushing the boat in front of him like a wheelbarrow—but of course, Gruesome only meant that Gilbert had rowed the boat. "Didn't Frisson take a turn?"

Gruesome nodded. "Short."

"No staying power," I agreed, "but I'll bet he got back into shape fast. Didn't he try to raise a wind?"

Gruesome shook his head. "Queen might know."

So Frisson had been afraid to whistle up a wind, because Suettay might have detected it and realized they were still alive. I gave him points for foresight, but subtracted them for underestimating his opponent—I wouldn't be surprised to find out Suettay had seen through his illusion.

A nasty suspicion occurred to me. "Did a new wind start up?"

Gruesome nodded, staring at me in amazement.

"Same thing happened to me," I assured him. "And it blew you here?"

"How know? How know?" Gruesome bleated.

"Just a lucky guess." I had remembered that I had told the wind to take me to Thyme. Apparently, this was where she lived. I had twisted the wind to blow me here, but I needn't have bothered—Thyme was keeping an eye out for any boat that came close enough to puff into her trap. My friends' arrival on this island was no accident, either. I had a sudden image of a spider again, but this time, it was a black widow. "So where are they? Frisson and Gilbert, I mean."

Gruesome started to answer, then shrugged helplessly and pointed inland. "In woods. In cage."

"Cage?" I stared. Jail? Frisson and Gilbert? A nearly-knight and a nouveau wizard? *"How?"*

Gruesome shrugged. "Woman."

"They were captured by a *woman*? Okay, I can understand that—I guess. But what kind of spell did she use?"

"No spell." Then Gruesome frowned, reconsidering. "Maybe spell."

" 'Maybe spell'?" I frowned. "How can you have a 'maybe' spell?"

"Fish-un and Gibbet see woman. She smile. Gibbet turn red, start shaking, go hide. Fish-un big-eyed, come to her. She lead him into cage. She chase Gibbet into cage."

So. She hadn't needed any magic, other than her own sweet self—or sweet body, I amended; the self was yet to be determined. Just the ordinary magic that any beautiful woman has naturally, or can learn.

Well, I was armored against it. I'd been worked over by champions and had accumulated some thick layers of scar tissue around my heart in the process. Any time a pretty woman started giving me the come-hither look now, all I had to do was remember what the other ones had done to me, and the beautiful lady suddenly seemed much less enticing. Okay, so maybe I had lost out on a good one that way, but I didn't really think so—experience had shown me that every time I'd fallen in love with a woman who turned out to be good, she tactfully and gently let me know it wasn't mutual. I attracted neurotics and sickies, women who wanted to use me for their own twisted purposes, and the hell with what it did to me.

What can I say? Like will to like? I hated to think that. But if it was true, all the more reason to stay single. Which I had.

"Thyme," I informed Gruesome. "The woman's name is Thyme."

"Time?" Gruesome asked, frowning. "Day? Week?"

Well. I hadn't known he had grasped the concept. Apparently the spillover from that spell I'd thrown at Gilbert had done more than I'd known. I felt a chill, wondering just how much else Gruesome knew that I didn't know about. "You might be right," I conceded, "but I thought she was named after an herb. After all, she's a nymph."

"Nimf?" Gruesome screwed up his face in trollish concentration.

"A nature spirit," I explained, "a personification ∴
fertility—or at least sexuality. She's not really human, she's
supernatural—and, thank Heaven, can't leave this island. She's
tied to the plant whose life energy she embodies."

That was too much for the poor troll. He just shook his
head, looking frazzled—or shook the upper part of his torso,
anyway. "Like Saw say. We go break cage?"

"We can try," I said slowly, "but that brings up another
question. Did you try to break them out?"

"Me try break!" Gruesome nodded with vigor—something
like bowing. "She touch cage, and cage bite Goosum. Jump
back and fall—plants tied around feet."

"The cage bit you?" Then I remembered—that was how you
explained an electric shock to a toddler. Thyme had touched
the cage, and it had given Gruesome a jolt. "Was the cage
made of wood?"

"Yuh! Wood! Sticks!"

So. Anything made of plants, she could use to work magic.
I laid a bet with myself that the "sticks" were still alive, plants
that she had just told to grow into a huge box. "And while you
weren't looking, the grass tied itself around your legs?"

"Yuh! Legs! Arms, too, after fell! Try get up, grass pull me
down! Roar!"

He gave a sample, letting loose a bellow that shook some
nearby rocks and left waveforms in the sand. I winced and reminded myself to conjure up some mouthwash for him.
"How'd you get loose?"

"Woman tell Goosum go stay near water, watch for Saw.
Find him, eat him!"

"Saul!" I stared. "Me?" How the hell had Thyme known I
was coming?

Exactly. Maybe she had a message from the Other Side.

Or maybe she had asked Frisson. From what Gruesome said,
he was so besotted he would have told her anything. Of
course, he also would have told her that the moon was made
of green cheese, if that was what she had wanted to hear, but
she seemed to have overlooked that possibility.

Then the rest of what Gruesome had said percolated through
to my undernourished brain. Something about if I showed up,
he was supposed to have me for dinner. I swallowed thickly
and looked up at him. Was that a hungry gleam in his eye, or
was I just imagining it?

CHAPTER 25

I wasn't imagining the drop of saliva that hung on his lower lip, but Gruesome was always drooling, anyway—I told myself. Myself wasn't really listening, though—it was paying too much attention to the cold, trickling dread that was pooling in my midsection. I started talking, slowly and soothingly, but getting faster and louder as I went. "Gruesome. This is Saul speaking. You know, Saul? The nice guy? Your buddy? The one who always lets you have time off to go hunting? Who stopped the nasty sorcerers who were throwing whammies at you?"

Gruesome nodded, but he still looked hungry. A huge slab of tongue lolled out and smacked around his mouth in a circle, cleaning up the drool with a sucking sound that lanced from my ears straight through my gizzard down to my boot soles. I talked faster.

"Gruesome," I said. "You remember the fairy folk? The ones who put a spell on you? That you would never eat people again?"

Gruesome frowned—apparently, it was a less-than-pleasant memory—but he nodded.

"And remember the spell I laid on you?" I knew I was treading on thin ice, but I had to take the chance.

"Spell." Gruesome nodded. " 'Member. Yah."

"Those spells make sure you can't eat me, or even try to be mean to me," I reminded him.

"Spells no good no more," he informed me. "Time woman do something. Goosum no feel spells hold him back no more."

Alarm thrilled through me, five alarms with all the fire

301

trucks already gone. The nymph had something to do with time, indeed. She had reached back into Gruesome's personal past somehow, countering the fairies' compulsion spell and my own binding spell. I started to edge away. "Uh—you aren't really all that hungry, are you, Gruesome?"

"Plenty hungry," he assured me.

Frantically, I tried to remember that binding spell.

"But Goosum no eat Saw," he explained. "Maybe yummy, but friend. Saw save Goosum, Goosum save Saw. If eat, no have friend."

I heaved a sigh and began to relax a little. Gruesome had realized that you can't have your friends, and eat them, too. "I—I'm really glad you had that insight, Gruesome." Gruesome shrugged, somewhere up above his face. "Food plenty. Friends few. People yummy, but deer yummy, too. And sheep and bunnies. Even fish."

And, of course, there was no shortage of finny dinners in the vicinity. Cautiously, I asked, "Eaten any good fish lately?"

"Yuh!" The tongue came out to slurp again. "Big fish, big as Goosum! Fin in middle back, pointy nose, teeth like Goosum. Yummy!"

A shark? He had fought a shark and won? Talk about eat or be eaten!

And it had only made one lunch?

I decided to make sure Gruesome was with me if I wanted to go wading.

I looked up at the big guy, studying him closely. Yes, the hungry gleam was there, but so was something else—some deep-seated, total trust, some light of admiration. It hit me with a shock—Gruesome had me on a pedestal. To him, I could do no wrong.

I felt shaken. I also felt like running for the hills. When someone is that loyal to you, you have to be loyal to him, too. Friendship means responsibility. Friends mean commitment. I felt as if the quicksands were running, sucking me down.

Then I remembered that I was here *because* of a friend.

With a shock, I realized that, somewhere along the line, I had let myself become committed. Okay, Matt might not have thought so, but apparently I had.

Well, no, it wasn't complete commitment. If I'd been mad at him, I wouldn't have hesitated to run out on him—if he weren't in trouble. Of course, Matt never made any demands on me when he wasn't in trouble, except for company, which was mutually agreeable. Come to that, he hadn't made any demands when he *was* in trouble, either—this little excursion had been my own idea.

Suddenly, I realized that this big, ugly troll saw more virtue in me than I did—but I wasn't about to tell him his mistake. Instead, I felt humbled and unworthy, simply because a living creature could value me more than his own strongest instincts.

I was touched.

So, of course, I couldn't let him know about it. I stepped closer in spite of the rank aroma, reached up to slap his stony hide, and said, "Come on. I hereby release you from any compulsion to patrol the seacoasts looking for me. After all, you've found me, so that order doesn't apply anymore. Let's go find our friends."

But he balked. "Saw?"

"Yes, Gruesome?"

"Could make spell 'gain? Don't like hunger for friend."

I swallowed, and agreed very quickly. I rattled off the spell—after all, if he wanted temptation removed, I wasn't about to argue.

Of course, I still didn't believe in magic. I looked him up and down, frowning dubiously. The glint was still in his eye. "I don't think that worked."

"Oh, yuh! Yuh!" he assured me. "No feel hunger for Saw now! Ev'thing else, but not Saw!"

"Or our friends, either?" I figured I'd better run the spell twice more, with Frisson's and Gilbert's names, just to be sure.

Then I reconsidered. I'd run the spells again—*after* we'd found them. The spur of hunger might help overcome the remains of Thyme's compulsion to stay on the coasts.

"Friends! Yuh!" Gruesome said, with enthusiasm. "Go to friends! Now!"

And he plowed off into the undergrowth, heading inland and going fast.

I hurried after him, rehearsing the spells under my breath. After all, if Gruesome thought his hunger for me had abated, then it had, right? The magic worked in his mind, not his stomach—but it worked. Who was I to argue?

I could imagine how it must have been—Thyme appearing out of the jungle foliage, clothed in nothing but a vague notion, and Gilbert turning bright red as he spun about to rid his eyes of a sight that kindled desire that threatened to overwhelm all his ideas of the noble life. Frisson, however, labored under no such handicap—he stared like a hooked fish, probably gulping like one, too, and drifted toward her like a zombie. Not terribly difficult to manage, either of them, no.

Would *I* be?

I had time to consider the answer as I followed Gruesome into the bush. It wasn't a jungle here—the Mediterranean isn't far enough south—but it was certainly a rain forest of a more temperate disposition. The trees and flowers were all familiar to my North American eyes, but there were a lot more vines that I was used to, winding around the trunks and hanging from the limbs. The underbrush left off after a dozen yards or so, but the soil sprouted flowers everywhere there was a patch of sunlight. Their perfume filled the air, stirring memories of late-night dates and feminine companions who let down their hair in more ways than one, and let down . . .

No. I clamped down on that thought hard, and thought about oranges with great intensity. Maybe it was just the landscape, or maybe it was an enchantment—autosuggestion? But in either case, Thyme was softening me up, getting me into a sensuous mood, preparing me for her appearance.

Was I getting paranoid? And what did I mean, "getting"? Or was I arrogant? Or was it just wishful thinking?

All at once, the trees were gone. We stepped out into a sloping meadow with a stream running through it. I looked around, dazzled by the riot of blossoms all about me and the horde of butterflies of all patterns and hues, huge and iridescent. The perfume filled my head, making me feel giddy. I reached frantically for some reminder that I was under attack. "Gruesome! Where're Frisson and Gilbert?"

The troll just grunted by way of answer, but he also pointed toward the banks of the stream. I looked, then looked again; what I had thought was a grove, was something quite else. The trees were scarcely more than saplings, but they grew so closely together that only the skinniest of men could have slipped between them. Of course, Frisson was the skinniest of men, but Thyme had taken care of that problem, too, because vines almost as thick as the trees wound between the trunks, rambling up and down and wrapping around each upright, to form a very effective cage. Up above, about eight feet off the ground, branches grew out almost at right angles, tangled with more of the vines. Yes, it was a live and growing cage, just as I'd guessed, with plenty of shade to protect the prisoners from the sun, grapes for them to eat, and a meander of the stream close enough for them to dip up water to drink. But it was bedecked with the huge, gaudy blossoms that smelled so intoxicating and must have constantly been filling them with sensuous feelings that verged on desire. I wondered about pheromones—and how poor Gilbert's dreams of virtue were holding up under this assault.

Not too well, at a guess—there he was, kneeling in a corner, facing the bars, arms thrust through to give him something to lean on, hands clasped in prayer. His eyes were closed, his lips were moving soundlessly, and there was sweat running down his face.

The heat, no doubt. Of course, he was rather pale . . .

But where was Frisson?

There, flat on the floor of the cage, facedown, the most dejected-looking heap of rags I'd seen since the flash flood hit the thrift shop. He lay so still that a shot of alarm juiced through me—but as I came closer, I heard him moan. I relaxed—a little. "Frisson! Gilbert! We've got to get you out of there!"

Frisson jerked up off the floor. "Master Saul!"

Gilbert spun about. "Wizard! A rescue! Take us out from this cage!"

"My fondest wish," I reached out to grab a vine and shake it. "This doesn't look all that strong, Gilbert. One cut with your sword, and . . ."

"I have it not."

"Huh?" I glanced at his scabbard. Sure enough, it was empty.

He reddened and dropped his gaze. "The witch . . . She took it from me when I averted my eyes."

And struggled with his libido, no doubt, trying to erase the afterimage of that beautiful body from the insides of his eyelids. I nodded. "She's disarmed belted knights in her time, I bet. Nothing to be ashamed of. Well, this is no sword, but it'll have to do." I pulled out my clasp knife, popped it open, and began to saw at a vine.

It shrieked.

I yanked back the blade as if I'd just cut into a power line. "Holy Hannah! It's *really* a live one!"

Gilbert looked about with sudden hope. "Hannah? Is there a saint come to help us?"

Frisson lamented, "Certainly it is alive, Master Saul. Are not all vines and trees?"

"Well, yes," I said, "but they don't feel pain." I'd been following the research, and there was still no definite evidence of a nervous system in plants. "And they certainly don't scream!"

"All plants do, on this nymph's isle." Frisson sighed. "The very stones cry out to her. 'Tis thus she knew of our coming."

"Oh, did she really!" Not that I had thought these two would have been terribly good at adopting a low profile, anyway.

"Aye," Frisson said. "She appeared before us, stepping through a screen of leaves so that she seemed to have come out of thin air. She wore a gown the color of her skin, yet of velvet, so soft that it seemed to beg to be touched . . . stroked . . . caressed . . ." He swallowed thickly.

"Spare me, poet," Gilbert groaned.

But Frisson didn't hear him; he was staring off into the immediate past and wishing it were the present again; his longing was naked in his face. "She stepped from beneath the trees, and her every movement was an invitation to that dance that ends only with two bodies conjoined, hip to hip and chest to breast. 'Welcome, wayfarers,' said she. 'Will you not tarry with me a while?' "

"I could not force mine eyes away." Gilbert dropped his head in shame.

"I could not wish to," Frisson said in rapture. "Indeed, I could only wish to gaze at her more, to breathe the perfume of her presence . . . and touch . . . for she came closer, much closer, and reached forth to caress my cheek, breathing, 'Will you come with me, then?' 'Anywhere,' I answered on the instant, and she laughed, low and in her throat. Her finger trailed fire across my cheek, touched a flame of pure pleasure to my lips—but alas, it died as she took her hand away, turning about and swaying off toward the trees. I followed on legs that felt like stumps, so clumsy had I become, and there was naught in the world for me but the roll of her hips as she left.

"But that movement slowed and stopped; she turned with a frown to my friend Gilbert, saying, 'Come with me, then, handsome stranger.' 'Nay,' quoth he, his eyes averted. 'I have taken a vow never to touch woman.' 'Why, then, you will not be forsworn,' said she, 'for I am not a woman, but a nymph.' 'You are an object of venery,' quoth he, 'and I have sworn to be celibate.' 'Surely so great a vow cannot be binding when made by one so young,' and her voice was a purr. 'Come with me and learn why you should not have given it.' 'I am true to my word!' cried he, and spun about, his back to her. I could see the anger in her eyes, though she banished it quickly. Then those hips began to move again, and I followed, entranced, but she went around in front of Gilbert and stepped close, so quickly that he could not turn away. Instead, he staggered back as if she had struck him—and she stepped close once more. He backed away yet again, and had not stopped when she stepped in, and thus they went, him backing away before her with myself following after. I blush to say it, but I did not realize my friend's pain—for all there was in my world was that graceful, slender back, and the swaying of those hips, and . . ." He swallowed thickly again. ". . . my dreams of what those clinging skirts might hide."

I was hanging on his every word; this was better than a porno video. "So she took you to her house?"

"Nay; of a sudden, she turned to face me, and I saw Gilbert stumble to a halt and whip about, away from her. She beckoned, and I came in delight—but she stepped to the side, and I went on past. I whirled, but she was backing away. I cried out and followed, but this lattice came up between us, and I could only throw myself against it and cry out with my loss, reaching out to touch—and there was a vagrant caress of some velvet swelling that set me afire from head to toe, but it went away . . ."

Gilbert moaned, squeezing his eyes shut.

". . . and sweet, full lips tickled the palm of my hand, and were gone. 'Bide you there,' said she, 'till I have need of you; for I've one to toy with already, and will have no need of aught but he, till I have done with him. Pray for him to fulfill my desire, that I may more quickly come for you.' I cried again, plastering myself against the trunks and reaching out so hard I thought my shoulder must crack. But she only laughed again, and leaves rustled, and she was gone."

"I bade him not pray," Gilbert said, his voice tight in his throat.

"Did you truly?" Frisson turned to him. "I did not know. There was naught for me but the sense of aching loss, and I closed my eyes, that I might treasure the memory of the sight of her the longer."

"So she boxed you up right and proper," I said. "Does she feed you?"

"Not herself, alas—but some barky monster that speaks not, and fills the air with musk."

Interesting—she had a guard. A plant, from the sound of it, but I didn't think his classification would help us much. I glanced up at Gruesome and decided that with me there to goad Frisson into working magic, or at least to read his verses for him, there was an even chance. "Well, I don't like to cause anything pain—but there has to be a way to get you out. Which end opened up to let you in?"

"Yonder." Gilbert pointed. "I remember, for as soon as I could go no farther, I turned about, to rid my sight of that corrupted witch—and saw that I did stare at a tree with a double trunk."

I looked; the curves of the trunks suggested a man and a woman approaching one another in intimacy; I could imagine how they swayed, when the wind blew. How could Gilbert have missed it?

Because I had a dirty mind. In fact, the fruit on that tree looked like the epitome of sensuousness to me, the double swelling globes elongated just enough to suggest human anatomy, and covered with a downy softness that fairly begged to be stroked. I shook my head; dirty mind, as I've said. "I don't suppose you've eaten any of that fruit?"

"I did try," Gilbert admitted, "but when I reached out to touch, it did withdraw, ever tantalizing, ever just beyond reach."

"Figures," I muttered. After all, I knew that plants had sexuality, too. "Well, if the other end is the door, let me take a look and see how it's fastened." I went down to the end of the cage, pushing past a lot of leaves—it had been nice of her to leave them with a roof—and inspected the corners. Sure enough, the corner-post trunk was right next to a vertical length of vine, almost as thick. There were at least a dozen creepers weaving back and forth between the two of them, though, and they were barky and looked tough. I stared, at a loss. "I hate to cause pain to a living being . . ."

"Do not," Frisson said quickly. "I will wait, I will wait gladly, I will endure a thousand days, if only at the end, she will come to bid me amuse her!"

"How hollow of you!" Gilbert cried. "Would you rush to sin, false man?"

"I am a poet," Frisson said doggedly. "I hear you speak of

sin, but with the memory of that splendid form within me, the words have no meaning."

"They have to me!" Gilbert strode over to me and gripped the vines, shaking them with sudden rage, straining at them with strength that spoke of sublimation and should have moved half a ton. He had some effect, too—the vines keened, so highly pitched that it went right through my head.

"Leave off!" I cried. "You're hurting them!"

"What matter pain, when virtue's at stake?" Gilbert raged. "What matter the pain of a plant, for Heaven's sake?"

"Yes, for Heaven's sake!" I shouted. "I thought you were a Christian!"

He froze, staring at me blankly. "Why, so I am!"

"Then isn't charity as high on your list as chastity? Isn't it just as important that you not hurt another living being, as that you keep from having sex?"

"Nay," he said, "for sex—" He winced at the word, but forced himself to use it. "—sex is one among the means by which we are hurt, or hurt one another! To take a woman's virginity is to hurt her most shrewdly, to steal her greatest treasure and break her heart—and therefore, to take a man's will hurt him likewise, though he know it not! Even to fornicate with one *not* a virgin, will surely hurt her heart—or his, for that matter—and will cause that hurt whether she and he deny it to themselves or not! 'Tis to be used, exploited!"

Now, that struck me as a sick attitude. I really wished I could disagree with him.

Unfortunately, I couldn't—not if I was really trying to be honest with myself. What he had said was possibly true and fitted my own experiences. Of course, it was sick nonetheless—or was it the exploiting that was sick?

"There are limits," I argued. "Under the right circumstances, sex can be a wonderful thing."

"Aye, if both are in love, and wedded!"

"Love is not needed," a throaty, musical voice behind me said. "Only desire need be felt."

Now, to call that voice "musical" is like saying that champagne is old grape juice. It was lilting, it was transporting, and most of all, it was stimulating. It resonated in my loins and set up a charge that shot up to make my head giddy.

So, before I turned around, I made a stern effort to get control of myself, reminding me that she was just another woman who was looking for an angle to get what she wanted out of me, while giving as little of herself as she could. Thus buoying my concept of manliness, I turned slowly, saying, "Nymph Thyme, I presu—"

I couldn't finish the word. The descriptions hadn't just failed to do her justice, they hadn't even leveled charges. She was even more beautiful and seductive and sensuous than they'd said—and nobody had mentioned her face, but for a few seconds, I couldn't notice anything else. Her face was heart-shaped under glossy black hair that tumbled down about her face and shoulders; her sloe eyes were huge and slumberous, shaded by long, thick lashes under delicate, arching eyebrows. Her nose was a delicious, tip-tilted confection that fairly begged to be kissed, and her lips were wide, full, dusky red, and aching to be tasted. Her gown was very low cut, but that mass of black hair tumbled in to fill what the dress revealed, allowing only tantalizing glimpses of cleavage between softly swelling mounds, which fulfilled every promise a man could ever have dreamed of as they strained the fabric of a velvet bodice that was the exact same shade as her skin. Frisson had been right—it fairly compelled me to reach out and touch it.

But I fought the compulsion and forced my eyes to stay on her face. The ripe lips parted, moistened, and breathed, "Come, lordly gallant! Will you not tarry with me, to enter my abode and taste of my pleasures?"

Believe me, I was tempted. Tempted? I could barely keep my feet from moving. But I must admit to a certain incipient panic underneath it all, the old conviction that whatever she was really after, it wasn't entirely for my own good. *Angelique! Save me!*

After all, what's a true love for?

And she did save me—or the memory of her, anyway. Pale and smoke-thin as her wraith was, it still outshone in beauty and allure this gorgeous wench in more-than-full color right before me. How? Maybe it was Angelique's innocent faith in love and her sheer goodness. Maybe it was the sweetness of her spirit. Most likely, it was all of it rolled into one, the total-ity that was that single wonderful being, Angelique.

Whatever it was, the memory of her protected me against the vamp right then, dimmed Thyme's attraction to bearable levels, and made me aware all over again that I was confront-ing a magical being on her home turf, and that the attraction I was feeling was anything but natural.

That being the case, I needed to fight magic with magic. "Frisson! Give me a verse!"

A grubby, spider-leg hand pushed a scrap of paper into mine. I snapped it open, tore my gaze off the purring vision before me, glued it to the letters, and chanted,

> "Lovely wanton! Could I command
> Troops of knights from every land,
> They'd bow before you, and admire
> Each curve so sweet that wakes desire!
> Swaying or still, clothed or bare,
> Your lips, your eyes, your raven hair,
> Your breasts, your thighs . . ."

I stopped right there. No use helping the enemy, now, is there?

I should have realized. What else would Frisson have been writing about while he was stuck in a cage on Thyme's island? What else would he have been thinking about?

I was on my own. And I didn't want to work magic. That might have demonstrated that I believed in it, which I was determined not to do.

But, hey—if they were somebody else's words, that wasn't my doing, was it? Even if I made a few changes.

All right, so I was rationalizing—but logic wouldn't help me out of this bind.

Kipling would.

> "A fool, there was, and he made his prayer
> (Even as you and I!)
> To a rag and a bone and a hank of hair
> (We called her the Woman Who Did Not Care),
> But the fool he called her his lady fair
> (Even as you and I!).
>
> A fool there was and his goods he spent
> (Even as you and I!)
> Honor and faith and a sure intent
> (And it wasn't the least what the lady meant),
> But a fool must follow his natural bent
> (Even as you and I!).
>
> And it isn't the shame and it isn't the blame
> That stings like a white-hot brand.

It's coming to know that she never knew why
(Seeing at last she could never know why)
And never could understand."

The nymph stared at me in disbelief. "I? Be without mercy?"

"You don't really give a damn about what happens to the men you use," I said. "It's the same effect, no matter the cause."

"To be sure, I care! I seek only to give as much pleasure as I take!"

"Yeah, but you don't think about the aftermath." Still, I was getting the idea—I needed a stronger verse.

And quickly—her eyelids were drooping, and she was sashaying closer. Behind me, I heard Frisson groan. Before me, I could hear her begin to sing, in a voice that awakened every hormone I had and made each one thrum through my blood. I missed the words, but they didn't matter.

Of course they did! I tried again.

"Her true love hath her heart, though she not his:
A poor exchange, one for mere liking given.
She holds his dear, but hers he seems to miss,
Yet dotes she on him, and for his love is driven."

She stared at me, those huge, marvelous eyes growing even more huge. Then they filled with tears that overflowed and ran down her cheeks as she turned her face away. "Alas! How can I be true to love, who know only the pleasures of the body?"

I stared appalled, and behind me, Frisson cried, "Wizard Saul! You are a beast, to make so beauteous a damsel cry! Lady, wait! For I shall comfort you!"

"I could not ... could not accept ..." she sobbed, "for I have ... I have one whom I ... Oh! What is this pain in my breast?"

Frisson let out a cry of despair. "Wizard! You have destroyed my hope! My hope of a few hours alone with this nymph!"

"I have?" I looked from him to her, totally confused.

She looked up at me, tears flowing. "Aye, for I burn within for the sweet and gentle monk who dwells now in my house. What have you done, Wizard? For I can no longer bear the thought of coupling with any man save him—and he will not surrender to my blandishments! Oh! What is this pain?" And she pressed a delicate hand over those glorious breasts.

"It is her heart," Gilbert said, with heavy satisfaction, behind me.

"A heart!" She stared up at him, appalled. "In a nymph? Nay, I prithee!"

It made sense. In a fertility sprite that was ready for any encounter, anything resembling memory, or lingering fondness for any one male, would definitely be a liability.

I decided to be a little more direct.

> "Now this is the law I shall give you,
> And bound to its mass you shall stay—
> For the head and the hoof of the law,
> And the haunch and the hump is—obey!"

Her eyes went wide in sheer horror. "What would you do? No man may command me—for I must command every man!"

"Not anymore," I said severely. "Just try to disobey now."

"I shall go!" She turned on her heel.

"You will stay," I said quickly.

She froze, one foot up in the air. "I . . . I cannot . . . summon the will!"

"No," I said softly. "My magic compels you." Actually, I had a notion it was sheer suggestion, but why should I have told her that?

"I shall summon my own magic!" she cried. "I shall enchant myself free!"

"Watch out," I warned her. "Give me any more grief, and I might find a way to give you a soul."

It was pure bluff, of course—even agnostic me knew that only God can make a soul—but it straightened her up and put the light of terror into her eyes. "Oh, nay! You would not make me mortal!"

"Any way I can," I assured her, "so let's not make it necessary, okay? Just show us to this houseguest of yours."

Foreboding shadowed her face. "What wish you with him?"

"We need a consultant." I chose my words carefully. "I understand he's an expert."

"He is? At what is he expert?"

I took her in from head to toe in a single glance. "Nothing you're interested in—but I'm afraid he's not learning anything you have to teach, either. As the phrase goes, I don't think the two of you have any common area of interest."

"But we have! I need simply convince him!"

I eyed her askance. "Not having too much luck at it, are you?"

She flushed, and snapped, " 'Tis purely a matter of time. He is male, is he not? And any male will succumb to me, given Thyme."

Frisson made a mewing noise behind me.

"Prove it," I said. "Show him to us—but first, let my friends out."

"Wherefore should I?" But her feet were already moving toward the cage, and a look of alarm spread over her face. "How is this! I do not wish it!"

"But I do," I said softly. "My spell, remember?"

"No mortal wizard can have power o'er me! Not here, on mine own island!"

"Guess again," I said, still softly. "Sorry to have to do this, but we really can't take the time for an extended persuasive campaign." Especially since, if we did, I was afraid I was the one who would be persuaded. "Just let them out, there's a good nymph, okay? Then introduce us to this houseguest of yours."

We came through the musk-scented forest, out of the trees into a meadow of grass mingled with mint, and saw her bower.

"Bower" is the only word that could describe it. I suppose it was technically a house—but with a house, you expect the wood to have been cut down. This one was made of trees growing side by side, with just enough space between them for windows. The boughs intertwined overhead to form a very snug roof—evergreen, I noticed. I didn't think winter would do much here except rain, but she was ready for that.

And, of course, flowers. Each tree trunk held a climbing vine that sported blossoms of all hues—the blue and purple of orchids, the red and white of roses, the yellows and oranges of melon flowers. It was a gay and dazzling profusion, and its perfume filled the air.

I didn't see how any man could get a lick of work done in there, let alone think about anything but sex.

We came in the front door—a wider-than-average opening between two trunks, shaded by a huge evergreen bough—and stepped into the bedroom.

Actually, I don't think that bower had anything but a bedroom—it was all one room, and it was floored with heaps of cushions. Oh, sure, there was a low table, just big enough for dinner for two, though it was low enough that you pretty much had to lie down and prop yourself up with an elbow, Roman-fashion, and there were a few other horizontal surfaces filled with knickknacks—at a guess, one was a vanity, and the other was a wine cabinet. There was a tapestry, too, hiding a large space at the far end that might have served as a closet, though I didn't get the impression that our hostess was big on clothes. Neither were the figures on the tapestry.

But most of the floor space was taken up by a huge bed that looked to be solid padding eighteen inches thick, the softest and most inviting bed I've ever seen. For that matter, the whole room was one big invitation, and I didn't see how any man could ever summon the resolution to leave.

Which made it all the more stark a contrast, to have a high writing desk and a stool over against one window, a roll of parchment bathed in a ray of sunlight that lanced down over the shoulder of the brown-robed monk who sat there, industriously scratching away with a quill pen.

CHAPTER 26

I stared.

He must have felt my gaze—or heard us enter, and what man could keep from looking up at Thyme? But he saw me, and Frisson the hollow-cheeked and Gilbert the gaunt, right behind me. He stared in surprise. His face was round and pleasant, but creased with lines of strain. There were a few gray hairs mixed in with the brown around the bald circle of his tonsure. His face broke into a glad smile. "Why, 'tis company! How welcome are they!"

"Scarcely at all." Thyme pouted. "Are you so easily distracted from me, man of letters?"

"Nay." He turned a fond gaze on her. "Naught could command my attention for long while you are with me, lovely one—nor is any company lacking. Yet novelty is always pleasant, and new company stimulating."

She flushed with pleasure and lowered her gaze. I had to give him points for gallantry—and for diplomacy. That mention of "stimulation" ought to win him her willing cooperation in having a chat with us. Poor thing, she didn't realize that the stimulation he meant was purely mental.

"Sit down, sit down!" He gestured toward the low table. "They may, may they not, mine hostess?"

"Aye," she said unwillingly, "though not for overlong—for there are matters I wish to speak of with you, the two of us alone."

Which was, no doubt, the topic she always wished to speak about—the two of them being alone together. Very much together.

"To be sure, to be sure!" he climbed down off his stool and joined us as we folded ourselves tailor-fashion around the taboret. Gruesome slouched in the doorway, shifting uneasily from one foot to the other and blocking the view.

I glanced at the writing desk—current research was always a good conversation topic, even if you didn't understand the answer. "What are you working on there?"

"Only copying out my breviary," he said, and must have seen the look of blank incomprehension on my face, because he went on to explain, " 'Tis the book that contains my office—the prayers that I must read every day, and which I must contemplate."

"Really," I said. "How long does that take you? Per day, I mean?"

He shrugged. "Scarcely an hour."

An hour? A full hour of prayer every day? I tried to hide a shudder and thought up another question. "Why are you copying it out?"

"Why, for that I fear I will wear it out, if fair Thyme keeps me here overlong."

"I shall." She made a face. "You have ever your nose thrust in that small dusty volume!"

"Alas!" he agreed, almost meeting her eyes—and suddenly, I understood. Saying his office was about all that was keeping him from giving in to her temptations. I figured he was probably reading a lot more than one hour each day.

"Drink, my guest," Thyme purred, setting a flask of amber liquid on the low table. Gold glinted within its depths, and the light shimmered on its surface. If it wasn't an aphrodisiac, it should have been, just by its looks.

"How good of you," the monk said. "Will you pour, pretty one?"

Thyme leaned forward with the bottle—which brought a gasp from Gilbert, as he quickly averted his eyes, and a whine of agony from Frisson—and poured with ill grace. "They shall have to share one cup, good man, whiles you and I share the other—for I have only the two."

"Oh, we'll manage," I assured her, and lifted the cup for a sip. It hit my stomach with a jolt, bounced, and felt as if it blew the back of my head off. Coconut milk? Sure! Fermented coconut milk, to the point where it must have been a hundred proof at least. Sort of a natural piña colada—and come to think of it, there was an overtone of citrus to it.

Frisson reached for the cup, but just in time, I remembered what any beverage in Thyme's house might do, and covered the cup with a palm. "No, pal, you've got it bad enough already." That won me a dirty look from Thyme.

The monk ignored it. "What brings you to this island?"

"An ill wind," I quipped, "but I made it blow good."

I expected puzzlement and a suspicious glance, but the monk only nodded, as if he understood. "You are a wizard, then."

I felt a chill down my back; this guy understood too much, too quickly. "No, not really. In fact, I don't even believe in magic. I just pretend when I have to, toss out a few rhymes when I've run out of any other way out."

He smiled, amused. I felt a flash of irritation, but I had to admit it was mostly shame—it sounded pretty hollow, even to me.

"You may equivocate with yourself, sir," the monk said softly, "but you cannot equivocate between God and Satan."

"Now, hold on!" I bridled. "You trying to say there's no middle way? That you're either a hundred percent good, or a hundred percent evil? Well, I don't buy it, brother!"

His gaze stilled totally, and he looked so intently into my eyes that I thought he was trying to see into my brain. "Why would you think I had not taken my final vows?"

Now it was my turn to go on the ropes. I stared at him, thinking fast, churning up what I could from my medieval history course. It didn't help that I wasn't Catholic—but I did seem to remember something about the difference between a monk and a priest. I'd said "brother," and he'd thought I was using his title—or what I thought was his title.

Or what he wanted Thyme to think was his title.

That's right, a brother hadn't taken his final vows yet. Maybe that included the vow of celibacy?

Well, I wasn't about to blow his cover. "All right, so you're a father. But not my father, Reverend!"

"Certainly any priest is your father in faith."

"Only if I belong to your church—and I don't."

Gilbert recoiled. "Paynim!"

The monk held up his hand, eyes never leaving mine. "Nay, good brother—for so I see you are, by your tonsure. Nay, our friend may be a Christian indeed, but of an eastern church. Is that not so, Wizard?"

I thought fast again. How far east did he want? After all, my parents' church had sort of started out in New England—well, England, really, and that was plenty far east from where I was living just now—if you went all the way around the globe. "Another sect," I said. "Another branch of Christianity. That's what I was raised in. Sure."

He frowned, catching the equivocation again, but all he said was, "I cannot continue to call you naught but 'wizard.' I am Friar Ignatius. And yourself?"

"He is the Wizard Saul." Thyme leaned forward, taking the opportunity to intrude herself into the conversation—far more of herself than was good for Friar Ignatius' peace of mind. "His comrades are Squire Gilbert and the madcap Frisson— and that huge monster who lurks in the doorway, he calls 'Gruesome.' "

"Rightly, too." The monk took the excuse to glance away from Thyme and the primrose path, and look up at the troll. "How comes he to your service?"

"He tried to ambush me when I was crossing a bridge," I said. "Being new to your country, I didn't know any better. By accident, I called on the fairies, and they enchanted him so that he no longer wants to eat people, and they bound him to my service."

"I thought I had detected some such unseen bonds upon him." Thyme frowned prettily. "Yet I thought I had untied them. How comes he to be so bound again? Can you explain this, Friar?"

It was no accident that she had switched the question from me to him; in all courtesy, Ignatius couldn't help but look at her. His glance dipped to her décolletage for just a split second, then leapt to her face and held there with frantic intensity. His face tightened, and I realized where the strain lines had come from—he was bound and determined to be true to his vows, but he wanted her so badly that it was physical pain.

She knew it, too, the witch. Her smile heated up several degrees; her eyelids drooped more, and her lips seemed to grow fuller and more moist even as I watched. She leaned a little further forward to offer a better view—but Friar Ignatius' gaze stayed fixed on her face. I was awed by such iron self-control.

Behind me, Frisson whimpered.

"I can only guess, pretty hostess," Friar Ignatius said calmly, though his voice cracked a bit, "that Wizard Saul knitted up those bonds again."

"Yet how could he do so?" she murmured, deep in her

throat, reaching out to touch his hand. "On my isle, my magic must needs be supreme."

The hand didn't move, but the monk's whole body shivered. "There are some magics that are of great force no matter in whose domain they are said, sweet hostess." His voice seemed to roll and caress over that word "sweet," but he kept his gaze glued to her face. His voice cracked, though, and his whole body was tense.

"Yet there are some enchantments that must needs be stronger in my presence." Her touch moved up to his chest. "Must they not be supreme in my own garden?"

His voice was almost a groan of torment. "Nay, sweet lady. The object of an enchantment can strengthen any magic. If the troll wished the spells to be reestablished, his own will would aid the Wizard's weaving."

And, by inference, if Friar Ignatius was determined to resist Thyme's charms, they couldn't bind him, whereas Frisson's will went hand-in-glove with Thyme's. No wonder he was so completely spellbound.

I couldn't help wondering about Friar Ignatius, though— either he had the will to virtue of a saint, or he was something of a wizard in his own right. I decided to give him an out. "That's right. It seems Gruesome has taken a liking to me during our travels. He asked me to reestablish the spells."

It gave him an excuse to look away from Thyme; it broke her charm. She looked daggers at me, and I felt them stab through my nervous system all the way to my groin; but Friar Ignatius was saying, "Even so. His will reinforced your spells. It was not one who worked against the strength of Thyme and her island, but two."

Did I detect a plea for help there? "You seem to know quite a lot about magic, Friar. You must be a wizard, too."

But he shook his head. "I am but a student, Master Wizard—"

"Anything but a master. Scarcely an apprentice."

That won me a smile. "I but study the ways of magic and the workings of it. I can tell you much, but I lack the talent."

"Talent?" I stared. "It requires a talent?"

"Aye. Do not any of the arts?"

"Well . . . sure." I swallowed, collecting my wits. "It's just that I thought it was a . . . uh . . . more of a science."

"Odd choice of word." Friar Ignatius frowned. "However,

'science' means 'knowledge,' and surely the practice of magic requires that, too—at least, if it is not to bring disaster."

"Well, where I come from, 'science' means more than just a collection of facts. It organizes them and generalizes—it works out rules for using forces."

Friar Ignatius lifted his head slowly. "Fascinating! That is the very approach I attempt!"

I began to see why the Spider King had sent us to him. "But if you've worked out those kinds of rules and methods, anybody should be able to work magic—they shouldn't need talent!"

"Any practice requires talent, Master Wizard," Friar Ignatius countered. "We may not realize some of them, for they are so common—there are few indeed who cannot cook, though there are a few who fail in so much as frying an egg, no matter how much they learn nor how hard they try. There are few men who cannot wield hammer and chisel to craft things of wood—yet again, there are some who fail. There are some who lack those talents, and whose efforts come to naught, even at tasks that most of us regard as simple."

I remembered my own attempts to fix my car, and held my peace—especially since he had mentioned cooking; I remembered what had happened the last time I had tried to boil rice. "And you lack the talent to work magic?"

"Oh, not completely." He waved the notion away. "By long and arduous practice, I have mastered a few simple spells—and any peasant can mix a few herbs while muttering a charm to mend a sprain, or cure a cold."

"Oh, really?" The pharmaceutical companies back home would have loved to get that one.

"You did not know?" Friar Ignatius looked more closely at me. "Yet you walk boldly through the worst of Thyme's spells."

How had he known that? Probably one of those "little spells" he had mentioned.

"You are surely a wizard of power," the Friar summarized. "You must have great talent, Master Saul."

"Aw, shucks." I dropped my gaze, putting on my bashful act. " 'Twarn't nothin'."

"Nay, 'twas a great deal." Friar Ignatius frowned. "Do you truly know so little of the craft you practice, Master Saul?" He stiffened, suddenly becoming aware of something, and peered more closely at me. "Whence come you?"

I just stared at him for a second while I weighed alternatives. Then I decided I had nothing to lose and said, "Another world."

"Do you truly?" he breathed. "And does magic work so differently there?"

"Scarcely at all," I admitted. "In fact, we've managed to do without, by studying the world around us and organizing that knowledge into the science I told you of. I suppose we've had to replace magical strength with knowledge and skill—but we've found ways to work some wonders, anyway."

"And with that method of thought, coupled with a strong talent, in a world in which magic *does* work ... Nay, small wonder you are a master wizard, though you know so little of it!" The monk glanced at Thyme and glanced away, lowering his eyes and flushing; but she stiffened, eyes widening in alarm.

He didn't have to say it; it was plain for all of us to see: *Can you get me out of here?*

"Why, how is this?" Thyme demanded. "In all this world, there's scarce a man who would not give all he had to be where you are, and to taste of my charms! As would you yourself! Admit it, shave-pate—do you not burn to embrace me?" Her voice deepened, growing husky. "To stroke and caress me, to let your hands taste of my body while your mouth tastes of my lips, and then to—"

"Why, to dwell in sadness, so sorely afflicted?" the monk groaned. "Cease to torment me, fair one! I beg of you!"

"I will grant your wish when you grant mine." Her voice was a silken caress, unrelenting. "Speak truly, Ignatius! Do you not wish to learn the pleasures of my body?"

"Alack-a-day, how shrewdly I do!" he moaned. "When you are near, my mind seeks only to fill itself with the sight and sound and scent of you—but my soul yearns yet toward Heaven! Do not tempt me, beauteous one, for your charms are torment to me, who cannot have them!"

"Yet you can," she breathed, reaching out to turn a soft hand across his. "They are yours whenever you wish it!"

"Nay, for I must needs be true to my vows!"

"As you wish," she teased, brushing against him.

Ignatius shuddered, and cried, "Nay, not as I wish, but as I will! Oh, how cruel you are to me, fair nymph, to torment me with pleasures I have forsworn! Cease this sweet torture, I beg of you!"

"Ah, well, as you will, then," she snapped, nettled—and, suddenly, somehow, she was no longer a torch of desire, but only a very beautiful female. "I cannot move you whiles your will holds firm. You are maddening, Ignatius!"

"I regret that I cause you pain." He lowered his eyes.

"You do not regret it sharply enough." But her gaze kindled with mischief again.

Suddenly, I understood. "He intrigues, doesn't he? The only man who has ever resisted your blandishments."

"The fool!" Frisson moaned.

"Oh, there do be some few others." The words were ashes in her mouth. "There was a man with a strange gleam in his eye, who turned upon me and beat me till I fled; I found him quick passage on a ship I summoned by storm. And there was another monk, a friar in a white robe, who declared me to be a devil, a succubus, and sought to banish me by long and hateful verses. This island was a miserable and barren place while he lived."

I thought about asking how long that had been and how he had died, then thought better of it.

Friar Ignatius was shaking his head and muttering. "I could never do such a thing, no! Nay, she is a good woman, a sweet woman, and I confess to great fondness for her."

"But not so great as to surrender to lust," she said, with a sardonic smile. "What is this new emotion you have kindled in me, monk? For I have never before laughed at mine own downfall."

"Frustrating," I said, "isn't it?"

"He chafes me no end," she agreed, "yet not as I would wish. Therefore shall I keep him here in my bower, until he gives in to his feelings, surrenders to sweet sensation—for if he does, he will fall fully in love with me, abjuring his vocation and even his religion."

"Since the one follows the other," I murmured. "Just can't resist a challenge, can you? Isn't a temporary lapse into sin good enough for you?"

Thyme shrugged, which set up secondary wave effects that were entirely too harmonious. "When first he came here, mayhap—yet now, my pride is affronted. I must have his total, abject devotion."

"You have it! 'Tis yours!" Frisson exclaimed, his eyes burning.

She glanced at him with a flicker of long lashes and a lazy

smile. "Many thanks, man of song; yet 'tis he who has pricked my pride, not yourself. Nay, I must become the most important object in his life, or feel myself to be a woman of no worth."

"But you are! You are sweet and kind!" Friar Ignatius almost put his hand on hers, but held it back just in time.

"Sweetness of temper is the least I offer you," she returned, "and the kindness of your taking is not the kind I would receive."

"He got under your skin right from the beginning, didn't he?" I said.

"Aye, but only in metaphor, more's the pity. Oh, he was but a mild diversion to me at first, naught but another shipwrecked man; in truth, he was least and last—least of interest to me, and last of all his shipmates, the captain and crew. Yet when I had done with them and sent them on their way to deflower maidens no more—"

"You destroyed their desire?" I stared, eyes wide.

She gave me a cynical smile. "Know, poor male, that the fulfillment of your fantasies would end them."

I wondered just what she had done to those sailors. Had they been so thoroughly sated that they could never work up a good case of lust again? Or would real women pale into insignificance, after her? "Finished with them? What did you do to them?"

"Sent them all packing," she assured me. "My magic repaired their ship; my island replenished their larder. I wished them fair winds and sent them coasting away in their ship, chastened and much less likely to despoil women."

Of course, they might also go on a campaign of rape to reprove their masculinity to themselves, but I didn't think Thyme had considered that. In fact, I didn't think she considered anything about anyone but herself. "Then you found Friar Ignatius wasn't willing."

"Aye," she said with bitter resignation. "Him, I could not seduce, and that made him a thing of fascination to me. So when I bade his fellows farewell, I kept him here, to amuse me—yet I've found naught of amusement, and less of satisfaction."

"And never will, I fear." Friar Ignatius sighed. "My regrets, sweet one."

"But you rose to the challenge," I interpreted.

"Aye," Thyme said, "and would warrant that he did, too, though he allows me no proof of it."

I understood. She'd had supreme confidence in her femininity, in her limited way—but that limitation covered a deep insecurity; it was only a bubble. Friar Ignatius had punctured that bubble by his refusal and had become an affront to her self-esteem. The only way to rebuild her self-image as the ultimate femme fatale, was to seduce him—and since he wouldn't seduce, she was thinking less and less of herself every day.

He had a great technique for saying "no," though. Any woman but a nymph would have felt immensely flattered and been willing to give up.

But she *was* a nymph, and the real thing, too. I shook my head sadly. "I hate to be discouraging, but I'm afraid you're doomed to disappointment."

"I will never give in till he does!" she declared.

"Your tenacity is laudable," I said, "but your judgment is lacking." I hoped. "Either way, I'm afraid I really can't afford to give you the chance to prove your point, or his; I need his help."

"I shall ne'er let my true love depart!" she cried.

"But you will," I said softly, "because I'm a wizard—remember?"

Her eyes narrowed; she surged to her feet, throwing her head back and arms up, as if to embrace the sky. The sight was breathtaking, but I was braced for a move like that, so it didn't quite drive the verses from my head.

> "Dim lords and captains have I seen
> Who witnessed my spells, one and all—
> And say, 'La Belle Dame Sans Merci
> I have in thrall!' "

Thyme froze, then slowly lowered her arms and her gaze, to regard me with disgust and loathing. "Speak, then." Her voice was choked with tears. "I must obey."

"I bid you give this monk your leave to go."

"Why, so I must," she said with infinite reluctance, and turned to Friar Ignatius. "I am constrained; therefore you are not. You are free to go!"

Relief and joy flooded his face. She saw, and her own filled with hurt. Friar Ignatius leapt up with a cry of pity. "Poor wanton! Ah, I could wish I had not taken holy vows, that I might indulge my base desires with you! I am a man sworn to God and chastity; yet still my heart will ache for sight of thee!"

The hurt lessened in her face.

He caught her hand, eyes lit with fervor. "Never will I forget these sweet days, nor the hours of delight in your company! Nay, every minute near to you has been pleasure so sweet as to be almost pain, and I thank you mightily for this taste of bliss! Never will I forget you; ever will I treasure the memories of these months!"

The hurt was almost gone now, but there was an aching longing welling up in her; she could not take her eyes from his face.

He forced his own gaze away. "Wizard! Can you not lessen her hurt? Can you not give her sweet nepenthe?"

"Forgetfulness?" Yes, out of sheer pity, I could certainly do that much. Besides, I couldn't have her menacing shipping and sailors, trying to restore her wounded vanity. I turned to Frisson. "How about it, Fr—oh."

Frisson's face was so heavy with lugubriousness that he looked like a bloodhound. His eyes were huge and bloodshot, transfixed on Thyme.

"No, I think I'd better try to manage something myself." I turned back to the ill-sorted couple, remembered my evenings in the coffeehouses, and dredged up an old folk song:

> "In my garden grew plenty of thyme,
> It would flourish by night and by day.
> O'er the wall came a lad,
> And he took all I had,
> And he stole all my thyme away,
> Yes, he stole our sweet Thyme away."

It worked faster than I had expected; even while I was still singing, the "lad" showed up, his head poking above the wall of greenery not too far from the bower. Then his whole body appeared, climbing up a tree; he swung out along a branch and dropped to the ground. He was just a little shorter than Thyme, if you didn't count the horns—short goat horns, and goat's legs with cloven hooves on the end. Of course, with that shaggy hair from the waist down, he didn't need any clothes—which was just as well, since he wasn't wearing any. He was wearing a syrinx, though—a set of panpipes, hung around his neck by a cord.

Thyme glanced at him, then glanced again.

I wondered if I really needed the second verse, but I sang it anyway.

"In June, the red rose is in bloom,
  But that was no flower for me,
  For I plucked at the bud,
  And it pricked me to blood,
  And I gazed on the willow tree."

"The willow, symbol of lovers' sadness?" Thyme sighed. "Ah, well could it be mine!"

"What! Do I see the trace of melancholy on thy features?" The faun hopped up to her. "It must be erased—for a face so fair must not be careworn!"

She glanced his way, her gloom lessened by the flattery; but she said, "Why, what are you to speak so? Consider with care, foolish boy, for you are but a kid!"

"Mayhap, but I am a goat withal." A mischievous grin touched his lips. "Be mindful, sweet wanton—I will grow on you."

"Not if I can prevent it." She made a shooing gesture, irritated. "Begone, irksome child!"

"Alack-a-day!" The faun looked up at me. "Can you not aid, Wizard?"

"Could be," I said.

"Oh, it's very good drinking of ale,
  But it's far better drinking of wine.
  I would she were clasped
  In her lover's arms fast,
  For 'tis he who has stolen her, Thyme—
  Yes, 'tis he who has stolen our Thyme."

"What nonsense do you rhyme?" Thyme demanded, nettled, but the faun lifted the panpipes to his lips and began to blow.

It was a melody amazingly sweet, but also sad, weighted with a longing beyond his apparent years, and it conjured up words to match it, not quite clearly enough to voice, hovering just on the verge of consciousness, telling a tale of unrequited desire and aching yearning.

Thyme looked up, staring in surprise.

The faun began to weave from side to side, then to move his hooves in a slow dance.

Thyme followed him with her gaze, mesmerized. The lines of sadness disappeared from her face, and she began to sway in time to the music.

I reached out and grabbed one of the tree trunks that made up the bower. That music was getting to me, working its way inside and initiating its own ache in me, from heart to loins.

Thyme's swaying grew broader; she began to move her feet, following the pattern of the faun's dance. The music thrilled with hope, and the faun's movements grew more suggestive. Thyme followed, hips swaying more broadly, body curving and retreating, her eyelids growing heavy, a knowing smile curving her lips.

Behind me, somebody moaned; I recognized Frisson's voice.

Now the two were as close as dancers in a ballroom, weaving and swaying, advancing and retreating. All signs of care were gone from Thyme's face, and a musky scent was beginning to tinge the air. The dancers moved in unison, as if a single mind animated both bodies.

Out of the corner of my eye, I saw Frisson staring with eyes so wide that the whites showed all around, his face one instant from madness.

Thyme reached up to the brooch that held her dress fastened.

"Time to go." I grabbed Frisson and tugged, but he was rooted to the spot. I cried, "Gilbert! Help me!"

The squire shook himself, coming out of his trance. He flushed deep red, nodded, and took Frisson's other arm.

"Lift," I told him, and together we hoisted the poet's frozen form and moved toward the door. An agonized sound started in his throat, slid up to his mouth, and out his lips: "Noooooo!"

"Keep going," I said through clenched teeth.

"Nymph, keep me!" Frisson begged. "Use me, debase me—but keep me!"

She didn't even glance his way; her gaze was transfixed on the faun, her face glowing, her fingers fumbling with the brooch.

"Sweet nymph, farewell!" the monk murmured, and ducked out the door.

Frisson gave a horrible groan as we pulled him through the portal and away, struggling in our hands. Gilbert held fast, his back resolutely turned to the scene behind him. That meant I was facing it; I saw the dress slip, saw a flash of pearly pink skin, before the glare of the noonday sun washed out all sight of the interior. We turned frontward and stumbled away, dragging Frisson with us.

Behind us, the music grew slower, even more heavily sensual, setting up a rocking rhythm.

Frisson went slack in our arms, sobbing, and Friar Ignatius let out a long and shuddering breath. "I thank you, Wizard. Of all the assaults my virtue has suffered on this isle, this was the greatest." His mouth twisted in a sardonic smile. "Though I must confess, 'tis cause for chagrin, to find I am so easily forgotten."

"Just think of it as proof that she was only using you," I suggested, "or wanted to."

"Yes. Well put." He nodded. "In that fashion, I am glad to know I was right to resist—glad in worldly terms as well as spiritual, for I was but a toy to her."

"Don't worry," I said. "She isn't interested in any of us anymore."

"Praise Heaven!" Gilbert shuddered. "And I thank you, Wizard! I was almost ensnared!"

Privately, I thought it would have done him a world of good, but I didn't say so.

CHAPTER 27

Frisson didn't manage to start working his legs again until we came in sight of the ocean. Even then, it was all he could do to stagger across the beach to the boat and collapse into it, sobbing. The rest of us heaved and pushed, driving it over the sand and back into the ocean, though I don't think we could have done it without that huge boost from Gruesome.

"In." I looked up at him, pointing to the inside of the boat. "I'll finish pushing off this time."

The shark mouth grinned; he was glad to be leaving. He clambered in and sat huddled in the bow, moaning in anticipation of seasickness.

"Get in," I told Gilbert and Friar Ignatius. They clambered over the sides. Gilbert sat down facing aft, took up an oar, and fitted it between the pegs that passed for an oarlock—and to my amazement, Friar Ignatius did the same. They pulled together, I shoved, and the boat's bottom grated free of the last of the shingle. I vaulted up and over the stern, and the two men of different cloths threw their backs into it, rowing hard.

The last echo of music died away. I wondered what was going on back in the bower, then thought frantically about apples—it doesn't do any good to try *not* to think about something; you have to think about something else instead.

When the island was only a thin green line on the horizon, Friar Ignatius panted, "Hold." He and Gilbert leaned on their oars, drawing deep gasps. When he'd caught his breath, Friar Ignatius said, "I thank you, Wizard. I'd have never won free by myself."

I knew why, too—he hadn't really wanted to. I couldn't blame him. "Glad to do it—but I had an ulterior motive."

"Aye." Friar Ignatius nodded. "You said you had need of my aid."

"That's right. You see, we're trying to stage a bit of a revolution—overthrowing the queen of Allustria."

For a minute or so, the only sounds I heard were the surf, and Frisson's last miserable sobs.

Then Friar Ignatius said, "Well." And, "Are you, indeed."

"Yes," I said. "You see, I fell in love with one of the queen's sacrifices and managed to keep her from despairing at the last second—and being a virtuous maiden, her ghost was headed straight for Heaven. Suettay couldn't stand to let a victim get away, so she kept the body alive. I'm trying to get Angelique's body back, but it's in Suettay's castle, so . . ."

"The only way is to overthrow the queen." Friar Ignatius nodded with grim understanding. "Well, I cannot say the goal is unworthy, Wizard Saul, though your reasons are somewhat less than noble."

"I always thought love was very noble—if it was real." I shrugged. "Besides, I'm not from your world, so I don't have any vested interest in your politics. This is entirely personal."

Friar Ignatius stared at me. "Surely any man has interest in the war between good and evil!"

"They're pretty abstract," I returned, "and for a long time, I wasn't even sure there was any such thing as real, genuine evil—I thought it was just the label I used for people who were opposed to me. Over the years, though, I've seen people, those I had nothing to do with, do some really horrible things to other people, sometimes just because they enjoyed it; so I'm willing to say there is such a thing as evil. Even so, it's not my problem, don't you see—it's none of my business."

But for the first time in my life, the words sounded hollow.

There was a racheting groan, and Frisson pulled himself up off the bottom of the boat onto a seat, staring past me at the thin green line that was Thyme's island.

I took a chance. "Feeling a little better now?"

He just sat there staring for a minute or so, then finally, reluctantly, nodded. "Aye. And I think I must thank you, friend Saul, for aiding me. I was ensnared."

"But you're still not sure you wanted to be freed," I said softly.

He shook his head, then let his chin sink onto his breast.

"Ay me! I could wish I were to die there, so long as she were to bestow her favors upon me! I could wish to have put her in a flask and taken her with me, that I might let her out whenever I wished!"

"You're not the first man to wish something like that," I said softly.

"You would let her out at once," Friar Ignatius said with the certainty of one who has been there, "and never put her back. You would waste away your life in dancing attendance upon her, Master Frisson."

Frisson shuddered, remembering. "How could that be waste!"

"Because you wouldn't accomplish anything," I said. "You wouldn't become anything in your own right—just one of her toys. Put it behind you, Frisson—as I said, you're not the first man to wish it, and you won't be the last." I turned to Friar Ignatius. "I don't want him to forget—and I don't want him distracted, not when we have so much menace facing us. You've studied magic—any ideas?"

" 'Tis not that I've studied magic alone," he said softly, " 'tis that I've studied God, and the Faith, and the soul." He reached out to touch Frisson on the temple. It was a very light touch, scarcely a fingertip, but Frisson went rigid, and the monk chanted something in Latin.

Frisson went limp, but the hangdog look hung lower.

Friar Ignatius took his hand away with a sigh. "As I said, I've not the talent."

"But I have?" I asked him. "Let me try.

"If the fool'd been stripped to his foolish hide,
        (Even as you and I!)
    Which she might have seen when she threw him aside—
        (But it isn't on record the lady tried)
    Some of him would have lived, but the most would have
        died—
        (Even as you and I!)

        Yet it wasn't the lady—a friend interfered
        (Even as you and I!)
    And rent him away from the one he revered,
    Before she could come in the scented dusk
    And suck out his juice, and toss out his husk—
    He turned from the lady, freed, unharmed,

Though not by his choice, but his friend's strong
arm
(Even as you and I!)"

Frisson stiffened like an I-beam again, then slumped in total
relaxation.

We waited, holding our breaths.

Slowly, the poet sat up, eyes wide. " 'Tis done! I am
healed!" He looked at me with a tremulous smile. "I cannot
thank you enough, friend Saul!" But he still looked sad.

"Anything for a friend," I said. "Besides, I need you func-
tioning, on the side of the angels."

Friar Ignatius looked at me in surprised approval. "I thought
you professed to be apart from good and evil, Wizard Saul."

"Not apart from them," I corrected, "just not committed to
them."

He smiled sadly. "You cannot have the one without the
other, Wizard."

"Oh, yes I can," I said softly. "There is neutral ground, and
I'm in it." I heard the after-echo of my own words with something resembling shock, but I plowed ahead anyway. "But that
doesn't mean I'm apathetic. I do care when I see people suffering, and I'm willing to try to help if there's a way I can. I'm
just not a fanatic, that's all."

"You cannot equivocate between God and the Devil, Wizard," he said softly.

I felt a chill on my back, but I shrugged it off. "Not here,
maybe. But you can keep the whole thing in perspective and
not let your zeal for the letter of the law distract you from the
spirit."

His eyes widened. "I thought you had no affinity for good,
Wizard Saul—yet you cite our Savior's words."

"Know your Bible pretty well, do you? Well, so do I, and
not entirely willingly. I had a good religious upbringing—good
in my parents' eyes, maybe."

"Then how was it not good?"

"Because it showed me too many fanatics, too many people
who are willing to do bad things, such as humiliate a kid pub-
licly and convince him that he's bound for Hell."

"That is a grave error," he said, his eyes huge.

I gave him a sour smile. "I wish there were more clergy like
you, Friar Ignatius."

He turned away, his face darkening. "Do not, for I am little use with a congregation, Master Wizard. In truth, if I so much as step up to a pulpit, my tongue cleaves to the roof of my mouth with craven fear, and I cannot utter a word."

I felt a surge of sympathy. "Hey, now—it's all right. We all get stage fright—and if you get too strong a dose of it, why, that's just not your talent. You know your own strengths, don't you?"

"Aye." He turned back to me. "I have a useless gift for pondering Holy Writ, Wizard, and am therefore skilled at explaining how the words of Christ, uttered a thousand years ago and more, may guide our conduct even in this latter age. Nay, mayhap not so useless, for other priests do hark unto me and find my words of aid in speaking to their flocks."

I stared. "You're a theologian."

"I would be loath to claim the honor," he said.

"And might thereby deceive people who have to deal with you," I said. "And you specialize in applying Scripture to daily life?"

"Aye, most especially in the use of the talents God has given others, for I am so lacking in them."

"So that's why you study magic," I said slowly, and a thought throbbed in my brain. "Does that extend to explaining how it works?"

"Aye, though in its essence, 'tis simplicity itself."

"Most great insights are," I said softly.

"Though the first step in that simplifying is to merely say what is magic, and what is not."

"Oh? What is not?"

"Prayer. If we pray for God to intervene in our lives, and if He sees fit to do so, we are like to think it magical, when 'tis more properly a miracle."

I frowned. "I haven't seen many of those."

"Oh?" He smiled. "Did you not speak of love for a maiden?"

I flushed. "That's ordinary, not miraculous! I mean, everybody—well, a lot of people fall in love. It's just hormones and sublimation, not . . ."

His gaze was very steady.

"Okay," I admitted, "so there's something there besides lust and compatible pheromones. It's still not exactly rare."

"Have you ever seen a baby born?" he asked.

"That's a natural process!"

"The creation of a new soul is not—'tis an act of God."

I tensed against an eerie feeling that was stealing over me. "I thought that was the phrase for horrible storms and earthquakes."

"Do you see God only as a destroyer, then? Or do you see each lightning bolt as a miracle?"

"I thought it was supposed to be the wrath of God," I snapped.

"Nay, though it may be His instrument, as virtually anything of this world may be—and as any good Christian must hope to be."

"Now, hold on!" I held up a hand to forestall him. "Are you trying to say everything that happens is a miracle?"

"Certainly not—but by the same token, a miracle need not be rare. It will nonetheless be a miracle, my friend," Friar Ignatius said, with that gentle smile. "I have seen hopeless illness cured, and not through the laying-on of hands, but only through prayer, and because it pleased God; I have seen melancholy lifted from a maiden's heart by the beauty of a sunrise; I have seen a man, bent on death, restored to the will to live by the song of a skylark. The grace of God can reach us all at any time, if we are open to it."

Revelation. "So that's what prayer is! Just turning on the receiver, opening a channel!"

"Odd terms," Friar Ignatius said with a frown, "but that is certainly an aspect of prayer. Not the whole of it, of course, but a part."

"The part that seems to pertain to the discussion at hand." I frowned. "So how *do* you think magic works?"

"By symbols and intent." He rested a hand on Frisson's shoulder, and sang,

> "Let your heart's pain ebb,
> Let it pass, let it pass!
> Be freed of love's web,
> Let it pass, let it pass!
> From the Mire of Despond be raised,
> And your heart be filled with praise
> And the past cleared from your gaze,
> Let it pass! Let it pass!"

Frisson looked up, startled, then turned to Friar Ignatius with a frown. "What have you done?"

"Only given you a song to ward your heart," the monk assured him.

Frisson held a level gaze a moment longer. "You have, and I thank you deeply. Alas, the wanton was fair! But in truth, she had thought only for her own pleasure, and none for my welfare. It is removed, now, though the memory of the passion is sweet . . ." His face darkened. "Alack-a-day, what a fool I made of myself!"

"You had a great deal of aid," the monk assured him.

Frisson smiled, and I stared in shock, for it was a sardonic smile, such as I had never seen on his face before. "I had small need of help, Friar Ignatius, for I've made a fool of myself many, many times in the past. Ah, so many!"

"Why, then, we are brothers," the monk said with a smile.

"Are we so? Nay, I think not—for you did cleave unto God's rules, and thereby did save yourself from shame."

"As the psalm says, 'The salvation of my countenance, and my God,' " Friar Ignatius said softly.

"For you, mayhap—but for myself, I played the fool roundly. In truth, I would be tempted to say that I could not have made a fool of myself, for God did."

"Say not so." Friar Ignatius' voice became stern. "The only true folly is turning away from God, Master Poet, and as long as you reach out to others, you have not done that."

"Even if they should spurn me? There is some sense in what you say." Frisson nodded. "But there are ways of reaching out, and there are other ways of reaching out. I think I must modify my techniques, Friar Wisdom."

"Friar Fool, say rather." The monk smiled. "For as long as we do live and breathe, we must needs be fools in some measure." He noticed my stare and turned to me. "What amazes you, Master Saul?"

I gave myself a shake and said, "Thought you claimed you couldn't work magic."

Friar Ignatius flushed and lowered his gaze. " 'Twas only a small magic, Master Wizard, such as a cotter might use."

I started to object, then caught his meaning—the "spell" had been as much suggestion as anything else. Convince Frisson that he had put Thyme behind him, and he did—for certainly, he believed in both magic and monks. Instead, I said, "Had that spell ready to hand, did you?"

"I did," Friar Ignatius admitted, "though I recast a few lines as I spoke. 'Tis a sovereign for many ills, Master Saul—for all things must pass, and it behooves us to speed their passing if they are not for our good."

It made sense, but it wasn't the kind of wisdom I was used to hearing from the West. "I was beginning to think you were this universe's equivalent of a theoretical physicist," I said, "but I'm beginning to suspect you're something of a psychologist, too."

Friar Ignatius frowned. "These terms are strange."

"Darn right they are. So, Friar Ignatius, just how do *you* think magic works?"

"As it will," he answered, "and constantly, for it sustains us all, though we know it not. 'Tis like some great, thick, unseen blanket that overlies the whole world, Master Saul, like a mist upon the plain."

I started to object to "overlies" and was about to suggest "englobes," when I remembered that to him, the world was flat. "So it's a substance, though a diffuse one?"

"Not a substance," he said, "but a kind of energy, like the thrumming you feel within you on a fair morning, when you are in good health."

I stiffened; he was describing a field force. "And this energy blanket covers the whole Earth?"

"Aye, but the energy within us can thicken and direct it, if we have the talent."

"How?" I frowned. "By thinking at it? That would make sense—thought waves modulating a field force . . ."

But Friar Ignatius held up a cautioning hand. "Not thought alone, Master Saul, but all of our bodies, every bit of our being. Our own energies fill us; they are not in our minds alone, or we could never walk."

I didn't like the way this was going, but Frisson did—his gaze was fairly glued to Friar Ignatius' face.

"A man born with the gift for it," the monk said, "can make the magic thicken, gather power from it, and direct that power as he wills."

"And how does he do that?"

"By the symbols that he chooses, to clarify his thinking and involve his whole being in his intention," Friar Ignatius said.

"Then what," Frisson asked, "makes the magic black or white, good or evil?"

"The purpose for which he intends it," Friar Ignatius replied, "and his motives for doing so. If a virtuous woman wishes to

heal, to help, or to protect another, then she appeals to God for
His aid in her deeds, and her magic will be white."

"How about if she's using it to kill an attacker?" I said.

"A good woman would not wish to kill." Friar Ignatius
turned back to me. "She would wish to protect herself and
would therefore only wish to stop or withhold the attacker. Her
spell might kill him, if that were the only way to stop him, but
her intent would be good, and her magic from goodness."

It sounded specious, but I didn't argue—I'd heard enough
about sex crimes to believe that a woman might very well kill
an attacker by accident. All she'd really be thinking about, of
course, would be stopping him—but if she hit a vital organ,
tough luck. I'd be the first to say it, and the last to deny it. "So
how can you tell if you're dealing with a wizard or a sorcerer?"

"You may know him by the symbols he uses," Friar Ignatius
answered. "If he inflicts pain to gain magical powers, if he
speaks of death and uses skulls and twisted blades and blood,
then his magic is surely ill, and aided by evil."

"Symbols?" I frowned. "I've only seen sorcerers use
words!"

"You may also see them brandish a staff or a wand," Friar
Ignatius said. "It magnifies the force of a spell, even as it magnifies the force of a blow."

I had a notion it had something to do with directing the
force, like an antenna, but it was not fair bringing electromagnetism into the discussion.

"But brewing spells with physical objects for symbols is
lengthy and cumbersome, though the magic is extremely potent," Friar Ignatius said. "In the field, a magician will rely on
words and gestures."

"But how could that do any good? How could physical symbols do any good, for that matter?"

"Because, Master Wizard, the symbol is the thing."

I stared and clamped my jaws shut. In my universe, one of
the cardinal principles of semantics was that the symbol was
not the thing. Well, other universes, other natural laws.

"The whole of one's being must be gathered together and
directed," Friar Ignatius explained, "that all the energies within
and around our bodies may form and fashion the magical energy to our purpose. Symbols are the tools we use to so solid-
ify our beings—and the more powerful the symbol, the more
fully are the various parts of ourselves gathered together."

"So whether we're drawing on God to help us focus our own energies is a matter of whether or not we want to," I interpreted.

" 'Focus'—an excellent term!" Friar Ignatius clapped his hands. "I should have thought of turning to mathematics for my concepts! I thank you, Wizard Saul."

I shivered, wondering what I had done. This "magic field" he was talking about seemed to be this universe's equivalent of electromagnetism—and I knew darn well what our own physicists and engineers had been able to do with electricity and magnetism, once they had started shaping their thinking according to mathematical principles. What would happen here, if Friar Ignatius started applying math to magic?

Amazing things, I didn't doubt—because I had a very strong suspicion that it really was possible to manipulate that magic field without drawing on either good or evil. It was an impersonal force, after all—the personal element came when you tried to draw on the power of supernatural beings to help you control it. Besides, I was still trying to think of those beings as imaginary—in which case, they served as very, very powerful symbols.

Powerful, indeed—they tapped directly into the subconscious. I thought of my hallucinatory guardian angel and shuddered. "I wouldn't be so extreme," I said easily. "After all, we're talking about an art, not a trade. So words are symbols, and poetry concentrates meaning—so the better the poetry, the more powerful the spell?"

Frisson's eyes were so wide they almost bulged.

"Aye," Friar Ignatius said, "and poetry that is sung, is more powerful still."

"Sung?" I frowned. "How does that work?"

"Because there is order in melody," Friar Ignatius explained, "that adds its strength to the order of rhyme and meter; and because song is felt throughout the body, and thereby incorporates all of our energies."

My spirits sank; I had a tin ear. But Frisson's face lit with delight. "I have a passable voice."

"Then bend your thoughts toward God and goodness," Friar Ignatius said, turning to him. "Meditate on Him, that your magic may be for the benefit of others, and the strengthening of goodness."

Frisson gazed at him, eyes glowing, and nodded. "Aye, for we go up against great evil, Friar Ignatius."

"The power of goodness must needs be greater than the power of evil," Friar Ignatius rejoined, "for it doth draw on God, the Ultimate Source."

I sat bolt upright. "You aren't trying to tell me that good will always triumph over evil!"

"It will, if all other elements are equal," Friar Ignatius said. "No demon can stand against an angel, and white magic is much more powerful than black. But it is more difficult to be good than to be wicked, and more difficult to master white magic than black. Fasting, prayer, self-discipline, returning good for evil—these are difficult. To give in to anger and the lust for revenge is easy."

I thought about the Taoists and Zen Buddhists, and kept thinking.

But Frisson spoke. "We must needs confront a vile sorceress and her minions, Friar Ignatius. We will need all the strength that God can lend."

"His grace is there for all," the monk murmured, "if we will but be open to it."

"I think," Frisson said, "that I must learn to pray."

For some reason, that sent shivers down my spine. I tried changing the subject. "Was this why the queen had Thyme tie you up?"

Friar Ignatius turned to me, a strange light in his eyes. "So you have guessed that, too, Master Wizard! Yes, I had wondered—though I cannot prove that. Still, 'tis quite possible that it was the queen of Allustria who drove our ship to the nymph's isle—for she could not damage me herself, as long as I remained devoted to God."

"And if anybody could break that devotion," I said, "it would have been Thyme. But why did the queen want you out of the way? Was she afraid you might convince some of her sorcerers to repent and start working toward sainthood?"

"As do we all," Friar Ignatius reminded me, "if we do not despair. That is possible, Master Saul, but I think it more likely that she wished me imprisoned so that my ideas of human life would not spread."

"Ideas about the riddle of human existence?" I frowned. "How could that hurt her?"

Friar Ignatius bowed his head, hiding a smile of bitter amusement. When he looked up again, his face was bland and his smile gentle once more. "I have gathered wisdom from the East and from the West, Master Saul, and let go of those parts that I did not feel consistent with the whole. What is left is somewhat irreverent; indeed, those in positions of power might think I mock them, or the very notion of their right to authority."

"You mean you've come up with ideas that are a threat to the queen?" I frowned. "How?"

"Because, taken together, they add up to the notion that folk need not depend on the crown for their sustenance or safety, but only on God, on themselves, and on their neighbors."

"Decentralization!" I stared, thunderstruck. "My lord! No wonder Suettay's out to get you! You're threatening her bureaucracy!"

He frowned. "What is a 'bureaucracy'?"

"Government by desks," I said. "Behind each desk sits a clerk, but they come and go, and the desks stay. Each desk has a bigger desk it answers to—the more powerful clerks answer to other more powerful clerks, and on up to the queen herself."

"Then you see clearly, Master Saul." Again, he gave me that strange, close look. "You know that her clerks do make her the center of authority of the land and give her control over the least of her subjects, no matter how far from her castle they may be."

"I'm familiar with the basic idea, yes."

"And with the notion that each subject must do as he is told, without question?"

"With the notion, yes. Not with the fact—my countrymen tend to do a lot of questioning, and complaining, too, and sometimes they even manage to go around the lower desks and go right to the top and get satisfaction."

His eyes glowed. "A marvelous people! Small wonder you are the one who can aid this land!"

"I didn't say I was one of the ones who succeeded." I stirred restlessly. "On the other hand, in my own world, I've heard of countries where the people don't dare complain, or even ask any questions. Allustria's like that, huh?"

"Aye—and if you know the manner of it, then you must be able to imagine what would hap if each of those subjects were convinced that he was the master of his destiny, and that he himself had the duty of choosing what he would and would not do."

I could feel my eyes snap wide. "*That's* your theology?"

He shrugged uncomfortably. "A part of it, yes. But 'tis truly quite old—Christians have always believed in free will, believed that 'tis for each of us to choose whether to sin or not to sin, whether to work toward Heaven or lapse toward Hell."

"But a tyrant like the queen can gain a lot of mileage if she can convince her people that they're all bound for Hell already, so they might as well do what she says and keep from having pain in this world—and gain anything she's willing to give them for rewards."

"Even so. And, too, I have come to believe that folk should be governed by their own consent and consensus, by discussing matters till they can agree, following the example of the holy hermits who abide nearest them. Thus they would live according to the common law they create together, and by the Commandments of God."

"Revolutionary!"

" 'Tis a brave notion, and devoutly to be wished." Frisson was pensive. "But how could it come to be, Friar Ignatius? Such a transformation in people's thoughts could not be worked in a single night, nor even a decade."

"Even so," the monk agreed. "If it can come about at all, it will be by the patient example of men and women dedicated to God—and I do not, of course, believe it can come to be completely or perfectly as I see it. Only in Heaven may we be perfect, one by one or all together. Still, I do think we can hope to improve greatly as the years roll. 'Twill be a long process, and slow . . ."

"But even in its early phases, people would want a better government," I said. "You're giving them the idea that they can expect to be treated as worthwhile human beings in their own right."

"But of course," Friar Ignatius murmured, "for that is what they are. Every soul is infinitely precious, Master Saul—precious to God, and therefore should be precious to anyone who calls himself Christian."

"Should be," I noted. "And, of course, there's the minor problem of whether or not your ideas will work unless everybody tries them all at once—but even a small dose would be enough to bother the bureaucrats. They see people as numbers, not souls."

"A fascinating notion." Friar Ignatius frowned. "So you can understand, Master Saul, why the queen would wish me gone."

"Oh, sure! She wants people to believe they're stuck being whatever they were born as—and if they were born serfs and peasants, as the vast majority of them were, it's not going to do them any good to try to be anything different, or to even protest against what the authorities tell them to do."

"Which is to say, that they have no free will, not even such lesser forms," Friar Ignatius agreed.

Interesting that he thought social mobility and social action were minor. "Of course, it *is* awfully difficult to become anything you're not born to—and society does everything it can to keep you in place."

"Difficult," the monk agreed, "but not impossible. Our birth and our talents, and the moral teachings given us by our parents and clergy—these are among those things given us, over which we have no control. Still, a soul who strives, and who uses wisely what she or he is given, may yet do great things."

I frowned. "How about if he's born with a really vicious temper, a lust for power, and a sex drive that just won't quit?"

Friar Ignatius shuddered. "I have heard of such men—nay, I have met them. But even one so accursed may win to Heaven through devotion to God, and adherence to His Commandments."

That, of course, was what really mattered, to him—free will was there so we could choose to sin or not to sin, to fly or to burn. I was seized with the vision of the pinball machine of life, with the balls and the laws of force and motion being determinism, and when and how I hit the flappers being free will. "I think we should tilt."

All three of them looked at me as if I'd lost my marbles. "What did you say, Wizard?"

"Uh, nothing," I said quickly. "Strategy for the revolution. How long before we get to the mainland, do you think?"

Only a day and a night, as it turned out. There were some storms with some very odd timing, boiling up out of a clear blue sky—but Frisson was clearheaded again, and we had some idea what we were fighting. I fished through my sheaf of parchments and handed him a couple of odes in praise of sunshine, and he improved on them as he recited, and for some reason, the foul weather blew over almost as quickly as it had come.

Still, it did seem kind of odd to me that the queen should let us make it back to the mainland with no worse trouble than that.

I mentioned this to Friar Ignatius right after we had hauled the boat past the high-tide mark and started hiking inland. "It may be that she has little time to spare for us," he told me, "even though we may be the greatest challenge yet to her throne."

"Aye," Gilbert agreed. "If the Spider King and the Gremlin have done as they promised, she will be far too busy to spare us much attention."

"Good point." I turned to the nearest large spider—we were hiking through a marshy meadow, and the arachnids seemed to be everywhere; the stiff grass was ideal for mooring webs. "Tell the Spider King we're back, will you?" I said. "And we'd like to know what's going on."

My buddies glanced sidelong at me as if they were wondering about my sanity again, but they'd met the Spider King, too, all except for Gruesome and Friar Ignatius, so they kept their peace. Which was very wise—the spider was busy mending the rim of her web, but she turned and scampered straightaway back to the center—and disappeared.

Friar Ignatius stared at it for a few seconds. Then he whipped his gaze up to me, stared for a few seconds longer, then glanced back at the web.

Gilbert squared his shoulders and cleared his throat. "There is small time to debate," he said. " 'Tis long and far to Allustria, and we have only our legs."

He took the lead, and we filed off after him.

About half an hour later, we were coming up to a stand of trees. Just to the right of our path, a really splendid web was strung between two saplings, four feet in diameter, with a spider whose body was the size of an old-fashioned dollar. We glanced at it in admiration, then looked again.

Woven into the web were runes. They spelled out, "Gaze."

"Gaze?" I frowned, staring. "Gaze at what?"

"Thus." Friar Ignatius beckoned, and we turned aside from the path, heading for the sound of a brook that had been paralleling our path for the last few minutes. The monk scouted along its edge until he found a small pool that had formed between some rocks. "Here, poet," he said. "Craft a verse that would tune a pool to the king's mind."

"Uh, I think . . ." I pulled out the sheaf and riffled through, then yanked a slip. "Here, Frisson!"

The poet pursed his lips, absorbing his own verse again, then spouted it out, with improvements:

> "Water, water, most contrary,
>   Help this televisionary.

Let no image now be sinking,
But show us what the king is thinking."

I did a double take, but he was right—"television" was
Latin for "seeing at a distance," though not quite in the way
my culture meant it. I looked down at the pool, almost daring
it to show me something.

It clouded and darkened, then cleared, but stayed dark, a
deep indigo—and in its depths, images formed. My gaze
locked onto them; I couldn't have forced myself to look away
if I'd wanted to. And, of course, I didn't want to; to say the
least they were compelling.

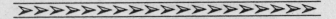

CHAPTER 28

We saw a mob of peasants beating up a squad of soldiers in a village square. It was unbelievable, until the pool showed us just one villager swinging a cudgel down at a soldier. The man-at-arms stabbed at him with a pike—but the peasant's cudgel whacked right on the haft behind the head, and the shaft broke.

"The Gremlin!" I breathed. After all, our perverse friend specialized in making things break down at the crucial moment. Admittedly, he was better with high-tech devices—the more complicated they are, the more things can go wrong—but he was managing pretty well with what he had.

The battle disappeared, and another army swam into view—but in this one, the soldiers were fighting among themselves. A knight rode about the fray, trying to knock combatants apart with a mace, but his horse tripped, and he disappeared into a melee of flailing arms. The images grew larger and larger, floating out past the edges of the pool, till I could see an over-turned kettle next to the ashes of a campfire. The kettle was empty. Then the fighting soldiers swam back in, growing smaller and smaller until I was looking at an overhead view of the churning mass of soldiers. Suddenly they streaked past me, and the images expanded again, until I found myself looking down into a trio of farm wagons. They were filled with hay. Apparently, the quartermaster had bollixed up the order, sending horse food instead of people food, and the soldiers were starving.

"The Gremlin!" Gilbert breathed.

"Maybe," I said, "but I think he's getting expert advice."

346

The fight dimmed and faded, and another picture grew in its place. A peasant, wearing a green tunic with yellow hose and a tall cap, was going from door to door, looking very confused as he scooped gold pieces out of a bag and handed them to the peasants. The recipients stared, unbelieving, then broke into huge smiles and heaped thanks on the donor—but he was already turning away toward the next cottage, looking very frazzled.

"He is a tax collector." Gilbert frowned. "Wherefore does he give money, rather than take it?"

It almost seemed as if the pool had heard him; it clouded up, then cleared again, showing us a view of a big room. We were looking at it from high up on the wall, and we saw a mob of men in rich-looking robes milling about half a dozen tables with checkerboard tops. There was a lot of gesturing, and I could imagine the noise. It looked like one of those television news shots of the New York Stock Exchange just before closing time on a bad day.

" 'Tis the exchequer," Friar Ignatius murmured.

Oh. So that was where the word "checker" came from. Now that he mentioned it, I could see colored disks on some of the checkerboards, like beads on an abacus, and serving the same purpose. This was a counting room, and these men were clerks. "What are they arguing about?"

I shouldn't really have asked; I knew the answer as soon as I'd thought of the question. They were blaming one another, of course, trying to pass the buck before one of them got caught with it.

The pool seemed to have heard me, though—as if in answer, it magnified the big desk in the center of the room, the one without a checkerboard, where a man with a gold chain around his neck was scribbling furiously on slips of parchment and handing them to the nearest of a group of boys, who twisted their way between furiously arguing clerks to hand the slips to men who were still sitting at their counting tables, moving stones about frantically, trying to look busy. As one boy carried his parchment, it swelled till it filled the pool, and we could all read, "Take two pennies from each peasant." But even as we watched, the words "Take" and "from" were blurring, the pen strokes writhing into new forms that made the message say, "Pay two pennies to each peasant."

"What spell is this?" Frisson stared, amazed.

"The Gremlin again," I said, "though I think he might be getting some advice from the Rat Raiser."

The scene rippled and disappeared, and another one steadied in its place. This one looked a lot like the first, except that the tables didn't have checkerboards inlaid into them, and the men milling about wore richer and more colorful clothing—mostly doublets and hose; I only saw one or two real robes. Most of them were also wearing mail shirts that gleamed at the necks of their tunics and showed between belt and hose.

" 'Tis the command post of an army!" Gilbert exclaimed, staring.

"And judging from the quality of the clothing, this is the high command," I agreed. "It looks a lot like the other room."

" 'Tis in the queen's castle," Brother Ignatius breathed.

Gilbert frowned. "How is this? Knights and lords, scribbling on parchments?"

"It's called centralized command," I said. "They put their orders in writing, and couriers run them to the generals in the field."

"They fear the field will come to them," Gilbert said, "and shortly, or they would not be wearing mail."

I hoped he was right.

A general finished dictating to a clerk, who was scribbling on a parchment. He poured sand on it, dumped the sand, made sure the sheet was dry, and handed it to a courier who headed for the door, slipping it into a pouch as he went—but not quite quickly enough to keep the pool from magnifying it, and we watched it change from "Conscript five male peasants from each village" to "Discharge five male peasants to each village." Then the parchment slipped into the dispatch case and was gone from sight—but even as it did, the scene rippled and changed to a view from up high, showing a long stretch of dirt road with twenty or thirty soldiers ambling along with their pikes over their shoulders, laughing and slapping one another on the back.

"Men released from arms?" Gilbert cried. "In the midst of a war?"

"Seems Queen Suettay made a mistake by turning her commanders into bureaucrats," I said. "She made them vulnerable to the Gremlin—and the Rat Raiser, of course."

"The Rat Raiser! Can this soft-handed clerk best even knights in the field?"

"Not in the field," I corrected him. "Only before they get there."

The scene rippled again and changed to a paneled room with a richly dressed man sitting behind an elevated table on top of a dais. Before him stood a bruised man in rags and chains, flanked by two well-fed men in green and brown.

"Foresters," Gilbert breathed, "and a county magistrate."

"A courtroom?" I asked.

"A knight's court, mayhap," he said, "though a simple knight can scarcely be termed to hold court."

"Well, it certainly is serving the purpose." I couldn't help but feel sorry for the poor peasant in front of the bench. "What did this guy do, to deserve being arrested?"

"The two men to either side of him are forest keepers," Frisson said. "I warrant the peasant was caught a-poaching." He sounded as if he spoke from experience.

I caught my breath. I'd always thought the medieval forest laws were unfair, even though I had to admit the game laws of my own day and age made no sense. Still, making sure deer and pheasants aren't hunted to extinction was a far cry from making sure they were reserved only for the aristocracy's tables and amusement.

This time, however, justice seemed to be adhering to the spirit rather than the letter; the knight was gesturing, and the foresters stared, aghast. The knight pounded on the table, getting red in the face, and the foresters reluctantly turned to strike off the peasant's irons. He stood, dumbstruck, staring at his reddened but naked wrists; then a forester gave him a shove toward the door. He stumbled, but turned the stumble into a run and got out of there before the knight could change his mind.

The knight, for his part, was still red-faced, only now he was glowering at a parchment that lay beside him on his high table.

"The Rat Raiser again!" I grinned. "He told the Gremlin how to louse up the judicial system—from Suettay's standpoint, anyway."

"Aye." Frisson smiled. "Merely dispense actual justice."

The scene rippled again, and we found ourselves looking down from overhead at two long battle lines stretched out across a meadow, facing each other. At the head of each rode a man in armor, with a whole squadron of silver lobsters behind him on heavy-duty Percherons.

" 'Tis the duke of Degmaburg!" Gilbert cried. "I know his arms!"

"Only a duke?" I frowned. "Not a minister of some sort?"

"Nay. He was too strong to depose, though not to corrupt. He is one of the few of the old nobility who has held his station under the sorcerers' reigns."

"And now he sees his chance to reestablish the old line," I breathed, "meaning himself."

Even as I said it, the duke's horse began to canter forward. His squad of heavy armor heaved into a trot right behind him, and the peasantry leveled their pikes and began to move forward.

But Gilbert was frowning. "How is this? The queen's knights are far behind the line of men-at-arms! What can they do there?"

He was about to find out—for just before the duke and his knights struck, the peasant line opened up like a gate, and the horsemen hurtled through. Suettay's armored division snapped their lances down and tried to work up to a quick trot— apparently they hadn't planned on having to fight. But the duke and his men were going too fast to stop; they slammed into the royal knights, unhorsing a few, then dropping their lances and grabbing for maces and broadswords. It turned into a melee after that, with the knights chopping one another to filings.

Meanwhile, back on the front lines, one of the noncoms lowered his pike and held out a wineskin. The advance wavered; then the duke's troopers dropped their pikes, reached for the wineskins, and pulled out some hardtack. In a few minutes, they were laughing and chatting with their opposite numbers, having a regular party while they watched the lobsters open one another's shells.

"How can they think they will not be punished?" Gilbert wondered.

"Nice question." I pointed to the silver melee. "Here come their masters."

The knights were riding back full-tilt, and those broadswords rose and flailed down at their own men. They hit . . .

And broke.

Snapped clean across, just as if each sword had been a brittle antique. The knights stared at the remnants of blade attached to their hilts, then roared and pulled out their maces.

The heads flew off on the first swing.

The rankers' arms shot up, presumably with a cheer; then their pikes raised and stabbed, some finding chinks in armor, some jabbing between saddle and tin pants, levers to tip knights out of saddles—which they did. Then each knight disappeared in a cluster of soldiers, and pikes rose and fell.

Gilbert was pale-faced. "Soldiers striking down their own knights!" It was the ultimate threat to him.

"Suettay's harvest," I told him, knowing it would be reassuring. "She's trained her army to get everything they can for themselves and prey upon the weaker, killing off anybody who gets in their way. She forgot that she might not always be the stronger."

But the queen's side hadn't dispensed with all its strong-arms yet; a sorcerer in a midnight robe banded with gray stood up, waving his arms.

"A man of the second rank." Frisson frowned. "This may be their undoing, poor devils."

"Maybe not," I said. "Don't underestimate the Gremlin's capacity for making things go wrong."

Suddenly, a rain fell—a very localized rain; it seemed to envelop only the sorcerer. He clutched his hat and ran, but the storm followed him.

I frowned. "What kind of rain is that? It looks yellow—no, brown, when there's enough of it! And it foams . . ."

"Ale!" Frisson cried.

The sorcerer fled, pursued by foot soldiers who stopped every few paces to dip up the puddles he left behind him.

But they were already growing smaller in the gazing pool; the field dwindled, forests leaning in from the sides to hide it. Then the treetops began to look like waves in a pool as they shrank away, and kept shrinking. A patchwork quilt of farmland moved in around the edges, still shrinking until it became a plain flat area of yellowish green with dark-green masses of forest and clots of dots that were towns made of houses. The blue shimmer of the Baltic appeared at the top of the pool, with the white beard of the Alps below. Ribbons of blue marked the boundaries, and I found myself looking down at Germany as I knew it. But the picture kept on expanding, including Austria, Hungary . . .

"The Holy Roman Empire," I whispered.

"Holy no longer," Friar Ignatius said grimly, "and 'tis odd that you should couple the empire with Rome, for Hardishane refused to accept the crown the pope would have given him.

He did revere the pope and his bishops, for he was a man of faith—but he held that the churchmen should no more partake of governance, than he should of ministry, and that 'twould be as great a catastrophe for the one as for the other."

I whistled. "Brave words, for the time! How did he avoid being excommunicated?"

Brother Ignatius shrugged, and Gilbert said softly, "Who would have dared excommunicate Hardishane?"

I took it that Hardishane was this universe's answer to Charlemagne, and had been just a little more deft than the Frankish king—or a little more paranoid. I decided I wanted to learn more about him—but now wasn't quite the time.

An area of the map was growing in the screen—the southeast, where the Alps gave some security to the smaller kingdoms and principalities that would someday be Switzerland, in my universe. We seemed to be going in for a close look at the sector that would have been the Dauphin—the bridge between France and Germany. I wondered why—but as the view swelled, we saw a long dark line snaking out of the mountains into Allustria. The line was moving—and as it swelled, I could make out the gleams of armor and spear heads, then individual knights and soldiers. It was an army on the move.

"The army of Merovence!" Gilbert cried. "Praise Heaven!"

But the view went past them, a pair of mountains swelling, then their tops flanking the screen. There the view steadied, and I saw soldiers in the same colors as the marchers below standing on crags, bows in hand. Among them stood men in homespun tunics, looking as hard as the rocks they stood on, bearded and booted against the cold.

"The montagnards have thrown in with Merovence!" Gilbert cried, "and the Free Folk with them!"

"The Free Folk?" I frowned.

"Behind the soldiers," Friar Ignatius prompted.

I looked, and realized that the gray-green wall I had taken for rock had a head and a tail—and wings! So help me, it was a dragon!

But it was growing smaller in the pool, and the scene blurred as we swept along the line of the army. It steadied again, and a dragon floated by, filling the pool for a moment, its wingspan vast but still nowhere near enough to support such a huge body. Was magic in the air, here?

Yes, of course. If Friar Ignatius was right, raw magical power filled all of space, like the hypothetical ether of early electronics. I mentally kicked myself—I had known that! And if there were a magic field that surrounded the whole Earth, why wouldn't life-forms have evolved to take advantage of it?

I resolved to keep a closer eye on the local fauna.

But the view was narrowing again, the individual soldiers growing larger as the view swept on to the head of the file— and I saw a sight that stung like a slap in the face. At the head of the column rode a knight whose long blonde hair streamed out from under a steel cap with a crown around it.

" 'Tis Queen Alisande!" Gilbert yelped. "The queen of Merovence herself!"

My heart leapt into my throat. "Isn't that a little dangerous?"

"Nay." Gilbert pointed. "See who rides beside her."

On the lady's right hand rode a man in midnight blue, emblazoned with stars and crescent moons and comets, though he wore a steel cap instead of a pointed one. "A sorcerer?"

"Nay, the Lord Wizard!"

"I notice he's riding a dragon," I said. "Thought you said they were the Free Folk."

"They are, and the fabled Stegoman is the Lord Wizard's friend, not his slave. And, see!" Gilbert pointed; on the other side of the Queen rode a knight all in black, on a midnight charger.

"Sir Guy de Toutarien!" Gilbert crowed. "I know his blank shield."

"Black armor and a blank shield are pretty anonymous," I demurred.

"Aye, but what other Black Knight would ride beside Queen Alisande of Merovence? Nay, all do know of that blank-shield knight, Wizard Saul! 'Tis he who aided the Lord Wizard to overthrow the vile usurper Astaulf and his sorcerer Malingo, to set Queen Alisande again upon her ancestral throne!"

I could see there was a lot of old news I was going to have to catch up on.

"Thereafter," Frisson said, his eyes glowing, "they two worked among the folk of Ibile and shook the throne so sorely that Queen Alisande could ride in, depose the false sorcerer who had taken the crown, and restore the rightful heir."

I was beginning to see a pattern here. "Who is the rightful heir to the throne of Allustria?"

"None," Frisson mourned. "Suettay's ancestor slew them all, root and branch, when she usurped the throne."

"All?" I stared. That didn't equate with the medieval tradition. "You sure there wasn't maybe a baby hidden someplace? Raised as a peasant, possibly?"

"Three, but the sorcerer-queen found them all out and slew them in cold blood. Then her daughter slew her mother before the whole court, took the throne, and sent knights straightaway after the last babe of the cadet branch, and his mother."

"So. No heirs." I frowned. "That gives us a problem, doesn't it?"

"We shall find a fit monarch," Friar Ignatius said with certainty.

I wished I'd shared his confidence.

The scene dwindled, and the Alps sank out of the picture. A long river swam to the center of the pool, then grew larger until we saw a battle going on at the eastern end of a bridge. The space around the bridge grew larger and larger as the invaders pushed back the defenders, and a steady stream of reinforcements poured across the span. In the thick of the fighting rode a silver knight with a golden circlet about his helm.

"King Rinaldo of Ibile!" Gilbert cried.

But the battle was already shrinking; soon we were watching a blur of greenery speed by. It steadied and swelled; we found ourselves watching a thread of brown emerge from the mass of leaves, growing until we saw a road through a forest, blocked by a tollgate. There were five carts drawn up, waiting to get through, but four of the drivers were gone, and the fifth walked the line, soothing the mules. Then the other four men came out of the tollhouse, shaking their heads. Together, all five men put their shoulders to the tollgate, heaved, and forced it up. Then they mounted their carts and drove on through.

"How is this?" Gilbert frowned. "Have they overpowered the witch-clerk and gone their way? How so? And know they not what will hap to them when they are caught?"

"Nothing," Frisson said slowly, "if the witch-clerk was gone."

I stared, then remembered the sick toll-witch I'd cured.

"Shall not bandits fall upon them?" Gilbert asked.

The trees blurred, but the road remained clear; we were looking at something happening farther down—a cloud of dust, with struggling men and swords and staves dimly visible though it, slamming and hacking in rage at one another.

"Two mobs of bandits!" Gilbert cried. "They fight to see who shall have the right to despoil the merchants!"

"And they're making enough noise so travelers will have

sense enough to stay away." I nodded. "The winner will probably be so weakened that he won't try to ambush any five who
have sense enough to band together."

"But do they not fear the magistrate?" Frisson asked.

The scene shifted to show a magistrate's house with a dozen
men standing about impatiently, waiting for the door to open.
Finally, they knocked, then knocked again, then pounded in-
cessantly.

"Magistrate's not home," I said.

"Is he out hunting bandits?" Frisson wondered.

"Nay," Gilbert answered, "for his stables are full, and his
men stand idle."

I looked at the area behind the courthouse. Sure enough,
there were a dozen men in leather armor, shooting at big round
targets and taking halfhearted swipes at one another with oaken
staves.

"How shall the merchants resolve their disputes now?" Friar
Ignatius murmured.

Apparently, the merchants were wondering that, too, because
they were talking among themselves with a lot of gesturing.
Finally, they gave up and walked away, discussing matters
among themselves. They sat down in the village square, ten of
them watching while two stood up and began to argue.

"They have set up their own court!" Frisson cried.

"Sure," I said. "Who needs the magistrate, anyway?"

"Only the queen," Gilbert murmured.

The pool showed us a few more such scenes—borders with
people crossing freely, ignoring the watch house nearby; farmers selling produce off the back of their carts, with no tax-
gatherer in sight; a mob breaking into a courthouse and
burning the records. All these official buildings were empty.

"Where are the clerks?" Frisson breathed.

There they were, stumbling down the road, propping themselves up with staffs, meeting one another and going along in
company, holding one another up.

"They are all sick!" Friar Ignatius said.

"So many of them, all at once?" Frisson was wide-eyed.

"Of course!" I crowed. "The Gremlin—he's an expert at
disrupting systems! He spread a plague among them, that attacks only bureaucrats!"

So it seemed. Half the witches in the land had gone off, sick
and stumbling. Their skin was yellow, their faces disfigured
with pustules and pockmarks, their hands with open sores.

"Why aren't they staying in bed?" I asked.

"To wait for death and Hell?" Friar Ignatius shook his head. "Better to force themselves to search."

"Search?" I asked. "What are they looking for?"

The file of witches in the pool suddenly paused, everyone straightening. Then they were pelting pell-mell down the road, or rather, hobbling as fast as they could. The ones in front fell at the feet of a tinker who had been coming toward them, ragged and clattering with pots hung about him. The impact of two or three people bumping onto his shins and grabbing at his cloak was enough to knock off his broad-brimmed straw hat ...

And to reveal his tonsure.

"He is a priest!" Friar Ignatius breathed, "a holy man who goes in disguise, for fear of the queen and her men!"

"Her men have found him," I said. "Apparently, they know the signs."

But they weren't arresting him—they were babbling, gesticulating. The priest recovered from his shock, his face turning from frightened to grave, and he held up a hand. The sick ones fell silent, and he pulled out a piece of cloth four inches wide and six feet long—a stole, the priest's badge of office. He hung it about his neck, then stepped around to the far side of the cart, beckoning to the first witch. The woman hobbled after him.

The others began to line up in front of the improvised confessional. There was some struggling for place, but it was rather halfhearted. They just didn't have the energy.

"They don't think he can cure them, do they?" I asked.

"He can cure their souls," Friar Ignatius answered. "They may suffer for hundreds of years in Purgatory, mayhap even thousands, through all the tortures they have wrought in this world, and more; they may burn in fires as hot as those of Hell—but someday, they shall be released, purified, to rise to Heaven. They will not be damned for eternity, when the priest has heard their confessions and given them God's forgiveness of their sins."

"Ironic," I said, "when you stop to think that these very men and women were probably hunting him only yesterday."

Then I heard the echo of my own words and stilled, amazed, as I realized how much courage that wandering priest must have. He had been going about secretly ministering the Sacraments for years, knowing he might be arrested any day, taken away to die in torture. But he had kept on, because the few good souls there still depended on him.

He needed that courage more than ever, now. He was rocking back and forth as if he were receiving punch after punch, but he held on to the side of the cart, grimly hearing the long tale of the witch's sins.

"What's hurting him?" I asked.

"Devils unseen," Friar Ignatius said, lips thin. "They will not give up their prey easily."

The confessing witch began to jerk about with blows from unseen hands, too—and talons; streaks of red began to appear on her cheeks and hands. On the other side of the cart, the line of witches was beginning to rock, too.

"We must aid them." Friar Ignatius joined his hands, bowing his head and closing his eyes.

"What . . . ?" I started to ask, but Frisson touched my arm, and I fell silent.

In the pool, the invisible punches stopped. The witches cowered together, looking about them, wide-eyed.

"Angels fight the devils," Frisson murmured.

Friar Ignatius made the sign of the cross and looked up.

"The angels won," I said.

"Of course," Friar Ignatius answered with a glowing smile.

On the far side of the cart, the priest was able to finish hearing confession in peace. He bowed his head in prayer, then made the sign of the cross over the penitent, no longer a witch. The woman rose and tottered away, face upraised—and transfigured, shining with relief and joy.

"Now she may die with a lighter heart," Friar Ignatius murmured.

I stared at him. "Pretty heavy-duty magic you worked there, Friar!"

But Ignatius only shook his head. "No magic at all, Wizard Saul. Only prayer."

"Only," I echoed dryly.

The shriven witch was shuffling slowly down the road now, joined by a second. A third rose from confession and joined them.

"Where are they going now?" I asked.

"To seek a physician, I doubt not," Friar Ignatius answered. "Their souls being healed, they shall seek a cure for the ills of the body."

"So they won't go back to their jobs?"

"Certainly not, Wizard. They cannot do so without once again selling their souls."

Which pretty well did in the bureaucracy—at least for a few days, until Suettay could find new recruits. But by that time, the combined revolution and invasion would be over, and there might be no Suettay to do the recruiting.

The line of witches and the toiling priest were already shrinking, the map blurring, until a band of bright blue showed at the bottom of the pool—the Mediterranean. A belt of greenery began to grow, separating into individual trees at the edge of a meadow, then a silver line grew into a brook—with four men and a troll at its edge, staring down at something.

"Why, that is ourselves!" Frisson cried.

"Hold on," I said. "I think we're about to get our marching orders."

Because the scene was shrinking again, the blue band of sea disappearing. The forest swam across our gazing pool and down, and we found ourselves looking at the line of a road that swam up through what I thought of as Yugoslavia. Little black dots were converging on the road, black dots that resolved into men in homespun as the scene expanded again—homespun tunics, with scythes and flails over their shoulders.

"An ambush?" Gilbert frowned, tensing.

"No," I said. "I think they're recruits."

They were. We found it out even while we were in the forest. We followed the trail around a huge old oak—and suddenly they were there, a dozen peasants in green and brown, with bows and daggers instead of scythes.

"Outlaws!" Gilbert scowled, reaching for his sword.

"Hold on." I caught his hand and held the sword in its sheath. "I think they want to parley."

They did; the leader came forward, hard-faced and wary. "We wish to return to our homes," he said, "but we cannot, whiles this brutal queen and her henchmen rule."

"We could change that," I told him, "maybe."

"And what is it that may be?"

"An army," I said. "If we get enough men, we'd stand a very good chance. The Spider King is helping us, and he's getting advice from some experts."

So we went on down the road, but with a dozen armed men at our back.

A little farther on, an old hag suddenly broke through onto

the trail and came tottering toward us, just barely keeping herself upright with a makeshift crutch, one clawed and spotted hand reaching out. The outlaws shouted, "The Witch of the Rock!" and leapt into defensive positions.

"I am Suettay's clerk no longer," the old woman wheezed as she came closer. Then she erupted in a spasm of coughing. I caught a whiff, and recoiled—what had she been eating for breakfast? Silage?

And she was tottering toward me! I backed off, fast.

"Oh, withdraw not from me!" she cried, staggering forward a few more steps. Then she went into another coughing fit, overbalanced, and fell on her knees. That didn't stop her, though; she kept coming on her kneecaps, hands uplifted, imploring. "Heal me! For are you not he who dares to heal a witch?"

"Uh ... I've been known to do it." I glanced at Friar Ignatius. "But only when the witch is ready to repent and abjure her witchcraft. I mean, my cures don't work as long as you're sworn to the Devil's service. Besides, what point is there in my healing a person who's going to turn around and throw a whammy at me the next minute?"

"Oh, I would not do so!" She had to break off to cough again, deep racking barks that shook her whole body. They passed, and she wheezed. "I would ne'er repay good with ill!"

"Then you're not much of a witch—"

"I am not! I wish to be no longer! I fear the gaping mouth of Hell, with its leaping flames!" She coughed again, then turned to Friar Ignatius. "Are you not a priest? Then shrive me, I pray! That even if I die ere he doth cure me, my soul will not burn in Hell for eternity!"

Friar Ignatius gazed at her for a long moment, then nodded. "Come aside."

She tried to get up to her feet to come after him, but ran into another coughing spell and didn't make it. She fell back, and his face turned somber. He waved the rest of us away and drew a stole out of a pocket in his sleeve. Draping it around his neck, he went over to the pitiful sobbing heap and knelt down by it. He made the sign of the cross and recited, "*In nomine Patris, et Filius, et Spiritus Sanctus.* What would you confess, my child?"

The word "child" rattled me—and so did the stole. I sidled over to Frisson and said, "Guess he's more than a brother, eh?"

"He never said he was not a priest," the poet returned, low-voiced. "What illness does this witch have, Wizard?"

I studied the woman, who was muttering a mile a minute to Friar Ignatius, between coughing spells. "Hard to say without asking her and thumping her chest—but at a guess, I'd say it's tuberculosis. Could be pneumonia, but I don't think she'd be able to move this much if it were."

"Would not her demonic master give her wards against such?"

"Only if he had a good reason for keeping her alive—and she's just an underling, not one of those who set policies that make thousands miserable and tempted to resort to evil. Why prolong her life? This way, he gets her soul that much sooner."

At least, that made the kind of sense Frisson could understand. Me, I didn't believe any of it—not the bit about the Devil, nor the stuff about magic. But he did, and I needed to communicate in his terms. "Her lungs are filled with fluid," I said, "and there are tiny creatures in there that are making her body malfunction to keep the goo pouring in. Think you could craft a verse that would kill them off and dry up their habitat?"

Frisson's eyes lost focus. After a few moments, he pulled out parchment and quill. I obligingly turned my back to give him a writing surface and said, "Say it while you write it out—I think we need quick work, here."

He began to mutter while he scribbled. I couldn't quite catch the words, except for "sere" and "sec" and just plain "dry" now and then—but I could see what was happening to the hag.

The racking coughs that kept interrupting her confession grew fewer, and even as I watched, her skin began to regain some color. The feverish glint faded from her eyes, but they didn't fade to dullness—they brightened, with good health. She didn't begin to gain weight, of course—that would take a few good meals. Every day. For a couple of weeks.

Finally, she stopped talking and bowed her head, trembling. By this time, she was looking so healthy that I figured the trembling had to be remorse—or fear, that Friar Ignatius might withhold forgiveness.

And he did look severe. No wonder, if half of the things he'd heard were as bad as I was guessing. But he nodded slowly and began a soft-voiced dialogue with the witch. She nodded, answering him in monosyllables, seeming to wilt even more with each answer. At last, satisfied, he nodded and began a short monologue. I couldn't hear any of it, but I guessed he was telling her what she had to do as penance. Give her credit, she didn't even wince. In fact, when he was done, she looked up in surprise; then, at his admonition, she began to mutter a prayer. Friar Ignatius closed his eyes, tilting his head back, and muttered his own prayer. It lasted just a little longer than hers; then he spoke a few final words, making the sign of the cross toward her—and, so help me, she made it, too, crossing herself from forehead to abdomen, then from shoulder to shoulder. She bowed, saying something, then pushed herself to her feet, turning away . . .

And tottered.

Gilbert was there to catch her by the arm. "Stand still a moment; let your limbs grow used to keeping you upright again."

"They do!" She stared, amazed. "I knew confession was good for the soul—but for the body, too?" Then she realized what she had said and turned to me. " 'Twas you, was it not? You healed my body as he healed my soul!"

"Not this time," I said, and gestured toward Frisson. "This is the man you want to thank."

"I do, oh, I do!" She threw herself at Frisson's feet. "Thank you a thousand times, good master, a thousand thousand! You have given me back my life; you have given me a chance to atone!"

"I . . . I rejoice," Frisson stammered, "yet 'twas done at his behest!" He pointed to me. "I would never have thought of the manner of it by myself! Praise Master Saul!"

"I shall, I shall!" She swiveled to me, salaaming, and I had to move fast to get my boot out of kissing range. "I cannot thank you enough, nor praise you enough! Oh, how can I ever repay you?"

"By helping other people," I said automatically. "Go through the countryside as long as you can, and look for poor people to help."

"But I have no magic to aid them with! Ah, would that I did!"

"No magic, no," I said, "but you may find that simple labor is enough. Certainly you can listen to people's troubles and try to comfort them. And if you meet any other witches, you might mention how much better you feel for abjuring witchcraft."

The former witch looked up in surprise, then stood slowly, her face firming with resolution. "Even so, then. While life and breath remain, I shall do what little I may. Farewell, physician! Every night and morn, I shall praise you in prayer!"

She turned away, moving off down the road, standing much straighter than she had, and seeming to gain strength with every step.

Friar Ignatius stepped up beside me, watching her go. "That was well done, Master Saul. You have wrought well this day."

I shrugged. "I just don't like seeing somebody in pain, if I can do something about it, Reverend. But you seem to have done pretty well, too."

"Only the duties of my office." Friar Ignatius folded his stole and put it away, shaking his head. "It was the fear of damnation that brought her to me. Like so many, she had never really thought of the tortures of Hell, never let them seem real to her, until she was nigh death."

"Whereupon she came to me to prolong her life, to stave off Hell."

"Aye, but once having thought of Hell as real, she knew the fear would never leave her, for she would come to the flames and demons someday." He shook his head. " 'Tis not the best of reasons for abjuring Satan and witchcraft, but 'twill serve."

"You'd rather she wanted to confess out of sheer remorse, eh?"

"Aye—so I was at pains to remind her that Purgatory is just like Hell. The fire is the same, the agony is the same—but the soul in Purgatory will one day be freed and rise to Heaven, whereas the soul in Hell will never have an end to his tortures. There is no hope in Hell."

That reminded me of Dante's Hellmouth, with the slogan over the door, "Abandon hope, all ye who enter here"—but it also reminded me of Dante's version of Purgatory, which was much less drastic than Friar Ignatius'. Either way, though, was better than torture that never, never ended.

"I could understand why a witch would definitely prefer Purgatory," I said, "no matter how long she had to stay there."

"A witch, or any sinner." Friar Ignatius nodded. "And all those who govern this land, and all those who are their underlings, are either witches or sinners."

I winced at the thought of all the people I would be sending to Hell in the process of trying to stay alive myself. "All of a sudden, I hope you become very busy, Reverend."

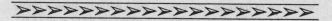

CHAPTER 29

I changed my mind the next day. The bureaucrat witches and warlocks started coming out of the hedgerows, quaking with the terror of Hellfire and calling to Friar Ignatius to shrive them. Most of them were sick, too, so I suggested gently that we handle it methodically—he took them in for confession, then sent them on to me for healing. Frisson quickly built up a catalog of verses; all I had to do was describe the visible symptoms, and the shaken but joyful penitent would describe the invisible ones, and Frisson would flip through his booklet of verses, finding the symptoms and handing me the appropriate poems. Some of them were very odd, but they all worked.

"It's amazing that you can keep coming up with so many verses that exactly fit the situation," I told him during a lull.

He shrugged. "When the inspiration seizes me, Master Saul, I write what it will have me scribble; I do not think of its use. Natheless, I cannot help but think that this must be very poor poetry, if it comes so readily, and is so utilitarian."

"You've been listening to the critics too much," I grumbled. "Take a look at your impact instead."

And we started out on the road again, with me wondering who was the really important person in this party.

They came in groups of four and five, and by the second day, they were showing up every four hours or so. In spite of anything Gilbert or I might say, Friar Ignatius always insisted on stopping to hear confession. "Aught else," he told me, "would be to forswear my vows. I must not turn away a single sinner; 'tis a part of my vocation to reconcile them with God."

"My vocation is staying alive, and it's definitely a part of that to dethrone the queen," I retorted. "In the long run, that will save a great number more souls! The more often you stop, the longer it will take us to get to her capital, and the longer she'll have to gather her forces and fortify her castle—not to mention preparing an ambush with overwhelming power!"

Friar Ignatius shook his head serenely. "You still think in terms of this world, Master Saul, and fail to see that this battle will most truly be won in the domain of the spirit."

"That may be, Reverend, but a hail of spears and arrows in this world can very effectively prevent us from joining battle in the next."

"It shall not," he assured me, with amazing authority, "for the strength that underlies those spears and arrows is the power of evil. If we counter that fell force, the spears will never be thrown."

I would have argued, but the man had so confounded much charisma that for the life of me, I couldn't think of a comeback. I thought one up ten minutes later, of course, but it didn't do much good then. I saved it for our next argument, but he had a comeback for my comeback, and hit me with one more argument that I couldn't think up an answer to just then. That was the way our exchanges went, all the way to the capital—I was always one answer behind him.

And it was driving me crazy, because our progress was slowing to ten miles a day.

"Is it my mistake," I asked Frisson, "or are we running into the whole harvest of the Gremlin's epidemic of witch diseases?"

"It may be," Frisson said slowly, "or it may be simply that those who are ill and in terror of death and Hellfire have begun to hear of you and have come to seek you out. Those who fell ill would never have thought to attempt to survive, if they had not heard of your work; they would have died in despair, forgetting that they could repent."

I stared. "Come on! Word can't have spread that fast!"

"You underestimate the power of rumor," he returned. "Yet there is another explanation."

"Probably much more believable."

Friday shrugged. "The witches were bound to Suettay's service by their demonic master, and I would hazard the guess that some of the power that maintained them came from her. Now, though, the land has begun to rise against her, and she has withdrawn the power that upheld them, gathering all her strength unto herself, for her final battle with you."

"Just what I wanted to hear," I muttered, "that she'll be worse than ever, next time I meet her."

"It is a compliment, in its way," Frisson assured me.

"Then I think I could use a few insults. Well, let's move on."

We did, but they kept coming. I hadn't really registered the fact that the whole bureaucracy here had been corrupted—or recruited from corrupt individuals, all having sold their souls to Satan. And of course, it took a lot of people to run a completely oppressive totalitarian regime. They came in all shapes and sizes, some of them young, some even young and beautiful, but most middle-aged or just plain aged. Frisson explained it to me.

"Most despair late in life," he told me. "Till the middle of their lives, they cling to the notion that God will give them worldly success of one sort or another—whether they deserve it or not—even if it be nothing more than the kind regard of other folk. But when they do look back on their lives and realize that nothing has come of their attempts to live virtuously, that they have not gained fame or love, many then do turn 'gainst God in bitterness and swear themselves to the Devil's service, if he will give them some advantage over their fellows while they live."

"And they stop aging?"

"Their bodies, aye. Few think to have their lost youth back, and Satan will not give it to most who ask, for he has their souls already; they yearn so strongly for power or wealth that they will sell themselves to him even without the inducement of youth or beauty. But some are tempted by no other lure than that—though once corrupted, they turn to greed for power and wealth quite easily, even to the illusion of strength that comes from deliberate cruelty."

To me, of course, all this was just part of the massive hallucination in which I found myself. But even in my terms, I was beginning to understand that "selling your soul" could be more than a metaphor, or even a literary image; it represented dedicating yourself totally to yourself, to the gratification of your own drives and urges, to getting what you wanted no matter what it took, no matter who you had to hurt or betray or grind down—and no matter who you had to flatter, or whose boots you had to lick. No matter, indeed—you planned on getting back at them when you'd climbed over their dead bodies to get their power. It made me shudder: I knew too many people like that, even in my own world.

Not that any of our successful treatment cases were any great argument for youth culture. There were a few women who must have looked really beautiful before they were hit by the smallpox that brought them to us—or the cancer, or the mild stroke—and there were a few men, too, who still looked so good, even in the grip of tuberculosis or syphilis, that they made me think of Dorian Gray. But after they repented and recanted, they looked more like his picture—for a few minutes. Then they aged rapidly, very rapidly. Fortunately, the pretty ones usually made it out of sight before they collapsed. The others just turned to dust right before our eyes. It made me shaky, I can tell you.

Most of them, though, just confessed and came over for healing, which we usually managed before they'd aged too badly. Then they went their way, jubilant if old and ugly. Beauty didn't matter to them much by then—they knew they didn't have long to live and were only interested in making amends.

Gilbert and I started getting very tired of fighting crabs, though fortunately the giant crustaceans didn't get any smarter. Gruesome didn't, either, but he developed quite a taste for crunching shells. He almost developed a taste for shellfish, period, but I managed to stop him in time and get him to realize that whatever the crabs had been doing inside the sick people, they were apt to do inside Gruesome. He started getting really angry at them then, with very salutary results.

Actually, I had to admire the repentant witches for their courage. To haul themselves for a week's stumbling journey, or more, took a lot of determination in itself, even if most of them did use the tatters of their authority to press peasants into giving them rides; some even managed to intimidate the gentry into express trips with horse-drawn vehicles. Some had to come on foot, though, and they did—but no matter how they traveled, they made the journey with their private demons hounding them every inch of the way. It must have taken enormous grit—though the fear of Hellfire may have helped there.

The devils never showed themselves to anybody but the remorseful witches, though, after those first few encounters with my guardian angel. They knew that, as soon as one of the Heavenly Host stepped into the picture, they were bound to lose.

So the devils' only real chance of keeping the frightened witches to their contract was to intimidate them into staying away from priests and healers—or to hit them with so much despair that they would figure they couldn't possibly be forgiven, or had no way out of the contract, that they were going to Hell and there was nothing, but nothing, they could do about it. I suppose that worked on quite a few of them, but of course we never saw any. We heard about it, though, from the ones who lasted.

The witches weren't the only ones who showed up. The first nonoutlaw volunteer showed up our second morning. All he carried was a flail and a pack of journey rations, but he looked grim and told us he had come to fight the queen. Turned out the local warlock had ruined his family with taxes, debauched his sisters, and driven himself and his parents into living in a shelter that was basically a large basket, working from sunup to sundown to pay the taxes he claimed they still owed—and they didn't dare fight back.

"With you, however, I dare," he told me. "I may die, but I will at least bring down a soldier of evil before I do."

" 'Twas not the fear of death that held your arm, then?" Gilbert demanded.

"Nay, but the thought that my death would accomplish nothing. What have I to live for? But I would die for a purpose!"

"Come with us," Gilbert said.

There were three more waiting at the outskirts of the next village. By evening, two more groups had joined us.

After that, they came in constantly. At every traffic circle, every milestone, there was another group of three or four, waiting to join us with scythes, flails, and stony expressions. Gilbert cross-examined them while Frisson muttered spells that tested them for truth. We found a few ringers, sent in by Suettay's ministers to infiltrate us, of course. They didn't last long.

"Don't kill him!" I shouted as a dozen peasants fell on the spy. "You can't fight evil with evil—you'll just be selling out to it!"

But the spy pulled out a knife as long as your arm and lunged at the nearest peasant, shouting a spell. The knife took the peasant in the chest, and the spell sent the rest of them writhing on the ground in agony.

Gilbert stepped in and chopped the man's head off.

After that, I didn't argue.

The next day, a peasant came in, doffed his cap, and showed us his tonsure. This time it was Friar Ignatius who did the cross-examination, including handing the man a crucifix and listening to him say the Apostles' Creed. He passed the test, then helped hear confessions. The next day, another showed up, and by the end of the week, we had six monks. They saw the chance to unseat Suettay and came to add the strength of their prayers to our magic and Gilbert's army. Friar Ignatius assured me that they would multiply our effects tenfold. Given the crazy set of natural laws at work—or should I say, supernatural—I didn't doubt him.

Then a peasant showed up, wild-eyed and white-lipped. "They come, my masters, they come!"

"What do you speak of, man?" Gilbert grasped the man by both shoulders, holding him still. "Who comes?"

"The Army of Evil!" he cried. "Footmen and knights! There are too many to count, and they have two sorcerers to strengthen them!"

My ragtag army broke into a hullabaloo—but I didn't see anybody who looked like running. They were all grim, most eager—even a few who were trembling with fear but determined.

There were only a few hundred of them, though.

"How many is 'too many to count'?" I asked Gilbert.

"For a peasant?" He shrugged. "It could be a few hundred, or many thousand." He turned back to the man. "Were they on the road?"

"Aye! I heard them coming afar off and hid in the bracken to watch! They came on and on and on, four abreast! I waited till they passed, counted as high as I could, yet still they came on!"

Gilbert nodded. "How long was it till they passed?"

"How long?" The peasant looked startled; he hadn't really thought about it.

"As long as it takes you to go from your hovel to your field? Or as long as a Mass?"

"Between." The peasant's brow furrowed. "Not so long as the Mass, but longer than the journey to my field."

"A thousand at least." Gilbert released him. "You have done well. How have you managed to come to us before them?"

"They go by the road. I know the land and have come across the fields. They march; I ran."

Gilbert nodded. "They will be here within the hour, surely—probably far sooner. You have done well, fellow. Go whet your scythe among the others; we will need it to be sharp ere long."

"I will!" Battle lust gleamed in the youth's eye—enough to make me shudder. He hurried away to join the others.

I stepped into a quick huddle with Frisson, Gilbert, and Friar Ignatius. "We knew this was coming, I suppose."

"Aye," Frisson said, looking as scared as a cat who has used up eight lives. "We set out to march 'gainst the queen, did we not?"

"And we knew we would face her army, soon or late," Gilbert said. "In truth, 'tis amazing they have not come upon us before; I have expected them with each nightfall."

"Nightfall?" I looked around. "Yeah, it's almost sunset, isn't it?"

"Assuredly," Friar Ignatius said. "The Army of Evil is at its strongest in the hours of darkness."

"So we have to hit them hard and fast and roll them up before night." I looked around at our peasant encampment, frowning.

"You have an idea," Frisson stated.

"Well," I said, "if they're being so polite as to come straight down the road, they must be expecting an ambush, mustn't they?"

"They would not fear it," Gilbert said grimly, "not with their numbers."

I nodded. "All the more reason to give them what they're expecting. What's the best kind of ambush you could prepare under the circumstances, Gilbert?"

The squire frowned, thinking for a few minutes, then turned away to the peasants. "Ho! How many among you can strike a bird on the wing with a sling?"

"I," a dozen men said at once, and fifty more were only half a beat behind them. By that time, all the rest caught up, and the word "I" rolled through the whole camp.

Gilbert nodded, satisfied. "So I had thought; small birds are the only game that is not forbidden to a peasant." He raised his voice. "Seek out sling-stones, and be sure your pouches are full! Then get you up into the trees on either side of the road, and hide you well!"

The excited murmur rose to a surf roar as the peasants got busy hunting up pebbles.

"Good idea." I nodded. "Put them where the troopers can't come to grips with them."

"Aye," Gilbert said darkly, "but they are sure to have archers. It would take but a volley or two to fell all my men."

"Oh, I think we can provide them some measure of protection. Just have a squad ready to block the road in front of them. That's where it's apt to get messy."

Frisson stared. "What manner of protection can you craft thus?"

"An invisible shield," I said. "Let them batter themselves against it and wear themselves out."

"A good thought!" Gilbert looked surprised. "Whence came that notion, Master Saul?"

"Oh, just a kind of fable I heard once." I didn't think I should try explaining about television and toothpaste commercials.

"But not for long." Frisson looked disappointed. "Surely their sorcerer will dissolve it."

"Yes," I said, "but we could build a wall within a wall within a wall."

Now Frisson looked startled. "That could hold—yet not long enough for the whole of the battle."

"Yes, but I think it'll keep their sorcerer busy long enough for us to get the drop on them."

Frisson frowned. " 'Get the drop'?"

"Take them by surprise," I said. "Sneak in an extra punch. Gain an advantage."

"Ah!" Frisson nodded. "And how shall you do that?"

"Too complicated to explain. I'll have to show you—after we've finished making the shield." I turned away. "So let's get busy—we need to stake out a very long perimeter."

It turned out we had just the boys for the job; somebody ran and borrowed a plow, and Gruesome pulled it while another fellow guided, following Gilbert. He paced off a line five hundred feet long, which didn't seem like enough for an army that took fifteen minutes to walk past, but he assured me they'd all come cramming in at the first sign of action. When they had plowed up one side of the road and down the other, then across to make an H, I took a verse Frisson had started some time before, but that had stayed in my mind rather oddly—probably because the rhythm of its meter was the kind of thing you can't get out of your mind for an hour, and when you do, it keeps coming back. I had scrounged up six feet of string while they'd been plowing, and now I sat down by the campfire and wove a cat's cradle while I chanted:

> "From this furrow, let there rise
> A wall unseen, invisible
> But proof against the foeman's cries
> And weapons, but divisible
>
> By all my allies, who may pass
> When outward bound. Be as mica,
> Or a sheet of one-way glass,
> Hard but clear to light, or like a
>
> Membrane semipermeable,
> Warding stench and halitosis,
> Admitting none, though unseeable.
> Let objects out, though, like osmosis!"

I didn't like working magic myself, mind you, hallucination or not—but these were concepts Frisson just didn't have. He was helping with the weaving, though, so I didn't have to admit it was all my doing.

"I see naught." Gilbert was peering anxiously into the darkness.

"Of a certainty," Frisson said, grinning. "He said it would be invisible, did he not? But look yonder!" He pointed up at the stars. "See you not how they twinkle?"

"Stars do ever twinkle! They forever have!"

"Aye, but growing larger and smaller? Surely there is something between them, like to the haze that rises from a hot rock in midsummer!"

Well, he had the concept, anyway. Call it what you will, a force field is a force field.

"Now comes the tricky part." I put my hands together and dropped the cat's cradle. "Gilbert, send men out to charge the wall and see if it's still there."

Suddenly, the squire looked scared. He turned to the peasants. "Ho, Willem! Kurt! Baden! Take you each a band of men, and set out for the furrow!"

They did, not asking.

I turned to Frisson. "When did he learn their names?"

"As soon as they came in," Frisson answered. "I do not think he knows them *all* by name, but he has picked out the leaders, and certainly knows each of them."

I decided the Father-General had sent me a live one. Not bad, for an eighteen-year-old kid.

The peasants went out—and came back real fast, looking spooked. They conferred with Gilbert in low voices. He nodded, satisfied, and came back to me. "The wall holds. Kurt was able to leave it, but not to come back."

"Good," I said. "Send him a hundred men and tell him to send them up into the trees to either side of the road. They'll have to go around behind, of course—the invisible wall is rooted all along the furrow, and if they try to climb in from the road, they'll just bounce back. Get another fifty men in the trees on this side of the crossbar, ready to pick off anybody who gets through. Not that I think anybody will, you understand—but just in case. Keep another fifty ready to charge out between us and them, and the rest hidden in the forest ready to pounce."

"And what of the sorcerer, Master Saul?" Frisson asked.

"You saw that sculpture I was just making with the string?"

"Aye, though I would not term it art." Frisson frowned.

"Make up your mind whether you're an artist or a critic, will you? Okay, we'll call it a model. Have you ever played the two-person version?"

"Aye, when I was a child."

"Well then, let's get childish." I picked up the string and started weaving. "Here's how it goes . . ."

The army came marching down the road, singing a deep baritone chant that somehow reeked of menace. We sat in the road ahead of them, our hearts in our mouths, Frisson taking the cat's cradle from me with trembling fingers. Gilbert stood behind us, ostensibly watching the road, actually ready to signal his slingers. He was nervous, too, but he had said he was more worried about some hothead striking too early than about his own safety.

The vanguard saw us, raised a shout, and came running.

Gilbert waited until they were only fifty feet away from the furrow plowed across the road, the pounding of their boots filling the night, before he signaled.

A hail of stones shot out of the trees to each side of the road. Then fifty peasants pounded out into the road between us and the oncoming soldiers, and started slinging.

Howls of anger and pain erupted from the army, but the soldiers in front bellowed in rage and charged down on our bodyguard. Their halberds swung down . . .

. . . and bounced off a surface they couldn't see.

They bounced hard; most of the weapons struck their owners, or the men behind. They bellowed again, but this time, there was as much fear as anger in the sound.

Their mates, back along the road, loosed a volley of arrows at the trees along each shoulder. The arrows darted up . . .

. . . and bounced.

They fell back, but they fell hard, with almost as much velocity as they'd had when they hit; it was a resilient invisible wall. So the points scratched and pierced soldiers, not peasants. The soldiers howled in surprise and alarm—and another hail of sling-stones fell on them, striking on foreheads and temples, denting helmets and breaking collarbones. Soldiers fell with shouts of pain. More of them fell in total silence, out cold.

The sorcerer reared up in their middle, shouting a chant and making passes.

I took the cat's cradle from Frisson. He stuck his thumb up in the middle, and I chanted,

> "Blest be the tie that binds
> That man who'd work us ill,
> By sorc'rous spells unkind.
> Now, let his tongue be still!"

As I finished the last line, I pulled the strings tight, imprisoning Frisson's thumb.

The sorcerer's chant ended in a frantic yell, as something invisible pinned his arms to his sides. He struggled to free himself, tripped over a fallen soldier, and rolled on the ground, squalling and bellowing, inarticulate.

"Why can he not chant?" Frisson asked, huge-eyed.

"Because I paralyzed his tongue," I answered. "Hear how his yelling keeps making vowels sounds? He's trying to chant a spell, but he just can't form the consonants."

I kept the pressure on Frisson's thumb, only letting up a little when it started turning blue. I waited, grinding my teeth, till the yelling and rattle and clatter had diminished and turned into groaning.

"They are all down," Gilbert told me. "Shall I send men among them to kill those who still live?"

Still live! I hadn't stopped to think that those sling-stones had probably killed a fair number, not just knocked them out. "No," I said, then cleared my throat to stop my voice shaking. "No, it's more important that we get to the capital. Besides, most of them are just peasant boys who were pressed into the army against their wills. They will probably be more than glad to run on home if they have the chance."

"Like enough," Gilbert agreed, "but to have that chance, the sorcerer must die."

The words hit my stomach hard enough to make it sink to my boots, but I knew he was right. Leave the man alive, and he'd just rally the remains of his army to strike at our backs. "Couldn't we give him a chance to repent?"

"Aye, but even so, we must kill him then. If we do not, he will likely renew his bargain with Satan as soon as we are out of sight."

I knew he was right, but I still hated to give the go-ahead. "If we kill in cold blood, we've started selling our own souls to Satan."

"That is true of slaying the peasant soldiers," Gilbert said inexorably, "but it is not true of their master. The knight and the sorcerer must die, or they may find a way to murder us all."

"Yeah, I know you're right." I sighed. "Take Friar Ignatius and a dozen men to guard him. And pass the word when you've got the sorcerer hog-tied, so I can let up on Frisson's thumb."

Gilbert stared at the imprisoned digit, then said, "You are truly amazing, Master Saul, and Master Frisson, too."

"Only because we don't do things the way we're supposed to," I told him. "It throws everybody off stride—and makes 'em madder 'n Hell when it works. Go send somebody to Purgatory, Gilbert."

He did.

That wasn't the last army we faced, of course, but it was the easiest. The next army got crafty and surrounded us on all four sides before it marched in chopping. But we had the best intelligence in the country—a couple of dozen local peasants, who knew the terrain as well as they knew their dinner bowls. They came in unbidden, with exact details of troop placement and strength—so when the army swooped in on our camp, all they hit were a couple of hundred simulacra that turned back into sticks of wood at the first sword-stroke. Then our treetop peasants cut loose with their slings, and the archers barely got off one volley before they were all felled by flying pebbles. Of course, their sorcerers had dispelled my invisible shield before they even charged, so we did lose a dozen men—but they lost two thousand.

The third army tried to draw us into a trap by having a dozen pretty maidens doing a fertility dance involving taking off their clothes in the moonlight, but Friar Ignatius and his fellow monks went through the camp quickly, telling the peasants in no uncertain terms that in this case, at least, feminine pulchritude really was a wile of the Devil. Our men kept ranks and marched on by, to the great indignation of the young ladies, who yelled catcalls and insults after them—until Frisson and I finally managed a spell that showed them as they really were, without the demonic cosmetic spells. When our peasant boys got a sight of the naked, withered old hags and young but very ugly girls they really were, they all shuddered, looked away, and praised Friar Ignatius at the tops of their voices.

The army charged out in pursuit, of course, but they weren't really trying—they knew they didn't have a chance. They were right, too—Frisson and I changed the ground in front of them to bog, and they all floundered down in the mire. Their sorcerers firmed the ground up fast, of course, but they forgot to pull their men out first, and most of them were trapped hip-deep in hardpan. A few unlucky ones were completely underground, but I think their mates dug them out. They didn't have anything better to do, after all—our army was long gone.

Besides, we were two thousand strong by that time, with more coming in every night—and older peasants constantly bringing in baskets of provisions. I was having nightmares, remembering the peasants of the First Crusade and all the burglaries they had committed on the way to Constantinople, trying to keep themselves fed. I talked to Gilbert about it, and he understood immediately. He set up a system of command ranks, making each officer or NCO responsible for the conduct of his men. Then he appointed a few MPs, to patrol the perimeter of the vast mob and check to see if anyone was getting out of line. A few did; he expelled them from the troop and left them to the tender mercies of the peasants they'd robbed.

Because a mob it was, even with Gilbert's impromptu chain of command. There wasn't time to drill them, but he did manage to get across the idea of marching in order, teaching his officers a few marching songs to help. Frisson grew very thoughtful, was seized with inspiration, and dashed off a few poems that he then proceeded to sing to Gilbert. Gilbert loved them, gave them to the officers, and we marched along singing. They could hear us a mile away, but we weren't exactly any big secret, anyway.

After the second day of orderly marching, Gilbert was beginning to look worried. I took him aside and asked why.

"They have not attacked again," he told me. "Surely the Army of Evil does not intend to let us pass unchallenged!"

"Haven't you heard what your men are singing?" I asked.

He frowned. "Aye, but what has that . . ." There he broke off, turning to stare out at his army as they marched past, singing:

> "Sons of Might and Magic,
> Will you let this tragic
>   Moment pass from history?
> Hearts that know uniqueness,
> Will you let this weakness
>   Daunt you with its mystery?
>
> Onward, onward! Never shall the foe
> Dare come near, as in serried ranks we go!
>
> All step as one, unbending!
> Strength wells up, unending!
>   Enemies shall distant be!
> Never shall we tire
> Until this sovereign dire
>   Shall be hanging from a tree!"

"Why, they dispel attack!" Gilbert cried.

I nodded. "It would take an awful lot of black magic to squelch that much enthusiastic spell casting. On top of which, they're giving themselves constant energy input, and keeping themselves in order."

"Amazing, Wizard!"

"Yes, isn't he?" I nodded at Frisson. "But don't try to convince him of it; he thinks he's just writing what comes to him."

Still, I worried. Two thousand enthusiastic peasants were good protection on the march and could be very useful for general brawling—but they weren't going to stand a chance against disciplined, professional troops.

Which was exactly what we saw, when we came up to the top of the ridge that overlooked the capital. There it lay, a half-mile-wide town with a river flowing through it and a huge castle on the hill in its center. It had a high, thick wall all around it, and between the wall and us, a solid band of troops a hundred yards thick.

We stared, appalled, and I whispered, "How are we going to get through this?"

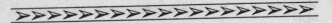

CHAPTER 30

"Surely we have strong enough numbers to force a passage." But Frisson didn't sound too sure.

"We have not," Gilbert assured him. "They outnumber us by five soldiers of theirs for every one of ours, at the least—and theirs are trained and seasoned veterans, whiles ours are boys who have come straight from the plow."

"But our men believe in our cause!"

"And these soldiers believe in the profit they shall gain by victory," Gilbert returned.

"Surely the love of money is not so strong as the will to be free!"

"Perhaps not—but when 'tis coupled with skill and strength, it will suffice." Gilbert turned a grim face to me. " 'Tis for you to say, Master Saul. What may we do?"

"Why," I said slowly, "we'll just have to find some soldiers who are even better than they are."

Gilbert smiled bleakly. "Well thought, if we could find such so quickly. Yet even if we could, we would need very many, for greater skill and strength mean little, in the end, 'gainst such numbers."

"Not entirely true." I was thinking of Crécy and Agincourt. "Besides, we don't have to wipe out the whole army—just force our way through to the gates and knock them open."

"And how shall we do that?"

"It was one of the first verses Frisson wrote, and I've been saving it for just such an occasion."

The poet looked up, startled. "Which . . . Oh! My angry verse 'gainst the walls built by wealth and might, to pen the poor!"

"Yes, and the refrain about tearing down the walls—I think you even made some references to Joshua and Jericho."

"I can only trust in you for such," Gilbert said slowly, "but if you say it, Master Saul, I am sure it shall be done."

My heart sank. I hated the idea of having people depend on me—it resulted in responsibility, and responsibility involved commitment. But there wasn't much choice, now.

A shout went up from my "army." Looking up, I saw a double file of soldiers coming over the ridge a quarter of the way around the valley, at least a mile distant, with knights at their head and rear. Their armor and weapons clashed and clattered, and their chanting came to us faintly over the distance, too faintly to make out the words, but I went cold at the sight of them. "Just what we need—enemy reinforcements!"

"And more coming in all the time, I doubt not," Frisson said, very nervously. "Whate'er we are to do, Master Saul, 'twere best if 'twere done quickly."

"Yet where are we to find these skilled soldiers you spoke of?" Gilbert asked—and, with a sardonic smile, "Have you a receipt for such an one?"

" 'Receipt'?" I frowned—then I remembered that it was an old word for "recipe." I could feel inspiration strike—or in this case, memory, of an evening watching Gilbert and Sullivan's *Patience*. My grin grew. "Yes, now that you mention it, I do." And I began to pantomime taking ingredients off shelves and mixing them in a bowl, as I recited:

"If you want a receipt for that popular mystery
  Known to the world as a Heavy Dragoon,
  Take all the remarkable people in history,
  Rattle them off to a popular tune."

I proceeded to do so, running quickly through the first verse, and putting in a quick chorus:

"Take of these elements all that is fusible,
  Melt them all down in a pipkin or crucible,
  Set them to simmer and drain off the scum,
  And a heavy dragoon is the residuum!"

"Aye, guv'nor!" a beery voice said two feet above my head. My buddies drew back with a moan, looking up. Even Gruesome muttered with nervousness.

There he was, chestnut stallion and all—six feet plus of re-
splendent dress uniform and ferocious mustache.

"Just in time!" I grinned. "Assault the enemy—they're
down below you! Cut me a way through to the gates of the
city!"

"As you sye, Capting!" the dragoon bellowed, wheeling his
horse toward the nearest footman. "God save the Queen!"

And he rode full-tilt down the slope and into Suettay's infantry, laying about him with his saber. Gilbert shouted and
galloped to back him up.

I would have, too, but I knew the enemy was too many for
only three men and a troll, even if one of those men was a dragoon. I signaled Gruesome to wait, and before Gilbert even hit
the first rank, I chanted:

> "Let us have a thousand like him!
> Appear here now, his taste to cater!
> Multiply him; thousandfold,
> By ditto, Spirit Duplicator!"

They appeared with a huge shout, charging after their proto-
type with flourishing sabers, and slammed into the enemy with
a crash like the meeting of two tidal waves. Gilbert churned
back out of the press, looking dazed. Somewhere at the front,
a joyous Cockney voice bellowed, "Just like Waterloo!"

Gilbert came panting up along their back trail. "They have
no need of me. A most amazing company, Master Saul!"

"Sure are." I grinned. "Forward the heavy brigade!"

The enemy soldiers were trying to rally their men, but the
explosions of the dragoons' muskets had them spooked. They
drove into the press, clearing the way in front with musket
blasts, then widening the path with their sabers. Pole arms
reached for them, pikes stabbing and halberds slashing, but the
dragoons mowed through the shafts as if they'd been butter,
and their horses struck out with steel-shod hooves. A few arrows found their marks, and a few dragoons fell, but not many.

Then, suddenly, they were almost to the gate. The press of
dragoons began to part, leaving a clear path paved with fallen
pikes.

"Time to move," I pointed out, and Gruesome bellowed and
waddled forward. I turned to Gilbert. "Let's go!" He bawled to
our peasants.

The dragoons cleared before us to my shouted commands,

and Gruesome plowed through to take the point with Gilbert just behind and to his right, a dragoon just behind and to Gruesome's left. They bored into the enemy army like a diamond bit, fire and armor, and the dragoons carried away the military detritus they churned up. It was a mad quarter hour, with the enemy pulling back from Gruesome's roars and teeth and trying to cut in from the sides, only to meet Gilbert's and the dragoons' blades, before the dragoons pulled in to chew them up. My head filled with shouting and the clash of steel . . .

Then, suddenly, we were through, with the city gates in front of us.

I pulled out Frisson's poem and chanted,

"Really break, locks! And really break, bolts!
And really break, gate that we come nigh!
And as we come to this double door,
'Twill break itself quite handi-ligh!"

The wood began to crumble even before I'd finished. Splinters shredded loose, then kindling-sized chunks, as gravel began to fall from the great stone blocks to either side.

The Army of Evil let out a huge roar and crowded in behind us and on all sides.

The peasants were in the center, shielded by eight hundred surviving dragoons, and the medieval footmen weren't making much progress against the case-hardened steel and flashing hooves of the Victorian heavy cavalry—but for every one my horsemen killed, three more popped up in his place. Dragoons went down—slowly, but steadily. They chopped and stabbed frantically, desperately outnumbered. The stones of the walls were flaking, but slowly; glancing back, I was seized with the sudden overwhelming fear that the soldiers of corruption would wipe us out before the wall crumbled. I turned, pulling out my clasp knife for whatever it was worth, and readied myself for a last-ditch fight.

Then, suddenly, a howl of fear and disgust erupted in the distance.

"What comes?" Frisson gasped.

"If it can affront such soldiers of sin," Gilbert said, blanching, "how can we stand against it?"

But Gruesome, looking out over the field from several more feet of height, rumbled, "Old ones come."

"Old ones?" I frowned; it didn't make sense.

Then I began to hear the wailing that overrode the cries of disgust, a wailing that came closer and closer as the wall above turned into a trickle of sand—closer and closer, until I could make out words.

"The Witch Doctor! Where is the Witch Doctor? Bring us to the Witch Doctor."

"Witch Doctor?" I turned to Frisson, staring.

The poet shook his head. "I know naught, Master Saul. I have never heard of such a thing."

"Well, I've heard of it," I allowed. "A witch doctor is a pejorative term for an African shaman, a sort of combination priest and physician . . ."

My peasant army parted with cries of fear, pressing back against the dragoons and their horses, who were chopping gleefully at an enemy who was shrinking away. A channel opened through my plowboys, and down that corridor stumbled a pack of people horribly disfigured by disease, some doubled over with pain, some limping on crutches, but led by a dozen or more people with missing fingers, missing hands, missing forearms, hobbling because of missing toes or feet.

"Lepers!" Gilbert gasped.

And they cried, "Bring us to the Witch Doctor! We repent, we abjure our witchcraft! We will no longer serve Satan! But bring us to the priest who will shrive us, and the Witch Doctor who will heal us!"

"We don't have a witch doctor!" I bleated. "No Africans at all! Maybe there's one in the city—I wouldn't know."

"But the priest, we have." Friar Ignatius stepped forward, and his monks came up behind him with very purposeful strides.

"Friar!" I yelped. "We're in the middle of a battle!"

"Then we shall help you win it!" a tall, decaying man cried. "We have magical powers no longer, but only shrive us, and we shall throw our bodies against their swords!"

"I don't think they'll let you get close enough to stab." I eyed them askance, then turned to Friar Ignatius. "But they might die laughing. Brother, can you spare some time? Some way to keep it down to a minute or two?"

"Certes." Friar Ignatius stepped in front of me, calling out, "Kneel, those of you who can!"

Gruesome pointed over the ex-witches' heads, rumbling, "Sojers come!"

"Of course! The contagious cases opened a clear path for them!" I groaned. "The wicked warriors are filling it in!"

"Do you all repent your evil works?" Friar Ignatius cried. The answer rolled forth from a hundred throats: "Aye!"

"Not queen's sojers," Gruesome insisted. "Them fight queen's sojers."

"Huh?" I looked up, thunderstruck. "Reinforcements for our side? But how . . ."

"Never ask." Frisson's fingers bit into my arm. "The Spider King said he would summon aid."

"Ego te absolvo!" Friar Ignatius cried. "I absolve you of your sins!"

The ex-witches cheered with joy . . .

. . . and with a roar, the gates collapsed.

Gruesome loosed one last blast and charged into the city, with Gilbert hard on his claws.

"After him!" I cried. "Nobody will want to get close to you! If you really want to help, here's your chance!"

The ex-witches cheered again and charged through the gates. It wasn't a very fast charge, but it was good enough. I wiped a sodden brow and breathed thanks that I'd managed to shake them.

My peasants shouted triumph and boiled through after the witches, sweeping Frisson and me along in their wake.

The citizens got out of the way fast, and our bloodthirsty boys were too bent on revenge to think about looting yet. They ran through the streets bellowing, Gilbert leading them on toward the huge turrets that rose ahead. Soldiers appeared in the streets, but they couldn't muster more than a few dozen, and our plowboys just rolled over them. I was in the middle of the mob, so I saw the results as I strode on by—dead peasants, and dead soldiers, some of them trampled. I ignored them and put them out of my mind. Time enough for remorse later. There was no way to win a battle without killing men.

But did the battle have to be won?

I remembered how Suettay had tortured Angelique; I remembered the squad of bullyboys that had tried to beat me up. I remembered the peasants ground down by the vindictive warlock-bailiff, and I knew, *Yes.* Suettay had to go.

Which meant this battle had to be fought.

And I could see, from the hard faces all around me, that all my peasant men had just such memories to spur them on—many, I suspected, worse than mine.

Then, suddenly, the walls of the castle were before us, and the drawbridge was rising. The walls above bristled with the home guard's pikes, and I knew crossbows were being leveled at us. Worse, I knew that the army we'd broken through was on its way to take us in the rear. We had to get into that castle, and get in fast. I had to kill Suettay before her army caught us.

"Gremlin!" I shouted.

He was there suddenly, obscene and chuckling. "Fear not, Master Saul. I have rusted the locks of the crossbows; I have blunted the heads of the arrows. The mortar that holds that wall together is parched and crumbling, and the great windlass that hauls the drawbridge chain is crumbling, even as we speak, of dry rot."

Then he was gone, and my peasants started recovering their nerve. I locked my knees to keep them from collapsing and reflected that, occasionally, it's nice to have the Spirit of Snafu around—if he's on your side.

I heard a distant crack. The drawbridge halted its upward rise, poised, then came thundering back down.

My army cheered and charged into the gatehouse tunnel. The first dozen rammed scythe blades into the arrow slits. Screams echoed in the tunnel behind, and we streamed through into the courtyard with only a few arrows striking my men.

There, we met Suettay's army, drawn up and waiting.

My men bellowed with joy—at last, a chance to strike out at their oppressors. They plowed into the army, and in seconds it had turned into a melee of individual combat. Military discipline didn't amount to much in that churning mob—and the plowboys turned out to be just as expert with their scythes as any soldier with a halberd.

Frisson's hand bit into my shoulder. "We dare not tarry, Master Saul! Valiant though they are, these peasants will be torn to bits—especially when the outer army finds them!"

"Right! We've got to hit their central power source!"

Frisson frowned. "You speak of Suettay?"

"Yeah! She's in there somewhere! But how do we get to her?"

Air shimmered, and the Rat Raiser appeared before us. He became solid and stumbled, reaching out to catch my arm, steadied himself, and looked up, a bit wild-eyed. "The king has sent me to take you to the witch!"

"Good idea!" I turned back to Frisson. "Change us all to rats!"

"But . . . but how are we to—"
"Never mind; let me try!

"Wee, sleekit, slinking, skulking beasties
We shall become, long-tailed and feisty!
Large rats, who scurry off so hasty, In hurrying hassle!
To run and chase through byways nasty, Within this castle!"

Sudden pains wracked me—Burns' revenge, no doubt. My vision blurred, and I had a dim sight of things growing larger and larger about me. Then, suddenly, the world stabilized, and there were huge feet thundering toward me. I shouted with alarm, and raced for the wall . . . only it came out as a squeak, and I was running on all fours. Running pretty well, too—but I wasn't thinking very clearly. I was only aware of my frantic fear.

Then I was up against the wall, and I turned at bay, terror churning into savagery—but none of the huge feet were anywhere near. Instead, I saw a bunch of giants duking it out, cutting each other up with huge knives. It didn't make much sense to me, so I put it out of my mind; all that mattered was getting to the evil queen, who had sicced all those cats on us.

Cats?

I looked around, fear of felines stabbing through my entrails. I relaxed with relief—there were no cats in sight, nor even their terrible reek.

Reek?

Now that I had a few seconds' respite, I realized that I was wrapped in a world of aromas. For a minute, I was rapt indeed, spellbound at the richness and variety of the environment: horse's sweat, men's sweat, fear scent and battle scent—and under them all, the huge catalog of ordinary, everyday aromas: this morning's breakfast, porridge and sausage and river fish; last night's dinner, roast mutton and black bread; dung and lilacs and birds and more, more and more. I was dazzled, frozen, entranced . . .

. . . until I recognized the scent of dogs.

Dogs! Dogs chased rats! I was tense with fright in an instant. I looked around me frantically—but I didn't see any dogs, and I realized the smell was coming from far away, so I started to relax.

Until I noticed the two huge rats a few feet away.

I whipped about, turning to run—and saw something long

and hairless. I froze, realizing that it was part of me. I had a tail!

Then I remembered: I was a rat. Why, I wasn't sure, but that made it okay to be with other rats. I turned back, and saw one of the other rats just doing the same thing, only he was quivering. His coat was dark brown, and he was smaller than the other one, who was huge, as rats go—I guess. He was also mangy and moth-eaten and scarred, with patches of fur missing. He was looking at the two of us with definite contempt.

Suddenly, there was a huge din at the gate. I whirled, heart beating a mile a minute—and there, high as a mountain, came riding a knight in black armor, and beside him, a knight who had a sword in one hand and a stick in the other, mounted on a dragon, an authentic, actual, fire-breathing dragon! I squealed in terror and huddled back against the wall.

Then, behind the two knights, came a knight with long golden hair and a golden circlet around her helmet. Behind her, soldiers and knights boiled through the gate.

The dragon roared, bellowing a thirty-foot tongue of flame. Enemy soldiers howled with pain and turned to run. The knights rode after them, chopping wherever a soldier or enemy knight turned to fight, and the footmen pounded after them, spreading out and rolling up Suettay's soldiers.

None of it made sense to me, though—I just cowered, looking frantically for a hole to hide in. After all, I had no more brain than a rat.

A stinging blow jolted me out of it, and I turned, instantly angry—to see the big, mangy rat slapping the smaller brown rat. Then he whirled back to me, baring his teeth. I hesitated and, when the big rat saw he had our attention, he squeaked, "Follow!" and turned to scamper away down the nearest drain.

I followed, numb with the realization that I had understood his word; he was still speaking human language—and I could still comprehend it.

The drain led into a sewer. We scampered through increasing darkness, lit occasionally by another drain. Then it grew almost pitch-black, but I was surprised to see that I could dimly make out the form in front of me. I remembered there was supposed to be another one, and glanced back. Sure enough, the brown rat was still following.

Then the tunnel opened out, and we were in a sort of round chamber with other tunnels opening off it. The big rat in front of me was squeaking up a storm. I edged to the side, so I

could see around him, and realized that he was facing three
other rats, almost as mangy and unkempt as he was—and
smelling to high heaven! They regarded us with eyes that were
definitely unfriendly, but that turned almost worshipful as they
turned back to the big rat in front of us. They squeaked something that must have been assent, because they took off and led
the way into one of the tunnels, single file, and the large rat
followed them.

We followed him. After all, there wasn't much choice.

I found out later that, while we were creeping through the
sewers, the good guys were conquering the capital. Behind
them, the citizenry broke loose in celebration—turns out there
weren't very many of them who'd been happy with the sorceress' rule. In fact, most of them had lived in fear and trembling,
and there were very few who hadn't suffered from her depre-
dations in one way or another.

The good guys charged into the keep, their resident wizard
fending off Suettay's spells with his own.

Of course, Suettay wasn't really concentrating—by that
time, she had other worries: me, and Frisson.

It took us a while to qualify as major headaches, though.
First we had to get done playing catch-the-tail with our leader,
that being the only way we could keep track of him in the total
dark, as we ran along through drainpipe, crack, and cranny. It
was tough going, but our rat bodies seemed built for it.

Finally, we came out into dim light. Looking up, I saw
rough rocks projecting above us in a sort of ladder. I realized
later that it was a tunnel made by a series of cracks inside
those walls, and the "rungs" were the back ends of the stone
blocks that made up those walls. At the moment, I didn't have
enough brain power for that, of course—I just accepted it.

Our guides started hopping nimbly from one projection to
another, just as if they made up a rat's staircase.

My ratty heart quailed, but the big rat got behind me and
snarled and gnashed his teeth, and I jumped.

Up we went, rock after rock, as my heart beat faster and
faster and my breath came harder and harder. Finally, our
guides crawled out onto a sort of shelf and went scurrying
away into some more darkness. Trembling with exhaustion, I
followed.

Thick black closed around us again. I followed the scrabbling of claws ahead. Then, suddenly, a reek hit me, one that

went right through my head. I recoiled, but the big rat behind
me snarled, and I forced myself to go forward again, trembling
from sheer fear this time, not exhaustion. What kind of un-
earthly smells were these? It wasn't like the warm, homey ef-
fluvium of the sewers, or the musky, delicious garbage-reek of
the other rats, but a nose-searing, brain-tearing mixture of
smells that cut like saws and stabbed like needles.

It got to our guide rats, too. They cowered away, quivering—
but between them, I saw the hole between two stones, with
ruddy orange light glowing on the other side.

I cowered away, too—that's where the horrible smells were
coming from.

The big rat behind me squeaked with angry menace. No go;
I cowered harder.

Then a searing pain shot through my behind, just above the
tail, and I shot forward with a squeak of agony. The bastard
had nipped me! I recovered, scrabbling on all claws just short
of the hole—but something soft and massive struck me, and I
jammed into the hole with an outraged squeal.

And I do mean into—it was as tight as a bottleneck around
a cork! How the heck did the real rats expect me to get
through this? But I stretched, and found that my body suddenly
became amazingly slimmer; my ribs seemed to compress, and
it was hard to breathe for a moment, but with all four sets of
claws pushing and pulling, I oozed through that hole as though
I'd been greased.

Out! At last! I leapt aside, to let the next one come out . . .

A tearing yowl filled the world, and something huge and
reeking plummeted down at me.

I may not have known that smell, but my body sure did.
Cat!

CHAPTER 31

I squealed in terror and ran.

The cat yowled with delight and leapt after me. I tried a quick U-turn around a table leg, doubling back; the cat's claws scrabbled on the stone, and I dashed for the next table leg and went up it like a monkey up a tree. The cat spat in fury and leapt up after me, knocking an alembic to the floor; it shattered, but I was already running for the other end of the table, squealing in terror. The cat gave a meow of delight and plunged after me. Beakers and thuribles tipped and smashed; foul-smelling powders went flying. That slowed the cat down a little; he sneezed several times, pausing for each. By the time he got his nose clear, I was back on the floor, dashing for the protection of a huge caldron. I shot between it and the wall, and realized that it was hot—there was a fire under it! But the cat was too angry to care; it shot through right behind me, and yowled in pain and anger as its tail hit a burning ember.

Any distraction helped! I made another U-turn around the caldron, hoping the cat would be a little more circumspect about the circumference. It wasn't; it charged even faster for being all the hotter.

Broom! And a shelf above it! I dashed up the broomstick. The cat barreled into it with a snarl, but I leapt a split second before the broomstick went flying. Up I soared, up and up, front claws stretching for the shelf, it coming closer and closer . . .

. . . then receding farther and farther. I fell. Panic surged through me; I writhed in midair, saw the floor coming up at me, struggled frantically to reach a chair five feet over—

And hit. Hard. On stone.

I blacked out for a second; my ears rang, then filled with a yowling that seemed to echo through all the world as the cat pounced. My vision cleared just in time to see sharp teeth closing on me. Pain stabbed through the back of my neck; the monster jerked me off the floor, claws coming up to rip out my belly . . .

The cat screamed, and I shot down to the floor again. I was no fool; I landed running, glancing back . . .

. . . to see the cat streaking after two other rats, with a spot of blood on his tail.

I felt insanely grateful. I hadn't known a rat could.

These weren't your average rats, of course—they were very, very smart. Just before they got to the stone wall, they split apart, dashing for opposite corners. The cat slammed on the brakes, scrabbling to a halt, then paused a second, trying to decide which rat to chase. She opted for the smaller one.

Definitely, those rats were as smart as humans.

Wait a minute—they were humans! And so was I! My minuscule rat brain had lost track of that fact while I was being chased! Suddenly, I remembered that I'd understood the big rat, that it had spoken human words. If it could, I could, too. There wasn't much room for memory in that little brain, but it did serve up the couplet I'd prepared for just this occasion:

> "See as thou wast wont to see,
> Be as thou wast wont to be!"

I couldn't remember the rest, but it didn't seem to matter—two human beings suddenly shot up from the rubble in the corners, where the two rats had hidden. The cat tried to pause in mid-pounce, yowling frantically, heading right toward Frisson's navel. He caught it, grinning, then murmured, "Poor tabby!" and stroked its head.

The cat yowled in total bewilderment and struggled to be free.

The Rat Raiser advanced from the other corner, hands outstretched, bloodlust in his eye.

Frisson let go, and the cat leapt down, dashing for cover. The poet stepped in front of the Rat Raiser, holding up a hand. "No! She was only doing her duty!"

The Rat Raiser narrowed his yellow eyes, lips drawing back to bare his oversized, yellowed teeth.

"We have other game to hunt!" Frisson scolded. "You are human again, and cats are the least of your worries!"

The Rat Raiser suddenly looked apprehensive. He looked about him with quick, furtive glances, then stared, pointing. "There!"

Frisson looked, then turned to lance a finger at me, snapping,

> "See as thou wast wont to see,
> Be as thou wast wont to be!"

The room changed perspective amazingly. The furniture shrank, becoming only tables and chairs instead of a forest again. The cat dwindled from a monster to a pet. Of course, I just barely noticed this—most of my mind was too busy feeling the pain as I suddenly grew 600 percent. I clenched my teeth against a minute's agony, as my body stretched upward and filled out, mushrooming. Then only the after-aches were left, and I was human again. I heaved a shaky sigh and tried to pull my limp self back together, looking about me, marveling at the fact that I was still dressed. Come to think of it, so were Frisson and the Rat Raiser. Maybe the spell had changed our clothing into fur?

I looked about me, taking in the shattered glassware on the top of a table that was surely the alchemist's equivalent of a lab bench, the array of powders and miscellaneous ingredients racked on shelves against one wall—some of which I was sure I wouldn't want identified—the fire under the caldron and the stench arising from it, the long table against the other wall, with Angelique on it . . .

Angelique!

She lay strapped down on the table, the marks of torture still upon her, dress ripped open, the clotted blood still dark in the center of her poor bruised bosom. The instruments of torture lay ready, thumbscrews by each hand, the boot open and waiting near her foot, and it wasn't a table she was strapped onto, it was a rack!

By her head was a small, clear bottle, within which churned a mint-green mist. My stomach fell—could that be her soul, the ghost with whom I was so ardently in love?

"We've got to get her out of there!" I was by her side in an instant, fumbling with the straps on her wrists, but they were riveted, not buckled. Exasperated, I pulled out my clasp knife and started sawing. "How do we get her spirit back into her body, Frisson?"

The poet pulled out his sheaf of newest poems and leafed through them, frowning. He pulled one out and recited,

> "Undivide the sundered rents!
> Unite the disparate elements!
> Churn into a bound Gestalt,
> Mind and spirit, blood and salt!
> Banished ghost, repatriate!
> Soul and corpse, reintegrate!"

Nothing happened.

"Nice try, but no cigar." I sawed at a leather bond. "What else have you got?"

Frisson flipped through his scraps and pulled out another one.

> "Tie the free
> And holy-day rejoicing spirit down
> To the ever-haunting importunity
> Of business, where it should be bound
> And has from birth—its body, lifelong city!"

He looked up from the verse and stared.

Nothing happened. The body lay still, the mint mist churned inside its bottle.

"Pull the cork," the Rat Raiser suggested.

"Of course!" I slapped my forehead with the heel of my hand, then grabbed the bottle.

It wouldn't move.

"A spell!" I stepped over to the bottle. But I wasn't about to waste time trying to break it—it didn't matter where the bottle was, as long as the ghost could get out. I twisted the cork.

It wouldn't twist.

I stuck the tip of my knife in it and levered. Nothing, not even a chip.

" 'Tis enchanted," Frisson opined. "What luck with her straps?"

"None at all; the knife doesn't even scar the leather." I looked up, frowning. "You mean . . ."

Doors slammed open, front and back, and guardsmen boiled in, hard hands reaching for us, pikes stabbing, and behind them, Suettay slammed the door closed, crowing, "Taken! Taken in my trap, like the rats they are! Slay them, slay them out of hand!"

I grabbed up the boot and threw it at the nearest guardsman; he fell. The Rat Raiser snapped out of his horrified trance and caught up broken glassware off the lab table, hurling it at the soldiers. I fell into fighting stance with my knife, my stomach sinking, knowing I didn't have a chance, but Frisson was flipping through his anthology, pulling out a scrap, and chanting,

> "Where are the friends to guard our backs,
> Coming strong, through wind and wrack?
> Where are the hearts who know no peer?
> Marching close! To us be near!
> But where are the friends of yesteryear?"

"Right here!" a muffled voice shouted on the other side of the door, and the wood turned to powder. A dot of light shot in, so brilliant that it hurt my eyes, and a voice straight out of a synthesizer sang, "A rescue! A rescue, friend to friend!"

"Demon!" I cried in delight.

Behind it came Gilbert! And behind him, the Black Knight I'd seen from a low angle just after I'd turned into a rat. After him strode the knight with the long blonde hair and the golden circlet—I was shocked anew to realize she was a woman!—and the blue-robed knight who had been on the dragon. Outside, a roar filled the antechamber with flames.

The guardsmen inside cried out in fear.

"It cannot come in!" Suettay sawed the air frantically with her hands, chanting.

"We are in already!" the Blue Knight snapped, sword stabbing out at her midriff—but one of her guards snapped out of his funk and beat down the blade.

All about, the knights were taking on the footmen, chopping down halberds and smiting down enemies. Sure, there were only three of them and one squire, but they wore armor. And that confounded dot of light was swooping from one soldier to another, and each one it touched just fainted.

"Loose the corpse!" the Blue Knight shouted, and the spark swerved off to settle on Angelique's bonds.

The Blue Knight disposed of Suettay's bodyguard with a chop and a thrust, beat him off, and spun to Suettay again, chanting,

"They that have power to hurt but do help none,
  That do not the thing they most do show,
  Who, hurting others, are themselves as stone,
  Unmoved, cold, and to remorse quite slow."

Suettay froze.

The Blue Knight spun to me. "That won't hold her for long,
but just enough to— Paul!"

I knew the voice, and a second later, the visor snapped up,
and I knew the face. "Matt! What the . . . What are *you* doing
here?"

"Saving your bacon, and just incidentally wiping out a depraved and vicious usurper! My queen had a vision telling her
to go help the Witch Doctor, because he could cure Allustria
of witchcraft!"

"Great! Can you find him?"

The cackling laugh of gloating triumph snapped me out of
my sentimental reunion. I whirled, to see Suettay holding Angelique's freed corpse by the arm while she pulled a pink flask
out of her robes. "Fool! 'Twas a captive sprite in the bottle, not
the girl's spirit! Her soul is here—and is now gone!"

"Max!" Matt yelled. "Stop her!"

"How?" the arc-spark sang, but Suettay was chanting something in that obscene arcane language, making lewd gestures
and turning transparent.

So was Angelique's body.

Frisson shouted out,

"Five hundred feet of beaten ground
  With walls and towers are girdled 'round.
  Within them, let this queen be bound!
  In a tower will she be found!"

The witch queen disappeared.

Her soldiers cried out in despair, stepped back, and threw
down their weapons. "Mercy! Quarter! Quarter!"

I howled.

"I am sorry, sorry!" Frisson cried. "I had to act, and 'twas
all I could think of at that moment!"

"You did very well," Matt assured him. "There wasn't exactly time for a literature search; at least we know where she
is."

"Do we?" The blonde woman stepped up, looking severe.

Her voice was a rich alto. "There are four towers. How shall we know to which she has gone?"

"Bind them!" the Black Knight snapped to Gilbert, who set about lashing soldiers with a will. The Black Knight stepped over to us. "There are four towers, and four of us. Do we each seek out one turret! Matthew, take the east—Your Majesty, the west, and I'll take the south." He turned to me. "To you lies the north. Farewell!"

"Right!" Matt charged out the door, with the other two right behind him.

"Hey, wait a minute!" I yelled after them. "We can get there much faster if . . . nerts!" I was talking to an empty door frame. I turned back to Frisson. "Quick! A new verse!"

"An old one!" Frisson flipped, pulled, and handed it to me. *Cherchez la femme!*

I took the parchment and read the verse.

"Even from her bondage, my lady's voice cries;
Even from the gaol's jaws my frantic heart replies!
I ask, and have—I seek, and find
The golden lass who fills my mind!
I seek, and find—I've sought, and found!
Take me where my true love's bound!"

For some reason, the words held my attention more strongly than they ever had—this in spite of the frantic crawling fear I had for Angelique. Somehow, I knew she was in greater peril now than she had been since the day she had died—but my gaze was riveted to the paper, holding each word as I read it in a savage contrast of blackest black and whitest white. I couldn't have torn my gaze away until I finished chanting it. Then I could, and I did.

Frisson was beside me. We were in a very large room with curving walls—another laboratory, one far more elaborate than the first—and there was Angelique's corpse, stretched out on a table, with the little pink flask beside her rib cage and Suettay bending low over her, hands outspread and moving in strange patterns as she chanted slowly in a deep, heavy tone.

Her real laboratory! In a flash, I understood. The other one had only been stage dressing, a trap to catch me—and I had walked right into it!

Fortunately, so had Matt and his friends.

Suettay's mumblings were making the air dark with gather-

ing magical force. I could feel tremendous power brewing all
about me; it made my hair stand on end in more ways than
one. It didn't take much thinking to figure out what she was
doing—pushing Angelique's soul back into her body, but this
time, without any chance of escaping. The instruments of torture stood ready at hand, along with a long, curving knife.

She was going to sacrifice Angelique all over again!

I snapped out of my daze. If ever I'd needed help, it was
now!

But Frisson had beaten me to it. He was already chanting.

"Come away, come away,
  Hark to the alarm!
  Come in your war array,
  Wizard-at-arms!
  Come with companions of magic and might!
  Come with the queen, and your friend the Black Knight!"

Just as he finished, so did Suettay.

The magic field seemed to implode with a soundless concussion that staggered both Frisson and me—and the bottle turned
clear, the corpse's eyes fluttered!

"Why!" I shouted at Suettay. "With a battle raging about
you and a kingdom falling—why stop to torment this one poor
girl?"

"Because only thus may I snatch victory from the jaws of
disaster!" Suettay glared at me, a finger spearing out toward
my heart—fortunately, ten feet away. "Even now, when I complete the ceremony, he will grant me power sufficient to hurl
you all to perdition! Beware!"

She raised the knife. I shouted, and would have leapt at
her—but just then, Angelique sat up as far as her bonds would
allow, blinking about her, bemused—and I caught my breath.
Even battered and bruised, her face was so lovely that it held
me spellbound. Oh, it was the same face that I'd been seeing
all along—but it was real now, made of flesh and bone, and
vivid in a way her ghost never had been, even in the darkest
night.

Suettay screamed with triumph, snapping the knife up high
in her right hand, the left pressing Angelique back down as her
scream turned into a stream of syllables that I couldn't understand, and the knife swept down . . .

Behind me, a voice snapped, "Max! Destroy that knife with a sudden case of metal fatigue!"

The dot of arc light shot over to the knife, touched it—and as it slammed into Angelique's ribs, it turned to dust!

Suettay screamed in rage and frustration. She swatted at the arc light, catching it in a fist—and screamed as the spark tore through the flesh, shooting out to hover in front of her, spitting, "Foolish mortal!"

Beside me, Frisson was chanting,

> "Come as the winds come, when
> Forests are rended!
> Come as the waves come, when
> Navies are stranded!
> Come in your wisdom, scholar audacious!
> Come now to triumph, Friar Ignatius!"

Suettay screamed in rage and frustration.

The air glittered; then Friar Ignatius was there, stumbling and reaching out to brace himself against the lab table.

Suettay took one look at him and screamed again.

Sir Guy and Gilbert leapt from behind me to opposite sides of the table, grabbing Suettay by the arms and shoving her back against the wall. She shrieked in rage, then shouted a verse, and a million bits of steel appeared, hovering over her—darts, to hurl at both knight and squire!

But Matt stepped up beside me, chanting,

> "What whetted vision mocks my waking sense?
> Hence, sharp delusion! Enchanted points, hence!"

The bright field split and started to swoop toward knight and squire—and disappeared.

Suettay shrieked another verse, hands twisting, fingers writhing, and Gilbert and Sir Guy cried out, letting go of her and frantically trying to loosen their armor, which began to glow with heat. Freed, the witch crowed with triumph, stretching her arms—but the tall blonde knight stepped up, slamming her back against the wall and pinioning her wrists, as Frisson yelled,

> "You must stay the cooling charm,
> Or you may burn out quite!

Chilled be your metal, hot to warm,
And cease to give out light!"

Sir Guy and Gilbert groaned with relief and stepped up to
help the blonde knight.

Suettay was on the ropes and she knew it. She screamed another verse, in anguish . . .

And something exploded in the middle of the laboratory.
The cloud of reeking smoke shrank in on itself, and a huge
devil stood there, hurling hot coals at the knights, leveling a giant pitchfork, and bellowing, "As you have called, my master
sends me! Get hence, feeble mortals! Do not impede this emissary of the King of Evil!"

The knights turned as pale as Angelique's ghost and ducked
flying coals, but they stood firm, the blonde crying, "You have
no power over us, minion of evil! Get hence!"

Suettay screamed, thrashing in their hold.

The devil growled and advanced, lifting his pitchfork.

"Angel!" I cried. "If ever you wanted to interfere, now is
the time! Appear! Help! Please!"

"I thought you would never ask, man."

I stared. It was my angel, all right—I recognized the basic
face, the glow, and the wings—but he was dressed in a chambray shirt, blue jeans, and boots. He had always had long hair,
of course, but now he had a beard, too.

Matt darted a quick, incredulous look at me. I spread my
hands and shrugged.

The hippie-angel grinned, holding up a palm. "Get back
where you came from, pestiferous porter! Go back to Hellmouth, and don't ever come up here again!"

The devil bellowed in rage, turning its pitchfork toward the
angel and hurling—but the points bounced off the angel's
palm, and the devil convulsed in sudden agony, screaming in-
coherently as he faded away.

Suettay cried out, loud and long, but it was a howl of despair.

"Even now, there is salvation for you." Friar Ignatius
stepped up, reaching out to her.

The angel turned toward them, beaming—literally. His light
spread out a ray toward the witch-queen, but she turned and
hissed at him, and the ray hovered just short of her.

"The grace of God will not be imposed upon they who wish
it not," Friar Ignatius assured her, his voice surprisingly gentle.

"Yet be assured, even now God will forgive you, and save you from the fires of Hell."

"*Save* me? Fool!" Suettay spat. "I have been a queen of witches, and I shall be a queen in Hell, too! Kill me if you will, for my soul will not writhe in torment, but quiver in delight at the cruelties it imposes on those spirits too weak to do great evil!"

"Never believe such a lie!" Friar Ignatius' face turned severe. "All human souls that go to Hell, go to eternal torment! Satan takes delight in torturing those he seduces to his realm— delight, though no joy, which he cannot feel!"

" 'Tis you who lie, pawn of Heaven!" she spat. "Do not seek to dissuade me—I shall remain true to my master!"

"Turn away from him, I implore you!" Friar Ignatius reached out. "Repent while you can!" He touched her arm.

She screamed in rage and pain—he was so pure that his mere touch sent her into agony. Seeing this, he yanked his hand away, but Suettay shouted a verse and, with a titanic heave, shook off the knights. They fell back, but they caught themselves against the wall and scrambled to their feet, drawing their swords.

But Suettay was growing, swelling, her form stretching upward, higher, even as we watched.

The blonde knight shouted and leapt in, sword thrusting— straight in under Suettay's breastbone, stabbing upward.

The witch screamed, twisting. Then the point must have burst the reins to her heart, for her eyes dulled, and her body deflated, shrinking back to its normal size, sagging down over the blade—but the scream went on and on and on as the body sagged to the floor, too heavy for the queen of Merovence to hold up. That scream turned into a shriek of triumph, then faded away, crying, "Master! Master! I come to your reward!"

The chamber was quiet a moment.

Friar Ignatius shook his head, face very sad. "I have lost another soul, another of God's creations."

"It was not you who lost her, Friar, but herself," Frisson said quietly. "She was so far gone in false pride that she would not admit defeat, so saturated in evil that she would not reach out to God's grace. She had truly given up belief in goodness or in love, even as simple fellowship—so there was no one through whom she could reach out to God, and no one whom she would not wish to torment for her own twisted pleasure."

"And so dedicated to deceit that she would not see the lie

Satan had foisted on her as blandishment." Friar Ignatius nodded heavily.

Then, distant, faint, but very clear, a scream rang out, rang through all that reeking chamber, through each of our minds, making our hearts sink, for it was Suettay's voice in agony so intense that it shook me to the core—agony, but with the shock of betrayal. It was a scream that seemed to go on and on, and hadn't slackened a bit as it faded from our hearing—and, I suspected with dread, would go on for eternity.

It seemed still to ring through us for a very long time, but the room had actually been quiet for several minutes before I looked up at my guardian angel and said, in a last feeble attempt at protest, "Eternity is a very long time."

He nodded sadly. "Yes, Paul. It is."

CHAPTER 32

"Look," I said, "you didn't have to show up as a hippie. Who do you think you're kidding, anyway?"

I caressed Angelique's hand while I said it, though. She sat beside me in the courtyard—anything to get away from the stench of that laboratory—eyes glowing, head resting on my shoulder. She'd been in a great deal of pain when she "woke"—not the sharp pains of present torture, which we'd headed off, thank Heaven, but the aches of old ones. It was enough to make me mad at Suettay all over again, and ...

"I shouldn't be glad she's suffering," I told the angel. "Suettay, I mean. But I am—after what she did to my Angelique." I was able to say "my" with only a passing qualm, somehow.

"You should be above such sentiments," the angel murmured.

"I know," I said, "but I can't help how I feel—and it's better to be honest about your feelings. Hey, man, I'm human, too!"

"Yeah, you are," the angel acknowledged. "But you're a good human."

I frowned. "I said, you don't have to look and talk like a hippie. I know you for what you really are, man."

"Yeah, sure," the angel said, "but if I didn't look like this, you couldn't sit there and call me 'man.' "

I took a deep breath. "Okay, so it sets me more at ease, and I can relate to you better. But there are times when it's more important to be looking up to an angel, than to be comfortable."

"True, true—and when those times come, I'll be glad to

show up the way you expect, halo and wings and all. But for the moment, I think we need to be able to get down and clear a little more."

"The way I expect?" I looked at him sharply. "What's your true form?"

"I don't have one," he said right back. "I'm a spirit, remember?"

"Okay," I said impatiently, "how would you look to me if I were a spirit, too?"

"Like whatever you expected, man."

I bit down on my temper. Angelique reached over with her other hand, stroking mine. I know she meant it to be soothing, but it was anything but. It did serve as a nice distraction, though, and I couldn't remember to keep being angry.

The angel smiled, proudly—and that irked me all over again. "Look, I'm not a good man! So don't go smirking like that."

"No, you are," he contradicted. "At least, you're a decent and humane man. For example, you wouldn't really want Suettay to suffer for eternity, would you?"

That gave me pause. I stopped to consider, consulting my inner feelings. "No," I said at last. "A good long time, yes—long enough for justice. But not forever."

Angelique stirred beside me, nestling a little more firmly against my arm.

"You'll have to stop distracting me," I told her, "or I won't be in any shape to talk to an angel."

She looked up to give me a heavy-lidded, pinfeather smile, then closed her eyes, looking very content.

"So what happens now?" I asked the angel. "What do I do?"

He shrugged. "Whatever you want—and, I hope, whatever you really believe is right. I don't run your life, Paul . . ."

"Saul," I grated.

". . . I only try to shield you from the Tempter and sway you back to God."

"You've been doing pretty well so far," I admitted. "Anybody who can keep me on the straight and narrow . . ."

". . . doesn't really have all that hard a job," he finished. "Ask your friend Matt."

"I'm asking you!"

"But there isn't any more need for me to stick around—at

least, not so you can see me. So long—but remember, I'm with you for life!" And he disappeared.

"Cop-out," I snarled after him, then thought about the term. He *was* sort of a Heavenly cop . . .

"Your friend gone?" Matt came clanking up.

I looked up at him. "In a manner of speaking. He says I should ask you."

"Anything." Matt clapped me on the shoulder, looking straight into my eyes with a grin. "But there are some boys over there who have a question for you."

"Boys?" I looked around the courtyard, frowning. Queen Alisande's knights were cleaning up the castle, rounding up evil stragglers, with a dozen of Matt's junior sorcerers along to help. We head honchos could take the weight off our feet for a while.

Not a very long while, though. A hundred yards away stood a small army of heavy dragoons—at least five hundred. I winced at the thought, hoping there were more still alive—if "alive" was really the term for a magical construct. I certainly owed them. I went over to see what they wanted. "Good afternoon, Sergeant. What can I do for you?"

"More work for us, Guv?"

I remembered looking up toward the dragoon's back trail during the battle, seeing their dead lying fallen, fading even as I watched, disappearing.

"No," I decided. "Return to quarters."

The dragoon saluted and whirled his horse, turning back to his fellows, bawling orders. I chanted after him,

> "To whatever barracks stores them,
> Let these soldiers now retreat to,
> With soft cots and pensions for them,
> And full store of beer and eats, too!"

A heat haze seemed to spring up, enveloping the dragoons, thickening to mist, then London fog. When it cleared, they were gone, leaving behind them only a cowering wreckage of moaning men-at-arms and fallen knights.

"As if they'd never been," Matt whispered.

"Retired," I corrected. "Maybe not to Heaven, but to one heck of a Limbo!" I turned to him and caught his hand. "You found me in the nick of time."

"I knew when you'd arrived in this world," he said, squeezing back. "I talked Alisande into moving out the next day."

I was amazed at how firm his clasp was—amazed at his having enough strength to walk around in all that armor, in fact. "You've put on a lot of muscle in the last three days."

"Three days to you." He turned, strolling back to Angelique and the seats we'd found, by the wall of the keep. "Four years, for me."

I stared. "Four *years*?"

"Time moves at a different rate here, I guess," he said, "or there's a differential between our two universes."

I just stared at him for a moment, as he sat down, right where the angel had been—or still was, for all I knew. The thought gave me a chill, but I shook it off and said, "So what's been happenin', man?"

He started telling me. It took a while.

When he was done, I just sat there, dazed.

" 'Tis a most amazing tale," Angelique murmured by my shoulder. "We had heard some echo of it, we folk in Allustria, but not all."

"You wouldn't," I said. "Suettay wouldn't have wanted it known that evil sorcerers and usurpers could be beaten." Then, to Matt: "So that tall blonde with the crown is the queen of Merovence—and your wife?"

"Finally," Matt affirmed.

"Yeah, after she kept you waiting three years." I felt indignation for my old friend, but I tried to assure myself that long engagements just meant more-solid marriages. "So you're the king?"

"No, just the royal consort—and Her Majesty's Wizard. She was very insistent about that. So was I, in fact."

"Yeah, I wouldn't want that much responsibility, either."

Angelique looked up at me, shocked.

"That doesn't mean I won't accept any," I hastened to assure her, and she relaxed with her smug, lazy smile again.

"So how'd *you* get here, Paul?"

I grinned. "You first."

Matt returned the grin. "Too much studying. I started concentrating on that piece of parchment so much that it began to make sense—and when I looked up, here I was."

"Same thing," I said. "I got worried about you, and I couldn't find any trace, so . . ."

He flushed. "Sorry, man."

"Hey, it's okay, it's okay—now. I ran out of leads, so I started studying the new parchment that showed up ..."

"New parchment?" He sat up straight, frowning. "What new parchment?"

"You know, the one that said, 'Hey, Paul, drop me a line ...'"

"*That* one?" The frown deepened to a scowl. "I just wrote that out when I was feeling homesick one night. When I went to throw it in the wastebasket the next morning, it was gone. How'd it get to you?"

"Don't know," I said slowly, "but I could make a guess. There were an awful lot of spiders in your apartment. One of them bit me while I was translating the parchment. I blacked out, and woke up here."

"The Spider King!" He stared. "I thought he was just a legend!"

"Oh, he's real, all right, and he lives in some sort of dimensional nexus. I think he wanted to clean up the situation here in Allustria, so he ..." I broke off as Matt's gaze drifted, his eyes brooding. "What's the matter?"

"The Archbishop," Matt said slowly. "A spider bit him, and he fell ill. I had to go cure him—and while I was working on him, he grabbed my sleeve and demanded to know if I had ever met a single man who had a genuine sense of integrity."

I stared in horror. "You didn't give him my name!"

"Well, yeah," Matt said uncomfortably. "Funny thing is, when he got well, he didn't remember a bit of it—not surprising, the temperature he had."

"But I'm not a saint! I'm not a good guy!"

"No," Matt said slowly, "but you have a sense of self that won't quit. You won't let anybody infringe on you, in any way. Makes you pretty abrasive sometimes, in fact."

Angelique moved a little away from me, eyeing me warily again.

"Not true," I assured her. "He always did have too high an opinion of me."

"No," she said, "he did not."

I turned and frowned deeply into her eyes. "Then how come I'm in love with you?"

"I ken not." She gazed back, and her eyes seemed to be all there was in the world. "But I rejoice."

Then she broke the gaze, and her spell, by turning to Matt. "Can you not explain this, Lord Wizard?"

"Only by logic," he said slowly, "which has its limits—but if he is compulsively true to himself, and has nonetheless developed an obsession for you, then there must be something about you that fulfills some element of himself. Probably more than one."

"You traitor," I growled at him—but Angelique had gone heavy-lidded and self-satisfied again, cuddling up to me, so I didn't really mean it.

Matt knew that; he only smiled. "Don't blame me, Paul. It's not my fault if you have an instinctive sense of psychic balance, some gut drive for keeping the harmony between all the parts of your personality."

"Yeah," I admitted. "You claimed that was why I was attracted to Zen. I kept telling you that it was Zen and Taoism that gave me that sense of balance, not the other way around."

Matt shrugged. "Cause, effect, or a positive reinforcing cycle, it doesn't matter. You've got it, and when it's threatened, you lash out at whoever does the threatening." He nodded to Angelique. "Take care, mademoiselle. He gets mean sometimes. He mellows out pretty quickly, though."

"I thank you." But her equanimity didn't seem at all disturbed. "I shall be mindful of it."

I think I might have felt a little easier if she'd seemed worried.

"So you've got the instinct for walking the ethical tightrope," Matt summarized.

"Yeah," I said with chagrin. "Gave my guardian angel enough grief with that. He kept trying to get me to commit myself to the side of the angels, and whenever he did, I went out and committed a sin."

"At least, a sin by his rules," Matt amended. "I don't think you ever really did anything all that bad."

I glared at him. "I keep telling you, I'm not a saint!"

"Yeah, and someday you'll get yourself to believe it, too. No, no, I take it back." He held up a palm. "Let's just say you're only a fundamentally decent, honest, and caring individual."

I was just beginning to get really sore about that, when Gruesome came waddling up, grinning from ear to ear—well, from side to side. "We won, huh?"

Matt scrambled back fast.

"No, no, he won't hurt you," I assured him. "This is Gruesome . . ."

"He sure is!"

"No, that's what I nicknamed him. He's my friend." I was startled to hear myself say it, but I guessed I was right. "If he has a name in Trollish, I can't pronounce it."

"He doesn't." Matt still looked very nervous. "They don't have enough intelligence."

"Oh, he has a name all right. Some fairies used it to enchant him so that he wouldn't eat people anymore," I assured him, "and by the time a nymph named Thyme removed the spell, he'd started thinking of us as friends instead of snacks." I turned to Gruesome. "Tell you what, old fellow—I can transport you back to the bridge where I met you, and you'll fit in with your fellow trolls again."

"No! No!" Gruesome shook his head—well, upper half— from side to side rapidly. "Goosum no like trolls no more! Well, maybe females," he added as an afterthought, "but only for little while, now 'n' then. Goosum like people!"

"That's what I'm afraid of," Matt muttered.

"Goosum like people for friends! Goosum want stay with Saw 'n' Fish'un!"

"I think that can be arranged," I said slowly, trying not to let him see I was touched. "But you'll have to let me renew your anti–people-eating spell now and then."

"Sure, sure! Goosum no like sojer-taste, anyway!" He made spitting noises.

I wondered how he had found out.

"I think," Matt said slowly, "that he has really begun to think of you and your companions as friends."

I nodded. "All I have to do is broaden the scope, extend the feeling to all mankind."

"I dunno," Matt said dubiously. "It hasn't worked on people."

"Yeah, but he's a little more direct," I said. "Somehow, his trollish nature's been modified. He's basically pretty decent now."

"As are you," Angelique murmured sleepily.

I bridled, then remembered that I didn't exactly want her to think differently. "Fundamentally, maybe—but it's buried pretty deep."

"Then I shall delve," Angelique answered.

I turned to her. "I thought that was my job."

She blushed.

"If that's your idea of a sin . . ." Matt began.

"Hey, that's what we were taught when we were kids, right? At least, in our universe."

"Oh," Matt said brightly. "You've figured out this is all real, eh?"

I backed fast. "Well, that's what the Spider King said. I still think it makes more sense to declare this all to be one huge, massive, hallucination."

"If it is," Matt said, "your subconscious is a great one for details."

"I *have* run into a few things I didn't know about," I admitted. "That doesn't mean this is all real."

"No," said Matt, "but that isn't the question that matters."

I frowned. "Then what is?"

"Can you return to our native universe? If you can, then this could all be a dream—but if you can't, then you're stuck here, and whether it's real or not, you're going to have to behave as if it were, or you're going to collect a lot of pain."

"Good point," I said, frowning, "but it's true of our own universe, too. No, the real question is: Do I *want* to go back?"

Angelique stirred against me, in just the wrong way. I turned to her. "What do you think, Prime Distraction?"

For answer, she reached up and pulled my face down to hers, giving me that long, long kiss I'd been dying for, but had been embarrassed to go after in public. I sat stiff for a moment, taken by surprise—but then I recovered, loosened up, and began to do a proper job of it.

Finally, we came up for air, and I heard somebody whistling. I glanced over and saw Matt surveying the courtyard, entirely too casual about it.

Gruesome, though, was more direct, as usual. He was watching us and grinning like a watermelon.

I turned back to Angelique, and her glowing eyes became my entire universe again. Suddenly all that mattered was whether or not *she* was real.

"Never leave me," she breathed, her voice husky but imperious. "Never leave me, while I hold breath!"

"Or maybe not even after," I agreed. "I wouldn't even think of it—again."

She smiled and turned her face up for another kiss.

Some time later, I lifted my face an inch or so away from hers, breathing hard and ignoring Gruesome's chuckling. "I warn you, though—I'm not going to put up with any nonsense about postponing the wedding for any three years."

"Neither," she said, "will I."

And her lips drifted up toward mine, parting, drawing mine down toward them . . .

Just then, a trumpet blew.

We got up, turning to look.

Queen Alisande was standing over Gilbert with a drawn sword—and he was kneeling, with his head bowed. Threat! I leapt for them, my heart in my mouth.

But Matt clapped a hand on my shoulder. "Easy, easy. She means honor, not harm."

I hesitated—and in the delay, the Black Knight, next to the Queen, cried out, "Know ye all that this squire, hight Gilbert, of the Order of Saint Moncaire, hath proven himself in combat! By striving and arduous campaigning, he hath given evidence of his tenacity, of his virtue, and of his dedication to goodness and God! Therefore on this day, here in the place of battle, the queen of Merovence shall do him honor!"

Alisande laid the sword on his left shoulder, then on his right, intoning, in that clear alto voice that made me realize what Matt saw in her, "I hereby dub thee knight!" Then she lifted the sword—and slugged him with a quick left hook. His head rocked, but he held still.

I didn't. I almost leapt for her right then. Fortunately, Matt still had hold of my shoulder—because she went on to cry out, "Rise, Sir Gilbert!"

My erstwhile squire rose, flushed with pleasure and honor, and bowed low to his queen.

I relaxed and joined in the cheering.

When it slackened, the queen beckoned—and Frisson stepped up!

"Until we can find the last legitimate scion of your last legitimate monarch," Queen Alisande called out, "I shall be your queen!"

A huge massed cheer went up.

I wondered how long they would feel that way. What was the dividing line between liberation and conquest, anyway?

"Yet I cannot stay to govern you in person!" she cried. "Therefore I shall appoint for you a viceroy, to rule in my place, and the place of your own king—one who has proved his wisdom in this long struggle to displace the usurper, and proved his steadfastness and loyalty to right. I give you the Viceroy Frisson!"

This time the yell was even more heartfelt than before. Fris-

son looked about him, damn near panicking—then saw me and
gave me the most doleful, pleading look of his life. I smiled,
nodding, hoping I looked as reassuring as I intended, trying to
make him realize I'd stand by him—and it must have worked,
because he relaxed, just a little, recovered his composure, and
turned to wave at the crowd. In fact, I saw him straightening
and seeming to grow larger and more poised, even as they
cheered.

The shouting died, Frisson stepped aside—with alacrity, if it
must be told—and Friar Ignatius stepped forward. He raised
his hands, crying, "Let the infirm of body, but affirmed of
heart, step forward!"

Everybody drew back, no one wanting to get in the way of
the sick ex-witches. They tottered forward and knelt.

"I shall hear all your sins and shrive you all one by one,"
Friar Ignatius declared, "but for fear that some might die even
while I spoke, I conferred upon you all conditional absolution.
Yet now we must heal your bodies, that your pain may cease.
Master Saul, come forward!"

"What? Me? What for?" I demanded.

"Why, to heal them, of course!"

"Oh, yeah, sure! Come on, Frisson!"

I stepped forward—and the witches cheered, then began to
chant, "Hail the Doctor of Witches! Hail the Witches' Doctor!"

The crowd took it up. "The Witch Doctor! The Witch Doctor!"

I just stared, thunderstruck. "Not me!"

Matt frowned at me. "You mean you didn't know?"

And then he began to laugh.

ABOUT THE AUTHOR

"A wandering Catholic, aye,
A thing of texts and catches."

Early in life, Christopher Stasheff found a catch in almost every point of Catholic dogma except the main ones, and has been spiritually wandering ever since. He has a lot of doubts about the Church, but only questions about the Faith.

One day, he realized that most of the medieval fantasies he read seldom mentioned the Devil, and never God. He vehemently maintained that wasn't the way medieval Christians really saw the world—they saw God everywhere, in everything, and the Devil always lurking, looking for an opening—and that authors really ought to write their fantasies a little closer to reality. Then he realized that, being a fantasy author, he was stuck with writing his next story that way.

He spent his early childhood in Mount Vernon, New York, but spent the rest of his formative years in Ann Arbor, Michigan. He has always had difficulty distinguishing fantasy from reality and has tried to compromise by teaching college. He tends to prescript his life, but can't understand why other people never get their lines right. This causes a fair amount of misunderstanding with his wife and four children. He seeks refuge in fantasy worlds of his own making and hopes you enjoy them as much as he does.

Available now in bookstores everywhere.

THE SECULAR WIZARD

by Christopher Stasheff

Published in hardcover by Del Rey Books.

Turn the page for a sneak preview of
the latest volume in Stasheff's
A WIZARD IN RHYME series . . .

PROLOGUE

The tall roan stallion looked up and nickered. The other horses crowded to the doors of their stalls to watch Accerese the groom as he came into the barn with a bag of feed over his shoulder.

A smile banished his moroseness for a few minutes. "Well! *Someone*'s glad to see me!" He poured a measure of grain into the trough on the stallion's door. "At least *you* eat well, my friends!" He moved on down the line, pouring grain into each manger. "And well-dressed you are, too, not like we who—"

Accerese bit his tongue, remembering that the king or his sorcerers might hear anything, anywhere. "Well, we all have our work to do in this world—though some of us have far less than—" Again, he bit his tongue—but on his way out of the third stall he paused to trace a raw red line on the horse's flank with his finger. "Then again, when you *do* work, your tasks are even more painful than mine, eh? No, my friends, forgive my complaining." He opened the door to the fourth stall. "But you, Fandalpi, you are . . ." He stopped, puzzled.

Fandalpi was crowded against the back wall, nostrils flared, the whites showing all around its eyes. "Nay, my friend, what . . ."

Then Accerese saw the body lying on the floor.

He stood frozen in shock for a few minutes, his eyes as wide and white as the horse's. Then he whirled to the door, panic moving his heels—until he froze with a new fear. Whether he fled or not, he was a dead man—but he might live longer if he reported the death as he should. Galtese the steward's man would testify that Accerese had taken his load of grain only a few minutes before—so there was always the chance that no one would blame him for the prince's death.

But his stomach felt hollow with fear as he hurried back across the courtyard to the guardroom. There was a chance, yes, but when the corpse was that of the heir apparent, it was a very slim chance indeed.

King Maledicto tore his hair, howling in rage. "What cursed fiend has rent my son!"

But everyone could see that this was not the work of a fiend, or any other of Hell's minions. The body was not burned or defiled; the prince's devotion to God had won him that much protection, at least. The only sign of the Satanic was the obscene carving on the handle of the knife that stuck out of his chest—but every one of the king's sorcerers had such a knife, and many of the guards besides. Anybody could have stolen one, though not easily.

"Foolish boy!" the king bellowed at the corpse. "Did you think your Lord would save you from Hell's blade? See what all your praying has won you! See what your hymn-singing and charities and forgiveness have brought you! Who will inherit my kingdom now? Who will rule, if I should die? Nay, now I'll be a thousand times more wicked yet! The Devil will keep me alive, if only to bring misery and despair upon this earth!"

Accerese quaked in his sandals, knowing who was the most likely candidate for despair. He reflected ruefully that, no matter how the king had stormed and threatened his son to try to make him forsake his pious ways, the prince had been his assurance that the Devil would make him live—for only if the old king lived could the kingdom of Latruria be held against the wave of goodness that would have flowed from Prince Casudo's charity.

"What do I have left now?" the old king ranted. "Only a single grandson puling boy, not even a stripling; a child, an infant! Nay, I must rear him well and wisely in the worship of Satan, or this land will fall to the rule of Virtue!"

What he didn't dare say, of course, was that if his demonic master knew he was raising little Prince Boncorro any other way, the Devil would rack the king with tortures that Accerese could only imagine—but imagine he did; he shuddered at the very thought.

"Fool! Coward! Milksop!" the king raged, and went on and

on, ranting and raving at the poor dead body as if by sheer rage he could force it to obey and come alive again. Finally, though, Accerese caught an undertone to the tirade that he thought impossible, then realized was really there:

The king was afraid!

At that, Accerese's nerve broke. Whatever was bad enough to scare a king who had been a life-long sorcerer, devoted to evil and to wickedness that was only whispered abroad, never spoken openly—whatever was so horrible as to scare such a king could blast the mind of a poor man who strove to be honest and live rightly in the midst of the cruelty and treachery of a royal court devoted to Evil! Slowly, ever so slowly, Accerese began to edge toward the stable door. No one saw, for everyone was watching the king, pressing away from his royal wrath as much as they dared. Even Chancellor Rebozo cowered, he who had endured King Maledicto's whims and rages for fifty years. No one noticed the poor humble groom edge his way out of the door, no one noticed him turn away and pace quickly to the postern gate, no one saw him leap into the water and swim the moat, for even the sentries on the wall were watching the stables with fear and apprehension.

But one did notice his swimming—one of the monsters who lived in the moat. A huge slaty bulge broke the surface, oily waters sliding off it; eyes the size of helmets opened, gaze flickering here and there until they saw the churning figure. Then the bulge began to move, faster and faster, a V-shaped wake pointing toward the fleeing man.

Accerese did not even look behind to see if it was coming; he knew it would, knew also that, fearsome as the monster was, he was terrified more of the king and his master.

The bulge swelled as it came up behind the man. Accerese could hear the wash of breaking waters and redoubled his efforts with a last frantic burst of thrashing. The shoreline came closer, closer . . .

But the huge bulge came closer, too, splitting apart to show huge dripping yellow fangs in a maw as dark as midnight.

Accerese's flailing foot struck mud; he threw himself onto the bank and rolled away just as saw-edged teeth clashed shut behind him. He rolled again and again, heart beating loud in his ears, aching to scream but daring not, because of the sentries on the walls. Finally he pushed himself up to his feet and saw the moat, twenty feet behind him, and the two huge baleful eyes glaring at him over its brim. Accerese breathed a

shuddering gasp of relief, and a prayer of thanks surged upward within him—but he caught it in time, held it back from
forming into words, lest the Devil hear him and know he was
fleeing. He turned away, scrambling over the brow of the hill
and down the talus slope, hoping that God had heard his un-
voiced prayer, but that the Hell-spawn had not. Heaven preserved him, or perhaps simply good luck, for he reached the
base of the hill with the alarm still unraised and sprinted across
the plain toward the cover of the woods.

Just as Accerese came in under the trees, King Maledicto finally ran out of venom and stood trembling over the corpse of
his son, tears of frustration in his eyes. Yes, surely they must
have been of frustration.

Then, slowly, he turned to his chancellor. "Find the murderer, Rebozo."

"But Majesty!" Rebozo shrank away. "It might be a demon
out of Hell . . ."

"Would a demon use a knife, fool?" Maledicto roared.
"Would a demon leave the body whole? Aye, whole and unde-
filed? Nay! It is a mortal man you seek, no spawn of Hell!
Find him, seek him! Bring the groom who found my son,
question him over what he saw!"

"Surely, Majesty!" Rebozo bent in a quick servile bow and
turned away. "Let the groom stand forth!"

Everyone was silent, staring about them, wide-eyed. "He
was here, against the stall door . . ." a guardsman ventured.

"And you let him flee? Fool! Idiot!" Maledicto roared. He
whirled to the other soldiers, pointing at the one who had spoken. "Cut off his head! Not later, *now*!"

The other guardsmen glanced at their mate, taken aback,
hesitant.

"Will no one obey?" Maledicto bellowed. "Does my weak-
kneed son still slacken your loyalty, even in his death? Here,
give me!" He snatched a halberd from the nearest guardsman
and swung it high. The other soldiers shouted and dodged even
as the blade fell. The luckless man tried to dodge, but too
late—the blade cut through his chest. He screamed once, in
terror and in blood; then his eyes rolled up, and his soul was
gone where went all those souls who served King Maledicto
willingly.

"Stupid ass," Maledicto hissed, glaring at the body. "When
I command, you *obey*!" He looked up at the remaining, quaking guardsmen. "Now *bring me that groom*!"

They fled to chase after the luckless groom.

It was the chancellor who found and followed the fugitive's trail to the postern and down to the water's edge, the company of guardsmen in his wake.

"Thus it ends," sighed the Captain of the Guard. "None could swim that moat and live."

But Rebozo glanced back fearfully at the keep, as if hearing some command that the others could not. "Take the hound into the boat," he ordered. "Search the other bank."

They went, quaking, and the dog had to be held tightly, its muzzle bound, for it squirmed and writhed, fearing the smell of the monsters. Several of them lifted huge eyes above the water, but Rebozo muttered a charm and pointed at each with his wand. The great eyes closed, the slaty bulges slid beneath the oily, stagnant fluid—and the boat came to shore.

Wild-eyed, the dog sprang free and would have fled, but the soldiers cuffed it quiet and as it whined, cringing, made it smell again the feedbag that held Accerese's scent. It began to quest, here and there about the bank, gaining vigor as it moved further from the water. Its keeper cursed and raised a fist to club it, but Rebozo stayed his hand. "Let it course," he said. "Give it time."

Even as he finished, the dog lifted its head with a howl of triumph. Off it went after the scent, nearly jerking the keeper's arm out of its socket, so eager was it to get away from that fell and foul moat. Rebozo shouted commands, and half a dozen soldiers ran off after the hound and its keeper, while a dozen more came riding across the drawbridge with the rest of the pack, led by a minor sorcerer in charcoal robes.

Down the talus slope they thundered, away over the plain, catching up with the lead hound, and the whole pack belled as they followed the trace into the woods.

They searched all that day and into the night, Rebozo ordering their efforts, Rebozo calling for the dogs, Rebozo leading the guardsmen. It was a long chase and a dark one, for Accerese had the good sense to keep moving, to resist the urge to sleep—or perhaps it was fear itself that kept him going. He doubled back, he waded a hundred yards through a stream, he took to trees and went from branch to branch—but where the hounds could not find his scent, sorcery could, and in the end they brought Accerese, bruised and bleeding, back to the chancellor, who nodded, eyes glowing, even as he said, "Put him to the Question!"

"No, no!" Accerese screamed, and went on screaming even as they hauled him down to the torture chamber, even as they strapped him to the rack—where the screaming turned quickly into hoarse bellows of agony and fear. Rebozo stood there behind his king, watching and trembling as Maledicto shouted, "Why did you slay my son?"

"I did not! I did never!"

"More," King Maledicto snapped, and Rebozo, trembling and wide-eyed, nodded to the torturer, who grinned and pressed down with glowing iron. Accerese screamed and screamed, and finally could turn the sound into words. "I only found him there, I did not kill . . . AIEEEE!"

"Confess!" the king roared. "We know you did it—why do you deny it?"

"Confess," Rebozo pleaded, "and the agony will end."

"But I did not do it!" Accerese wailed. "I only found him . . . YAAHHHH!"

So it went, on and on, until finally, exhausted and spent, Accerese told them what they wanted to hear. "Yes, yes! I did it, I stole the dagger and slew him, anything, anything! Only let the pain stop!"

"Let the torture continue," Maledicto commanded, and watched with grim satisfaction as the groom howled and bucked and writhed, listened with glowing eyes as the screams alternated with begging and pleading, shivered with pleasure as the cracked and fading voice still tried to shriek its agony—but when the broken, bleeding body began to gibber and call upon the name of God, Maledicto snarled, "Kill it!"

The blade swung down, and Accerese's agony was over.

King Maledicto stood, glaring down at the remains with fierce elation—then suddenly turned somber. His brows drew down, his face wrinkled into lines of gloom. He turned away, thunderous and brooding. Rebozo stared after him, astounded, then hurried after.

When he had seen his royal master slam the door of his private chamber behind him, when his loud-voiced queries brought forth only snarls of rage and demands to go away, Rebozo turned and went with a sigh. There was still another member of the royal family who had to be told about all this. Not Maledicto's wife, for she had been slain for an adultery she had never committed; not the prince's wife, for she had died in childbirth—but the prince's son, Maledicto's grandson, who was now the heir apparent.

Rebozo went to his chambers in a wing on the far side of the castle. There he composed himself, steadying his breathing and striving for the proper combination of sympathy and sternness, of gentleness and gravity. When he thought he had the tone and expression right, he went in to tell the boy that he was an orphan.

Prince Boncorro wept, of course. He was only ten and could not understand. "But why? Why? Why would God take my father? He was so good, he tried so hard to do what God wanted!"

Rebozo winced, but found words anyway. "There was work for him in Heaven."

"But there is work for him here, too! Big work, lots of work, and surely it is work that is important to God! Didn't God think he could do it? Didn't he try hard enough?"

What could Rebozo say? "Perhaps not, your Highness. Kings must do many things that would be sins, if common folk did them."

"What manner of things!" The tears dried on the instant, and the little prince glared up at Rebozo as if the man himself were guilty.

"Why . . . killing," said Rebozo. "Executing, I mean. Executing men who have done horrible, vicious things, such as murdering other people—and who might do them again, if the king let them live. And killing other men, in battle. A king must command such things, Highness, even if he does not do them himself."

"So." Boncorro fixed the chancellor with a stare that the old man found very disconcerting. "You mean that my father was too good, too kind, too gentle to be a king?"

Rebozo shrugged and waved a hand in a futile gesture. "I cannot say, Highness. No man can understand these matters—they are beyond us."

The look on the little prince's face plainly denied the idea—denied it with scorn, too. Rebozo hurried on. "For now, though, your grandfather is in a horrible temper. He has punished the man who murderered your father . . ."

"Punished?" Prince Boncorro stared. "They caught the man? Why did he do it?"

"Who knows, Highness?" Rebozo said, like a man near the end of his fortitude. "Envy, passion, madness—your grandfather did not wait to hear the reason. The murderer is dead. What else matters?"

"A great deal," Boncorro said, "to a prince who wishes to live."

There was something chilling about the way he said it—he seemed so mature, so far beyond his years. But then, an experience like this *would* mature a boy—instantly.

"If you wish to live, Highness," Rebozo said softly, "it were better if you were not in the castle for some months. Your grandfather has been in a ferocious temper, and now is suddenly sunken in gloom. I cannot guess what he may do next."

"You do not mean that he is mad!"

"I do not *think* so," Rebozo said slowly, "but I do not *know.* I would feel far safer, your Highness, if you were to go into hiding."

"But . . . where?" Boncorro looked about him, suddenly helpless and vulnerable. "Where could I go?"

In spite of it all, Rebozo could not help a smile. "Not in the wardrobe, Highness, nor beneath your bed. I mean to hide you outside the castle—outside this royal town of Venarra, even. I know a country baron who is kindly and loyal, who would never dream of hurting a prince, and who would see you safely spirited away even if his Majesty were to command your presence. But the king will not ask him for you, for I will see to it that the king does not know where you are."

Boncorro frowned. "How will you do that?"

"I will lie, your Highness. No, do not look so darkly at me—it will be a lie in a good cause, and is far better than letting you stay here where your grandfather might lash out at you in his passion."

Boncorro shuddered; he had seen King Maledicto in a rage. "But he is a sorcerer! Can he not find me whenever he wishes?"

"I am a sorcerer, too," Rebozo said evenly, "and shall cloud your trail by my arts, so that even he cannot find it. It is my duty to you—and to him."

"Yes, it is, is it not?" Boncorro nodded judiciously. "How strange that to be loyal, you must lie to him!"

"He will thank me for it one day," Rebozo assured him. "But come, now, your Highness—there is little time for talk. No one can tell when your grandfather will pass into another fit of rage. We must be away, and quickly, before his thoughts turn to you."

Prince Boncorro's eyes widened in fright. "Yes, we must! How, Rebozo?"

"Like this." Rebozo shook out a voluminous dark cloak he had been carrying and draped it around the boy's shoulders. "Pull up the cowl, now."

Boncorro pulled the hood over his head and as far forward as it would go. He could only see straight in front of him, but he realized that it would be very hard for others to see his face.

Rebozo was donning a cloak very much like his. He, too, pulled the cowl over his head. "There, now! Two fugitives dressed alike, eh? And who is to say you are a prince, not the son of a woodcutter wrapped against the night's chill? Away now, lad! To the postern!"

They crossed out over the moat in a small boat that was moored just outside the little gate. Boncorro huddled in on himself, staring at the huge luminous eyes that seemed to appear out of the very darkness itself—but Rebozo muttered a spell and pointed his wand, making those huge eyes flutter closed in sleep and sink away. The little boat glided across the oil-slick water with no oars or sail, and Boncorro wondered how the chancellor was making it go.

Magic, of course.

Boncorro decided he must learn magic, or he would forever be at others' mercy. But not black magic, no—he would never let Satan have a hold on him, as the Devil did on his grandfather! He would never be so vile, so wicked—for he knew what Rebozo seemed not to: that no matter who had thrust the knife between his father's ribs, it was King Maledicto who had given the order. Boncorro had no proof, but he didn't need any—he had heard their fights, heard the old man ranting and raving at the heir, had heard Prince Casudo's calm, measured answers that sent the king into a veritable paroxysm. He had heard his grandfather's threats, seen him lash out at Casudo in anger. No, Boncorro had no need of proof. He had always feared his grandfather and never liked him—but now he hated him, too, and was bound and determined never to be like him.

On the other hand, he was determined never to be like his father, either—not now. Prince Casudo had been a good man, a very good man, even saintly—but it was as Chancellor Rebozo had said: that very goodness had made him unfit to be king. It had made him unfit to live, for that matter—unsuspecting, he had been struck down from behind. Boncorro wanted to be a good king, when his time came—but more than anything else, he wanted to live.

And second only to that, he wanted revenge—on his grand-father.

The boat grounded on the bank, and Rebozo stepped out, turning back to hold out a hand to steady the prince. There were horses tied to a tree branch in waiting, black horses that faded into the night. Rebozo boosted the boy into the saddle, then mounted, too, and took the reins of Boncorro's horse. He slapped his own horse's withers with a small whip, and they moved off quietly into the night, down the slope, and across the darkened plain. Only when they came under the leaves did Prince Boncorro feel safe to talk again. "Why are you loyal to King Maledicto, Rebozo? Why do you obey him? Do you think the things he commands you to do are right?"

"No," Rebozo said, with a shudder. "He is an evil man, your Highness, and commands me to do wicked deeds. I shall tell you truly that some of them disgust me, even though I can see they are necessary to keep order in the kingdom. But there are other tasks he sets me that frankly horrify me, and in which I can see no use."

"Then why do you do them? Why do you carry them out?"

"Because I am afraid," Rebozo said frankly, "afraid of his wrath and his anger, afraid of the tortures he might make me suffer if he found that I had disobeyed him—but more than anything else, afraid of the horrors of his evil magic."

"Can you not become good, as Father was? Will not . . . no, of course Goodness will not protect you," Prince Boncorro said bitterly. "It did not protect Father, did it? In the next life, per-haps, but not in this."

"Even if it did," Rebozo said quickly, to divert the boy from such somber thoughts, "it would not protect me—for I have committed many sins, your Highness, in the service of your grandfather—many sins indeed, and most of them vile."

"But you had no choice!"

"Oh, I did," Rebozo said softly, "and worse, I knew it, too. I could have said no, I could have refused."

"If you had, Grandfather would have had you killed! Tortured and killed!"

"He would indeed," Rebozo confirmed, "and I did not have the courage to face that. No, in my cowardice, I trembled and obeyed him—and doomed my soul to Hell thereby."

"But Father did not." Boncorro straightened, eyes wide with sudden understanding. "Father refused to commit an evil act, and Grandfather killed him for it!"

"Highness, what matter?" Rebozo pleaded. "Dead is dead!"

"It matters," Prince Boncorro said, "because Father's courage has saved him from Hell—and yours could, too, Rebozo, even now!"

There was something in the way he said it that made Rebozo shiver—but he was shivering anyway, at the thought of the fate the king could visit upon him. Instead, he said, "Your father has gone to a far better place than this, Prince Boncorro."

"That may be true," the Prince agreed, "but I do not wish to go there any sooner than I must. Why did Father not learn magic?"

"Because there is no magic but evil magic, your Highness."

"I do not believe that," Prince Boncorro said flatly. "Father told me of saints who could work miracles."

"Miracles, yes—and I don't doubt that your father can work them now, or will soon. But miracles are not magic, your Highness, and it is not the saints who work them, but the one they worship, who acts through them. Mere goodness is not enough—a man must be a saint, to become such a channel of power."

Prince Boncorro shook his head doggedly. "There must be a way, Chancellor Rebozo. There must be another sort of magic, good magic, or the whole world would have fallen to evil long ago."

What makes you think it has not? Rebozo thought, but he bit back the words. Besides, even Prince Boncorro had heard of the good wizards in Merovence, and Chancellor Rebozo did not want him thinking too much about that. What quicker road to death could there be than to study good magic in a kingdom of evil sorcery?

"Will Grandfather ever die?" Boncorro asked.

Rebozo shook his head. "Only two know that, Highness—and one of them is the Devil, who keeps the king alive."

The other, Prince Boncorro guessed, must be God—but he could understand why Rebozo would not want to say that name aloud. Not in this kingdom—and not considering the current state of his soul.